Meant to Be

SARAH GERDES

RPM Publishing

Seattle, WA

Copyright © 2019 Sarah Gerdes

All rights reserved.

ISBN-10: 1-7329503-5-0
ISBN-13: 978-1-7329503-5-1

Library of Congress cataloging-in-publication data on file

Printed in the United States of America

First American Edition 2019, reprints 2020, 2022, 2023

Cover design by Lyuben Valevski
http://lv-designs.eu

ALL RIGHTS RESERVED. NO PART OF THIS BOOK MAY BE REPRODUCED OR TRANSMITTED IN ANY FORM OR BY ANY MEANS, ELECTRONIC OR MECHANICAL, INCLUDING PHOTOCOPYING, RECORDING, OR BY ANY INFORMATION STORAGE AND RETRIEVAL SYSTEM, WITHOUT WRITTEN PERMISSION FROM THE PUBLISHER.

P.O. Box 841 Coeur d'Alene, ID 83816

Meant to Be

CHAPTER 1

White snowflakes whipped around Danielle as she walked to her front door, the circular flips and swirls of the delicate frozen water identical to her emotions since leaving Lars' office. It was her fault he'd asked to end their relationship, her inability to let go of the past and her fear of the future colliding, blowing up their bond like a blizzard. Many sincere apologies later, he'd ended the discussion with a kiss and a statement he couldn't make any more promises.

So, did I really convince him to stay with me, or was he just delaying the inevitable? She clicked the lock over, feeling the rush of heat from the entryway, glimpsing the water of Lake Zurich through the bay windows of the living room.

Danielle heard Emma encouraging Monroe to help gather the books on the floor, first in English, then in Swiss-German. She placed her purse on the hallway credenza, feeling remorse and embarrassment, regretting her immature actions that made the discussion necessary. *Yes*, Lars had slipped while ice climbing, and *yes*, she'd reacted predictably, emotionally, then physically pulling away from him. It was the collateral damage of losing Andre, her fiancé and father of her daughter, to an accident the week before they were to be married. Lars had talked her through the stages of fear, tried to hold her, and keep her communicating with him, but no. She retracted first, then ignored him, finally refusing to see him when he showed up at the home of Andre's parents where she'd been. By the time Layda convinced her to talk with Lars, it was already too late.

"Do you know what it's like to have a child's bedroom in your own house with no child?" Lars had asked her when he'd finally taken her call. "To have started a new life, believing I could reclaim what I once lost only to have it ripped away?"

Lars' voice had been shaking from his own pain, each word grating on Danielle's emotions like a razor on glass. Danielle didn't blame him. His trust was gone. *I destroyed it.*

Monroe came zooming around the corner in a walker Georgy and Layda had gifted her, a pint-sized scooter she moved with increasing speeds on the shiny, concrete floors. Emma was right behind her.

Danielle switched into mom mode. "How was your Friday?" she asked the older woman who was wiping her hands with a towel.

"It was perfect." Danielle bent down to lift Monroe when she came near, but the ten month-old scooted out of her reach at the last moment. She laughed, watching her go, unwilling to chase her in heels still wet from the snow. "She will be ready for pre-school soon," Emma predicted.

"You think?" asked Danielle, a wistful tone in her voice. "I thought pre-school isn't until three."

"Well, maybe not this year, but she could benefit from interaction with other children. I did some checking with Layda and we found a few programs…"

Danielle loved the subtlety of the Swiss culture. "Let me guess. You already have something for me to look at?"

Emma smiled with the wisdom of a grandmother coaching a new mom. "I'll get you the list and my things."

In Emma's absence, Lars' words about having a room for Monroe brought to mind the Saturday afternoon the two of them had spent choosing the decorations for the luxurious bedroom, from the canopied bed, to the matching floor rug and chair. It had been like a honeymoon, laughing over the smallest details like the baby wipe dispenser. He wanted the most expensive model because it had more settings even as she argued a degree or two on a baby's butt didn't matter.

It had been easy and wonderful, filled with the excitement of a future together.

When Monroe raced by again, Danielle put her foot out, stopping the scooter, and lifted up her daughter. She planted an awkward and completely unsatisfying kiss on Monroe's cheek before depositing her back into the harness, laughing as she went back down the hall.

"Just wait until she's driving," said Emma with a smile. Danielle groaned, accepting the piece of paper with a list of local events for toddlers, scanning it top to bottom. After a moment, she asked if parents could come. "Of course, but activities are only during the week."

Danielle was disappointed but unsurprised. Children would typically be with their parents on the weekends. "Well, maybe in the late afternoon," she said hopefully.

When Emma had gone, Danielle realized her feelings about Lars were like a helium balloon. His hug and kiss were the equivalent to a shot of the lighter than air gas, lifting her hopes upward. Their deflated relationship could rise again, a bit at a time. All it required was work on her part and consistency and forgiveness on his.

Well, a few changes to his habits wouldn't hurt, she thought, slipping off her shoes.

CHAPTER 2

An hour later, her good friend told her not to dwell on the possibility of Lars changing.

"He told you he couldn't make promises once already, Danielle," said Stephen, "and prior to that, had said he never committed to giving up his sports of choice, ice or rock climbing. To think he will do so now, when he already gave up on your relationship once is…"

"Delusional?" she offered.

"You said it, not me."

Monroe cried from the other room, and Danielle listened to Stephen continue to talk even as she addressed her daughter's predicament. Her little hand was stuck between the slats of the bed board as she refused to drop a toy on the other side. Danielle had to forcefully remove the musical ball, causing Monroe to momentarily shrill, but subsided when she picked her up and put the ball in her hand. Perching Monroe on her right hip, she walked with her daughter back into the kitchen, keeping the phone on mute as she placed Monroe in the high chair. A bowl, a raw egg and small swifter later, her daughter had happily splashed most of the egg outside the bowl, but was occupied.

When Danielle heard a click and a female's voice, she realized Stephen wasn't alone. It was Saturday morning, well before the restaurant opened. "I'm so sorry, I didn't think you'd already be at the restaurant."

"I'm not. I'm not going in until three today, can you believe it?"

"What?" she exclaimed, genuinely surprised. "How is that even possible?"

"When one has priorities Danielle, anything is possible. Even getting to the restaurant later than normal."

Only one thing would get Stephen away from management duties, and it was his new, almost-family situation. "Then I'll assume you are out with Eva, shopping for baby items?"

"You assume correctly," he said, causing Danielle to chuckle, the joy of his statement cutting through the clouds in her day. She was happy for him, his unconventional situation notwithstanding. "Now, getting back to the situation at hand."

"Ugh," she groaned. "I keep telling myself I'm not that pathetic, but I just really want the blunt opinion from the brother-I-never-had, the kind Lani used to give me but she was never as nice or as diplomatic as you."

"You want more than just a listening ear, correct?" When she convinced him she could handle it, he continued. "Danielle, you aren't addressing the real issue. As Lars said, abandoning his sports of choice and taking up another one might only make him resentful. That's independent from overcoming your own fears. Forgive me for saying this, but it's like you can see the chair in the room but are refusing to sit on it."

"That *was* awfully diplomatic," she teased, her humor designed to soften the impact of his words.

"Danielle, you both continue on this path and you'll be forcing a situation that isn't sustainable. Sleeping together as your fear remains and his resentment grows. How is that good for either of you?" She remained silent. "And imagine if you got unexpectedly pregnant?"

"I changed my mind. I want the diplomacy." He chuckled while she bit her inner cheek. "You are so like my dad."

"A compliment, I'm sure. Danielle, let me give you a glimpse of the future. You are going to go through the stages of loss, just as you did with Andre. After Lars came back into your world, he held off becoming intimate with you because he wanted to be sure your emotional state could handle it; that you weren't moving too fast back into romance. And what did you do?"

She inwardly groaned. "I convinced him I could handle it."

"Yep. And now you're going through what you probably should have confronted before—truly dealing with the death of Andre so you can live a fulfilling future." As she listened to Stephen, she was forced to acknowledge that Lars was once again right. "That's why you need to get up and over this emotional rock wall of your own, by yourself. He can't help you and he knows it."

"I should have let fate take its course. We should have broken up."

A pause preceded Stephens comment. "Do you see any other way to mature independently?"

In the last two hours, Danielle had tried to avoid the nagging voice within her that repeated Lars was rarely wrong. His foresight and perspective were unmatched.

"It's not what I want," she said plaintively.

At this, her perennially even-tempered friend laughed. "You think anyone chooses to be single when in a perfectly healthy relationship?" he asked.

For a moment, her attention was diverted from her own situation to his. "You referring to Lani?"

"Who else? Other than the fact she got the thriving restaurant she wanted, then left me for Max because he was the swinging single who didn't want children, that breakup, as ugly as it was, put me on a much better path." Danielle was full of admiration for his perspective and some skepticism that he was taking his current situation in stride. "Who knows?" he continued. "You might find that sometimes the most unconventional situations are the healthiest."

"Explain, please."

"Happy to. Because Eva and I aren't emotionally tied at the hip, we are partners in the truest sense of the word. We have one goal, and that's to raise a healthy, happy child."

At this, Danielle couldn't help herself. "Are you telling me you don't ever sleep with her? I don't believe it. She's too beautiful and you're too handsome. I mean, that's where it started in the first place."

"Actually, it started with us being friends for years, before I even knew Lani."

"Okay, friends first. But what's unreal to me is how you even make it work with Eva when you are still in love with Lani?" she asked, genuinely curious. "Because we all know you are. Even Lani knows it!"

"Intellectually, it makes perfect sense. Just because Lani fell out of love with me and into bed with Max doesn't do away with the memories or love. It happened to coincide with Eva and I both needing someone with a caring heart and warm arms. We were there for each other. Babies can happen when sex is involved, so whether my relationship with her continues from friends to something more remains to be seen. But there's no pressure."

Danielle almost envied Stephen's situation, but doubted it would ever work for her. "You Swiss are more logical than the average American," she told him. "Lani and I, to our advantage or detriment, are passionate and known to be a bit more emotionally driven."

"Don't use that as an excuse not to look at yourself closely and do what you can. Regarding Lars, he has to determine if you and your relationship are worth altering or not."

"Without me pressuring him," she interjected.

"Exactly. You both need to step back and walk the road alone for a while. Explore the notion of dating other people. Heaven knows half of Andre's hockey team would be lining up at the door, along with several of the club managers in town."

"What about work?"

"What about it? You trade away and he's still the managing director. No issue. In fact, he told you he didn't care who you slept with in the office as long as didn't affect your numbers on our first day, right?"

"You can't be suggesting I go running around with guys at work."

"No, but you have no rules against doing so. The more important message I will give you is to get ok being single. Too many people jump into unhealthy relationships because they aren't comfortable being alone. You met Andre your second day in Zurich, at our restaurant no less. You have had no more than a few weeks here and there of being single. I'm not sure you even know how to do it."

Danielle burst out laughing. "Okay, you have definitely taken the blunt brother thing too far."

"Good. Then I've done my job. In the meantime, work during the day and live a little at night." Then Stephen turned it down a notch. "Now, changing subjects, we'd been planning a surprise 30th birthday party for you and were present when Lars told you about it. It's still a few months out, but I'm thinking it might not be such a good idea now."

"Agreed, which means I'm going to be in some backroom bar entering my thirties by myself."

"No," he countered. "You get Johanne and Dario dancing. And don't forget Lani. She can be there for you."

This was precisely why she loved Stephen. The man was so kind-hearted he could look past his own hurt with his ex-wife to encourage an on-going friendship.

"Actually, your former wife is likely my former friend." Danielle told him about her conversation with Lani just before she met with Lars. "It went nuclear when I declined to invest in her already struggling restaurant, my own issues taking precedent. She said I was pulling the Andre-death card, expecting sympathy from everyone, and essentially screwing my relationship with Lars with my own inadequacies."

"You're right," Stephen said dryly. "That was nuclear."

Danielle heard a door open and shut, then Eva's voice in the background. "Stephen, who would have thought you and I, of all people, who were once both in thriving relationships, would each have children with neither of us married, or in my case, even partnered?"

"Does one have to be in love to raise a child, or is it enough to be good friends and good parents?"

For that, she didn't have a ready answer.

CHAPTER 3

The following morning, the sky was blue and the roads clear, the efficiency of the maintenance crews one more thing to love about her adopted Swiss town. She called Georgy, asking if they'd like visitors.

"Are you going to arrive in time for lunch?" joked Monroe's grandfather.

"I can if you have food," she bounced back.

"Layda is bringing home cheeses and meat from the market. Do you want to stay overnight? We can give you a grandparent night off if you'd like. Perhaps with Lars?"

"Georgy…" she said. She was so grateful Georgy had fully embraced Lars as a part of her world, the hole of his son's death partially filled by a man he'd known far longer than herself.

"My dear, I know how busy you are, and I know you need to continue having a life which, as Monroe's grandparents, we are encouraging you to do."

"If you only knew," she replied.

"Oh? Something happened?"

"Yes. We can talk about it later, if, and only if, it's not going to cause stress in your life. That's the last thing you two need."

Danielle made it over to Georgy's by eleven, opting to drive instead of using her all-purpose stroller. The snow was too deep, despite the cleared sidewalks, and she wanted her overnight things in case she decided to stay.

And what else am I going to do? Sit at home, wallowing in her hot bath of depression, thinking of Lars at his chalet in St. Moritz staring at the Matterhorn or being comforted fireside with the two individuals who loved her like a daughter.

"Hello, dear," greeted Layda, kissing both her cheeks. Monroe excitedly stretched her arms to her grandmother and Danielle smiled. Andre was not here with her in person, but his parents would be with her for the rest of their lives.

"And you," Danielle said, embracing Georgy, exhaling loudly as he squished her.

"Losing weight again?" he grumped. Danielle shook her head and asked Layda if she could make the salad dressing for lunch today. "That will get you another slice of dessert my dear," he promised.

"Good. I'll take it and yours," she retorted with a smile.

Lunch was an informal affair, eaten in the breakfast nook of the lakeside house. When Layda offered to put Monroe down for her nap, Georgy put his hand on Danielle's forearm.

"Now, when were you going to tell me?" He raised a bushy eyebrow at her, waiting. She thought he was referring to her tone on the phone. "About leaving MRD?"

She blinked. "I'm not leaving the top investment firm in Switzerland quite yet."

"Noel said you might."

She sighed, pursing her lips. "More of his wishful thinking," she smirked, "and proving that the whole Swiss-discretion thing has gone right out the window." It had been nice not thinking about what she was going to encounter at work on Monday. Still, given Georgy's decades-old friendship with Noel, the founder of MRD, he might know more than she did.

"Did he tell you anything else?"

"No. He only mentioned Lars said you might want to be let out of your contract, and the way Lars described it, Noel was going along with Lars' recommendation. Was that of your own making? The last time we spoke, you weren't ready to leave."

"I still don't want to leave, but that may now be a possibility. Lars clearly didn't tell Noel it was because he was preparing to dump me." At Georgy's look, she quickly added, "As in, end our personal relationship, which he has done."

He stared at her the way a sage does, processing her words and expression. He then turned paternal. "Does this have to do with what's been going on over the last few weeks?" Danielle could see he wanted to help, but didn't want to cross her personal boundaries. "If you can't, or don't want to talk to me about what's happening, what about Layda? I know you have had some good conversations in the past."

Danielle smiled sadly. "You both have been so great about my…dating. But I don't want to hurt either of you."

"My dear. You lost your parents. We lost our son. Are these things easy? Of course not. But we are a family now. Let her be there for you, if you can." His hand was still on her arm when Layda walked in to the room.

"Georgy, that's a thoughtful look."

Danielle held his eye for a second then winked, looking up at Layda as she sat down. "He's just trying to see how long it's going to be until I move out of MRD and into the family fold."

Layda shook her head. "As always."

"How about we go over what you have planned for Monroe's birthday party?" Even though it was six weeks away, Danielle wanted to focus on something fun for a change.

"That's my cue to depart," said Georgy, standing.

"You can't leave now," reprimanded Danielle. "This is the good part!"

"My dear, I've already agreed to riding in a sleigh in the mountains. I certainly don't want to know any more details."

Danielle's eyes were bright and wide when she turned back to Layda, all concerns about Lars gone. "A sleigh?" she repeated, dumbfounded. Layda grinned back.

An hour later, Danielle was sipping chamomile tea as she leaned back in a comfortable chair in the sitting room. She'd thoroughly appreciated and supported all that Layda had planned, delighted at having a woman in her life who so embraced the role of grandmother, and who was now essentially her mother. Her father's words came to mind, and she mentally repeated them now.

"Men will come and go," her father had said, "but family remains forever."

"Layda, can I bring up the subject of Lars, and specifically, what's happened since our last conversation?" Danielle was comforted to see Layda look interested and open. She moved to a seat opposite Danielle, her back to the lake.

"The last time, you told me to face my fears and talk with Lars but I came to you too late. I'm now taking the proactive approach, hoping I can get ahead of the game by soliciting your advice first."

The compliment was accepted and Danielle proceeded.

"I called Lars as you suggested. He refused to talk to me and for the next few weeks avoided me at work. Yesterday he called me into his office, offering to let me out of my contract with the firm, essentially ending our relationship." She paused, taking a sip of tea, staring into the liquid for a moment. "Layda, remember how you said you take pills to get over the fear of something happening to me and Monroe? I can't do that, and I know it would only make you worry more if I did. But…I think I need to see a counselor. Someone who can help me work through this, because with or without Lars, I can't live like this."

Layda then did the unexpected. She set down her own drink and moved next to Danielle. Without a word, Layda hugged her. "I'm sorry," she said, and Danielle's emotions overwhelmed her. When she stopped crying, Layda left the room, returning with a black, leather notebook. On a piece of paper, she wrote out her recommendation. Then she sat beside Danielle, her look one of focus.

"Now, I do have a thought I'd like to share. You need to go out."

"Excuse me?"

"Yes, I said that," she confirmed, her eyes narrowing slightly. "You, Danielle Grant, need to go out. You are an attractive, smart woman, who should not let the opinions and emotions of a man like Lars hold you back from enjoying your life. Not now, and not ever."

"I…" Danielle stammered, unsure what to say. *Thanks, or you're crazy?* "Are you sure about this?"

The perfectly coiffed, platinum blond hair barely moved as Layda nodded. "One hundred percent. I respect Lars but you hold your head high and make your presence known in this town, in your own right and on your own merits, because you may not have the last name Mettleren, but you have the attitude and backing of this family. Not to take away from Lars, but as he, himself once said to you, there are plenty of attractive men in this town." Danielle nodded. Those were indeed the words he'd once uttered.

"Well then," Layda said decidedly. "You see how this week goes. You be the one to make the decision to move forward, with all that entails.

Show him what you are made of. And if you believe he is on the same page as you regarding being single, then you have my full support to explore a world beyond him, just promise me one thing." Danielle nodded expectantly. "You don't you look back, not once, at least for the time being."

Danielle found a bit of humor. "This is where the strong, Swiss female comes in to play, I take it?"

"You bet your American fanny it is." Danielle put her hand to her mouth and let out a squeal of laughter. She'd never heard Layda swear before, and in such a profound, strong way. She threw her arms around Danielle and gave her hard squeeze. "You can and will do this."

Danielle was sure going to try. She had no other choice.

CHAPTER 4

Monday Danielle arrived at work before six and kept her ear set in, her eyes focused on the terminal in front of her as bodies moved past the glass wall to the hallway. She thought she caught Lars go by, but that was because of the cologne that permeated the air, not a visual sighting. At ten, Johanne appeared.

"You have a minute?" His look was pensive, an unusual expression for her former peer, now manager.

"For my boss, I always have a minute." He sat in front of her desk, legs crossed one over the other. "Nice glasses," she complimented. "They match the hue of your pants. What does that make, seven pairs of glasses?"

"Nine," he corrected with a wink. He glanced over his shoulder then back at her and she schooled her countenance appropriately. "I saw a meeting notice that had you as the subject, the other two were Lars and Noel. Did something go down I should be aware of?"

The fine line between dishonesty and privacy was a fine one.

"No, not really. They thought I wanted to leave and were going to let me out of my contract." His eyebrows raised expressively.

"What in the world would give them that impression? Wait," he said, lowering his chin, dropping his voice. "Are you involved with someone, *again?*"

Danielle couldn't help snickering at his tone. "I wish. Quite the opposite in fact. I have no one now."

Johanne's jaw dropped. "But just a few months ago you were back with Mr. Anonymous." Her grin was ill-timed. Lars walked by at that moment, but he continued staring straight ahead. No collegial drop-by's today. Danielle decided to keep it light.

"Don't try and keep track of my dating life. I can't."

He watched her for a few moments, and she had the distinct impression that after knowing her nearly two years, he guessed there was more to the story than she was letting on.

"So you say." With one more mischievous look, he left and she continued trading. Lars didn't stop by that day, or the next. She had resigned herself to the notion she'd rarely, if ever, talk to the man outside the weekly meetings. By Wednesday, the stress of consciously avoiding him had ebbed. It wasn't until Thursday morning, ten minutes before the weekly meeting with the traders that Lars did stop by.

When the two-tap came, she visibly jumped. "I'm sorry," he apologized, his tone and manner professional.

"No problem. What's up?"

"Mentoring," he said, remaining at the door. She gestured to her chair and he shook his head. "This will only take a minute." He did move in the doorway slightly, shutting the door halfway. Lars didn't want the office to hear what he had to say, but he didn't want to appear overly friendly with her either. Fair enough.

"Margaret would like you to spend more time mentoring the new traders---" he paused, putting up his hand to forestall her objection. "I know, but as the new co-managing partner directly under me, she gets to make the decision. I know it's been hurting your numbers, but this would be temporary. Before you ask, I said yes, but will make accommodations for the request."

This was all business, with his bottom line and her income the focus.

"Such as?" she queried, her voice flat.

"I've asked Johanne to reframe your quota and required that he drop you off the schedule for every non-essential client meeting."

"That doesn't yield happy clients. Why would you do such a thing?"

Lars' shoulders raised with dissatisfaction. "Because the new traders, while good, are struggling with the environment of wealth management for individuals and families."

"What did Margaret expect?" she asked, leaning back in her chair. "Their specialty is corporate funds. Expecting them to immediately come up to speed on our expertise is unrealistic for them, and honestly a bit insulting to the rest of us." His lips pursed. The merger of Velocity with MRD had been of his making. To insult the results was to insult him. "I'm not intending to denigrate you, by the way. It's reality."

"I'm not disagreeing with you, and yes, it's reality, one that Margaret and I didn't anticipate, but now need to work with."

Her eyes narrowed. "And I'm the one that's being loaded with the consequences, even though you, me and the overall downstream commission checks of support staff will be affected. Even Glenda, who is vital to me and relies almost entirely on my trading for her commission checks." In this world, she was more than his equal; she was his superior. "How about an alternative solution? You ship them off to an intensive two-week boot camp. The short-term loss of the trading will be more than made up by the long term results. But this piece mealing is like death from a thousand paper cuts."

"Can a person bleed to death from paper cuts?" he asked. As much as she didn't want to smile, she couldn't help it.

"I haven't personally tried it out, but I know it would be as miserable as hell." He smiled in appreciation, his olive skin stretching above his cheekbones, crinkling the corners of his eyes. *Turn it off. He's the boss, not my boyfriend.* "Seriously. Run the numbers," she encouraged. "I bet the firm will come out much further ahead choosing that route as opposed to me trying to be both mentor, teacher and worker-bee at the same time."

"I'll give it some thought."

She rolled one thumb over the other and glanced at the clock. "Are you telling me this now because you are going to announce it at the meeting, which is in five minutes?" He gave her a nod. "Well. I know you can be superhuman. Maybe you can run the numbers in that time."

"Danielle," he said, his voice and demeanor altering entirely. She stopped moving her fingers, waiting. "Thank you."

"For what? Trying to help you make more money and not decimate my bank account in the process?"

"For being yourself. I wasn't sure…"

"If I could be mature? I know. I deserve that."

"Yes, you did. Now," he said, his brisk tone returning. "I need to see what I can do about those numbers."

Danielle returned to her screen, eyes focused but mind elsewhere. He came, they'd talked, and she hadn't broken down, gotten angry or acted vengeful. She'd played it cool, just as Layda had advised. Another glance at the clock told her she could make one phone call before heading to the conference room. It took her only a few seconds to find the piece of paper Layda had given her with a name and number of a therapist. If she was going to work on improving herself, she didn't have a minute to waste.

CHAPTER 5

Danielle took a seat at the large, oval conference room table, facing the lake, not her preferred position, but she'd arrived just before the door was shut and had to take what was available. That meant sitting by Margaret, who led the meeting, giving the reports for the week prior. Glenda passed out papers to the traders around the table, and Danielle joined the others in following along with her comments. Lars looked at his phone most of the time, glancing up when a question was asked Margaret couldn't answer.

"The numbers are below our projections…" Margaret said, proceeding to identify what groups were underperforming and the specific results from each trader.

That can't feel good, Danielle thought to herself, looking at those for the team members for Velocity. She personally liked Jacob and Georgiana, and had spent considerable time with both of them, but numbers don't lie. And as her old boss David said, no one is your friend until the numbers post. "….we have a few changes we'd like to make to address this," Margaret paused, turning the floor over to Lars.

"We'd been planning on increasing the hours spent with some of our experienced traders from the MRD side but are now considering another option." In her peripheral vision, Danielle saw Margaret shift in her seat. Either Lars was catching her by surprise, or Margaret wasn't on board.

"We'll be getting back to the group with specifics, but suffice it to say we are going to choose the least intrusive, most effective route for the firm to increase profit immediately."

The remainder of the meeting was standard client account activities, which ones had reduced their total under management or transferred accounts out of the firm. This caught Danielle's attention. She looked at the page in front of her again, this time her focus not on the non-performing traders but the total under management.

"We're down four billion from last month?" she asked out loud, unable to hide her surprise. They certainly weren't coming from her accounts; it was the Velocity side.

"Any idea where they are going?" asked Johanne.

"Internal," answered Margaret.

"Family offices, you mean?" Danielle clarified. The woman nodded, and the room went silent. The trend of high net-worth clients taking their entire wealth away from investment banking and wealth management firms had been on the rise. Danielle knew one family out of India employed two-hundred full-time employees managing their vast resources. They recruited people like herself and paid her three times as much just in salary.

Margaret thanked the group for their hard work and Danielle went back to her office.

"Danielle, may I speak with you for a moment?" It was Margaret making her first stop ever at Danielle's office.

"Of course." Danielle sat down, plugging in her news feed to the international trading feeds as she waited for Margaret to speak.

"I understand you are having issues with spending more time with the people from Velocity?" Danielle wouldn't have characterized it that way and doubted Lars positioned Danielle's comments in any way but a favorable light. They may not be in a romantic relationship, but she felt sure he wouldn't throw her under the bus. An unmotivated trader was an unprofitable trader.

"It's a financial fact that the less time spent trading is in direct correlation to revenue."

"Your quota would go down in correlation with that effort, however."

"Which doesn't serve the company or myself, but it's immaterial. The firm will make the decision and we'll proceed accordingly."

"Will you?"

Danielle thought through her words. Margaret had been the former managing director at Velocity, no small feat for a woman in her mid-thirties, a position envied by men ten years her senior. The outward exterior of composure didn't mask her ambition, which was now being displayed. Either Danielle was on board, or she wasn't, and Danielle had the distinct impression Margaret was going to take it personally if her team members were not helped.

"I will reiterate, the firm will make the decision and we will proceed accordingly." Danielle spoke at a pace just slightly slower than she'd previously used, as though Margaret's ability to understand English was lacking. The woman's eyes lowered, her only response before she left the office.

Danielle kept her lip lines flat as she began trading. The woman deserved it. Arrogant *and* pushy; two traits Danielle didn't have much time for. She'd tell Johanne about it this weekend, maybe at the club.

Her spirits and numbers were higher the next day until noon, when she saw a calendar appointment on her schedule for the hour prior to the closing of trading. She saw the description and hit the speed dial for Lars, skipping right over Johanne and protocol.

"Do you have a moment?" she asked when he answered.

"Yes. In person or the phone?"

"It doesn't matter. I'm looking at my calendar and see that I just had an hour lopped off my trading, not just for today, but as I'm watching, an hour every single day for the next two weeks. I thought we talked about another option."

"We did, but Margaret made a persuasive argument for an in-person education from one of the best, as opposed to instructors who are mediocre." Danielle forced air into her chest, one breath, in and out.

"You ran the numbers and still made this decision?"

"Danielle, sometimes it's not always about the numbers." Those words had been said to her by this very man before, but under extremely different circumstances.

I wonder....no. It couldn't be. There was no romantic implication this time, with her, and it couldn't possibly be with Margaret. That much she was sure of.

"You are really telling me that you are making a decision where the numbers don't come first? We are talking about trading Lars, it's binary. Ones and zeros. If our clients fail to see the percentages returned that they are used to, they will leave, regardless of how well I or others have done in the past."

"I concur."

"Then what am I missing, other than the fact that my paycheck and bonus are going to be significantly reduced?"

"Sometimes people have to learn that their judgment is flawed and make a mistake or two."

Great. He's letting Margaret have her way and I'm going to be the one to suffer. "I get what you are doing and I'm issuing a serious protest. It's not right, and it's not fair to me in particular, and you know it."

"Yes."

Danielle realized it was futile to argue any further. At the beginning and end of the day, he was the head of the firm, and she, while their top trader for gold and currency, was only that. A single, replaceable employee.

She thought back to the notion of a family office. Georgy had been after her to create and run his family office since her required one-year employment contract with MRD had expired. Loyalty and Lars had prevented her from even considering that option. Now, with a daughter to raise alone, the last thing she needed was the time commitment that came along with managing a full-fledged investment firm, even one that had the Mettleren name behind it.

She sighed in frustration. Even if she wanted to, she was stuck working for someone else. She wasn't going to do that to Monroe, and MRD was still the best firm for wealth management in Switzerland, if not the world. She had a lot more to lose by leaving than by staying.

Danielle paused to close the door, turned up her dance music and got back to work. She wasn't going anywhere anytime soon.

CHAPTER 6

By the end of the day, she was mentally drained and emotionally frustrated. She'd sat with Jacob for thirty minutes, Georgiana another thirty, the last hour of trading wiped out as she attempted to explain to both of the traders some of the tricks of gold trading. Her own trades for the day were in the black, but only up a meager seventeen points, a bar well below her operating standard. All the while, she'd kept half an eye out for Johanne to walk by and give her a look of sympathy, or at least tolerance, for his override was going to be affected as well.

As she waited for her computer to shut down, she looked over her shoulder to the street below. A light snow was falling against the setting sun, the shimmer off the lake all that was romantic. In another month, it would be gone, replaced with budding cherry flowers from the trees that lined the pathway hugging the lake. The end of April though, she'd be on the water, like the first year she'd arrived.

Spring and new beginnings, this time marking her second full year in Switzerland and her thirtieth milestone.

On the way out, she stopped by Johanne's office. His lights were on, but he wasn't in.

"He's with Margaret," Lars said from the doorway of the nearest trader.

"Oh, thanks," she said to Lars, giving him a closed mouth smile. Perhaps Johanne was fighting for the right to get his trader back, but chances were high that he wasn't going to win a battle that Lars already lost. The woman might prove to be a force in her own right.

"Is it urgent? I could interrupt if need be." Lars was in his purely professional mode, the one he'd maintained at the office even throughout their romance.

"No. Nothing urgent. Have a good night." Crisp and professional, but not curt, the way she'd be had they never been involved.

As the elevator descended, she rethought their history. Part of the charm and intrigue with Lars had always been their bantering, the business conversation intermingled with double meanings and leading sentences, the intellectual stimulation greater than his looks, cologne and clothing.

Her phone rang on the way home and seeing the caller, she picked up.

"I understand you were looking for me?" Nice of Lars to have told Johanne. Exactly what a managing director would do.

"It was for no other reason than to commiserate, but since you're my manager and not my trading peer, you have to rise above these lowly complaints." Johanne groaned in a very un-boss like fashion, making her smile. "I'll take that as your non-verbal agreement so you don't get in trouble."

"No trouble that's not of my own making," he quipped. "I was giving Margaret feedback on her plan."

"How'd she take it?"

"Any guesses?"

"Probably the same way she took my feedback."

"Like a piece of ice sliding down the glacier onto her arse?"

"Johanne!" she said with a burst of laughter. She was glad some things hadn't changed with his promotion. "You're not going to get fired, are you?"

"No, because I told her that if you quit over this continued stupidity, they were going to have to make due with me, and I wasn't going to spend one ounce of my time training her sub-par traders."

"Wow."

"It gets better," he continued. "After Margaret left, Lars caught me and I told him the same thing. And I quote, MRD will lose its number one trader—that being you—and second in line, which would be me. I think he got the picture."

"Is it going to change anything?"

"No," he grumped, "not in the short term. Lars made a commitment and you know how he is about his commitments."

"Thanks for trying, my friend. I'll do my level best to share enough information to improve their numbers, but don't think for a minute I'm revealing my precious secrets."

"Yes. That's best saved for the dance floor. Speaking of which, do you have plans for the weekend? Ready to find a special other, perhaps?" She cleared her throat. "Guess that's a no. You going to tell me what happened to Mr. Anonymous?"

She giggled through her words. "Nothing juicy I'm afraid."

"Spill it. I have to know."

Danielle pulled into her driveway, grinning from ear to ear, despite the sorry circumstances. "My daughter is waiting to be fed dinner and Emma to go home. Later I'll give you some details."

"Promise?"

"Surreee," she drawled. "You get Margaret to end this obnoxious mentoring thing before the month is out and I'll divulge all. Promise."

That got him off the phone and she instantly regretted her promise. The last thing she wanted was for Johanne to know that the entire relationship with Lars had been going on right under his nose. Not that he'd be angry, but perhaps mildly hurt she hadn't confided in him.

One more thing to worry about.

That evening, after she put Munroe to sleep, she traded on the after markets for two hours not her standard three. She longed for the sauna at her old apartment, opting for a bath instead. As the suds crested to her chin, she closed her eyes, thinking of the deep, claw-footed tub in Lars' home. It was that night he'd told her that he'd waited a long time to take care of a woman like her. She wondered if he'd ever say those words to her again, or if they were being said to someone else instead.

CHAPTER 7

The next day, Danielle arrived at work, neglected to eat lunch and watched the clock with an almost neurotic awareness. She had fewer hours in her day, and ultimately, no matter how many trades she made, it didn't take away the fact that she was beholden to a new management structure who were dictating her schedule. Before she'd gone to bed, she placed a call to Georgy, revisiting the subject of a family office. Was he considering it? Did he have someone to run it?

"Anyone in my position is considering shifting to a family office," he'd told her, confirming the notion that billionaires had loyalty to one thing: making and keeping their money. "I do have several individuals in mind but have made only casual inquiries, nothing formal. Not to worry; I'm not going to put my best trader and favorite daughter-in-law out of work quite yet."

Danielle's sigh of relief wasn't entirely fabricated. While he didn't make up the majority of her client assets, his network in totality comprised a solid third of her volume.

After lunch, Johanne stopped by. "Going dancing with us this weekend? Now that you are single and all. "

"Let me get through this day and I'll think about the weekend after."

"Saturday night. Eleven. You know where."

"The cages or bust," she joked, a bit surprised that she didn't feel a stab of regret she wasn't going with Lars.

That's what seven weeks without intimacy will do to a girl. She wondered how Lars was handling the lack of physical contact with a woman—or was he lacking? From all he'd revealed, he was just as susceptible to a beautiful woman as the next guy. On one hand, she knew him to be dedicated and devoted to her, but seven weeks…. *No*, she decided. He was more like herself. He'd hold out for a woman he intellectually admired and personally respected. Life was too short and he was too smart to have flings.

The would be Max's role. Lani briefly entering her mind. It had only been a week since their argument, but it felt longer. On the way home, she was tempted to call Lani, knowing she'd be cooking at the restaurant and her cell phone would be tucked away and turned off. The better person to ask about her life might be Johanne tomorrow night. Given that he'd revealed he'd invested in her venture, he was probably talking with her on a frequent basis or at least having dinner at her restaurant, The Stinking Rose.

Danielle swapped thoughts of Lani with making pasta for dinner before heading over to Layda's. Georgy was traveling on business, and Layda enjoyed her company.

Monroe was on the floor in the living room and she in the kitchen when her mobile phone rang, the ringtone causing her stomach to drop.

"Are you calling to see if I'm going to come to work Monday?"

"No," Lars answered with a lightness in his voice. "I assumed you were going to be there."

She smiled. It was a first step. "You assumed correctly. But you must have work on your mind?"

"Actually, it's after hours and I typically have a bit more class than to call and talk about work. So therefore, I am calling to ask about you personally. I'm genuinely interested."

"Well at present, I'm making homemade spaghetti for myself and Monroe, trying to decompress from a rather tough three days."

"It will pass," he predicted, "which is what I emphasized to Johanne this afternoon."

"Good, because money is one thing. Demoralization is another."

Lars softly chuckled. "It's been three days of trading Danielle, not quite three hours out of your schedule. The bottom line is that the firm isn't going to change all that much, but I get your point."

"Do you?"

"Yes. From what Margaret related, you don't really want another boss."

"Was I that obvious?" Her sarcasm thick.

"Yes, but what wasn't obvious is how you are doing personally. How are *you* doing?"

"I made a promise in your office Lars, the latest in one of many I've made to you over the course of our…the time we've known each other. Part of that is trying not to let my personal situation interfere with work."

"Understood." He was proceeding cautiously, and they were once again entering new territory, one akin to being long lost friends and reconnecting, where the discovery was going to happen all over again, except the perspective and viewpoints were totally different.

"Danielle?" Lars prompted.

"I'm sorry, can you repeat that?"

"I was asking you stop what you are doing for a moment and talk to me."

She took her hands off the pot and forced a breath into her chest.

"Okay, I'm focusing."

"For the third time, how are you, *really*?" he emphasized.

"I'm starting the process, just like I promised. Layda has a therapist with whom I've made an appointment."

"Really?"

"Yes, really. And you? Any upcoming ice climbing events?"

"This weekend, actually."

Huh. "Well, good luck and be safe."

"I wasn't trying to get you off the phone by saying that. I've been doing a lot of thinking on the matter."

"That's good, because so have I," Danielle said. "You know how you said you can't make promises, well, as we pursue our independent courses, it's like we are walking our road alone for a while."

"A good analogy," he concurred. She would have preferred him to become unhappy at the prospect of being apart for an undetermined period of time.

She slipped a hot pad on her left hand, holding the large, copper pot as she stirred the thick meat sauce. "But you know, people who journey need to eat. I'll have enough for three tonight if you'd like to come over. Nothing fancy. Just food." For a split second, she thought it was fate that she was making this particular meal. The first time Lars came over, they'd enjoyed the first of what they thought would be a lifetime of spaghetti dinners as a family.

"Do you think that's wise?"

Danielle sighed. "To be truthful, I don't know what's wise any longer, Lars. I want to be with you but am afraid of what will happen if we're together and it makes an already unstable platform tip."

"All valid emotions given it's been only a week. Even so, we are two intelligent individuals. I'm wondering whether you think we should continue this way or not?"

Danielle slowed the stirring motion. "What way? Is this a subtle way of you suggesting I leave the company?"

"No, your job is secure. I'm thinking something entirely different."

Different than not dating but still working together? Her circular movements slowed further. "I'm all ears."

"During the last week, I've come to regret how I left things between us." She smiled, her emotional balloon lifting off the ground. Stephen was right; all Lars needed was a week to step back and think about the repercussions of what he'd said.

She tried to be cool. "How so?"

"To start, I realized that saying I couldn't make any more promises was vague." *You bet it was*, she thought, her smile wider. "What I'm saying is that I now fully realize how much damage was done."

Her hand stopped along with her heart. "I'm sorry, again," she interjected.

"I know you are, and I can say I'm impressed by your demeanor this week, which was purely professional but also fun, consistent since your arrival." His voice had gradually shifted from his personal bantering mode to his more objective tone. "I'm also pleased you have decided to see a therapist. That is a good step for you and your daughter." *Just me and my daughter?* "What I'm really saying Danielle, is that given the severity of the circumstances, I wasn't as firm as I should have been at the end of the conversation."

"The hug was firm," she said softly.

"Then you understand what I'm saying."

She was a mature woman, and visualizing Layda gave her a composure she didn't believe she previously possessed. "You are saying we are going to continue this way indefinitely. No romantic involvements or intentions. Co-workers at the office."

"And friends outside the office." Danielle didn't have any friends outside the office beyond Lani and Stephen, and Lars knew that better than anyone.

"You want to come over and talk about it?" she suggested hopefully, her last desperate attempt to salvage what they once had.

He had the grace to chuckle, but it ended in a sigh of finality. "When we learned Monroe was Andres' daughter you required the freedom to make your own choices and live your life," said Lars. "It worked out well."

She thought about the strategy he was describing, as though they were pieces in a game of chess. I move, he moves, we see where we end up. "And you believe this strategy of being apart is the best way to see if we will end up together again?" she asked.

"I do."

Monroe had toddled up to her leg, and Danielle bent down, stroking Monroe's soft hair. What blond she had in the last year had faded over the last six months, the brown coloring of her father becoming dominant and the blue in her eyes gradually overtaking the green, just like Andre's.

What would Layda counsel her to do and say? Danielle curled her fingers along Monroe's soft jawline, tickling under her chin. She landed a brief kiss on her lips, the action bringing a loving smile to her face. She had more than most single mothers could hope for: a healthy child, a great job, beautiful home, and unbelievable individuals whom she now viewed as her parents.

"Lars, I want you to know this. I loved you and our relationship, with all my being. So, if this is the last time I'm allowed to say those words to you and not feel uncomfortable, I want you to know that those feelings have been sincere and all I could ever have dreamed or hoped for." She looked deep into her daughters' eyes, seeing more of Andre in her than ever. "That said, I'm going to echo what you told me that day in the hospital. Even though we won't be together any longer, I will cherish what we had and move forward professionally."

"And as friends?"

A little bit of air escaped from her lips. "Like you, I can't make any promises on that front. I don't know what it means."

"You might find that it is possible to be friends with those in the workplace."

His tone was so distinctive, the sexy cadence exactly what had always attracted her to him; smart, wise and purposeful. It was also uncompromising. Their romantic relationship was now officially over.

The timer on the pasta went off over his last words, distracting Monroe, who let out an unintelligible word.

"I think Monroe needs you. Take care, Danielle."

Danielle blinked, working to keep her voice even. "Goodbye Lars."

She tried her best to keep her tears from falling, and over the next few hours, she did a good job until her head hit the pillow.

CHAPTER 8

Snow, two-feet deep, was a convenient excuse to stay inside. She'd called Johanne to cancel plans for Saturday evening, thankfully getting his voice mail. Layda called Sunday afternoon, curious about her state of mind after their conversation, and Danielle disclosed her final talk with Lars. Layda listened, expressing pleasure with Danielle's composure.

"Very mature and classy. He can't fault you for loving him to the end, just as he did you."

No, he couldn't.

Monday, Danielle had a new perspective on work, but it was quite different from her first days at the firm. Instead of unbridled enthusiasm sparked by a flame of success, it was dampened by the reality of storm clouds on the horizon.

Margaret walked by her office, the opalescent sheen from her blouse a perfect complement to her A-line, grey pencil skirt and matching pumps.

Italian, Danielle guessed, catching the elegant lines. The women couldn't be faulted on her looks. It was the personality aspect where she fell short. In that way, she was a complete oddity with the other managers Danielle had worked with here at MRD and before then at Russelz in the States. Although they were mostly men, intelligence and aggressiveness found a balance with joking around during non-trading hours. Danielle suspected Margaret was like this all the time; unable to relax her demeanor in the office with anyone.

In it to win it, she thought, the American phrase perfectly suited to Margaret.

At lunch, Danielle asked Glenda about a few of the local areas she'd heard about but not yet visited.

"You must go see the picturesque streets of Schipfe district, one of the neighborhoods of Old Town Zurich situated on the west bank of the Limmat," her Zurich-born secretary said. "The area is full of small shops with narrow walking-only streets along the Niederdorf." Danielle mentally took note as Glenda described another area of the old city located on the east bank of the Limmat. "It's kind of easy to get lost in the alleys, so bring your phone so you can use your GPS."

"My vote is the thermal baths of Thermalbad," said Johanne piped in from her right. "It's a in a former brewery with great city views from the rooftop."

"Both sound great," she said, regaining her enthusiasm.

Danielle turned to her office, assuming Johanne had appeared to talk business. Once inside, he sat down, legs crossed.

"Of course," he continued, as if the conversation hadn't stopped. "What you really need to do is go to the 'red district'" he put in air quotes. "It's on the Langstrasse, but I assure you, it remains generally friendly and without dangers for a…ah, single woman of your nature."

Danielle chortled at his phrasing, as though being single was a sexually transmitted disease.

"I'll wait on that one, thanks very much, but it's Monday. I can't imagine why you are telling me that now."

He winked. "Because next weekend is Valentine's Day, and I thought you'd want expert advice on what to do in this town, just in case you wanted to hook up."

Danielle put her hand to mouth, stifling a laugh. "Are you getting overrides from other traders, because you are being awful spry on the first day of the week."

He shrugged his shoulders. "A manager has to look out for his best trader at all times."

She thought about that for a moment. "So, what you're really saying is because my numbers are down, you need to get me back in the romantic sack so they move back up." His eyes grew bright as she leaned forward on her elbows. "As my number one platonic dancing partner, you need to know this now. Between my love life hitting the ground with the force of a cement block, and five hours of afternoon trading time off my books, we both better prepare for a dip in the money. Are you really worried about me or do you just want to get me out dancing and seeing Zurich's not-so-famed red-light district?"

At the question, his elevated eyebrows relaxed into a flat expression. "Margaret is after me."

"Even though this is all her fault."

"Indeed."

Danielle inserted her ear piece and touched the computer screen. "Then this will be her data point for what happens in pulling a trader off the boards, right?"

"Too bad we can't have you trade after hours for us instead of yourself," he grumbled.

"You caught that little change, did you?"

He grimaced. "It was pretty obvious. You doing it to prove a point?"

"Of course." He stood. They were as one on the subject of getting back at Margaret for hurting her performance. "Has Lars said anything about it?"

"No, and I don't expect him to. After all, he's the one who agreed with this approach in the first place."

The afternoon ended with her first dedicated session with Georgiana, the forty-one year old trader who was more demoralized than Danielle. She'd been top of her field with the corporate investment side, but according to Georgiana's replay of events, Margaret had essentially given her the choice of transferring to Zurich from Geneva and taking the job of a trader or be unemployed.

As they wrapped up the session, Danielle asked, "Are you enjoying Zurich?" she asked.

"Not yet, but maybe if I see more of the outside of this building than the inside, that might change."

"You have no friends or family here?"

Georgiana shook her head. "I have a few recommendations…" Danielle began, recommending a jazz club for music, a nightclub for dancing and Stars and Stripes for eating. She didn't mention The Stinking Rose, but then recalled they'd already been once on a company trip organized by Johanne.

"Thanks," Georgiana said gratefully. "What about the men in the office? Lars had said we can date who we want, but Margaret always frowned on that in the other office." Danielle looked past her, to the hallway. In a lowered voice, she spoke.

"Interoffice dating is indeed, a non-issue here," confided Danielle, "so you are welcome to explore that as an option. Personally, I have no experience in dating any of the traders, so I can't help you with who's single or not. But the person to ask is Johanne. He seems to know everything that's going on."

Georgiana smiled, grateful.

Stepping out of the building a few minutes later, Danielle pulled her collar up and hat down, the brisk wind carrying dusty flakes of snow.

"Hello Ms. Grant."

She turned. "Dominic!" He smiled, and she went straight up to him, giving Lars' driver a hug. "I'm American," she muttered. "I can do that." Stepping back, she asked how he'd been.

"No different. It's a little boring without you around." They shared a moment of silence.

Dominic adjusted his broad shoulders and twisted his neck to one side, the way a strong man expert in the ways of defensive tactics will do. He was not just Lars' driver, but personal bodyguard, and had been a figure in Lars' life for as long as Danielle had been in Zurich. There was only one reason he was parked out front, and that's because he was waiting for his boss.

"See you round," she said, her voice low.

At home, Danielle kept to her routine, trading once Monroe was asleep. It was still snowing outside, and it occurred to Danielle she needed to engage in another physical activity during the long winter season. Sailboarding was good, but it lasted only from late spring to fall, the other months she was a full-fledged office potato. She pulled up her calendar, seeing the first appointment with her therapist confirmed for Thursday, 3:45 p.m. It was barely enough time to finish trading, spend an hour with Jacob then take the metro over. Maybe the therapist would have a few ideas on a suitably strenuous activity to help her physical self as well as her mental well-being.

CHAPTER 9

Each day that passed felt like the sludge from the breakup with Lars was being diluted and filtered, producing a cleaner jet fuel. To her surprise, by Thursday, she was looking forward to her first appointment with Dr. Blatz. Instead of being anxious and impatient with Jacob when he sat down at 2:30 sharp, she felt calm, even generous with her time. The thirty-two year old had a fine grasp of the numbers, but that's where he was stuck. He didn't know how to expand his world outside of the latest quarterly reports. The Tuesday prior, she'd given him homework to take three of his largest clients and dig deeper into their industries, the goal to learn much more about them than what was publicly available.

"It's there," she'd told him. "You just have to take the time to find it."

She quizzed him about what he'd learned, and it didn't take long to discover that he'd not done what she asked.

"What you have is a start," she said diplomatically.

"A start? This took me three hours." This was what separates the leaders from the rest of the pack, she thought to herself. He must have sensed what she was thinking because his head tilted in curiosity. "How much time do you spend on your research?"

The double tap at her door prevented her from answering. She looked up at Lars. "Danielle, would you have five minutes to spare at the end of the day?"

"Yes, and exactly five, as I have an appointment at 3:45."

"Jacob, would you mind if your time with Danielle gets cut by ten?" Jacob gave him a nod and Lars left.

"Back to your question," Danielle continued, her mind on Lars. He'd once asked the same question when they were in his car, in what she'd categorize as their first official date. "During the week, I research and trade about three to four hours every night after work. On the weekends, between six and nine hours."

Jacob was silent. He'd pulled his lips to one side, letting her know he wasn't pleased by what he'd just heard.

"And since I can see you are wondering, the answer is no. I don't have a life." His lips relaxed with her comment. "There is really no way you can get the numbers I do without putting in the hours." Another phrase she'd used with Lars. *I have to stop bringing him into my thoughts.* "Back to this…" she said. They turned their attention to the screen, and he scooted his chair around to her side, watching as she pulled up one screen after another, drawing the lines between a corporation's financials and the source. As much as she'd told herself she wasn't going to divulge all her secrets, she knew Jacob wanted to succeed. But she also knew that if he chose to stay out late instead of putting in the effort, no amount of knowledge would ever get him to the front of the line.

Fifty minutes later, he stood, his light eyes dark with focus. "Monday?" he confirmed.

"That's what Margaret said, every other day, between you and Georgiana, switching the following week."

"How's she doing?" he asked, a competitive sound in his voice.

She stood up too. "Her numbers post on the boards tomorrow, just like everyone else."

"Right. Thanks again, Danielle. I appreciate it, especially knowing you don't want to do this."

"In this business, it's all about the numbers, Jacob. Don't take it personally."

She rang the buzzer outside Lars' office and turned the knob when the click sounded. He was already standing when she walked through, gesturing to the sitting area.

"I'll keep this short," he began.

"What's up?"

"I wanted to tell you that the decision was made to shut down client accounts at less than our fifty million mark."

"Interesting," Danielle replied.

"We made an exception early on, believing that your client base would grow, and it has." But certainly not by orders of ten or twenty, not even with her trading prowess.

"The letters went out last week, and I received a call from Max today. He will live, but it wasn't his money, per se. It's his families trust, and he's on the line to manage it."

"Letters?" she repeated. That was awfully abrupt. "Why didn't Johanne speak with them as the manager on the account?"

Lars used the palm of his hand to smooth out the fabric of his pants on his thigh. "Margaret thought it was unnecessary."

"Since when did Margaret start to know more about running a successful wealth managing and trading firm than Johanne, or certainly you?" He didn't answer the question, and Danielle couldn't help herself. "Lars, are you gradually ceding operational decisions to her for a reason, or are you on some sort of death wish for the company, because since the new year rolled over, I'm confused by what I see occurring."

"There is a difference between sharing management duties and decisions and ceding authority."

"Well, then may I ask another question? Am I the only recipient of her newfound authority, or is she sharing the money-reducing love around the company evenly?" Her look and tone were far more challenging than Jacob's had been the hour before.

"It may appear that you are taking the brunt of it—"

"Appear? What can be more factual than fewer zeros, Lars?"

"As I was going to finish saying, it's only short-term and will right itself. Even if other accounts didn't add up to fifty million francs, its far less than any one of your next client in terms of size."

There was no point in arguing. Lars was giving Margaret the rope to hang herself. She began to get up when Lars spoke.

"There is one other thing," Lars said. "The ring. I notice you are still wearing it." Danielle's thumb touched the bottom of the ring, which was on her fourth finger.

"Is that a problem?"

"No, I'm just surprised."

"Lars, you told me it was a reminder of all we had and the love we felt for each other, and to take it off meant…well…" She didn't want to say the words out loud. It felt odd.

"To take it off meant that you don't love me anymore," he finished for her.

"That's right."

She thanked him again for the update and left, gathering her things and saying goodbye to Glenda. She did still love him and had come to terms with the fact it was going to take some time for those feelings to go away.

And perhaps they never would, but only go dormant, just like her emotions had in the past. But then one day, that love might spring up like a new blossom, the ring a reminder and promise for the future.

Could it be that Lars was subtly implying she take it off because he no longer felt that way for her? No. He was clear when he gave it to her. This was about her feelings, not his. Could he really have expected her feelings to have disappeared in so short a time?

On her way out, she heard someone call her name. She glanced around and saw a wave from inside one of the cubicles.

It was Jacob. "I'm saying thanks again," he said.

"You are welcome. If nothing else its motivation to improve your numbers, being stuck out here should be it," she said, glancing around, her voice low. "Although why you are in a cubicle is beyond me. Wait. Don't tell me. Margaret doesn't believe in offices for traders?" He nodded, shrugging a shoulder. "Well, my old firm had the same philosophy, but it was slightly worse. There, I was in a bullpen with nine other traders."

His eyes rose, lifting up his lashes. "That wouldn't be so bad."

"Being in a bullpen?" she asked, mildly surprised.

"It would be endurable as long as you were in it, too."

The only response she could give was a laugh. "You keep going the way you are and I'll be demoted to just that, which I guarantee wouldn't make either of us happy."

She left him, and the conversation, behind her, still feeling the heat from her cheeks as she rode the elevator down.

CHAPTER 10

Exiting the building, she saw a familiar face.

"Hello again," she said to Dominic who was just getting out of the slate grey BMW stretch four-door sedan. "Ms. Grant," he greeted.

As she had to walk past him to the metro, she moved closer, conscious that if he were already out of his car, then Lars was close behind.

"You know," she said with a tone of earned familiarity. "Now that Lars and I are no longer dating, you can drop the Ms. thing." He smiled fractionally, his eyes alight with humor but his posture every bit the driver-bodyguard he was. "Or you can wait until you are off-duty and then just say 'yo! Hey-baby!'" Dominic coughed into his hand. "I know, you really miss my American-ism."

"You have no idea how much." She winked and didn't say another word, happy that she'd cracked his hard exterior. Danielle had rarely ridden in the car without Dominic as the driver because Lars lacked a license when they began dating, his being suspended due to the amount of traffic violations. It had continued throughout their journeys up to Lars' home in Zermatt, outside St. Moritz, so she and Lars could sit and talk the entire way up and down, or eat food and get work done. As a consequence, Dominic had been privy to their romantic interludes, but also their ups and downs, all experienced through his vantage point in the rearview mirror.

Not to mention the time he defended me against Andre.

It took Danielle longer than expected to find the office of psychologist Dr. Blatz, probably because the past scene replayed in her mind. After seeing Andre with another woman at the company function in St. Moritz, Danielle had thrown caution aside and enjoyed a drink with Lars. Four drinks and one gondola ride down the mountain with Lars later, she'd faced Andre in the parking lot who requested she leave Lars and allow him to drive her home. She'd refused, he'd touched her shoulder and Dominic had intervened. She'd felt safe in his presence and confident that all passing in front of his eyes and heard by his ears would remain confidential to his death.

After turning around, Danielle located the side street that wasn't as well marked as she expected. Arriving seven minutes late, she filled out the paperwork, knowing her fifty-minute appointment would now be down to about forty, give or take.

Just as well. The first time was likely a meet and greet anyway. Having heard about, but never participating in a therapy session, she had a good idea of what to expect. Or so she thought.

"Ms. Grant," Dr. Blatz said warmly, shaking her hand. His thick, salt and pepper hair contrasted with his youthful skin, a trait she associated with those born and raised here. "Hello Doctor." He invited her into his office, which was more like her living room at home. A couch along the wall, facing the lake, and two side chairs, one at either end. The doctor's own leather chair was in the center, allowing him to interact with the patient in any one of the three seating areas. She chose the couch, close enough to the end so she could rest her elbow on the arm.

They began with pleasantries, him asking how she had been referred to his practice. This begat a discussion about Layda and Danielle's relationship to the Mettleren family, and after the first ten minutes, Dr. Blatz knew about Andre, Monroe, and why she was now sitting before him.

"Death, dying and fear issues," she summed up for him. He gave her a slight smile, his blue eyes watching her, but not intrusively.

"Can I add on few other things we may cover?"

"Absolutely. I know it's not the Swiss-way or culture, but I'm all for the direct approach. Subtly hasn't ever worked very well for me."

"Then we will get along just fine. I would add avoidance, denial and fear of failure."

That got Danielle to laugh outright. "I agree! We are going to get along just fine."

Exactly forty-one minutes later, Danielle was making another appointment for the following week. Given the emotional territory they'd covered, she wanted to up the frequency of their sessions but Dr. Blatz cautioned against it.

"You will need time to process what we are discussing. Talking about emotions is far easier than dealing with them."

Wasn't that the truth?

When she returned home and greeted Emma, she was told her daughter was already down for the night.

"She didn't take her nap as usual, which means she might wake up bright and early."

"Or maybe she'll sleep until ten!"

Danielle was grateful for the unexpected time to herself. After a long bath, she sat on her bed, listening to background music as she traded in the afterhours market, mixing in more of the same, monotonous research she'd told Jacob about.

Jacob. Nice looking, a few years older than herself, and single. And he would remain that way, because she wasn't interested in a relationship with anyone at the moment, and certainly not with a co-worker.

The following morning at ten, Danielle received a text from Johanne.

It's V-day tomorrow You need to come out to dinner, we will be your dinner dates

She grinned at the series of emojis, ending with a big, red question mark.

let me check she texted back

He gave her a frowny face but then a thumbs up. Johanne was a good friend, she affirmed, thinking of her conversation with Lars. Unable to concentrate on the words in front of her, she logged out of her accounts and closed down her system.

Danielle then called Layda.

"That's exactly what you need to do, my dear. We will gladly be with Monroe. Stay out as long as you want."

Danielle was happy with the thought of going out with her two male friends on Valentine's Day. Johanne would choose a new place she'd never been, giving her the excuse to get dressed up and get out of the house, exactly what Dr. Blatz had recommended. He'd told her to get engaged and start making her life her own, starting as soon as she was ready.

Since she was going to be walking her own path for a while, it might as well be filled with a few great restaurants.

At eight-thirty on Saturday night, she and her two friends were seated at a high table at Dante, one of the trendiest cocktail bars in town.

"Did they name this after the poet or because they were trying to make it sound hot, like Inferno?" she asked her companions.

"It is hot, like me," Dario said dryly, causing her to laugh. The room was quickly becoming packed, the noise level increasing with each body now crowding the bar. Dimly lit lights dropped from the ceiling, the neon bulbs behind the well-built male bartenders all boasting ripped muscles. This was a place for the beautiful people of Zurich, she decided, and it didn't bother her one bit.

Unfortunately, the bar did have one downside. The drink orders were so slow, Dario and Johanne took turns counting how many times they stirred the ice in their glasses until the next order came.

"On to a new place," Johanne announced, tapping his phone. "I got us a seat at Bar Hotel Rivington. What?" he asked his on-again, off-again partner.

"If you want great espresso, yes, then by all means, but half the time the beer is warm," said Dario.

Seeing Dario's look, Johanne took out his phone again. "Try the Kronenhalle." Johanne rolled his eyes. Dario then turned to Danielle. "It's legendary not just in this town, but around the world. Johanne is resistant because it's favored by the older crowd and is typically chock full of artists, entertainers, writers—but it's like a throwback to the past. That said, it has the best escargot in Zurich. What's more romantic than a shell fish sautéed in butter for Valentine's?"

Johanne couldn't help but laugh as he dialed. "We'll never get in you know." Dario put out his hand for the phone.

"You need to know people, which I do."

Twenty minutes later, they were standing at the bar inside the Kronenhalle, an elegant setting within an imposing exterior. They'd just been served drinks when the maître d ushered the three to a table in the rear, by the window, "A preferred position for unique guests," murmured Dario to Danielle. Johanne overheard and coughed.

"You mean former friends." Danielle caught a glance between the two and let the inside joke alone.

"It is lovely," she observed, glad she was wearing a more tailored, sexy outfit of cream colored leather pants and a matching cashmere overcoat as opposed to a tight black skirt meant for dancing. Her friends were both in jackets, sans tie, each looking hip and sexy. "And Johanne, it's not all an older crowd. Half of the group is our age." Within the wood lined, floor to ceiling room, paintings from the masters hung in exquisite frames, the deep coloring offset by the ivory linen table cloths and champagne flutes. Red and white roses were everywhere in celebration of Valentine's Day, the delicate pastries, cheesecakes and other desserts all sporting a red, pink or white motif. She was so glad to be here with not one, but two handsome men. She didn't care a bit they were taken with each other more than her. In fact, it was the perfect situation for her unperfect life; companionship without the drama.

The menus came and she took their advice for appetizers and the main dish, enjoying their uninhibited conversation. They were on the subject of plans for the summer break when **Dario's eyes lifted from the rim of his cup and moved past her.** Johanne's eyes went to the point behind her, narrowing.

"Nothing of interest, Danielle. Just Lars and Margaret." As he closed his mouth, the lower lip dropped. "Margaret…" he said in a low, unhappy voice. "We both have her to thank for the present predicament of lower returns."

"Don't tell me," laughed Dario. "You can't afford your half tonight?"

Danielle smirked. "Guess you'll be picking up the tab for both of us Dario. Thanks for that." Dario winked and took a sip of his drink, making it clear he didn't mind.

"*Margaret*," Johanne said again, turning his focus to Danielle. "Do you know, Lars never brought up his engagement again after Andre's death? Maybe it was all because of that woman, who he'd obviously been working on with the merger."

"I know *you* never brought it up again after the one time in your office," she said, hoping to distract him.

Johanne nodded. "Because we merged with and integrated the new people in the office," he continued, putting the word *merged* in air quotes, hands low, by his chest, so as not to be observed. "Half a dozen times I've been at the office after hours, forgetting something or catching up on paperwork and I see Margaret's light is on. I go to the bathroom and guess what else? Lars' light is on too. She's not in her office. Where else could she be?"

"Coincidence?" she suggested flippantly.

"Is anything ever a coincidence with Lars?" Dario asked, taking a bite of his food.

"Nope," responded Johanne. "And she is now touching him on the arm, crossing the personal boundary space."

"And smiling rather wide," Dario added, giving the play-by-play.

"You two," she said, shaking her head. "While I find this reality show very entertaining, the more benign truth of it is that it's likely a business dinner. Perhaps her touching his arm is a way to emphasize something."

"Yeah?" murmured Johanne, his lips barely moving. "Look now and tell me if you think she's emphasizing. Fast!" Danielle put her cheek to her right shoulder and looked. Her mouth went dry, her stomach dropped and her legs felt weak. "What do you say to that?" he asked.

Danielle slowly and purposefully turned back around, a plastic smile of indifference melded on her face. "Clearly, a looser definition of merger may be in use here."

Of all the times and places to be, Lars was here, on Valentine's evening with another woman. Not that she really expected him to be home sulking, but really? On Valentine's? The ring and watch felt leaden.

Although her emotions propelled her to use the lady's room, she glued herself to the chair. There was no way in this world or any other she was going to be forced to acknowledge the two of them. A collegial touch to the arm was one contact which she would have no issue doing to Ulrich or Noel to emphasize her point. But for the managing director to put his hand on top of a woman's, at a table in public and leave it there? Every second counted in the world of business, and she abided by the three second rule. If the touch lasted longer than the time it took to inhale and exhale several times, there was more going on.

Much more.

The waiter came and they ordered dessert. Hidden at their table in the corner, and given Lars' evident focus on Margaret, Danielle found it plausible he'd not even seen them.

Lars moving on from her with Margaret shouldn't have come as a complete shock. If she were honest with herself, the very first day she met the woman at the front doors of MRD, jealousy, insecurity and fear had all registered and never truly went away. It had just ebbed and flowed with the rise and fall of her relationship tide with Lars.

"Why aren't you enjoying this more?" Johanne asked her, breaking into her thoughts. "I know that sassy, American attitude is never far from the surface."

"Perhaps my reluctance is because you're my immediate boss and it would be impolitic to discuss the managing director with you." Dario coughed and Danielle smirked. "Or, it could be that I'm simply above gossiping about the obvious."

"Oh, please," teased Johanne. "As if that's ever stopped you before. And lest you forget, I'm the boss who cage dances with you. You know," he said, his voice going a notch lower, "would you like to hear my expanded theory?" Danielle slid her eyes to Dario, her chest beating out of time.

"I'm ready to hear it," she said with false levity.

"Lars broke off the engagement and you were going to give it a play with him, but then Margaret swooped him away before you had a chance. Now your options are back to where they were before; limited to me and Dario for dancing, and Robin and every other manager at the clubs we frequent who keep buying you drinks and cajoling you to sing."

Danielle's eyes never left his, and she used every ounce of discipline to push up from the corners of her mouth into a fabricated smile. "If what you are saying is true, I should be devastated right about now, don't you think?"

Johanne shrugged. "At least a tad disappointed. Take a look now." Against all within her that counseled not to do it, she leaned forward, and turned her head slightly.

Lars was leaning towards Margaret, his right hand graduating from arm to neck. Danielle told herself to look away, but she couldn't. Margaret's smile grew broad as her eyelashes dropped and his lips reached her cheek. The pain Danielle felt was exquisite as she saw his own eyes close, his lips connecting with her skin. The kiss was short and impactful, like the punch that had gone into her kidneys.

"That's what I'm saying," muttered Johanne. Danielle should have stopped watching, but couldn't. Her eyes were still on him when he turned his cheek parallel to Margaret's, his eyes opening. Danielle connected with Lars' gaze, holding it for a moment, gratified her composure hadn't left her.

She felt nothing, her emotions having fled from the sun that Lars once was in her life. Margaret's eyes opened as well, probably wondering why Lars wasn't giving her any more attention. Unfortunately, she caught Danielle's eye as well. Danielle gave her the disinterested smile one gives a boss in a restaurant; acknowledgment without emotion.

"Too bad it was just one kiss," Johanne added, as though he'd been expecting more.

Danielle turned back to her friends. Johanne was focused on cutting the chocolate torte in front of him but Dario was watching her carefully.

"Johanne, I have a different theory," said Dario. "You want to hear it?"

"Oh Dario. No more," Danielle tried to say playfully as her insides were crushing against one another like a rock grinder. "Johanne just presented his and it came true. If history is any precedent, they might be making love on the table next." Johanne snickered.

Dario's eyes were level, and compassionate. "How about this? Remember when I tried to guess about the identity of the man who came after Andre? The one we never knew who it was?"

"Yes, I do," replied Johanne, who nodded as he took a bite.

"I'm thinking," continued Dario slowly, as if neither of them had spoken, "Lars was the man after Andre. Your *boyfriend*, as Johanne always called him. When you learned it was Andres' baby, that's when you became a single mother, without ever admitting the identity of the boyfriend. Then, when your father died, Andre came back in your life and you got engaged. Do you know it wasn't until a month before your wedding that Lars got engaged? He waited that long, thinking you wouldn't go through with the marriage. Then Andres passes, and by the new year, Lars is no longer engaged."

"An inventive storyline," Danielle acknowledged.

"You and Lars begin dating again, and all is well until Margaret enters the fray. What?" Dario asked Johanne, who was shaking his head in disbelief. "The timing matches up, almost perfectly to when you were talking about Danielle's numbers being up then down."

Johanne laughed out loud, but Danielle's emotions were fraying. In order to avoid Dario's inquisitive glare, she turned around in an attempt to prove her indifference. This time, Lars was focusing intently on his food, his back stiff and face severe while Margaret's countenance showed confusion. Danielle almost felt sorry for the woman.

"Do you see what your little narrative has done with the two of them?" Danielle inquired. "They were sitting there, happily enjoying a meal and us staring at them has gone and ruined it."

Dario was unrepentant. "Serves Lars right," he said. "His own line about not dating clients has ruined it for quite a few people, me and Johanne included. But thank you. I know Johanne will be grateful as well."

"Thanks for what?" she asked, genuinely surprised.

"For validating everything I just said."

Johanne looked between her and Dario in confusion. "What'd she just say? What'd I just miss?"

Danielle felt the hand of knowledge constricting its fingers around her heart. Dario had guessed it all. Now she had two options: lie to her good friends, who had seen her through singledom with all the highs and lows in-between, or come clean.

Johanne was still looking between Dario and herself when Dario spoke.

"How are you handling it?" he asked, his voice soft and sincere. Danielle bit her lip and glanced down at the table, caught off-guard by the emotional upheaval she was experiencing.

"Oh my God," murmured Johanne. "All that…that was true?" He leaned forward, his voice going to a near whisper. "Lars was the *boyfriend?*

Mr. *Anonymous*?" Danielle did nothing more than meet his eyes, curling her lips in tighter. "And you and he... *all this time*?" Her silence was all the answer he needed, for he sat back emotions crossing his face. Astonishment, understanding and now, with another glance across her shoulders, anger, the kind that comes from a brother who knows his sister has been betrayed.

Danielle leaned forward, placing a hand on his wrist in mirror fashion to what Lars had done with Margaret. "Johanne, listen to me. Lars was amazing. Emphasize was. He's moved on, just like Andre did before him. Don't you remember St. Moritz when Andre brought Eva?"

"Of course, but Eva was temporary, and look where that ended up. But you? Unreal." He held her eyes now. "You want to tell us what happened? Or rather, let me cut to the chase as your friend and immediate superior. Are you going to leave MRD?"

"Not now. It's the best I can do for an answer. As to what happened with us? Everything was absolutely perfect until he came in one Monday with his arm in sling." Johanne nodded. He'd remembered. "I lost it, and he didn't want to change his lifestyle which includes risky sports. I couldn't handle the notion of losing another boyfriend, fiancé or husband to an untimely death. We literally had the perfect relationship until his accident ended it all. Now…"

"You're just working and avoiding the past?" suggested Dario.

"Yes, that's exactly what I am doing. When I came around, he'd shut down. Time adds up and people move on. For good."

The three were quiet and Danielle guessed Johanne was working through the subtleties at the office he'd previously missed.

"I hope you aren't mad I kept a secret from you," she said quietly. "I had to."

Johanne gave her an understanding smile. "It's alright. You had promised not to give me any trouble as your boss, and my ignorance has been bliss. Besides," he continued with a little more levity. "I can't complain when your numbers still exceed the industry by a solid margin, even with your trading being sliced by this mentoring requirement."

"I do what I can to make it easy on you," she said sincerely. "Dario, since you have been the master guesser on all things romantic over the last two years, what do you think? Do you really believe Lars would take a date to this place, knowing how many professionals come here?"

"You mean is he serious with her?"

Danielle nodded, but before Dario could answer, Johanne spoke his mind. "It has been two months since you had sex?" She gave a nod. "I don't think he's serious," Johanne offered. "I don't want to be rude Danielle, but he could be sleeping with half the town and since you mostly stay at home and have limited your outings to jazz and dancing, you'd never know."

The notion that Lars wasn't monogamous was wholly disturbing, because his nature was to be with one woman, totally and completely. Then again, he'd previously admitted when she reconnected with Andre, he'd pushed himself out of the gate into dating women sooner than he should have. Maybe he'd done it again.

"Return the favor with Jacob," Johanne suggested. "That one's pretty obvious."

Danielle shrugged and took a drink, as much to push down the acid that had been traveling up her throat as to regain moisture for talking. "For now, gentleman, let's be clear on one thing. I'm neither sleeping with anyone in the office, nor anyone else, and the numbers are still up, to the greatest degree possible."

Although her tone was upbeat, a somber mood had colored the conversation. Fortunately for her, it didn't last long. Dessert was finished, the bill soon paid and they walked outside. Danielle wasn't sure if Lars or Margaret looked their direction, because the men were walking in front and behind her, effectively blocking her from their line of sight. A gallant gesture from her two friends who still had her back.

CHAPTER 11

Outside, her friends gave her a final hug and turned left towards the metro while Danielle paused to check her phone. A cough made her look up and she laughed, walking forward.

"We have got to stop meeting like this," she said, holding her arms out. Dominic's hug was longer than the last.

"You okay?" he asked her.

"I will be."

He gently pulled back. "I saw you walk in with Johanne and Dario, but I was too late to catch you."

She willed a crooked smile. "It was the exclamation point of finality on our relationship, but you probably knew that even the last time we saw each other."

"And before." It was his job description. The secrets he'd keep were not ones she wanted to hear. "I'd offer you a ride home if the circumstances were otherwise."

In the light of the streetlamps, the sincerity in his eyes cut through his tough external demeanor. She laughed. "I have a long way to go before I warrant a car and driver, but even then, I'm not sure that's my style. I'm sort of independent that way."

"That was part of the reason why Lars liked you."

No. Lars loved me.

Her emotional state must have reflected itself because he pulled her to him again, giving her a longer hug, telling her to be have a good night. "As best you can," he added.

Danielle took the metro home, walking the final two blocks in the heavy, late winter snow. Inside Layda's home, she made herself a cup of tea, then going into the living room and turning on the gas fireplace. It was a grand, wood paneled room, like many in such a stately, waterfront house.

"May I join you?" Georgy was in his robe and slippers, a snifter in his hand.

"I thought you were traveling."

"Trip ended early due to weather, leaving me halfway to my destination. Layda said you had not one but two dates."

"Correction. I had two men on one date. I'm fortunate that way."

Georgy chuckled, his deep voice rumbling as he made himself comfortable. "It's still early."

"Not for me. There's only so much a woman can eat, but I did enjoy experiencing new places." She stopped abruptly, correcting herself. "Well, one anyway. Not so keen on the Kronenhalle."

A bushy eyebrow raised. "Everyone likes the Kronenhalle, including me. The owners are also fabulous."

Stupid me. "Let me rephrase. The atmosphere, food and my immediate friends were divine. Let's say a few unexpected guests weren't so welcome." He raised an eyebrow and she took a sip of her tea. "Lars was there. With Margaret. Georgy, he kissed her, right there, in public."

"Did you expect this?"

She shook her head. "I expected a lot of things, but not for him to move on so quickly, and certainly not with the newest member of the management team. Remember how Andre hooked up with Eva, about five weeks after we broke up, taking her to the company party in St. Moritz? This is nearly identical. Georgy, is there something in the Swiss, male culture that dictates a man can only take so much—or rather, can't take not having anything."

Slowly, Georgy's expression lightened.

"It's not written down in a book, no. What I think you have experienced is the pragmatism of a man, regardless of the country or zip code therein. They just realize the limits of the situation and make a decision to go on, regardless of the feelings underneath." He paused and then continued. "Andre never stopped loving you, as I told you when you attended his hockey game. Do you recall what I said?" She nodded. "He took your break-up very hard and found solace with Eva. But that was temporary, lasting only a few weeks."

"You are suggesting Margaret is Lars' rebound romance?"

Georgy huffed a response. "I'm not sure his interaction with her would warrant the word *romance*. Don't confuse physical intimacy with emotion and especially not love. Neither Andre nor Lars are the type of men to have their hearts easily touched, and when that happened, it was very deep, lasting years, in the case of Lars. That doesn't go away overnight."

No, it goes underground, just as Lars himself once told me.

"Do you think I should stick it out?" Georgy raised an eyebrow at her question. "I mean, just keep loving him and waiting for him like he did with me?"

"My dear, he didn't wait. He started dating other women, even becoming engaged. He moved on, just as he encouraged you to do."

She smirked. "I hardly see myself getting seriously romantic or engaged in the near or far future."

"Be that as it may, sometimes, relationships leading up to a marriage are like rubber bands, contracting then extending, but the tie between the two individuals is always there. Have you ever wondered about the traditional marriage vows?"

"Georgy, I've never been married," she said with sarcasm.

"Fair enough. Through thick and thin. The rubber band analogy came from somewhere. You experience times of lean and plenty, but you don't break. You and he may not be physical with each other, and be so with others, but your emotional rubber band is there, as sure and true as anything could be."

She gazed at him intently. "You really think so?"

"You have a world to experience and explore. Trust me. As you enter your third decade, the experiences you've had thus far will serve as the foundation for a great house for the future."

Danielle felt a sense of relief and optimism at his words. Heartache and loss were, and are, a part of life's journey, pieces of a puzzle that was not yet completed.

"I have one last bit of wisdom if you'd like to hear it."

"Always," she said immediately.

"I've learned that if things are meant to be, it will work out, easily and naturally. It's never forced. And when something takes too much work or effort, or the wires keep getting crossed and issues arise, no matter how hard one tries, it's not destined to be. In those cases, you let it go, because the universe, God, or whatever you believe in, doesn't want you to take that course of action. That's ultimately how you will know. With any man, not just Lars, it shouldn't be a struggle. Marriage is hard enough."

She went to bed repeating his words: if it's meant to be, it will work out. Smoothly. Easily. The words gave her the peace she needed to sleep, quelling her thoughts of a life with Lars. Too bad she couldn't keep him out of her dreams.

Danielle woke to quiet. Snow was falling and she checked the weather on her phone. When storms lasted more than three days, it just became the regular weather. In three weeks, the snow would be gone for good and she'd be on the water in a wet suit.

She adjusted her hips, bringing one leg to her chest, stretching out her lower back. What she should concentrate on was being in good physical and mental shape because she wasn't about to place bets on her emotions.

Monroe made noises from the next room and Danielle got out of bed to change and dress her. The two of them went downstairs where Layda asked about her Saturday night with her friends.

Discretion, thought Danielle, the word synonymous with this culture. It had lovely and sad connotations, most associated with Lars.

"Did Georgy tell you want happened last night?" Layda nodded sympathetically. "This is what being a real mother is like, Layda. You get the highs and the lows and in-betweens of your almost daughter." Layda was making a Waldorf salad, chopping the apples and adding the walnuts.

"I agree with him," she said. "Do you recall when I said I thought Lars was destined for you? Well, all things will work out, or not, just like Georgy said."

Danielle held out her left hand, causing Layda to look down. "And this?" Danielle asked her.

"Do you still want him to think that you love him?"

"Given what Georgy said, a man's heart doesn't always dictate what he does with his body, which I get. But Layda, that's not how I operate."

"Certainly not," she said with a bit of disdain for that type of behavior. She put down the knife. "And even if you did, why give Lars the satisfaction of thinking you are pining over him while he's out roaming the town?"

Danielle blinked then giggled. "Layda, if someone were to have told me you possessed this wicked streak, I never would have believed it."

She pursed her lips innocently. "Who said wicked? I can be just as pragmatic as the next woman, which means…" she paused, her mouth open, as if expecting Danielle to insert the words.

"Taking control, and getting what you want?"

Layda's lips smiled in satisfaction. "Precisely." She resumed cutting the apples and Danielle placed the cheese on the platter.

"So, I give the ring back."

"And that watch," Layda added. "You could buy each of those for yourself several times over. He doesn't deserve to have you wear them now, don't you agree?"

She did.

CHAPTER 12

Monday, Danielle paid Johanne a visit in his office. She sat down in the chair opposite him and kept her voice low. "I have a favor to ask," she began, "but it's easy."

"I like easy."

"Make sure that my time outside trading is filled from the moment I arrive until I leave, and that I don't have to meet with Margaret or Lars for any reason."

"But—" he began. She held up a finger, stopping him.

"But you are my boss. My numbers are down. You're unhappy and so am I. You run pass interference for me with Margaret and Lars as necessary. Intimate that if they don't like it, they might be down one gold trader in two weeks." His eyes popped and she raised another finger, forestalling his comment. "It's a bluff, obviously. I'm not going anywhere. I just need some space after what we saw Saturday night. Fair enough?"

He gave a nod. "Fair enough. Speak of the devil," he muttered.

"Good morning," greeted Margaret from the doorway.

"Hello Margaret," Johanne said, glancing over Danielle's shoulder. "What can I do for you?"

"It's Danielle. I'd like to meet with you during the lunch hour."

Danielle turned around. "I'm sorry, Margaret. I have an appointment."

The woman stared. "It's not on the calendar."

"It's during lunchtime, and I don't input my personal events on the public calendar."

"Whatever it is, I can take care of it for Danielle," Johanne said briskly. "She's got her trades to be concerned with."

"I don't want to take up your time, Johanne," Margaret countered.

"That's my decision to make, don't you think?" The woman paused for a moment then gave him a flat-lipped nod.

"How to win friends and influence people," Danielle murmured after she'd gone, causing Johanne to curl his lips. "Thanks for saving me."

"I fear it won't be for long. Promise you won't leave?"

She held his gaze. "If this continues, no, I can't. But you will likely know before me if I make that decision, or if it's made for me, right?"

He confirmed the truth of it and she went back to trading. Unfortunately, Margaret didn't honor her word. She stopped by Danielle's office at 12:15. "I thought you had an appointment."

Crap. She'd been trading and totally forgot to leave for the fabricated event. "Shutting down now," she remarked casually.

Margaret closed the door, standing with her back to the glass wall. "It's no secret you don't like giving up your trading hours but it's only for another week, assuming their numbers are up."

"Trading is an interesting thing, Margaret. No one can assume anyone's numbers are going to be up, even mine." Danielle stood, making for the wardrobe that held her coats, boots and shoes.

"Since you've spent time with Jacob and Georgiana, they've shown significant improvement. That's good for them and the firm."

"I'm glad." Danielle pulled on her coat. She'd have to figure out somewhere to go. Maybe even a lunch outside the walls of this building. It would be a first-ever experience. As Danielle buttoned her jacket, she expected Margaret to say what she really had on her mind, but as she didn't, Danielle slipped her purse over her shoulder. "Is that all?"

"Just one other item. As Johanne has inserted himself between the two of us for management issues, I'm doing the same with Lars. To this point, you and he have had a direct communication, however we have agreed that I should be the one to take over moving forward."

"We being who? You and Lars?" Margaret inclined her head, a single nod of superiority reinforcing who was a managing partner and who was not. "It's a non-issue, Margaret. I have nothing that requires a discussion with Lars on any subject. Should something arise, Johanne will take care of it, with you or whomever you decide. I'm here at MRD to trade, and that's what you should expect."

"Good." Danielle stared her in the eye until the woman stepped aside. Without waiting for Margaret to leave or say goodbye, Danielle exited her office, informing Glenda she'd be back in an hour. After ten minutes of walking in the light snow, she realized she was half-way to Stars & Stripes and kept going. Her instinct was proven out; the restaurant was slow, it being a Monday and stormy outside. Stephen greeted her with a surprised smile and she moved to their special booth. After stripping off her jacket and brushing the snow from her hair, she went back to the kitchen and greeted Renaldo and the staff.

She kissed his cheeks, asking for a recommendation. "I'm starved and in need of some comfort food,"

He winked. "Mac and cheese with ham."

"I'll go to sleep!" she teased.

"You will have chocolate mousse that will wake you right up. Trust me."

She did, sending a text to Johanne as she waited. He replied in typical Johanne fashion.

Witch.

Danielle suspected Johanne's original word was replaced by the non-cursing auto speller of the iPhone, but it still got her to smile. Women bosses weren't all that different than their male counterparts: they always wanted to be the lead feline in the room, and if it took spraying their scent on their perceived competition, they'd do it.

While eating her lunch, she thought of another possibility. Lars had indicated he was going to give Margaret the opportunity to lead and manage, and that meant a certain amount of failure. In a world of numbers, that meant a risk analysis, which Lars used for all major decisions. Perhaps he'd figured the risk of Danielle leaving the firm was so low that Margaret could continue to cut her teeth on his top trader without adverse effects.

Stephen joined her and she related the turn of events.

"I am surprised by Lars being with Margaret," he admitted, his disapproval obvious.

"Sure you are," she said sarcastically.

"Let me clarify. I'm surprised he chose Margaret, not that he chose a woman. As I said before, a man can only take so much."

She grimaced. "It doesn't matter who it was, or is. The fact is that it was a public space."

Stephen was quiet long enough for Danielle to snap out of her almost pity-party. "Tell me," she said, unsmiling.

"Two things. First, you and he were never able to be in public together due to the sensitivity of Layda and Georgy's feelings. He might have let loose with a beautiful woman like you've said Margaret to be because he was pent up and honestly didn't see you. Second, with Margaret, has it occurred to you that you, Danielle Grant, simply don't fit the culture she wants at her firm?"

Danielle blinked. "I have no idea what you are talking about. In the world of trading and wealth management, nothing matters but the numbers."

He shook his head. "That's what it might have been like in the States, but here, it's subtler than that. No female trader, save you, has a child. You are outperforming all the other traders here and in Geneva. You have an upward career trajectory, which means partner, then her job."

"I'm a threat," she surmised.

"Add to that you don't have an obvious boyfriend. Johanne said he spotted Jacob's interest and if he has, so has Margaret. I wouldn't be surprised if she sensed or saw something between you and Lars as well."

Danielle wiped her mouth, taking it in stride. "I'm a double threat, to her job and the men in the office."

"One doesn't need to be a therapist to hypothesize she is either doing this consciously or subconsciously."

"And by 'this' you mean pushing me out of the firm."

"It's been three months since the merger, more than enough time for a new manager to have determined who they want on the team and who they don't." Danielle nodded, agreeing. Employees and even executives were pushed out of the workplace all the times for reasons that had nothing to do with job performance. "Think about it as discrimination, Swiss-style."

"Stephen, I had the best conversation with Georgy and Layda over the weekend, and the net of it was I have to let go what I can't do anything about. If what you are saying is correct, and I suspect it is, then whatever I want or think about the new environment at MRD is irrelevant. My thoughts won't change it." The front door opened and two sets of diners came in. "You better get going."

"Are you going to leave?"

She waved him off. "I'm flattered that everyone is so concerned I'm going to leave town, but the answer remains the same. The town, no, but MRD won't be long for this life in the new world order."

"Good, because Eva and her family have planned a baby shower in a few weeks, and you need to come and navigate all the guests we've invited." Her eyes popped, but his danced. "It's a bit early, because the baby isn't due until the end of August, but her dad has a big opening at the gallery and lots of out-of-towners will already be here." He gave her a hopeful smile.

"Yes," she drawled, rolling her eyes. "I'll be there."

He leaned over and lightly kissed her cheek. She enjoyed her chocolate mousse alone. Talking with Stephen was a strengthening experience, facing reality by verbally sharing it with a good friend. There really was no changing her work environment. But she could change some of the dynamics.

CHAPTER 13

It was two-thirty when Danielle's phone rang.

"Danielle, could you please come my office at your convenience?"

"I'm afraid not, Lars."

"Excuse me?"

Danielle picked the phone off speaker. "Per Margaret's instructions, all management interactions are now to go through her, not you."

"When did this take place?"

"Just before noon. And just so you know, I have no problem with that protocol. Johanne confirmed that all topics not having to do with trading would be handled by himself, and if she instructed him to work with her, instead of you, that is management's choice. I'm here to trade." Danielle counted the seconds before he responded.

"I see. This will have to be the exception to her new process. When are you available?"

"Is this going to get me fired by Margaret for insubordination?"

"No. I still have the senior position, reporting only to Noel."

"Then if you put that in writing, in email to me prior to the meeting, I will be available at 3:35, after Jacob leaves my office."

"Why the requirement for the email?"

She cleared her throat loud enough to be heard. "Because the consistency and environment in which I've worked for nearly two years has deteriorated, along with other relationships I've been able to rely upon. Therefore, if Margaret were to see us in the same office together, I want to show her, in writing, that you requested this, and under what terms and conditions the meeting was set."

Danielle knew her formality was being over the top, but it was like being out in public; prying eyes were everywhere, and she wanted a back-up plan just in case.

"I'm writing it now and you'll have it in thirty seconds. See you at 3:35."

Danielle put him and their upcoming discussion out of her mind, finding herself less annoyed than usual when Jacob entered her office. He pulled up his chair beside her, handing her a sheet of paper.

"What's this?"

"My homework for my teacher."

She scanned the document. "Much better."

"That's it?"

"I'll grade you on the homework after you pass the test, how's that?" Jacob's eyes glinted with competitiveness. He was going to rise to the occasion.

"I'm ready," he said, holding his gaze on hers.

She motioned for them to switch seats and he took over her console, switching to his account. As she watched, he showed her what a weekend of research had done to his returns.

"Twelve percent in thirty minutes," she said, pointing to the numbers at the top of the screen. "You aren't winning the Grand Prix yet, but you didn't hit the walls either."

"Better, then?"

He offered Danielle her chair back and stood to the side.

"A lot. You have the essentials and have applied them effectively. I'm not sure what you would have to gain by sitting with me Wednesday and Friday."

"Every little bit helps," Jacob pointed out.

"Then we'll see you in two days with more homework."

At 3.35 Danielle entered Lar's office, sitting across from him. Lars finished typing and clicked his screen dark. The shimmer of his emerald colored tie caught in the fading light. He looked at her directly, her eyes already on his. What had formerly captured her attention no longer held any appeal.

"I'd like to say thank you for continuing to be so focused on the job at hand. I know it's been rough." She acknowledged his comment with a tip of her head. "Jacob and Georgiana have been effusive about your generosity in discussing your trading methods, and I say with all sincerity, it's meaningful. Despite what Margaret has indicated, I do have the direct relationship with Noel, who has asked me to give you the opportunity to have a percentage of the business."

A weird twist. "Have you run this by Margaret?"

"You should have the paperwork next week," Lars replied.

"So, the answer is no, you haven't run this by her?"

Lars tapped the sheet on his desk. "We felt it best to propose it to you first."

Danielle ran through the scenarios as to why they would do such a thing, stopping mid-thought. It just didn't matter. Nothing about Margaret's management style was likely to change. In fact, having an ownership stake would probably make matters worse for herself and possibly Johanne.

"Have you offered, or does Johanne already have a stake in the company?"

"Not at this time."

She looked up at the ceiling, unable to help the smile from forming on her lips. "You are purposefully putting Margaret on my bad side and you want Johanne there is well?"

"That's not the intention—"

"But would be the side effect," she interrupted. "Lars, you may tell Noel that the offer is nice but won't be necessary." He regarded her, his mocha eyes remaining steady. "It doesn't behoove me to have an interest in this firm."

"How does the math work on that?"

"It doesn't," she said equally. "This isn't about the math, but I will express to Noel appreciation for the gesture when I see him next." She had nothing more to say on the matter, and guessed that the scenarios he was running through his mind would all lead to a deeper discussion as to her reasons for rejecting such an amazing financial opportunity. As Stephen said, it was unnecessary.

"Thank you, and I appreciate you staying late to speak with me."

"Certainly." She rose, an unexpected flame of anger shooting up her spine as his eyes went from hers right down to the paper in front of him. No mention of Margaret, nor a single look of regret or shame at his actions at the Kronenhalle. He was literally all about the numbers, just like David, her former boss, had predicted he would be. He was truly emotionless, which was fine, because that's exactly what she felt now coming to work every day.

Quickly and without pause, she slipped the ring from her left finger, along with the watch she wore on her left hand. She placed both on the paper between his hands, gratified he stopped moving, his head still down.

"You always said these things have trade in value. Maybe you can get a good deal for the next woman in your life."

She turned without waiting for him to respond, not knowing if he looked up or not. She stopped by her office, grabbed her coat, shut her door and took the stairs two floors down. She immediately found the bathroom, looked to see if she was alone then entered the far stall. Once inside, she breathed unevenly, her legs shaking and her eyes full of tears. She nearly fell to her knees, gripped the toilet bowl and threw up.

CHAPTER 14

Danielle's emotional state increased the hours she poured into work. She finished up the night at eleven thirty, rising at four-forty-five and was in to work by 5:30 a.m. Emma didn't mind, as her husband was on one of his two-week overseas flights. Danielle's conversations with Johanne were limited to updates, and the interactions with the senior partners non-existent. The double-taps at her door were now a thing of the past; what social banter had existed between her and Lars fading to memory.

She spent Tuesday afternoon with Georgiana, who she feared might not last through the spring. Her homework assignments were the same as Jacob's, but her drive wasn't there. What suited her to the corporate environment didn't translate to the individual wealth management world. Danielle told Johanne as much, expecting he'd do what was appropriate with the information. Either way, the end of the week would come and her mentoring would be over. Jacob continued to impress her, showing her improved figures Wednesday, dropping another hint he'd like to continue their time together, wherever necessary.

"Maybe we need a check in once a week," he suggested.

"Like a quiz?" she teased. The man was treading the line of being a gentleman while stepping his toe into the world of casual dating.

"Yes, maybe something we could do outside the office?"

"Maybe."

On Thursday, her second appointment with Dr. Blatz was half catch up, a quarter talking about how she felt and the remaining part her plans on learning how to confront situations.

"You progressed in terms of dealing with Margaret head-on," he complimented. "The same with Lars, but this is all distraction."

"How so?"

He smiled slightly. "That's why it's called avoidance. The here and now takes precedence over the underlying emotional catastrophe in the making; you building the wall around your psyche, which, over time, becomes so high, that no one can get in, and therefore, you don't get hurt, just as you did in college."

"Where I did nothing but work."

He nodded. "Leaving the reality of a former boyfriend and a late stage miscarriage in the past as you focused on the numbers."

"The numbers are my friends."

"One can't have a fulfilling life with ones and zeros."

Danielle uncrossed her legs, turning towards him. "I guess coping the best way I can is called avoidance. But tell me this. Am I supposed to go out with every guy who comes along, allowing myself to be hurt in a come-what-may attitude?"

"How else do you propose maturing through the possibility that injury and death, be it from one's own decisions or what is commonly called fate?" Danielle rolled one thumb over the other, thinking. "Let's approach this another way. Is this man, Jacob, attractive?" She nodded. "And from a personality perspective, engaging, in your line of work and interesting enough to date?" She nodded again. "Then other than the fear of failure, you have no reason to say no."

Her fingers paused. "Anything I say is going to come across as an excuse, isn't it? " Dr. Blatz smiled in agreement. "I think not wanting to cause drama in the workplace is a legitimate reason for not going out."

"Then let's choose another man in your circle. List off all the single, eligible men you could go out with." Danielle laughed, but he waited patiently. "Don't look at the clock. I don't have another appointment after you. I'll wait."

"Think beyond the friends of Andre," he encouraged. Johanne's words came to mind.

"The managers at the clubs we frequent."

"You have no workplace tie to them and they are new to your circle," he noted as positives.

She pointed out the downside. "They haven't asked me out."

"They will," he predicted. "Men are smart; they can tell when a woman is mentally single, whether or not she's wearing a ring on her finger. They can also sniff out insecurity or vulnerabilities. You aren't insecure, but you are vulnerable. There's a major difference."

She sighed with exasperation. "I'm still vulnerable but you want me to be out there dating anyway."

"I do," he said, invoking the Swiss stare that she'd begun attributing to an uncompromising position on a subject. "Even if you know up front it won't work out, give it a shot. You must purposefully put yourself in vulnerable situations to build the internal fortitude to have a lasting relationship. Otherwise…" he said, stretching out his hands as if it were obvious.

"Otherwise, what?"

"You will go right back to your life in Portland, Oregon, where you dated much older single men who didn't want a relationship lasting more than a few months. Is that the best for you? Is it the best thing for your daughter?"

Danielle knew the answer to each question, trying one last track.

"I can hold off on this for a while, can't I?"

"It's your life, Danielle. Only you can determine when you want to start living it."

She rode the metro home, noticing it was lighter outside than the week before at this time. The snow was continuing to melt, each day exposing more of the sidewalk, the trees branches changing from winter brown to spring red.

Like my life. Thanks to her small circle of friends and Dr. Blatz, she at least had a glimpse of the road in front of her, and what she needed to focus on. Her one sticking point was going out with men to essentially test them—and her—out.

"It almost seems unfair to Jacob," Danielle told Stephen the following day, catching him on his walk to the restaurant.

"They are doing the same to you, Danielle. It's what the rest of the world calls dating. You and you alone determine how far you are going to let the date go, mentally, emotionally and physically."

Danielle tried to remember that as she sat with Jacob for her last mentoring session of the week. When their time together ended, he asked if she'd done any more thinking about a weekly get together.

"I suggest dinner because in two months, I've noticed no one really goes to lunch."

She laughed. "I like your assumptive close, like I've already agreed to go with you."

"You have," he agreed confidently. "You've just been debating whether or not you want to follow through on your desires."

She was drawn to his confidence, the bit of ego reminding her of how Andre had asked her out on the first date to go dancing. "You think you know American women that well, do you?"

"Getting around my comment with a question only confirms my statement." Mid-laugh, she saw Lars walk by, papers in hand. She didn't throttle her enjoyment of the moment, and instead conceded.

"Your homework has served you well." A slight smile of victory graced Jacob's lips. "But no dinner. I'm always with my daughter. That said, if you find yourself out dancing one night, stop by Hive. No guarantees I'll be there, but it's one of my favorite clubs."

"Then dancing it is. It will be uniquely American."

"No. It's uniquely Danielle."

She closed down her system, feeling good. She'd taken the first step in playing the field, taking it slow; a meet up not guaranteed but a possibility.

On a mission to get home, she heard her voice called as she passed by the front desk. She turned, waiting until Lars reached her.

"You've officially finished with the mentoring effort, congratulations."

"I hope it was worth it to the firm," she said, glancing at her watch. It was a completely rude to not make eye contact with the managing director, but he'd left decorum in the past, so could she.

"Thank you for the continued dedication." She smirked. His words were so bland and meaningless, what was the point? "Yes?" he inquired. She shook her head, trying to remove the thought that sex with Margaret must be sucking the life out of the man, because the Lars she had known was engaging, witty and full of a magnetic attraction that couldn't be stopped. "Have a great weekend, Lars. Enjoy that wonderful place in Zermatt, and be sure to use that piano more than once a month. It's best when played." Without another word, she left. Two could play this game, and with Layda's image in her mind, she felt like she was recovering a bit of dignity.

Another idea occurred to her, though she waited until the following day to run it by Layda.

"I think that's perfectly wonderful," her surrogate mother said. "You are really going to be putting yourself out there."

"Do I detect a little bit of glee in your voice?" Danielle asked with her own sense of joy.

"Much more than a little."

Danielle was gratified, then grew a little unsure. "And you're sure that the venue is…I don't know, classy enough, I guess?"

Touching her arm, Layda said, "Danielle, the jazz club was classy enough for you and Andre to go there frequently, and for you to get on the stage and sing with Benny more than once. So yes, definitely follow through with your idea. Above and beyond allowing you to mentally escape on a regular basis, you may dramatically open your circle of friends.

"Now," she continued, guiding Danielle to the nook off the kitchen. "Georgy, come in here, please."

"Is it time?" he inquired. Danielle looked between the two of them, sensing something significant.

"Is everything okay?"

"Perfect, my dear," he said. "Layda?"

Layda's smile did little to calm Danielle's unsettled feelings. "Georgy and I have been busy considering our situation, and your place in our life. We have an invitation for you."

Feelings of flattery turned to an overwhelming sense of love as Layda described how they wanted Danielle to attend the opening night of the Zurich Opera with them, as well as the pre-opera social for major benefactors, followed with a short cocktail reception at the Kronenhalle.

"The end goal is to have you more intimately involved with the family charities," Layda finished.

"This is one of many we support," added Georgy. "Another is the art gallery owned by Eva's grandfather, because he rotates much of the work through the hospitals and cultural centers we also support."

Danielle glanced at Layda, catching another sly look. "You are making sure I have no choice but to get to know everyone in this town!"

"No," Layda countered. "Just all the important people." Danielle shook her head in disbelief and excitement.

"I feel kind of bad for making this comment, but your inclusion of me in the family is a lot more fulfilling than Lars."

"It's certainly different," intoned Georgy, as though uncertain about the word fulfilling. "I wholeheartedly agree with Layda that if Lars is going to be out on the town, you might as well be doing the same, and with your peer group, which is the upper echelon."

"Of course, if they bore you to tears…" Layda said.

"Or are twenty years your senior," interjected Georgy.

"You can just make the connections and think no more," Layda finished.

Danielle finally put her hands up, laughing. "Okay! I get it. Social butterfly of Zurich, spreading my gilded wings wherever you want. I don't even know where to start in saying thank you ahead of time, just for the experience!"

"Sweetheart," said Layda. "If you were my daughter, you would be attending all of these events with us, and then at some point, by yourself. You see," she continued, slowing her words. "We can't keep doing these things forever. We want to—and need to—" Danielle's smile faded as the tears began to fill Layda's eyes. She touched her arm, thinking Layda must be thinking of Andre, and how the two of them would have represented the family together, as a couple.

Georgy stepped in. "What Layda and I are saying is that we want to start the process of including you in all our efforts, not just the financial part. Someday, all of this will be yours. Do you understand, and more importantly, is this a responsibility you would like?"

Danielle struggled to speak as her throat closed in on itself. "I love you both so much. It's not a responsibility, but a privilege. I can't believe…" she started. "Through all that's happened, I'm so lucky to have you in my life."

The three shared a wonderfully awkward hug which broke when Monroe scootered her way in to the room. "If she becomes a race car driver, it's going to be all your fault," Danielle joked, wiping the last of the tears from her eyes.

"Since I'll be sponsoring the team, I also get full credit when she wins." Danielle gave Georgy another hug and got ready to go home and get her clothes for the evening. She had her own homework assignment for Dr. Blatz, and she was going to make sure she had it fully completed by the time Monday came around.

CHAPTER 15

Danielle drove slowly in front of the valet line until she caught the eye of one of the attendants. He lifted his chin at her, raised his arm and gestured for her to pull in and stop. She did, thanking him with a twenty.

"Alone tonight?" he asked in English.

"Yes, can you believe it?" she replied in German, feeling the exuberance that comes with having a plan and an approach.

"No, not really," he responded in his native tongue. She returned his wink, her eyes adjusting once she descended into the subterranean room. She'd dressed appropriately, wearing a form-fitting black skirt with black sued ankle boots, contrasting with a contoured, mocha colored cashmere top. It set off her deep red lips and dark eyeliner, the combination perfect for the lighting on the stage.

She looked and found exactly who she wanted. Robin, the tall manager with short, blond hair. He welcomed her warmly, kissing her on both cheeks.

"Hello, Robin."

"Danielle," he said, his appreciative glance taking in more than her face. "The bar?" he suggested.

He guided her through the dimly lit room, the dark unable to hide his lithe figure. *Former basketball player, or maybe tennis.* He gave her the best seat in the house, closest to the stage yet private on the far side. "I'll direct your guests when they arrive," he added.

"I'll be alone tonight." She glanced over at Benny, who was playing the piano, his soothing voice nearing the end of a chorus.

"Is that right?" She turned back to him, smiling. "A Mexican coffee to start then?"

"That would be divine. Thank you."

"My pleasure."

As he placed the order with the bartender, she was tempted to bring up her primary reason for being here, but thought her strategy would work better if she sang a song or two.

As the drink was being made, Danielle expected Robin to excuse himself to seat the stream of guests coming in, but he gestured to another man in the front to take over chaperone duties.

"You know, I've never seen another performer here other than Benny," she began. "Why is that?"

Robin leaned his back against the counter, surveying the room with the eye of a proprietor. "I can't find anyone who matches his standards."

"Seriously? In this town?"

"You'd be surprised. You must be expert on the piano, have a decent voice and be able to handle the crowd."

"A tough combination," she agreed. She could sing and play for hours, but bantering with the crowd, and in both German and English? Danielle had been banking on the unique factor of being an American in Zurich to pull off her plan.

"Why do you ask?"

She shrugged. "Just curious."

Robin accepted the drink from the bartender and handed it to her. "On the house," he said, glancing down at her left hand. It was absent of the ring Lars had given her, and he'd noticed. Time to act.

She met his eyes. "Join me?"

"I'd love to." He turned to order and she placed her attention back on Benny. The jazz man saw her and nodded as she raised her cup.

"I don't want to keep you from your job too long."

Robin lifted his short glass to her, and she clinked it with her own. "This is one of the finer aspects of owning the club. I set my own rules."

He'd just finished a sip when the host at the door gestured to Robin. He set his drink on the counter, excusing himself. She turned her attention to the piano bar, humming along with *Ain't Misbehavin*, the irony of the lyrics bringing a smile to her face. Benny added his own flair to the classic, and she adjusted her harmony to match his.

"That was lovely," complimented Robin as he rejoined her. "Will you sing tonight?"

Success. "I'll sing if you'd like me to."

"I'd like."

Danielle lifted the cup to her lips, her eyes sliding to the stage, feeling his gaze still on her like a weight until he gestured to Benny. "Now I'm going to invite my good friend up to the stage," Benny rumbled. "I see she's having a drink and can't say no."

Danielle leaned over to Robin. "Since this is for you, do you have any requests?"

"Dream a little dream of me."

Oh, man. I asked for it.

"Alright," she said. She thought through the lyrics, and all that it implied. As she approached the piano bench, Benny scooted over and she planted a kiss on his cheek.

"Hey gorgeous," he drawled. "Been a while. How you doing?" he asked in an undertone, playing the keyboard absently.

"Another boyfriend dumped me," she replied, taking perverse pleasure when Benny's head remained down but he changed the chords to Blue Moon. She laughed and nudged him playfully.

"It couldn't have been the boss man."

"Yes, the boss-man," she emphasized. "It was my fault though."

Benny scoured her face. "You don't seem upset."

She nudged him. "Right now, I'm not upset. In fact, I'm rather healthy, because I'm here with you instead of sitting at home. Now, let's sing. Robin made a request."

The level of noise in the club remained high until Danielle hit her first notes. She sang the words without putting much thought into the meaning until she reached the chorus. *But in your dreams/whatever they be/dream a little dream of me.*

As she sang the final words of the song, she wondered if she wasn't going to be intimate with anyone, how was she ever going to know if they were compatible? She intuitively felt that question was already answered at least for Robin. The handsome club owner was treating every other seemingly single, attractive woman the way he'd treated her.

The notion didn't prevent her from pitching him on the idea of filling in for Benny when the man needed a break, which she did after joining him back at the bar.

"You'd be available?" Robin asked, leaning on the counter. She ignored the double meaning.

"Not full time, but periodically. Until recently, my schedule wasn't conducive to being out more regularly. It is now."

When Benny took his break, Robin asked Benny if he thought Danielle could handle the crowd.

"Get up there now, woman," said Benny. "Let's see how you do."

"Now?"

Robin smiled his encouragement. "No time like the present."

It was his challenge that lifted her butt off the barstool. Robin followed behind her, lifting the mic as she sat down.

"We have an impromptu guest. You've heard her sing tonight, and now we will be entertained with her playing as well. From America to Zurich, a gold trader by day and singer by night, give it up for Danielle Grant."

Danielle gave him a wide smile, glancing beyond the blinding lights to the crowd, ready to take the plunge.

"I'm thinking *Crazy* to start," she began, "because I must be crazy to follow someone like Benny." The crowd rumbled with laughter, subsiding when she began to play. The noise died almost entirely when she began. Getting lost in the words, the emotions pushed up from her belly, filling her chest and emoting out of her mouth. Then she recalled the last time she'd sung this particular song. Benny had been playing and she was singing to Lars. The love she had for him might be dissipating, but her desire for a man to be beside her had returned.

Danielle felt her throat start to close, her heart constricting with the aching memories. She immediately changed the chords, cutting off the remainder of the song for another in the same key.

Not gonna make that mistake again, she promised herself. The applause was louder than it had been for Benny, and Robin, who had been standing in the darkness behind her, took the mic.

"You think we should keep her, then?" The applause increased. He glanced down at Danielle. "And you'll stay?" he asked into the mic.

"For another song."

Someone from the audience yelled a 'yes please,' and then random shouts 'will you' and one loud: 'I'll pay you double,' caused Danielle to start playing again.

Robin looked at the crowd, then her. "I guess that's a yes, then."

She laughed, flattered. "That's a yes." The clapping went up again, this time, in direct correlation to her happy factor.

CHAPTER 16

Over a late breakfast, Danielle gave Layda and Georgy the replay of the evening before, adding that to start, she would just fill in for Benny a night or two a week. "We'll see how that goes and graduate from there," she told them.

"My glamorous, multi-talented daughter," rumbled Georgy with undiluted pride. Monroe was eating from Danielle's lap, Layda and Georgy sipping coffee.

"Georgy, going back to your favorite subject, when I'm going to be ready to leave MRD, I believe it's a bit closer than it was two weeks ago."

Georgy gazed at her over the rim of his cup. "Do you mean it?"

"Bear in mind I'm not credentialled to lead an outside organization, but if it's only for a single family I can do it."

"Danielle, this is the moment we—Georgy and I, have been waiting for," Layda interjected. "We are serious about having you manage our family office, for all the Mettleren's, in Geneva and elsewhere. Yes, initially it would be a bit of work, but you could take it on gradually. We'd transfer the activity in increments." Layda looked at Georgy for confirmation.

"It would be staged, as Layda said, so as not to overly burden you."

Danielle laughed. "Georgy, how can this be? At the encouragement of you two, I just gave away what little free time I had on the weekends. Add that to the lessened trading hours I have at the office, and my numbers are really going to be down."

Georgy waved away the argument. "Let's be blunt. Your motivation has dropped along with the numbers. I've noticed your returns aren't what they used to be, and so have others." He put up a hand, forestalling her defensive posturing. "Not that we mind, my dear. Your returns are still higher by far than your nearest competitor. It's just that you've spoiled us."

"He's right," Layda said firmly. "But this is about more than the money. Our entire extended family has been concerned about your health and well-being since Andre passed away."

"You're implying that the network under my management, starting with your family, has been hoping for this the entire time?"

"I know I have," Georgy said with enthusiasm. "As David said at the funeral, everyone wants the best, you have no comparison."

Layda laced her fingers on the table, a light in her eyes. "It's going to be busy, I grant you, but I'll be here to help. Office space planning. Introducing you to our philanthropies. Your new evening entertainment."

"Being a mom," Danielle said with a laugh.

"Which takes precedence, another reason why you'll need help."

Danielle sat back, feeling a bit light-headed. "Which will leave zero time to get seriously involved with anyone. I love this!"

"Who said one had to be seriously involved?"

"Layda!" Danielle squealed. Layda shrugged innocently, but Danielle wasn't fooled. She had now seen the woman's true nature coming through, and she loved it. "Did you know those were my father's exact words when I'd been in Zurich about twenty-four hours?"

Layda was smug. "He was right. And so am I."

"Now that you two have it sorted, I'll propose six months for the transition," offered Georgy. "That would put it at roughly September, giving you the summer to enjoy yourself while taking advantage of everyone taking three weeks off in August."

Layda offered to put Monroe down for a nap, leaving Georgy and Danielle to talk details.

Georgy had watched her thoughtfully during her explanation. "The rising trend of affluent families creating their own family offices, or multi-family office is concerning for all wealth management firms, not just Velocity-MRD," he said without sympathy. "Their merger only hastened the inevitable by paying you less commission, splitting up part of the overriding bonuses to others, who deserve better. Think about Johanne. He's been there for years and his numbers are now going down, not up. It's the wrong decision, especially in this market." He shook his head. "One of the few errors by Lars that I've ever seen."

There are others, Danielle thought, but bit her tongue to keep her personal life out of the conversation. "Aren't you thrilled you are finally getting what you always wanted? Us working together?"

Georgy nodded his head, the extra layer of skin under his chin touching the top of his collar. "What would David think?"

"He'd say that I've moved the proverbial business and emotional Alps during my tenure at MRD and if I wanted to, could lead another organization."

"But?"

"But nothing, really. The real question is if your relationship with Noel will survive."

"He's been expecting it since he learned about you and Andre. As far as he's concerned, he got two more years out of you than he expected."

"When we get closer, do you want to be the one to tell Noel, or shall I?" Danielle asked. "I'm thinking me, if you can have some discretion for once!"

They agreed that when the time came, she would be the one to do it. "Now, the biggest question is this: would you like an office with a lake view?"

Danielle laughed, relieved. "Sure, just as long as you realize I usually keep my eye on the screen and not the water. Thank you, Georgy."

"For what? The view, or waiting you out?"

"Both."

"My dear, I always knew this would happen, just not when."

That evening, she watched the lights of the stars bounce from the water then up to her ceiling. Lars was so good at anticipating her actions, he might already be two steps ahead of her, setting up the backup traders in advance her ever communicating her intentions to leave. It's what she would do.

CHAPTER 17

Monday, Danielle arrived at work with a renewed enthusiasm, which grew when she reviewed the calendar. Margaret was in Geneva for the week, a bonus. And in addition, she now had a light at the end of a very dark tunnel. Georgy promised on all things Swiss and confidential that he was going to keep his mouth shut and not even hint to Noel that Danielle would be leaving. The summer was soon enough, allowing for the month of August to be the natural break. September would involve handing over the accounts. Of course, that's where the real hit was going to be realized. With her leaving, Velocity-MRD would be down nearly thirteen billion if all the Mettleren personal entities moved over with her.

Without Jacob or Georgiana to take her time, her trading went back up in the high double digits each day. She wasn't asked to attend a single meeting as promised, and she noted that Johanne was in his office less frequently than he had been in the past.

Wednesday afternoon, Glenda rang her office. "You have a Robin Allaman on the line. Would you like to take it, or is he a prospective client for me to schedule an appointment?"

"Good question," Danielle said out loud. "He owns a business here in town, and I do know him personally. Yes," she decided, "put him through."

"You must be pretty important to have your own secretary," Robin said.

"She weeds out the riff-raff," Danielle said jovially. "What can I do for you? Have you already decided to fire me?"

"Hardly," he answered, his voice smoother than at the club, where he'd had to speak above the noise. "Benny and I were discussing your schedule, and he brought it to my attention that he wouldn't mind a full night off once or twice a week. I know we discussed…"

Danielle's eyes slid from the computer screen to the water as she turned around in her chair. They wanted to put her in for a block of hours, two nights a week. Furthermore, Robin thought it would be good for the club to post her times on-line.

"Benny is hot and all, but a female entertainer might appeal to a moderate few." His dry delivery had her laughing.

"I thought you wanted more girls in your club, not less."

"Ah, Revenue 101 Danielle. The men are typically the ones paying, and we need more of them."

"Then stop giving out so many free drinks to all the pretty girls."

Robin laughed good-naturedly and agreed with her. He proposed Thursday and Sunday, but she countered with Wednesday and balked on Sunday.

"Mid-week is best for my mom-schedule, but why Sunday? Isn't that a dead night?"

"It's when all the out-of-towners arrive for business Monday and have nowhere to go."

"If I can have a shortened schedule, from six to eight Wednesday and Sunday, then I think we can swing it. But when summer comes, I make no promises."

"Great. Can you start tonight?"

She let out a silent breath of air. "I need to check with my caregiver, so let me call you back in ten." Emma was thoroughly supportive of Danielle, reminding her that Monroe went to bed at seven.

"You can come home from the office and eat, and spend some time with Monroe. You'll be fine."

Emma spoke matter-of-factly, much like Andre had done when supporting her to go back to work after Monroe's birth. *It would be fine.* The similarity comforted her, and without it, she might not have accepted the opportunity.

It's like another voice from the universe helping me get out of my shell.

She called Robin, confirming she'd be behind the piano at six, but did give him a prediction. "I still don't think having a female playing on a particular night is going to change a thing."

"I'll bet you a Mexican coffee you are wrong."

At three-thirty sharp, Danielle shut down her computer. Five minutes later, she was walking down the hallway when Johanne called out. She slowed by his office, expecting a short hello-goodbye.

"You heard the news?"

Her chest stomach clenched. "No. What news? Is it bad?"

"Depends on how much you have invested. Lani's business is failing, which means our investment is going up in flames. But I shouldn't feel so bad. You are going to lose more than me."

Even though she needed to leave, Danielle sat down in front of him. "Johanne, I don't know where you came up with that information, but I never invested in Lani's restaurant." In the time she'd been in Zurich, she'd never seen Johanne with an expression like the one he wore now. "Did she explicitly say I gave her money for the new restaurant?"

"She said the money came from you."

"I told her no, the same day Lars broke it off with me," Danielle confided, glancing over her shoulder, keeping her voice low. "She and I haven't spoken since. When she sold her portion in Stars & Stripes, one could make the case that my initial investment of a quarter million created her own value, but that's as far as the connection goes."

Johanne's face went flush with anger. "I should sue her for fraud."

"That would be throwing good money after bad. Don't bother," Danielle said. "She has no money or assets."

"What about her apartment? I could place a lien on it."

"It's one of Max's rentals."

Johanne muttered in German, the words so guttural she couldn't make them out. "Then I go after Max. He has millions, and now that he's no longer a client, it's a non-issue."

"If Switzerland is like the States, it will cost you two hundred grand to get back your one. Is that how you want to spend your time and money? No," she answered for him. "You can make up the money in a few days of trading."

Johanne grumbled again, taking off his glasses, inspecting the rims as though Lani were a spot he could rid himself of. Danielle thought of Lars' prediction when they learned of Johanne's investment; that Lani would lose everything and the investors along with her.

"At least you didn't invest more," Danielle said, trying to be positive.

"Unfortunately, I did. I ignored Lars." He paused, putting his glasses back on, reacting to her stunned look. "I had asked him about the restaurant business and told him about the investment. I'd already put in 100 and he counseled against it."

"How much?" she asked in a whisper.

"Another one-fifty. Dario put in two-fifty." She put her hand to her mouth. Together they were in half a million. "I know."

Danielle didn't want to end the conversation, but she couldn't be late. She stood, apologizing. "I have to go to my next job now." Johanne's eyes popped. "I'm filling in for Benny two nights a week, just a few hours. I need to clear my head of this place as much as anyone."

"Don't ever do that to me again," he warned.

"You always like my surprises," she deadpanned.

"Not when it comes to your job." Danielle was silent, and he caught it. "Seriously?"

"You have until September," she said quietly. "You are my friend first and my boss second. I just made the decision over the weekend, and it wouldn't have been right to keep it from you."

A breath of air escaped his thin lips. "It would have been perfectly acceptable for someone without integrity, like you-know-who. Dare I ask you which firm?"

"No firm. I'm going to work in-house with Georgy running his family office."

The back of Johanne's hand went to his mouth, covering a wicked chortle. "All if it?" Danielle nodded with a grin. "They will go apoplectic. Best news I've heard all day."

"Oh, and are you coming to the baby shower for Stephen and Eva? I just got my invite last week and a whole lot of us are on the guest list. It's either going to be epic or a massive bust."

He agreed. "Me and Dario can't wait to see you. Good luck tonight."

Danielle was buttoning her coat against the forthcoming chill, and when she looked up she saw a familiar figure on the other side of the double doors. They made eye contact, and smiled at nearly the same time. Dominic held the door for her.

"And I thank you." They walked on the sidewalk for a short distance, he to his car and she to the metro.

"You've been leaving early lately."

"Dominic, the great news about your position of hearing and seeing everything is I don't even need to say a word."

"True enough. Have a good evening."

She paused at his car. "I will, and you know why? I'm singing at a jazz club tonight. That's one thing I bet you didn't know. See you later."

At home, Danielle dropped her purse, took off her shoes and played blocks with Monroe for an hour, then enjoyed dinner with her and Emma, changing right before she needed to leave. She put one half of her hair up in a high pony, leaving the longer, looser curls around her shoulders. Thinking of the lights on stage, she chose a soft purple top with thick, horizontal stripes, the lines orchestrated to increase the appearance of her bust, which was never a bad thing. A pale lipstick with a thick, long-lasting gloss was all she added and was out the door by five-forty. She felt as though a new version of her life here in Zurich had begun, starting when Layda and Georgy included her in their family activities.

She opened the front door, the exhilaration of the cold air nothing compared to what she felt inside, the anticipation of adding to her life in ways completely unrelated to her home or office exciting.

CHAPTER 18

When Robin saw her enter the club, he left the bartender and greeted her with kisses. "And you think being here won't make a difference with the patrons?" he clucked, taking her coat and purse. "I'll put your things in my office and introduce you to a few of the staff. The stage is ready and waiting."

The counter seating at the bar was already full, as were half the tables. Robin checked the microphone, adjusting it to her direction. "Do you mind if I mix up the music a little?" she asked. "Maybe throw in some modern tunes."

"It's your piano."

Danielle turned on her iPad. She had the playlist, but would take requests, knowing that if she didn't know the chords, she could look up the song and play by sight. After Robin introduced her, she began with the chords made famous by Eta James.

"*At Last* is appropriate since I'm finally up on stage of my own accord," she began. "You are welcome to sing along if you feel inspired."

She closed her eyes, the soulful tune penetrating her emotions, just as it was intended. The moment she opened her mouth, and for the next forty minutes, Danielle transported herself out of the own life and into the world of the others in the room, thinking about their dreams and aspirations, hurts and desires. Each note she sang and word delivered were constructed to draw out the love inside, sending it to another, one who would catch it, embrace it and hold on.

Eventually Robin stepped in to the spotlight as the applause slowly died down. "Danielle will be back after the break." Danielle asked for her purse, and followed him to his office, then stopped by the lady's room. She reapplied her lipstick and checked her hair, satisfied with both. A quick call to Emma assured her Monroe was keeping to her normal routine. Danielle had no pressure to get home, but was going to keep to her eight p.m. end time.

Her phone showed two unread text messages and she checked automatically. "Lars was right, again," Danielle murmured. She walked to the bartender, asking Leon for a soda water. She stood at the far side, in the near blackness just beyond Robin's office. "Hey, girl." She looked up to see Johanne and Dario.

"What in the world??" she exclaimed, taking turns giving hugs and kisses.

"I'm taking pity on him," Dario said as Johanne ordered two drinks.

"He needs it."

"No," corrected Dario, "I need it."

She looked between the two men. "What's up?"

Dario answered. "After your conversation with Johanne, I did some checking. I agree with you about not going after Lani, but Max is fair game. Before you ask, Max and Lani are on the paperwork together, and so I'll be suing them both, her for what cash and assets she has, and him for my investment money. If that leaves her homeless, so be it. Cheers."

Danielle squeaked a little and raised her soda water. Lars was right, again. Lani was going to lose it all.

She checked the time and stood. "I have one more hour. We can talk after if you can stick around."

"I've got a day job," Johanne playfully griped with a smile. "We just wanted to show our support."

She shook her head, feeling the genuine affection from both men. "You two have a way of choosing precisely the right times for your displays. Thanks." They had given her a beautiful baby shower gift, attended her engagement party, provided a mourning arrangement for Andre's passing and attended the funeral. They'd been alongside her throughout, and she loved them for it.

"Why the tears?" asked Dario.

"Never leave my life you guys, okay?" Another hug and she was off, inhaling big and deep to stretch out her vocal chords. By the time she reached the glossy black Steinway, she had changed her mind as to what to sing next.

"My former boss told me once that friends are fleeting, but respect is eternal. I believe that the *right* friends are eternal, and love is fleeting." A whup from the back room caused her to smile and nod, her eyes glancing in to the darkness. "And sometimes, friends can be like angels, who watch over me…whether I know they are there or not. Don't mind if I take a few liberties with the words."

Gershwin's famous tune brought the crowd down to a quiet hum as she sang the first verse of *Someone to Watch Over Me*. By the chorus, she could only hear herself breathing. There's a somebody I'm longing to see/I hope that he turns out to be/someone to watch over me.

She continued the song, the last words fading as she realized that the words might go, but her emotions didn't have to. *There is someone out there, watching over me. I just have to find him.*

Danielle didn't suffer any adverse effects of playing at the club, and as she told Johanne, she even got in two hours of trading at home that evening.

"For myself, of course, so you won't get any benefit, but at least my numbers are up while I'm here," she said. "Changing subjects, was Dario serious? Is he really going after Lani and Max?"

Johanne nodded. "Do not mess with that man. He has a lot more money that I do, which is why he became a client in the first place. Now switching subjects again, I understand Lars has confirmed for Monroe's birthday party. You are a brave girl."

Danielle's eyes popped. "You know more than me."

He had no more information to share and suggested she speak to Layda.

On her way to Dr. Blatz, Danielle rang Layda. Something had to have happened to change her mind. It had, she learned. Lars had proactively called her up.

"It was a little awkward," Layda admitted. "I couldn't reasonably retract the invitation without coming across as vindictive." Danielle thought through the paperwork on the Mettleren charities. Lars was on half a dozen.

"Which wouldn't help you and your philanthropic work. I understand."

"I'm really sorry, Danielle. The alternative is I cancel altogether."

"No," she said, trying to sound calm. "I think it was my father who said major events likes weddings and funerals are the only times extended families get together nowadays. We need to change that to all celebrations, don't you think?"

"I do."

Danielle entered her therapist's room feeling unsettled at the notion of seeing Lars at her daughter's birthday party. But, as she told Dr. Blatz, her show the night before had been a success.

"How will you handle seeing Lars and the other men at events in general, not just this one?" her therapist asked. It wasn't what she cared about.

"My thoughts are on Robin and Jacob, actually," she admitted. "I'm physically attracted to one and mentally the other." Her sardonic look got the staid man to do little more than lift a finger of her to proceed. "I can't help comparing Jacob to Andre, because they say similar things, in similar ways and intonations. It could be the age and place in life of meeting both—neither married or having had kids…"

"But…" he encouraged.

"I feel like I already had that wonderful, first-time experience with one man and don't want or need it with another. Jacob needs a woman with whom it will all be a first time and special. And with Robin, again I compare him to Andre when we were at the club. Andre couldn't take his eyes off me. The rest of the world didn't exist, and that's what I need."

"And expect."

"Yes. Is that wrong, or bad?" she asked.

"It's neither, though it's unrealistic for someone who isn't invested in *you*." He had emphasized the word for a reason.

"Don't say it," she forestalled with a hand. "If I don't let them get close, they won't have a reason to make me the center of their world. In other words, avoidance."

A verbal confirmation wasn't required. "Now we have something else to talk about in the time remaining. Your birthday."

It caught her off-guard. "How do you know about that?"

"Your medical paperwork."

"You need to plan something yourself," he suggested. "Something with special meaning, either alone or with others. When a decade flips over, it's momentous."

To Danielle, her birthday seemed like a distant event, when in reality, it was weeks away. *Avoidance.* She was beginning to hate that word.

"Okay," she said, acquiescing. "I can plan something."

"Good. Include in that plan ice climbing." Danielle felt gut punched. "No, I'm not kidding. This is an American-style I'm-going-to-pull-my-big-girl-panties-up tool designed to start removing the wall of fear you have built up, block by block." She couldn't even gather the breath to argue, and he took advantage of it. "Part of your fear is lack of understanding."

"We fear what we don't understand," she mumbled.

"And you can't fully appreciate what you don't understand. In other words, you understanding the tools, technique and skills required to ice climb, along with the associated safety equipment, is going to help you deal with some of your fears. There are literally tens of thousands of people who ice climb every year, and probably hundreds of thousands who rock climb, and how many accidents do we hear about? Maybe one a year? Contrast that to motorcycle riding. The last statistic I read was 4,490 die from motorcycle accidents in the United States alone. Compare that with ice climbing. In two decades, twenty-one people died from ice climbing in Canada whereas 451 from avalanches worldwide. That averages about 14 per year, *one percent* of those killed by motorcycles."

She let the information settle. "I need to get my head on straight."

"You need to get informed," he corrected. "You don't risk millions of dollars in trading without having done the research."

Danielle contemplated all that he wasn't saying. Andre's death was part of a far bigger figure; Lars' was fractional by comparison. She probably had better odds winning the lottery than Lars dying in an accident.

"Here, take a look at this information when you have time. I circled two I thought looked interesting." She accepted the envelope. "You are making good strides, Danielle, and it's only been three weeks."

She tried to remember that as she went home, leaving the envelope in her purse. It wasn't until after Monroe was in bed, and she was in her pajamas did she return to the kitchen, looking at the purse as though it had a viper inside. Reluctantly, but determined, she took it out and read the paper. It was a list of ice climbing events, along with beginning courses.

"Crap," she muttered. Dr. Blatz had circled one of the courses, offered four Saturdays in a row. He'd also highlighted an event on a Saturday, her birthday. *He is out of his mind if he thinks I'm going to go ice climbing, learn to ice climb even.* The statistics were enough for him to make his point.

She promptly threw the paper in the trash and went to her bedroom, shutting off the light and pulling the cover up. A fitful hour later, she got up and retrieved the paper, smoothing out the edges. She'd better embrace what she couldn't avoid.

CHAPTER 19

Riding the metro into work the following day, Danielle tried not to think about ice climbing but failed, visualizing Lars instead. He had been doing it since he was a kid, and had endured minor accidents, one from a falling rock and another from softened ice.

Wanting to think of anything other than ice climbing, Danielle thought of Lani. Lars had bought out Lani's share in Stars and Stripes, the funds giving her the money she needed to invest in The Stinking Rose. Now her own two hundred grand was going down the tubes, in addition to Johanne and Dario's half a million. Wasn't there a way to salvage that money other than through a legal route?

She pondered the subject all the way to work, knowing that the only person she could speak to about it was the one she wanted to avoid the most.

Danielle waited until the morning trading rush was over, and then rang Lars' direct line.

"Yes?"

"I have a personal matter to discuss, and it's not about me. I'd like your advice, unless that's something you can no longer accommodate."

"I can. Phone or in person?"

"Phone is good," Danielle said, already switching to her headset. She went to the door and closed it nearly all the way, then returned to her desk. She began, jumping right in to the situation. The restaurant was going to close, all the investors were losing their money.

"Johanne has a lot to lose as you know, but Dario has even more." She told him about the quarter million. "Did you know that?"

He didn't. "So, between Lani's original capital and Max's, they were nearly in three quarters of a million dollars up front. Even if Lani were killing it every night, it would take years to make the money back. It was too bad he ignored me."

"He feels worse than you do, trust me."

"Since you are calling for advice, one option is to put their portions on the open market as you did with Andre, but with their poor sales, I don't imagine it will have any takers." He added, "Johanne makes a lot of money, Danielle. This isn't going to break him. To Dario, it's merely an irritant."

"Not anymore," Danielle said, revealing her knowledge that Dario suspected fraud and was ready to take Max and Lani to court. She expected him to say something, but he was silent. "Did you have any idea of this?"

"Let's say I suspected as much because of some of the financial transactions I'd seen Max conducting."

"Oh man," she exhaled, then straightened out her shoulders. "But of course, you would be one step ahead of the game. You always know everything." Danielle had spoken so matter-of-factly, she wasn't aware of how bluntly her words had come out until Lars chuckled.

"That's quite a compliment."

"It's true," she grumbled. Their non-romance status didn't impact the reality that he was a brilliant businessman. "Turning back to Max, was he stealing to cover the balance sheet or simply transferring money? I couldn't believe they were running through money that fast."

"Who knows? I am guessing they probably have one or two months of operating capital with Dario's investment, but it's anyone's guess."

"Early summer," she said.

"Just as tourist season kicks in."

"Lars, I have an idea."

"I'm listening."

"I was thinking one of them could approach the owner of the hotel where they are now located and offer to sell or transfer the business. Lani's forte is making great food, not running a business. At the end of the day, Max's participation is irrelevant."

"You still want to bail her out, even after all she's done?"

"I'm really trying to help out Johanne and Dario. They may still go after Max, but at least this way, she would have a place to work."

Lars paused. "Under your plan, she'd become the cook, and focus on just that."

Danielle laughed. "Yes, Lars, Lani would just be *the cook*. You think it's a bad idea, don't you?"

"There is that word you are so fond of. It's not bad, it's that I'm pleased you want to continue to support a friend who has been anything but reciprocal. Yet, I'm not surprised. You have a kind nature that never ceases to amaze. Back to Lani, I doubt she'd get anywhere making her case to the establishment's owners. She would be better served by having someone act as the liaison."

"Lars, I've not spoken with Lani about this, and doubt she'd even talk with me if I tried. Even if she was on board, she's unlikely to have the money necessary to pay a broker."

"No need."

"How do you figure?" Danielle asked.

"I'll do it for her."

"What? Why?"

Lars gave an easy sigh. "Because regardless of where we are now, I can try and be of help to someone you obviously still care about no matter how unworthy she may be of your affection." It was a completely unexpected and gracious offer. "It may also make her less bitter towards Stephen and Eva."

"You think she's going back to ask him for money?"

"I put nothing past that woman," Lars replied, the disapproving tone rising to the surface. "I'll tell you what. I'll contact the owners, whom I know, and broach the subject. If they are interested, it can move forward with some behind-the-scenes guidance on my part. You won't even have to be involved."

"That's really great of you Lars. Thank you."

"My pleasure. Now, I have something for you. Monroe's birthday party. Layda and I spoke, and I wanted to be sure it's okay with you if I attend. I'd like to."

"Of course." It's the least she could do after he offered to help out Lani.

"Danielle, you do realize why I'm attending?"

"Yes," she answered. "You are long-time friends with the Mettleren family, and this is what the Swiss do; preserve relationships no matter what."

"Half of that is correct. I am friends with the family, and I am also your friend. I want to preserve both relationships, hence, helping Lani is by association helping you."

She had no quick reply. The world of friends and men was not her forte. She thanked him for his work on behalf of Dario and Johanne. "I, and they, appreciate that very much. Do you think I should say anything to Dario and Johanne?"

"No. Let Dario put some heat under her seat. It might encourage a rapid resolution."

"Good point. Thanks again, Lars."

Danielle removed the headset, turning to look at the water. Strange. Lars was the first person she thought of for advice, and he'd willingly given it. The cynic in her whispered he wanted to keep her as a member of the firm, and the Mettlerens as clients.

"Going dancing this weekend?" Danielle swiveled the chair around, seeing Jacob. "I looked for you last weekend but you stood me up."

"I can't stand a person up if I haven't committed to a date," she replied gamely, easily replacing thoughts of her former love with the man before her—the one who reminded her so much of Andre.

"I don't want a commitment. I want a date."

Danielle blinked, unable to stop herself from chuckling. "You are very straightforward for a Swiss man."

"And you are very hard to get, especially for an American woman."

"I do have a thing called a little girl at home who I spend a lot of time with," she explained.

"I remember, and I also know you like to sailboard in wetsuits on cold days."

"Then you know my whole life story," she said, spreading her hands. "Nothing left."

"Yes. Dancing, Saturday night. Meet me there?" Not since she'd been in Zurich had a man been this straightforward.

"I will commit to keeping it open as a possibility, since I can't guarantee finding a sitter on such a short notice." He wasn't entirely satisfied by her answer but she lifted her palms in the air, ending the conversation.

Saturday would come soon enough. She'd decide on her evening plans later.

CHAPTER 20

As Danielle lay in bed, she reflected on the last three weeks. It had started out rough and rocky with Lars and Margaret, then sloping into a flat plain of existence. Her path ensured she would leave in a half a year's time, so she and Lars could now have congenial, productive conversations about work and shared acquaintances.

And Jacob had asked out her out. She rolled over, facing the lake. The piece of paper on her bed stand caught her attention, removing Jacob from her thoughts and putting Lars right back in. It was the sheet of ice climbing events from Dr. Blatz. There was no getting around his intention, and she suspected he wasn't going to let the subject go, which ironically, was why she was paying him. To help her grow up and get on with her life.

So be it.

The next morning, she called the company and learned it would cost her about five hundred francs for the gear and instruction for four, half day courses, all offered on Saturday, the fifth was a competition, included in the price and required for the certificate of completion. Of all places, the closest was in Zermatt. At the suggestion of the receptionist, she spent an hour reading about the terrain in and around Zermatt, learning it was perfect for beginners and experts alike. Not all climbing required going straight up three hundred feet, which surprised her. Much, if not most of the ice climbing was more about maneuvering the frozen ice water above the rocks and hillside, which made it more "technical" than going straight up.

As she continued to read, she pondered why Lars had purchased a home in Zermatt. He loved to ski, and St. Moritz was most famous for the slopes, but in the summer, the rock walls rimming the town ran clean from water. In effect, he climbed the same walls year-round.

She leaned forward looking closely at the pictures of kids as young as eight holding an ice ax, geared up in helmets, strung with a harness and ropes, their crampons affixed to their boots.

If they can do it, I can do it, she thought with a bit of competitiveness.

In the section on technique, she learned the riskiest part of the sport was the changing conditions; the very element that made it so thrilling, just as Lars had said. Climbing throughout the season on varied surfaces provided different handholds and footwork; one type for a frozen waterfall and another for using an ice pick.

Danielle felt the adrenaline build as she learned that the typical climbing time is 2-4 hours for beginners. Enough time to get in a workout but not be gone from Monroe all day long. Advanced climbers didn't necessarily go much longer, maybe five hours.

So that was how Lars was able to manage his competitions and return for their Saturday nights together. His long, lean body kept in shape through intense positions and technique. No wonder he was addicted to this.

Danielle took a deep breath and called the ice climbing center back, booking her orientation training course starting the following week. Her birthday would be spent in a competitive, graduation climb, signifying both physical and mental achievement.

It took a moment to decompress from the information. She'd pulled up her big girl panties as Dr. Blatz had so bluntly said, and was going to pull them higher on a frozen waterfall one week from today.

She heard a clink and a drop, and went into Monroe's room. Her little girl was sitting on the floor, playing with a toy. "Since when did you learn to crawl out of the crib?" she asked her daughter, grinning. Monroe put the toy in her mouth, then shook it happily. Her little girl was growing up, so should she.

Later in the afternoon, Danielle received a text from Johanne, asking if her plans included dancing with Jacob that evening, and if other men were invited. She confirmed ten p.m., enough time for the club to get going. When Danielle arrived at Layda's home, the older woman wanted to hear about the week's events, her animated responses causing the two of them to laugh like girlfriends.

"Can we come and watch you in the competition?" Layda inquired, expressing excitement about bundling up with Monroe and Georgy, making a night of it in Zermatt. "You have never been to our home up there, but now is the time. In fact," she continued, "instead of driving up and down to the mountain for the next month of Saturdays, why don't you stay up there? By the time you return, Monroe will already be down to bed."

"I never knew you had a home in Zermatt," Danielle said, "and it's such a wonderful offer, but that's more time I'd be away from Monroe, and a burden on you."

All humor left Layda's face before she spoke. A warm palm rested on Danielle's forearm. "My dear," she started, sounding very much like

Georgy. "If Andre were alive, he'd either be home with Monroe or he would have joined you, leaving her with me. Either way, Monroe is with someone who loves her, and you would be enjoying your alone time, which is exactly what Andre would have wanted. Isn't that true?"

"Yes, that was how Andre was," she stated.

"Exactly. Supportive and encouraging. So, you are going to start climbing ice walls with our undying support. It's still a lot safer than riding motorcycles any day of the week."

They had a moment of silence for Andre at her comment. "Well then," Danielle spoke, clearing out the emotion from her throat. "I may take you up on spending my Saturday nights at your home in Zermatt, but what I will do by myself at night I have no idea."

Layda gave her a coy smile and winked. "The home has a great hot tub and sauna, and the kitchen perfect for making lots of hot chocolate." Danielle grinned. It sounded divine. "And the last day, the competition, being on your birthday, is perfect. We'll have a family celebration and you can go out with the group or stay home. Whichever you prefer."

Danielle chose to ride the metro to the dance club, waving to the bouncer at the door who ushered her to the front of the line. "It's been a while," the large man said, drawing the rope back, kissing her cheek. "No friends?"

"I think they're inside."

"Stay even if they aren't," he said, already putting the red rope back in place.

The thumping beats grew louder as she walked up the stairs, the hanging stars and globes constantly shifting as the blue, red and green strobes shot around the room. She'd never gone to a club by herself before, always needing the companionship of another girl or man to help her feel comfortable.

If I can handle ice climbing, I can handle entering a club alone.

Danielle made her way to the bar, squeezing between the bodies. Her back was to the dance floor when she felt fingers on her waist. "You came." Jacob was beside her, his fingers lifting when she moved slightly.

The bartender caught her eye. "Your usual?"

"Yes, please."

"I'll have the same," said Jacob. Danielle caught the bartender's look, but Jacob didn't.

"Are you here with some friends?" she asked, glancing around for Johanne and Dario.

"Over there." She followed his line of sight, seeing two girls and a guy. "They are other traders who work in the Geneva office, down for the weekend. You?"

"I'm alone, although I think Johanne will be here with his friend. They tend to be my preferred dancing partners." Two cranberry and sodas were put in front of them. She picked one up and took a quick drink, not wanting to toast him the way she and Andre had done their first night out dancing.

"That's horrible. What's in this?" Jacob asked with a grimace.

"Healthy stuff," she said blandly, as he motioned for the bartender, asking for a vodka on the rocks. "You get used to it."

"But why would you want to?"

She laughed, swiveling on the bar stool, facing the cages. "I like to be in control," she answered.

He leaned with his back against the counter. "Same question applies. Why would you want to?" She only smiled in response. Lars would have understood, Jacob did not.

"There they are," she said, raising her hand. Johanne was on the side of the stage, his dancing techniques the envy of women and men alike. The song transitioned to an heavy, thumping tune.

"This is calling my name," she said. "I'll be back." She didn't want her first dance to be with Jacob. Johanne beckoned to her with one hand, pulling her toward him as she stepped onto the platform. Together, they moved in and out of the beats, up tempo then down, perfectly in sync. By the time she'd finished the second song, drips of sweat were gliding down the back of her top.

"Nice shoes," Johanne half yelled in her ear, and she nodded. They were half-boots made of snakeskin, the fronts open with straps all the way down and a thick heal. Modern with a flash of retro, perfect for dancing without breaking a heel. Leave it to Johanne to notice.

Danielle stepped down when Dario came up. On the way back, she took a detour to the lady's room, checking her hair. The high pony was in place, and she lifted the back off her neck, pulling it into the rubber band. If she wanted to continue the ultra-sexy look, she would have kept it down, but the desire to be cool won out.

"You didn't join me," she said to Jacob, who hadn't moved from his position.

"I'm not really into dancing, but I like clubs. You do it well, though. I'm impressed." Danielle thanked him, feeling the relief that came with disappointment. Unlike Andre, who refrained from drinking when she did, Jacob appeared to be on his second or third vodka. And who didn't like to dance?

It wasn't meant to be, she thought, at least not with Jacob.

CHAPTER 21

Before she fell asleep, Danielle's mind wasn't on Jacob, but Max. Did Lani have any idea he was being duplicitous, if in fact, he was? Danielle didn't want Lani to suffer for the next ten years because she hopped out of Stephen's bed and into Max's. Maybe she could reach out to Lani and just check in, see if she could raise the subject without giving away too much.

It was a dilemma she couldn't solve, but knew the person who could.

Danielle's opportunity to speak with Lars and see if he'd gotten any information on Lani and her restaurant didn't come until Wednesday, just before she needed to leave. Seeing him outside her office speaking with Glenda, Danielle called out. He turned, coming into the office.

"Can you shut the door, please?" She waited until Lars was inside. "It's about Lani, I'm thinking of calling and trying to reestablish something, just enough to see if she has any idea what's going on with Max." Danielle paused, seeing Margaret walk past. "FYI, Margaret just went by and saw us talking. Am I going to get fired?"

"It's personal, not business," Lars said flatly. "Please continue."

"Well, that's it. Do you think it will do more harm than good?"

Lars pulled in his cheeks as he pushed his lips together. It was undeniably sexy, something she'd not associated with him for weeks.

"Bluntly?" She nodded. "She's never picked up on any of your hints in the past, so why now? In fact, Lani may be so angry at you and paranoid, she might interpret your raising the subject of the financial state as a way to push the financial knife further in her side."

"Good point. You suggest saying nothing, then?"

He inclined his head. "If you value her as a friend, and believe that she'll emerge from this a better human being, then yes."

"And you wouldn't trust her."

"Would you?" he countered. Danielle knew the answer as well as he did. "Now I have news of my own," he said, his voice changing ever so slightly. "Over the weekend I spoke with one of the two owners of the Raven Hotel. He's uninterested in paying any money for the restaurant. It's common knowledge Lani's restaurant isn't covering costs, although they haven't missed their rent."

"He'd take it over then?"

"That's it. Lanie and Max would have to be happy to walk away."

"Whew." All the money would be lost, by everyone. "A hard pill to swallow."

"Worse if Max is committing fraud." Seeing her expression, he turned his head slightly. "Yes?"

"You're so diplomatic, but stealing is still stealing," she said.

"Never change your own blunt ways."

Lars left, and the next person to walk through her door was Johanne.

"I'm here on the request of my manager who shall not be named," he said, closing the door behind him. "You trying to get fired?"

Danielle sniggered in full view of Margaret, who was hovering outside Glenda's cubicle. "After all I've been through, Johanne, nothing is going to faze me anymore, certainly not the woman who wants me to quit my job, which is now abundantly clear, because she's hovering by Glenda's cubicle. And before you say another word, I invited Lars to talk about Lani and her debacle. He chose to do it in person, therefore it was a personal conversation, which is not governed by the rules of this company, or, Margaret."

Johanne gave a wicked smile. "Snap."

"Now let me give you the recap on Lars." When she finished, Johanne cocked an eyebrow.

"What I want to know is about him—you have a whole lot of—not sure how to say this diplomatically—man balls, to be alone in a room with Lars and have a conversation about Lani, all above board and seemingly professional."

"Honestly, Johanne. I have to give the man credit. His is being non-emotional, more like he was at the beginning of my tenure here."

"Oh!" said Johanne. "Non-emotional. Awesome."

She snickered. "Stop it. You're killing me."

"See you dancing again this weekend?"

"Afraid not. I'm facing my fears, so to speak, and will be going up to Zermatt and repelling over some ice this weekend."

"Whatever," he said dismissively, stopping when she stared at him. "You're serious? What happened? You decided one death in the family for Monroe wasn't enough and you want to compound that."

For just a split second, Danielle was quiet, the explosion in her head manifesting itself in a choice phrase she'd not used since being in Switzerland. Her cursing jolted him. "Swear at me all you want," he retorted, "but it's the truth. Are you eff-ing kidding me?" Danielle bit her lower lip. "And have you told Layda and Georgy?"

Danielle briefly closed her eyes, breathing in, finding her one-space.

"I'm going to back up and start by apologizing," she began. "My swearing was uncalled for. You are being a protective friend, which I greatly appreciate and love you all the more for. My reaction is because this is about me and what I need. Georgy and Layda not only want me to do this but are giving me their home to stay in for the next five Saturday nights." She paused. "Preceding this was visiting my therapist, who on week one gave me the homework assignment to get out of my shell. It led up to last week where he suggested ice climbing."

As she spoke, Johanne shook his head. By the time she was done, he'd stood up, a hand on his hip. She was ready to tell him more, about becoming a part of the Mettleren family philanthropic efforts and all that it meant, but he put up a palm.

"No. Stop. I don't want to hear any more."

Danielle was genuinely surprised. Of all people, she expected Johanne to applaud her for putting herself out on the edge, literally and figuratively, overcoming her demons, not being the home-bound nun he'd implied she was becoming in the months following Andre's death.

"But there is so much more to tell you," she said, "all of it really good."

Johanne turned, his face aggressive, which was a new expression, and she didn't like it.

"Nothing is good when you are literally putting yourself at risk in a way I can't even begin to comprehend. Do you remember how some of us were mad when Andre died, because he had a choice and yet he willingly got on that motorcycle, and it got him killed. You know better, and you are going to do it anyway. Wasn't you almost losing it when Lars came in with his arm in a sling enough for you?"

"But that's the entire point, Johanne," she said emphatically. "I can't let my life be governed by fear. I'll never be in a healthy relationship or be healthy myself if I don't."

"Exactly! You stay healthy by staying alive! This is—" he stopped in frustration. "I can't talk about this right now."

Danielle hadn't noticed Margaret had left, replaced by Lars outside Glenda's cubicle until then. Johanne strode out of her line of site, leaving her in the direct path of Lars who looked at her quizzically.

It's okay, she mouthed, pulling her upper lip under. Unlike his most recent visit, if he came in her office, it would be business, letting off a new stream of inner-office fireworks. This place is becoming full of all sorts of drama, she thought, the reality giving her a bit of humor. Who would have thought the trading desk of all places was going to turn into a soap opera?

CHAPTER 22

Going home for dinner and two hours with her daughter effectively cleared her mind of Johanne's words. In hindsight, it was wonderful he cared so much for her welfare. He just lacked the broader picture of how she needed to personally mature.

And he is just as misinformed about the statistics of ice and rock climbing as I was.

Well, it wasn't her mission in life to convince him she was capable and had a path she was going to follow. Ironically, his opposition gave her more conviction she was doing the right thing. That night, she played to a slightly larger group than the week prior, a fact noted by Robin.

"Word is getting around," he said with satisfaction.

"Do I get another ten francs?" she joked.

"You said you aren't here for the money." It was true enough. "See you Sunday."

The following day, Johanne didn't stop by, nor did Margaret. Then it came. The two-tap knock at the door.

"Numbers are looking good," Lars remarked. "All must be well." The statement was more of a question.

"All things considered, yes. Thanks for asking." He held her eyes a moment longer. "Seriously. It's all good. Growing pains."

"Do I need to make any changes?"

"Nope. Not a thing."

Lars had no choice other than to take her at face value and left. At her appointment with Dr. Blatz, she replayed the highlights of the week, and he focused on her emotions around men, the jazz club and ice climbing.

"With knowledge comes power," he said, regarding her interaction with Johanne and the ice climbing discussion.

"I thought the sister-saying to that was: the greater the knowledge, the more responsibility one has."

"It's all about choice and consequence, which is Johanne's main concern," Dr. Blatz added. "You are fortunate to have a good friend like him in your life."

Friday, the numbers posted on the boards and Danielle decided to drop by Jacob's cubicle. He hadn't stopped by once all week, out of regret for getting drunk Saturday or disinterest, she didn't know or care. Inside these four walls, it was all about the numbers.

"Great job this week," she said, putting her fingers on the top edge of the grey cubicle, peering over. He looked up, a smile on his face.

"I had a good teacher. Wait," he requested as she removed her hand from the rim. "Sorry about what I said the other night." She tilted her head. "The bad drinks. Not dancing. I wasn't much of a gentleman."

She smiled. "No, you weren't, but that's what getting together is all about, right?"

He nodded with evident relief. Beyond the physical attraction, they weren't a fit on even the most basic level.

Danielle closed the door to her office on her way out, taking the long way around the office so as not to walk by Johanne's office, or Margaret's.

The flipside was she did pass by Lars' office, but his door was closed as usual.

"Danielle," called out Ulrich. Her first and former manager had been largely absent from her life since Johanne took over the duties at the beginning of the year. Other than the few meetings they attended together each month, Danielle had no reason to interact with him.

"How have you been Ulrich?" she asked with a smile. She missed his dry sense of humor and unbending professionalism.

"I read something interesting about you recently."

"It couldn't have been in the arrest section."

"No, but it was nearly as disconcerting," he said. "I didn't know you were moonlighting at a jazz club." *Oh, man.* "Why are you looking so distressed?"

"For some reason, I was thinking my schedule would be buried in the back of local papers."

Ulrich swiveled his curved screen. A huge headline ran across the top, with her name and the jazz club right below it. "Rather unassuming, isn't it?"

Danielle's eyes popped in shock. "Wow."

He turned the screen back around. "They must be pretty impressed to give you that kind of publicity."

"Well, it's just two nights a week for a couple of hours, but it's fun and keeps my voice and playing skills up to snuff."

"Did you just start?"

"No, it's been a few weeks, now." The man didn't have to say the words to show his relief. She realized he thought she'd just begun and her numbers would dip. Now that he knew she'd been doing both jobs, the real reason he'd stopped her had proven unfounded.

"I suspect you'll have a packed house," he said, telling her to have a good weekend. She did the same, encountering no one else before she left the building.

That night, Danielle read stories to Monroe before rocking her to sleep in the chair in the living room. The fireplace was on, and she had a DVD of Cinderella playing with English sub-titles.

Saturday morning, it was snowing lightly and she periodically thought about Johanne. By now, she guessed he'd have talked with Dario about Lars' approach with the hotel. There was no doubt in Danielle's mind Dario would use his resources to go after Max, but first, he had to have hard evidence. That meant hiring a private investigator to get the facts.

She looked at the time. Lars had counseled her against calling Lani—or rather—intimated it would be futile. Danielle's stomach churned with a sickening sense of fear—exactly what Dr. Blatz told her to confront. She—Danielle—either needed to resolve the situation with her friend and have the relationship be healthy, or be done with it, thereby eliminating the uncertainty.

She punched in the number on her phone.

"Hey," greeted Lani, her voice neither angry or happy.

"How are you?" asked Danielle, trying to match neutral tones.

"Fine. What's up?"

As unprepared to make the call as Lani was to receive it, Danielle defaulted to honesty. "I've just been thinking about you and worried about the restaurant so I wanted to call. If you don't want to talk, or if this is a bad time, I understand."

The genuine approach worked, because Lani sighed. "Thanks, I guess. Life is life. The restaurant still needs time to gain a foothold, but we are looking good on the revenue side, so that's encouraging."

"That's great," said Danielle with false enthusiasm. Either Lani was being kept in the dark about the true financial situation or she believed things would turn around, which was not a sound business strategy.

"Well, glad to hear your voice," Danielle said, uncomfortable with asking more.

"You too."

And that was it. The short call gave her no comfort, but then it hadn't gotten personal, which might have turned into a fight. And she had to face the fear of her friend, which was another step forward in the right direction.

"Oh crap!" she said out loud. Whether it was subconscious or not, Danielle had utterly forgotten today was the first day of her ice climbing skills class.

Danielle arrived at Layda's home ten minutes later. According to Layda, the roads were clear and Danielle would make it up to the mountain with about twenty minutes to spare.

"You won't have time to go to the house and then back down to the train into the town," she said. "So park in Tasch and either take the train, or cab or limo and it's about seven minutes to town. You'll arrive just in time."

Danielle gave her a quick hug and kiss and was gone. Traffic was light as she drove out of town and up the pass, trains going through tunnels on her right. The majestic scenery would have been more enjoyable if she'd been able to stop and take pictures, but she was on a mission, one which she barely made.

Parking at Tasch was hard, the two-thousand plus covered stalls packed to capacity, the clear, cold day beckoning everyone in the surrounding area. Her tension eased up when a car backed out. Five minutes later, she was boarding the train for the five kilometer ride to town. When she arrived, she was led to an indoor room where four others were being instructed on their outer wear, and a young woman came to her assistance, helping her with the fit of the clothes, harness and shoes. She learned they were going to receive today's instruction mostly in a classroom, working on a solid ice face where the temperature was consistent.

"And therefore, no risk of injury," said the female instructor. The short woman looked to be in her early thirties, with a sun-worn but youthful face. Danielle's anxiety level went from moderate to low, then non-existent as the hours passed. Each and every technique for handling the ropes, placing a foot and hammering with a pick were explained, then demonstrated, and finally, attempted. First while standing on the ground, then two feet above, and then at the very end of the day, eye-height.

The youngest member of the group was seventeen, a young woman whose father and mother both died in a climbing accident. Danielle learned of the incident during the lunch break and couldn't stop herself from asking why the girl then wanted to learn the sport.

"My parents loved it and loved life," she said. "They died without regrets."

"I think that's the best way to go," commented a man without emotion.

It must be this culture, Danielle thought. Here, death and dying were a part of life, euthanasia was seen as merciful, not murderous. And to the young woman's point, everyone was going to die, so one might as well die when happy.

Danielle stopped mid-chew. She'd said almost those exact same words at a table full of close friends and family after Andre's death. He loved riding bikes.

The last hour went by quickly as they scaled up another ten feet, all giving one another high-fives after the descent. As much as she wanted to see Layda and Georgy's home in Zermatt, she yearned for the bed in their home in Zurich, and waking up with her daughter. She headed back to Zurich, content that she had the rest of her life to enjoy the luxury of being a part of their family.

CHAPTER 23

"What's going on?" Danielle asked Robin when she finally got through the door the next night.

"You," he said with a wink, offering to take her coat. Leon already had a soda water with lime waiting, and she thanked him, asking him the same question, receiving a similar response.

She approached the stage, thinking the heat of the crowded room had lifted the temperature another few degrees. Retrieving the microphone, the red light turned white and she spoke. "It's seriously hot in here, thanks to you all, and I'm wondering if you mind me slipping off my shoes, because if I don't, I may pass out."

Danielle heard Leon bark a laughter, but taking her shoes off did help. At the end of the night, Robin helped her on with her heavy coat.

"Here, these are for you. I thought it best to hold them for the end of the night. Business and personal cards."

"What for?" Robin searched her eyes. "I don't need them. This is something I do for fun, I'm not looking for work."

His expression changed to one of inquisitive admiration. "I don't suspect they want to hire you, at least not to play." Danielle leaned her head forward, sure she hadn't heard him correctly. "It's the men's information, well, and some women, I think. *Dating*," he said with emphasis. Seeing her make no effort to take the cards, he nudged them forward. "Here. Just take them."

"Throw them away," she said under her breath, blocking the view of the patrons at the counter, in case any of those had provided their cards.

"Nooo," he drawled. "I committed I'd pass them along, which I'm doing. What you elect to do with them is your choice." He leaned to her ear. "Give them to your friends if you aren't interested." She giggled, took the cards and made her way out of the club, waving to Leon. At home, Danielle removed the cards and placed the stack on the counter, not bothering to look. Why should she strike up a relationship with a stranger when she couldn't even keep one with a friend?

That question was still lingering in the back of her mind throughout the following week, and kept rising to the surface when Johanne looked either at his papers during team meetings, or at Margaret, who conducted. When Lars was present, he deferred to Margaret, except when questions where posed that only he could answer. Without Johanne to joke with, life within the walls of MRD was work, pure and simple.

On Thursday, Dr. Blatz applauded her ability to forge ahead, even with the temporary loss of Johanne, for that's what he believed it was. Temporary.

"Your instincts are right," he predicted, referring to Johanne's protective nature. "A man doesn't stop wanting to take care of loved ones just because he isn't chasing a wooly mammoth around." Danielle paused, doubting it was actually possible for her therapist to make the quip, then heartily laughed, especially since she pictured Johanne with anything but a hairy chest. Nicely manicured and sculpted was more like him.

"What do you think of Lars? Is it time to tell him?"

"Tell him what?" Danielle asked. "You mean about the playing or the ice climbing?"

"Either, or."

"No on both," she said firmly. "I want to have the satisfaction of failing or succeeding on my own. He can find out later, but by then, I'm sure it will be less relevant than it is now." If Dr. Blatz disagreed with her, he wasn't going to say it.

Friday was another good day for numbers, with Jacob inching up the return ladder. He was still a solid twenty points behind her, but he was consistent, and in the trading business, that was all that mattered.

"Bundle up more than usual," Glenda recommended, popping her head in the office before she left. "It's negative three outside right now."

"It's going the wrong direction," Danielle protested. "It's supposed to be getting warmer, not colder."

When it came time for Danielle to put her coat on, the office was quiet. She'd called Emma, asking for another half hour while she provided a report Johanne had requested. It wasn't difficult, just time consuming. She'd started relegating operational tasks to her time at work, preserving the hours outside for discretionary activities like personal trading and family.

Inch by inch she was retracting and redirecting her efforts towards a different future, one that included managing the Mettleren family wealth.

As she waited for her report to finish processing and print, she retrieved the calendar of events Layda had given her, leaning back in her chair, enjoying the quiet of the office. Believing no on to be around, she raised the volume of her ambient music.

The distractions in her life, from playing at the club to ice climbing so effectively filled her free time that she didn't have extra to feeling sorry for herself or wonder what Lars had been up to. She glanced up at the glass wall; half expecting to see him walk by, briefcase in hand. Of all the men she'd encountered over the last month, at the jazz lounge, dance club or here at the office, Lars still held more physical attraction than anyone else.

Is that emotionally driven or purely physical? She challenged herself, hearing Dr. Blatz's voice in her head. Physical, all the way. There was no denying how Lars cut a striking figure in his suits or out of them, his short hair, the top lopped to either one side sexy and professional. She imagined her fingers running through the mass, pulling him forward.

"Danielle?" Her eyes popped open. "Were you actually sleeping?"

She laughed, embarrassed at seeing Lars standing before her. "Daydreaming as my reports process. What's up?"

"Not much," he answered, "other than to check in with our top trader." Danielle glanced over his shoulder in an obvious way. "She's gone, as is everyone else save the security guard."

Free to be herself, Danielle said, "You know, it's a very strange environment in which I now work. You are being clandestine with your co-manager and girlfriend, my boss and friend has put me on ice and we are talking like it's just a normal Friday."

Lars leaned against the door frame, arms crossed, smiling. "Correction. She's not my girlfriend, nor am I being clandestine."

"Oh really? You waited until she's gone to talk to me, which means you are going around her, and if she's not your girlfriend, have you already dumped her? No wait, stop, I don't need to know this."

"Yes, you do," he smiled, "or you wouldn't bring it up, and furthermore, it's personal, so we can discuss it in the office without going against process."

"See," she pointed. "That was clandestine, right there."

He laughed in response. "Why has Johanne put you on ice? Something to do with what happened the other day? "

"Yeah." Her mood dropped at the answer, and he caught it. "He's unhappy about the way I'm addressing some of my issues regarding fear, and I'd like to leave it at that, if I may." Lars was unsure what to do with that information, his eyes moving between her own, then assessing her body posture. "It will pass in time, as all things do. Now, changing the subject, any update on Lani's restaurant?"

"Unfortunately yes. On my suggestion, the owner contacted Max and offered to take over the operations. Max declined. It's unclear whether or not Lani even knew about it." Danielle inhaled quickly and shook her head. The printer started up, the sheets coming fast, ending almost as soon as it started. She pulled them off, stacked them and placed them on her desk.

"Johanne's reports," she said.

"Danielle?" She kept her head down. She knew that tone of voice and what it meant, but that's not what she wanted, not now. They had just reached a point of constancy, and she wasn't about to alter it. "You can't look down forever." She chuckled and lifted up her eyes to meet his gaze. "I see you are going to be at a number of events with Layda and Georgy starting in April." It wasn't what she was expecting to hear. "Things must be going well with the family."

"They really have become my parents, as you once predicted."

"It implies quite a lot."

Danielle saw where this conversation might head and wanted to cut it off before it got there. "At some point, they are going to want to ease out of their philanthropic efforts, as you can imagine. I will be an interim place holder for Monroe."

"I think there's a bit more to it than that," he remarked, watching her.

Danielle looked at the clock on the wall, the hint less than subtle. "Well, I used to think that this culture was all about discretion," she said, standing, pushing in her chair. "But you have known the two of them a lot longer than I have. Maybe I should be the one asking you for insights as to my future."

Lars dropped his arms but stayed in place as she opened the wardrobe and put on her coat. "Danielle, I don't think you understand what it means when a family like the Mettleren's make a public showing like they are doing with you."

"We are a family, Lars," she answered, putting on her warm hat, trying to stay clear of words and phrases they had once used with one another. Danielle put her bag over her shoulder and pushed the door shut, looking at him expectantly.

"I'm happy for you," he said, moving aside.

"Thanks. Me too. Have a good weekend."

"You as well."

She walked down the hall and out the doors, wondering what he was planning on doing that weekend. Likely ice climbing somewhere very far from her own indoor instruction area, or well beyond the ice falls used for novices like her small group.

"Good evening, Danielle."

"Hey!" she greeted Dominic, going at a diagonal to him. She put out her arms and he hugged her back. "Have a hot weekend of chauffeuring planned or are you going to mix it up with a few parking lot fights?" He laughed the deep chested rumble of a man his size. "Seriously," she said, poking his solid chest. "You need to use this to make all your hard work pay off."

He purposefully puffed his chest out, causing her to giggle and poke it one more time. "Don't let your boss find out you have a sense of humor."

"Not helpful," he said in an undertone.

"That's my que," she whispered back, leaving him at his car.

The next day, Danielle arrived at Layda and Georgy's forty minutes before she needed to head up to the mountain. Georgy beamed like a proud father when she related her first ice climbing experience and nodded approvingly when he heard about Johanne wanting her to be safe.

"He'll come around," Georgy predicted, not unlike Dr. Blatz. Both fell silent when she related Lars' comments about her being at all the public events.

"I think he suspects our plan," Danielle confided.

"Of course, he does," rumbled Georgy. "He has known us too long to think otherwise."

Layda placed a hand on Georgy's shoulder, rubbing it lovingly. "It's more than that, Danielle. Lars is right. In this culture, when the next generation is brought in, it signals a transition to be sure. But with your background and our financial situation, he is assuming, or guessing, there is more to it than just passing the baton."

"Georgy, do you think Lars already talked about this Noel?"

"Probably. He'd be a fool not to, and we know Lars is anything but that. Trust me, I'm sure Noel believes this is out there on the horizon, but one thing is giving him comfort."

"Which is?" she encouraged.

"You can't run a brokerage or investment firm yourself, as you said. You need someone more credentialled and those type of people don't come along every day, nor are they cheap. Yes, you can run all our wealth aspects, but for trading, it will still be outside. Someone must hold those activities, until you, yourself want to get the credentials to do so yourself."

Danielle got it. "I can only take away so much business from him."

The conversation shifted to her plans for the night, and she told them she was likely to return as she had the previous week. "Don't push it on our account," advised Layda. "If you feel tired in the slightest, you stay overnight, agreed?"

Monroe was in her scooter when Danielle leaned down to give her a hug and a kiss, feeling another rush of gratitude. Even if Lars became a meaningful part of her life again, would it get much better than what she had now? She shut the door, leaving the question behind her.

CHAPTER 24

That evening, Danielle's shoulders ached and her thigh muscles were screaming, along with her calves. She learned that the right technique for ice climbing didn't require the strength she was used to putting into her sailboarding. In fact, when done correctly, ice climbing was a whole lot easier than her summer sport. As the group removed their outer gear, the instructor warned her she'd be sore in a few hours.

"I don't have to wait," Danielle responded. "I'm hurting now!"

In addition to her legs, the tendons between her wrists to elbows were killing her. She was going to require serious stretching if she expected to play the piano tomorrow night. Sitting in her car at the parking lot in Tasch, she phoned Layda for a recommendation.

"Actually, the best masseuse I can provide is up in Zermatt, not down here in Zurich."

"Seriously?"

"Danielle, what did I say earlier today?" Her tone was a bit of scolding with a whole lot of love.

"Yes, mom." Danielle expected a witty reply from Layda, but heard nothing. "Layda?" she asked, concerned. Then she heard a sniffle.

"I've... I've waited my entire life since giving birth to Andre to hear that from a young woman."

"I hope you don't mind," Danielle said, emotion making her voice waver. "It just came out."

Layda choked on tears and laughter. "Do I sound like I minded? Now, I insist that you stay in Zermatt. Here's the number, and her name is spelled Annali, but in the states, you say it Anna-Lee, all one word."

"Got it. I am going to try and be home as early as I can tomorrow."

"Danielle, I love you like a daughter."

"Because I am your daughter."

Another pause. "You made me cry again."

"I'm not sorry about that, and I love you too."

The unexpected, emotion-filled call over, Danielle held the phone in her lap and wept, feeling all the love that came with having a mother again after her own had died and all the heartache of having no one to share in the joy.

Later, Danielle lay on the portable massage table set up in the master bedroom of Georgy and Layda's chalet. She involuntarily groaned as Annali stretched and kneaded her sore tendons.

"In and out," Annali counseled, keeping her own breath in time with Danielle. "Take a hot bath then rub this on the area," Annali recommended when she was finished, giving Danielle a small jar of muscle relaxant.

After she left, Danielle dutifully soaked in the outdoor hot tub. Layda's home was in the same Petit Village of Zermatt as Lars' residence, but although she'd been up to his chalet a number of times, she wasn't familiar enough with the town to know if they were in the same area, let alone street. The homes were graciously spaced apart, but lacked gates or other privacy barriers. She suspected that one could walk around the entire area in safety.

After having a cup of hot chocolate, that's what Danielle did. The road was quiet, save for periodic bits of laughter drifting down from the residences. A silhouette occasionally appeared on a deck, hand raised with a drink and laughter, the scene repeated in hot tubs, the two most common outdoor activities in this luxurious area.

She snuggled within her thick, down jacket, unable to keep her thoughts from drifting back to Lars and playing the grand piano he'd engraved with her initials. Was it being enjoyed by another woman or sitting dormant, as he said it had before she came into his life? Dormant, she decided, occupying the corner spot in the living room in the shadow of the Matterhorn.

The thought gave her comfort until she walked under the balcony where a man was kissing a woman.

Being happy for others who were in fulfilling relationships was much easier when one was in love, she determined.

She kept going, the path darkening between the lamp posts. *Am I unhappy being by myself, or is this is just a part of learning to be alone?* She didn't feel anger or cynicism, and her outlook for the future was a positive one, where good things can and do happen; bitterness had no place in her life. Hope. That's what it was. All that she'd been through hadn't extinguished the light of hope for a happier time. As her former boss and mentor told her before she embarked on her move to Zurich, it could and would happen.

"That's what seeing Dr. Blatz is doing for you," Layda said Sunday at brunch as Monroe sat on her lap, tapping Danielle's face with her little fingers. "Finding contentment is challenging, no matter how much money or position or family one has."

After lunch, the four of them left the house, intent on spending the afternoon at the Swiss Children's Museum. The idea was better than the reality Danelle learned, over estimating the attention span of an almost one year old. The toys and teaching areas were largely too mature for Monroe, who moved between play stations with the interest of a gnat. Her grandparents, however, enjoyed themselves immensely, often picking up items they remembered from their childhood. As Danielle struggled with an increasingly disgruntled child, Layda apologized.

"I'm so sorry," she said with a little laugh. "I think Georgy and I are having far more fun than either of you."

"It was a success," Georgy remarked to Danielle, who touched his granddaughter's face. "We were out together as a family."

Georgy's words came to the forefront when Danielle entered the jazz club just before six.

"I told you," said Robin smugly, taking her coat and giving her a light kiss to the cheek. "The first sold out Sunday night we've ever had. Congratulations."

Danielle accepted the soda water from Leon, who tipped his head and winked. A full house had the wonderful trickle-down effect of more money for the waitstaff and bartenders. For the moment, Leon and the other staff were shining the light of love on her, but she needed to set expectations so they didn't think it would last.

"Robin, you do realize that come summer, I'm going to be spending more time with my daughter at the beach and on the water during the weekends, not inside a bar?"

"Of course," he replied. "No one wants to be indoors during the summer. Even us."

"What do you do then? Shut down the club?"

"No, we switch to seasonal hours and are only inside if it's storming. We have the outdoor patio in the back, which is presently covered by snow. Live bands, quartets and local musicians play. You can be a patron then, not an entertainer."

Danielle's sense of relief was profound, and she took to the piano with added enthusiasm. She'd never performed to a sold-out crowd at any venue and she felt the energy in the room. Sipping her drink, she glanced to the corners of the club, recognizing a few men from previous sessions. Setting the glass back down, she motioned to Robin.

"What's this?" she asked him, touching the bowl.

"It's for requests and money." She was about to argue, but he leaned closer. "Trust me, this will make you pin money. Listen and learn."

Robin stood by the piano, mic in hand. After he introduced her, he touched the bowl. "The way it works is you make a request, writing it on a piece of paper which you will find on your tables. It's accompanied by a monetary amount, which you give to your server. The person with the highest enticement gets his or her song played. Otherwise, Danielle will play what she wants." He turned to her. "Right?"

"Absolutely. And what a girl wants is this." Robin led the crowd in clapping as she began, *I've got a crush on you.*

"Yes, I do," Robin quipped, still talking to the mic. "But then so do the hundred other guys in here, so I'm in good company."

During the first thirty minutes, servers provided her with a steady stream of requests, depositing the cards and cash on the piano between songs. At first, the notes were single francs, then one five appeared, followed by a ten trumping the request. It became a game of outbidding, with more twenties and a fifty competing for the winning song.

"I'm now going to play *Take the A Train*, which is the highest bid with a fifty. Thank you."

"Wait." Danielle repeated the introductory chords, allowing for a male server to approach. He presented her with a 100 franc note and a piece of paper.

"While the 100 is appreciated, this song has too many memories for me, good and bad."

The server put another hundred on the piano. "He authorized me to go to 200 hundred," turning to the audience, as though support were going to pressure Danielle to sing.

"My piano. My prerogative," she said with a coy smile.

"Come on," Robin yelled from the back, encouraging others in the audience. She looked straight at Robin and shook her head a defiant no, although smiling. "Why not?" He challenged, taking the side of the anonymous customer.

"If you must know," Danielle began, talking to a room full of strangers. "I sang this song to a gentleman who broke my heart. How about this?" she said, playing *The man that got away*, when the entire room heard the shout.

"A thousand," yelled Robin. "Will you sing it for a thousand?"

"What is this?" Danielle questioned. "An auction for my vocal chords? The answer is no. N. O."

Robin was now walking up through the center of the room. He reached the piano, turning to the crowd, making a show out of counting out the one hundred-dollar notes. "Hard cash," he said, counting out the hundreds. "Is your heart worth a thousand?"

"It's worth a lot more." She responded, jutting her chin out in playful defiance.

"Two thousand," yelled Leon from the bar.

"Are you kidding me?" she asked, speaking in to the mic. She executed a run all the way up the piano, tinkling the top keys delicately. It got a laugh from those in the front, and she looked back to the bartender. Seeing

Robin's demeanor, she compromised. "I'll sing it, for five grand, half of which will go to charity," she said with another trill on the keys. "And I do not take check, visa or money orders."

Positive she'd nipped that one in the bud, she proceeded to sing the intended song, then *Gimme Lovin*, which reminded her of Lars just as much as Crazy, yet it was a lovely, sensual moment in his downtown apartment, a memory that was about as close to intimacy as she could get without the bad memories. Two songs later, Robin approached the stage again. He placed the mic at the center of the piano. "The patron got conviction about that song, left and returned with your ransom."

Only one man used to have that kind of conviction for her, and he was completely and one hundred percent out of her life.

"Let's see if it's all here," Robin said, theatrically, counting out the hundreds. "Danielle, I'd say it's all here, and you are singing *Crazy*."

In the midst of the inevitable, Danielle was happy for Robin, who had made the most of out the moment.

"A deal is a deal," Danielle grumped with aplomb. "And someone really must be *Crazy* for this song to pay that amount, but it is Switzerland. Land of the filthy rich. This is for *you*, Mr. Anonymous in the audience. Should I start weeping, you shoulder the responsibility."

The crowd was respectfully silent, as though they appreciated the vigor of someone willing to shell out five thousand francs for a song and the anticipation a woman might cry on stage.

Danielle hummed, swapping out her playful-but-resistant attitude to the sultry, soulful one required to do the song justice. The lighting changed, the hot burn of the white to the warm, softer red. She closed her eyes, feeling the mood. She'd always been admired as a performer because she intonated what she felt; to cut off her heart was to restrict her voice.

Think of the wonderful parts of Lars, she told herself, still humming.

Crazy... she began, *crazy for being so lonely...*

Her reluctance became a thrill, subtly opening eyes, spreading her sensual energy into the black, with words and gaze.

*I knew/ you'd love me/ as long as you wanted...*she continued, *And then...someday/ You'd leave me/ for somebody new*

Yes, that's what happened, but it was my fault.

I'm crazy/ For thinking that my love/ could hold you...

Yep. I'd been arrogant enough to think that Lars would stick around, just like Lani had with Stephen.

I'm crazy for tryin... Yep, I am crazy because I'm now ice climbing as I try to mature.

*I'm crazy for cryin....*No kidding. I almost lost it the last time I sang this song when Benny and Robin were testing me out, and here I am again.

Danielle turned her eyes to the darkness, channeling the past feelings of love for Lars to the future, believing her heart would eventually be touched by someone else, making her journey of love and loss worth it.

And I'm crazy...for lovin you, the final words of the song drifting off.

Real or imagined, she felt the audience were applauding her strength to overcome her own issues as much as they were her voice and the five grand. She'd never know and it didn't much matter. She'd made it through this part of the journey.

CHAPTER 25

Danielle asked Leon and Robin who had paid the money, but they weren't divulging and she left the club with the question lingering. She'd find out eventually, probably when it wouldn't matter a bit.

Monday was quiet, and on Tuesday Jacob stopped by to point out his returns. It wasn't until Wednesday that Danielle saw Johanne, when he showed up at her office.

"Dario wants to come see you Sunday night," Johanne said from the doorway.

"You're talking to me now?"

A twitch on his lip was the first sign of remorse for his outburst the week prior. "Maybe. Or it could be I'm just checking to see if you're alive is all. Don't go reading too much into it."

Danielle lips curled into a smile. "I love you too."

Georgy and Dr. Blatz were correct: Johanne was concerned and worried for herself and her daughter. That night, playing was uneventful but lucrative, and Thursday afternoon Dr. Blatz applauded her progress in his moderate way.

"You mean I still have more to learn?" she quipped.

"Keep up the momentum," he encouraged. She did just that, scaling the ice formations with her group of four that Saturday, pleased her legs and hands were less sore than the week prior. Danielle wasn't as exhausted as she'd anticipated, surprising Layda and Georgy by appearing at their home shortly after dinner. She stayed the night and Sunday, left Monroe with her grandparents before going home to change and make it over to the jazz club by six.

On her way, Danielle's thoughts turned to Lani. She was likely completely unaware of the tsunami that was soon going to hit. When the voice mail clicked on, Danielle left a message, identifying that she wanted to talk.

The evening wasn't as eventful as the previous Sunday night, but the crowd was standing room only.

"I didn't even advertise this time," Robin gloated.

At the end of the night, Robin asked her if she minded not playing on Wednesday night. A well-known local who made it big was going to be in town and was going to give a special performance.

"Awesome," Danielle said. "Maybe I'll come by just to watch."

As the week started, Danielle reflected it was now three months since she'd been with Lars and time to stop keeping track. Next weekend was her last instruction course and then the competition. Thrilled and nervous about the prospect, Danielle focused on her numbers at work, ignoring Margaret when she passed her in the hallway and spending her time at home on the floor with Monroe, engaged in learning activities. Every week the little girl was expressing herself more fully, almost always humming or singing when by herself.

Too bad she was going to be raised an only child, Danielle thought, one of the few down moments she'd had recently. Danielle always figured if she were to ever have kids, she would definitely make sure to have a couple; having had no siblings of her own. Oh, well. Life could be a lot worse. Look at Andre and Lars or herself: *All of us were only children and we turned out okay.*

Wednesday came and she arranged with Emma to stay late, just as if she been playing. It would be nice to sit at the bar for once and enjoy a drink, listening to someone else entertain.

Leaving the office, she called Lani again, ignoring the bit of anger that arose over the fact that her friend hadn't called back. Rise above it, she told herself. The person who had more to give needed to be gracious, not an emotional miser.

Danielle walked along the busy road until a car in her peripheral vision slowed to a stop.

"Need a ride home tonight?" called the driver through the open window.

Danielle put the phone away, giving Dominic a smile. "What are you doing?" He pulled over, the hazard lights going on. "Other than being completely illegal and driving one of your boss's cars?"

"The boss is gone. This happens to be my car."

Danielle approached, still smiling. "You have nice taste." It was a Porsche Cayenne turbo SUV with studs on the tires. "Are you sure it's yours?"

Dominic laughed. "Thanks, and I promise it's mine. Can I give you a ride?" Without waiting for an answer, the window began rolling up as he opened the door to get out.

She scoped him up and down, and grinned. He wore jeans over boots, a turtleneck and a dark leather and fur-lined coat. "Look at you. You're a different person when you're not in a suit. Magnificent," she complimented.

"That's a yes, then, you will accept a ride home," he said, touching her elbow. "It's cold outside and this will save you time."

Dominic opened the door for Danielle and she found the seats already warm. He'd remembered her affinity for the heated seats in Lars' car.

"You know, I've never sat in the front of a car with you," she observed. "This is weird." He laughed good naturedly, turning down the dance music. "No, that's a good song," she said, turning it back up. Their fingers overlapped, the volume going super loud. "I'm hands off! You go."

Dominic pulled onto the street, deftly navigating between the trolleys and cars and alongside the two bridges through the center of town. "I get so used to taking the metro," she said, "which only gives one view of the city. Half the time I forget there are other ways to get home."

Dominic laughed, taking a left up a road Danielle thought she'd been up once. "See that building?" he pointed. "That's where I live."

"Lucky you." He was on the trendiest part of main street, right above a boutique clothier, the stone and marble building elegant looking but with a hip vibe that said single, not family dwellers. "Do you hear much of the noise from the clubs down further down?" she asked.

"None at all. My place is like a fortress."

"Well, then it fits your image."

Dominic chuckled. "And what's my image?"

Danielle looked at his side profile, this being the first chance she'd ever had to do so. From the rear seats of Lars' car, she'd become familiar with the back of his head, not his face.

"Fierce," she stated. "Strong, powerful. My first impression of you was when I was walking across the parking lot and we encountered Andre, remember? Even in my inebriated state, I distinctly recall thinking you were a man who could hurt things with your hands, and I hadn't even seen your face then!"

A late season snow storm had rolled in from the Alps, the thick blobs coming down heavy. Danielle was grateful she hadn't taken the metro. As close as it came to her home, she still had to walk up two sets of stairs to the street to her house.

"These roads are terrible tonight," she remarked, seeing an emergency vehicle lights up ahead.

"Accident," he muttered and took a side street. "Most people have already taken their snow tires off. Not smart."

She asked him how long he'd been working for Lars, and if he ever got bored with the job.

"Sometimes, but I teach self-defense and also train on the side when I get a few hours here and there." Danielle's focus was on him and not the road. It wasn't until he turned on the blinker to turn up a side street did she realize they were almost at her old flat.

"I'm so sorry," she laughed. "I thought you knew where I lived. I moved, two times since then."

"That one got by me." Danielle gave Dominic the address, explaining where it was. He stopped the car and was in the process of turning around when another SUV came careening towards them, sliding sideways. Dominic spun the wheel with his left hand, putting his right flat on her chest and holding her in place as the car's backend went into a bank and stopped. The other SUV missed the left front of his car by an inch, slamming into the vehicle behind them, the crunching of twisting metal was as loud and clear as the adrenaline in her body. She'd never been in an accident before…and…

"Danielle?" Dominic asked. It hadn't registered that his hand was still on her chest, or that he was now leaning toward her. Only when he touched her chin with his left hand, turning her to him did she respond. And then, she lost it.

CHAPTER 26

Uncontrollable terror began in her chest, continued up her throat, then erupted as shallow breathing, as though an intruder had come into her life, stolen everything she possessed and had run out the back door before she could even scream for help. When she found her voice, racking sobs came out, not words. Dominic drew her close, one arm around her shoulders, the other by her waist, eclipsing the short distance between the two seats.

"Trigger," was the only word she got out between sobs. It was exactly what Dr. Blatz had predicted would happen—should happen—to get her past Andre.

It was ugly. It was unexpected, and it hurt.

Dominic's cheek brushed against her head and face as he nodded, the soft bristles reminding her of Andre's five o'clock shadow, increasing the intensity of her sobs. It took time, but Danielle's heaving finally relaxed into exhausted breaths which continued to catch in her throat.

A police car and ambulance arrived, sirens blaring and lights on, a uniformed man soon tapping on the window to ensure they were okay. He and Dominic were talking rapidly, using words Danielle had not yet learned. Once the officer understood Dominic's car hadn't suffered any damage, they were free to go.

"Is your phone in your bag?" he asked her.

"I don't need a doctor," she whispered.

"It's not that," he said, already looking for it. "Code?" he asked. She gave it to him. "Home number for Emma? Never mind, here it is." She listened as Dominic greeted Emma in German, explaining he'd been giving her a ride home and the present circumstances. It was better Monroe didn't see her like this.

"Yes, I think so," Dominic said. "Good idea." He sounded exactly like the man he was when protecting and driving Lars.

Watching Dominic put the phone back in her purse, Danielle asked what was a good idea.

"She said that I need to get you a drink and help you compose yourself. She can be there with Monroe as long as required."

"I can't go out anywhere like this," she said softly, pushing on her cheeks, feeling how full and puffy they were.

Dominic checked her seatbelt before he put the car in gear. "You won't be going out, but in. To my apartment, for as long as it takes and as long as you need."

"Will that get you in trouble…I mean, do you have to be at the airport or something?"

"Not for a few days," he answered, his expression focused. "Far longer than you'll require."

In the passing lights, she glanced at him. The reverberations of the tsunami like event still moved through her, though the waves felt like they were decreasing in size.

"I'm sorry you had to experience my breakdown."

Dominic's muscular, warm hand found hers and held it tight. "I'm the perfect person to be with you, for many reasons."

"Yeah," she said quietly. They were silent for the short drive. He lived not more than a mile from her original apartment in the city, overlooking the lake. He parked the car in the garage, then came around to help her out. She linked his arm, keeping it in place as they rode the elevator to the second story, letting go so he could unlock the door. Once he opened the door, he touched her back, guiding her in.

"Here," he said, slipping off her purse, setting it on the credenza. She willingly let him be in control, turning for him to remove her jacket which he draped on the chair in the front entry.

"I like your style," she said softly. Her voice sounded weary even to her.

"Clean lines appeal to me." Danielle felt his touch on her lower back as he directed her to a deep, off-white couch, draping a grey chenille blanket over her legs. He turned on the gas fireplace with the click of a remote.

"Very cozy," she complimented, quietly. The living room was roughly the size of her own, but here the view of the water was to her right, not in front of her, the focus on what was inside, not outside the room.

"I'm going to get you a drink. Any preference?"

"A Mexican coffee is the only think I can think of, but that's likely not in the realm of impossibility."

"Give me ten minutes." When she looked up to give a response, the words stuck in her mouth. She was having a hard time concentrating, but was unsure why. Dominic sat down on the leather ottoman in front of her, nudging her legs between his. He placed his hands on her knees, his grip light, but firm.

"Your pupils are dilated, and your words are slightly slurred. You are suffering from a moderate form of PTSD. If I were to take you to the hospital, they would just give you drugs, which is only going to delay, but not address, what you are dealing with right now. Does that make sense?"

"Yes," she murmured, then reflected. "You're so professional."

"I am professional," he said without humor. "Nothing is going to take care of this, other than time, Danielle. No one really understands this condition other than military personnel, or those who have suffered from tragedy, such as yourself."

"Have you?"

He rubbed her legs comfortingly. "I have, unfortunately."

"Does it ever go away?"

Dominic's look softened with empathy, but was still intense. "Not entirely. The memory is always there, but you train the mind and the body to deal with it. In my world we call it conditioning. It's no different than the conditioning you do for your sailboarding. So eventually, when the mind gets hit with an unforeseen event, or a trigger, you can handle it. It gets better, a little bit each time."

Danielle felt her lower lip tremble. "I don't want to feel this way again, not ever."

"I know. None of us do. But it's life." Danielle searched his face, knowing tears were going to come, and she closed her eyes. The couch depressed as Dominic came beside her, his arms pulling her into his chest. She found the crook of his neck, wetting his skin. He stroked her hair, the action comforting. Knowing that he had lost those he cared about and understood her pain eliminated what shame or discomfort she might have felt with anyone else.

"I'm going to make your drink," Dominic said. "Trust me, it will help the anxiety without dulling your ability to work tomorrow, which I know is on your mind." She nodded and he rose, moving behind her. Music turned on, the ambient sounds mixing with the clanging of a coffee maker and opening of bottles.

"You will have to make do with my whipping cream out of the bottle, but at least it's organic, as is the coffee, which is decaf." She didn't respond until he sat beside her. "I'm rather proud of my concoctions, but you will tell me if it tastes authentic."

She mustered a smile, holding the warm mug in her hands. "My first and only taste of this drink has been here in Switzerland, so I'd never know if it's the real deal."

He held her gaze, like a doctor examining a patient. "That's an improvement. You are joking."

"Actually, I'm serious," her tone was lighter. "Thank you." He watched as she drank, and she knew it was because he was going to catch her mug if she faltered.

"Again," he requested. Danielle took another sip, and he joined her. When Dominic appeared satisfied she was on her way to finishing the cup, he set his glass down.

"I'm going to help relax you, and I want you to concentrate on letting go. Don't worry about Monroe. Forget about tomorrow and work, because it will be there whether you show up or not, as it will every day thereafter." He removed one boot from her foot, then the other, rotating her legs on the couch until she faced him, her lower legs and feet on his thighs. "Your only job now is to sink back into the couch."

The smallest movement of her head made her slightly dizzy.

"Did you make this extra strong?"

"No. What you are experiencing is the accelerated drop of adrenaline in your system. Sparing you the hormonal details, your physical and mental self is now coming down, taking your energy with you. The alcohol will impact you more quickly than if your levels were functioning normally."

Danielle looked at him over the rim of her cup. He was so specific in the explanation; no judgement or worry for her state of mind. It was objective and therefore calming.

"Thank you for explaining." He rolled his thumbs on the ball of one foot, then the other, moving back and forth between the two. "I thought a foot rub was always supposed to concentrate on the entire foot, then go to the other."

Dominic pushed deeper with his fingers. "The best approach, actually, is to keep the muscles balanced and in-line with one another. Don't talk for a minute. I want you to feel and hear something for yourself." Dominic adjusted the position of her right foot and used both thumbs to slowly slide up the arch of her foot, from heel to toe. As he did so, it felt like his fingers were going over dozens of pea-sized nubs.

"What is that?"

"Holistic medicine will tell you that it's the body's way of coping with stress, and your liver, which is known to hold in emotional and mental toxins, is on overload." Danielle tried to digest that.

"I'm bottling it all up?" Dominic nodded, repeating the motion on the other foot. "And here I thought I was doing so well, progressing I mean."

Dominic moved his fingers between her toes, gently separating each one. She twitched. "It tickles."

"Your reaction tonight could have been a lot worse, Danielle. Imagine if you had been on the street alone and saw that accident with no one around to be your safety net." She winced, the reaction only in part because he'd moved his fingers to her inner calve. "Your tendons around your Achilles heel are uncommonly tight, which can cause injury as well."

"I'll stretch more," she said, her mind still on the scenario he'd just described.

"That won't help, not in the long run," he told her, massaging the muscle until she felt it release. "Stress goes from between the shoulder blades, into your lower back, over and around your hips, then down the back of your thigh, all pulling up and on the Achilles tendons. Add to that you sitting in your chair all day, at a presumably stressful job, internalizing all that goes on in that lovely head of yours and it shows up here," he said, rather humorously lifting up her heel. Her eyes were wide open when he gently lowered her foot back onto his legs.

"Are you a doctor in addition to a bodyguard?"

One of Dominic's hands rested on the top of her lower leg as he took a drink. "I do have my undergrad in biology and a masters in physiology, but stopped short of medical school."

"Was this before or after you dropped out of planes in camouflage?"

"Both and during," he answered factually. "We are like the States, where one can get training while being in the military, particularly for post graduate work."

"Which was in what?" she asked.

"Survival." He paused, a slight smile playing on his lips. "Driving getaway cars for important people. And occupational therapy. Treating the body."

Danielle handed him her empty cup which he set on the table beside him. After hearing that, her shoulders and back released into the pillows behind her. "That's what I wanted to see," he complimented. She was pleased her body was responding as he desired.

But she was now more curious than ever. "Tell me again why you are doing this for a living instead of owning or operating a training or medical facility?"

"Money."

"Sort of important." No one knew that more than herself. She snuggled her hands under the blanket and Dominic shook his head no. He moved closer to her, wrapping her feet in the bottom half of the blanket to keep them warm, adjusting it over her belly. He placed one of her hands under the blanket as well, taking the other in his palms.

"Let's get your circulation going," he said.

"Are you sure you aren't trying to put me to sleep?"

"I would take it as a compliment if you did. Close your eyes for a minute and relax. Don't ask me any more questions. Just enjoy what I'm doing. You need this for your mental and emotional health."

"You're asking me to be a good client?"

"That was a question," he scolded. Her eyes were open until he lightly put his palm on her forehead, drawing it down, closing her lids. "Feel the sensations of your skin and the muscles underneath. As I rub, visualize the stress, anxiety and fears going from your palm, up your fingers and out your tips."

"Where is it going to go?"

"Another question."

She giggled at his stern tone, and then tried to breathe deeply, doing as he asked. Dominic turned her palm over, starting at the base of her thumb, massaging the tissue in small circles, from the inside of her hand to the fingers, slowly and with intent. Up to the fingers, one by one, working the delicate muscles between the joints. "Piano playing hands," he noted, running his finger between along the webbing, which was tight. Other men had called her fingers thick, but the way Dominic said it, Danielle knew he approved.

"Now up and out goes the stress," he continued, his voice conveying satisfaction. She visualized all the toxic badness rushing down her veins and into the palms, continuing a race to leave her body through her fingertips like lightening from a superhero. Dominic had used his thumb and forefinger on the skin up to the tip, switching to his nail which is slid along the surface.

It could have been the power of her mind, or Dominic's touch and encouragement, but she felt the ends of her fingers beginning to tingle.

"That's crazy," she whispered. Dominic hummed a response, and put down her hand, beginning anew with the other one. "Can I open my eyes now?"

"No. Try and feel it all over again." She did, experiencing the same movement up and out, and finally, the tingling in her fingertips. She sighed at the end, and he set her hand down, leaving his palms on top of hers, a human warming pad. "I was hoping you'd fall asleep."

"Dominic," she said, opening her eyes. "I can't fully relax because I have to go home and work tomorrow. No amount of comfort is going to change that."

He flipped over his wrist. "It's just before nine. If you get home around midnight, you'd get five hours of sleep, with forty-five minutes to get ready for work and get in a normal schedule for you, if I remember your working habits correctly. True?" Danielle nodded her head. Dominic rose, went to the credenza and found her phone. He spoke with Emma, updating her on the arrival time. Returning to the living room, he took her cup in for a refill.

"Now you are free to fully and completely be at ease for three hours. At the end, I guarantee you will feel a whole lot better than you even now."

Danielle felt her entire body respond to his comment. "I'll take your word for it."

CHAPTER 27

Dominic left and returned holding a fresh cup of Mexican coffee. He reached out his free hand to her. "Are we going somewhere?" she asked.

"The bedroom. It's the only place where I can rub your back. If it's anything like your feet and calves, your shoulder blades are splitting in two, making all the work I've done on your tendons worthless."

As he helped her up stand up, his eyes hadn't changed their expression, but her body responded as if they had. From her inner thighs down, she felt the same tingling that had been in her fingertips.

It's the adrenaline, drinking and relaxing combining to create a temporary rush.

He walked ahead of her in the hallway without turning on the light. She felt unsteady, compelling her to grip the material of his shirt, not letting go until they entered the room at the end. The light revealed a king size bed with a high, cream colored leather backboard, six pillows of earth grey and taupe highlights against the mostly white comforter.

"This looks seriously comfortable, and *relaxing*," she teased. "I hope you don't take it personally if I fall asleep half way through your backrub."

"Like I said, it would be a compliment. Take a long drink." She did, handing the empty cup back to him. He set it on the side table, briefly resting his hands on her shoulders, before moving to her buttons. "You could do this yourself, but I'm more proficient than you at this present time."

Dominic proceeded to release the first button, his eyes focused.

"How can you be so non-sexual about undressing me?" she asked pointedly.

Dominic's look didn't change, and the movements of his fingers continued. "Because," he said slowly, "you have not given me permission to be sexual with you. My intent in bringing you over here was not to seduce you. It was to help you work through this difficult experience." The second button was released. "Massage therapy was to physically expel the impact of a very traumatic event." Another button released and he worked on the next. "To make it sexual would be like a bait and switch, and that's not my style. Not with someone I know as a client, but especially not with a woman I hold in high regard."

The last button opened the top wide and she looked at his eyes. His fingers never touched her skin as he moved the shirt outward, then over her shoulders, lifting it off while leaving the camisole untouched and in place.

Danielle moved a little closer to him. "And what does it take to give you permission to be sexual with me?" She continued to watch him. "And if you don't like that word," she went on, her tone altering with her state of mind, "how about *sensual*, which suggests boundaries are still in place but real feeling is involved?"

Dominic's hands moved to the back of her neck, and she closed her eyes briefly as she felt his thumbs trace her skin from down to her shoulders. "Is there real feeling involved?" he questioned.

Danielle's fingertips went under the bottom of his sweater, feeling his skin. "I've always respected and admired you," she answered softly, eyes opening. "You've been consistent and kind and protective," she continued, extending her palms on his stomach, feeling his muscles, gliding up to his chest, where she paused, watching his unchanged expression. "Now, I've seen a completely new side of you, understanding and compassionate. I want to see more, if you'll let me."

"It sounds real to me." Dominic stared down at her expectantly. He was placing her in control.

She slid her hands onto his shoulders, and he raised his arms overhead, allowing her to lift the sweater up. He removed it, the ripples under this skin and down his arms causing a wave of desire to flow through her body.

"Can I still stay for three hours even if I don't entirely relax?" she asked seductively.

At long last, Dominic's expression altered. His warm palms went around her waist and up her back. Her arms, already above his shoulders, dropped, her fingers moving through his hair as their bodies met, belly to chest. Danielle could barely breathe, her head light from the desire which consumed her.

"Please?" she murmured. Dominic answered her question immediately and with force, his lips crushing hers. It was the beginning of the most sexually rewarding experience she'd ever had.

Danielle was on her stomach, facing Dominic, who lay on his side, his head resting in the palm on one hand as his other caressed and massaged the inside rim of her shoulder blades. Even his casual touch was therapeutic.

"You really didn't plan this, did you?"

Dominic smiled, the slight wrinkles in the corner of his eyes increasing. "Yes. I planned a car careening towards us on a snowy night after I happened to pick you up. It was a diabolical scheme."

Danielle smiled, then groaned in pleasure. "Your touch is incredible," she purred, then involuntarily exclaimed, "ouch."

"Still trying to rub some tension out."

She smiled again. "I have any left?"

Dominic's brown eyes darkened as his lashes lowered. For a second, the air in her throat seemed to stand still. His fingers moved along her skin, pushing her hair back, then he touched her face. "You are so beautiful, Danielle. Until recently, I'd never seen you so close. It's no wonder he loved you."

It was not the mood breaker Danielle thought the statement might have been coming from anyone else.

She was still gazing at him as he leaned over, rotating with her as she turned on her back.

"Could *you* learn to love me?" she asked quietly, the alcohol giving her liquid courage. Dr. Blatz couldn't ask for more vulnerability than that. Dominic's knee was already moving her leg to the side when he bit her neck, gliding his teeth along the fine muscles, tickling her.

"I don't need to *learn* to do anything, Danielle. To know you better would be to fall in love." Danielle gasped as he augmented his comment with a bite, just hard enough to arouse her. She dug her fingers into his skin, pulling him into her, fulfilling their mutual desire.

CHAPTER 28

Danielle's euphoria lasted through the following day, barely diminishing when Margaret called an impromptu meeting announcing the reassignment of several clients, taking them away from Danielle and her counterpart in commodities, giving the accounts to Jacob and Georgiana respectively. Danielle's eyes shifted to Johanne, thinking that he might be happy because it meant fewer meetings he'd have to have with the clients as the supervising manager.

"Johanne, monthly meetings with clients will change to bi-weekly until further notice."

There goes that theory. Lars was out of the office, but with something as big as account changes, he'd had to have known and supported the action. The only thing that struck Danielle as odd was that Margaret chose to announce it with the entire team present. Client exchanges were normally done in writing, among the traders, because it only affected a few.

She's making a point of letting everyone know trades are being taken away from me. That afternoon, Johanne called her to his office, asking she shut the door behind her.

"We'll just pretend this is a manager-peer review meeting, when in reality, it's a gripe-session." Danielle smiled, genuinely unperturbed by the changes.

"Look at it this way," she began. "You are talking to me again like we're the friends we are, so if it took me losing fifty million in client accounts, that's fine. We're worth it."

Johanne blinked, then removed his glasses, shaking his head. "Oh no, you don't."

Danielle laughed. "Don't what?"

He put his glasses back on. "Don't you dare go falling in love again at a time like this. I simply can-*not* take you being triumphant when the world within these four walls is crashing down like Jericho and whoever his name was that led them."

She giggled. "A woman can only go so long *without*, Johanne. And the word love is *way* premature. We are at the getting-to-know you stage, which has proven we have excellent physical compatibility. And his name was Joshua."

Johanne was still shaking his head. "I can't believe what Margaret is doing. She is literally deconstructing this place before our very eyes."

Danielle crossed her legs, rotating her ankle as Dominic had suggested. "Johanne, don't you see what is happening? The woman is gradually pushing me and who knows who else out of the company. First, taking my time to mentor her people. Then having all contact go through you, followed by forbidding me to speak with Lars about work. Now she's resorting to reassigning my smaller accounts. I'm sure she'd have gone for the bigger ones but I have direct relationships with all of those, and they'd leave the firm entirely if I were gone."

Johanne looked stricken. "The end goal is for you to quit or get fired."

"That's what I think."

His face flushed with anger. "Well, I'm glad you are happy because I'm pissed."

Danielle leaned forward. "Johanne, let's be clear. I've been furious for weeks, since the day she arrived and I saw her making eyes at Lars. But you know what my therapist told me, and I learned this weekend? Anger and frustration have done nothing for me other than to jack my health, screw up my body and make it so I can't even see an accident without getting hysterical. So, let me share the hard-earned wisdom with you: let it go. What you can't change, move on or get past it; which, by the way, are almost the exact words on the chimes you and Dario gave me for Andre's funeral."

Johanne blinked. "You are right. I need to take the advice I gave you."

"And another thing," she continued. "What's the worst case? You choose to leave and get paid more for working less somewhere else? Dario would be thrilled, and you guys could concentrate on what to do about Max." Seeing his lips turn down, she asked him what was up with that.

"Dario had a private investigator look in to it. Although this is Switzerland, and it's all supposed to be hidden in the darkest depths of the Alps, he verified Max invested only a part of the money into the restaurant, the other funds diverted to marketing and publicity, which means he was buying more rental properties."

Her eyes lowered with disgust. "Not real subtle."

"No. But we can put a lien on those, sell them and get our money back."

"Lani is still screwed."

"She deserves whatever she gets," Johanne said without feeling.

"Reaps what she sows is the phrase," she corrected, devolving into laughter.

He waved her away. "Go. You aren't helping my mood at all." Danielle was still laughing when she rose. "Danielle," Johanne called as her hand was on the door. "I'm very happy for you. Honestly. You don't deserve the hand you've been dealt."

"Yes, I do, Johanne. If I had to experience these things to grow as a person, and maybe help others along the way, then yeah, I did need to go through this stuff."

Danielle called Lani on her way home, getting her voice mail for the third time. She would continue until Lani called her back. If the roles were reversed, Danielle would appreciate being given a heads up to the forthcoming tsunami of badness.

After her weekly session with Dr. Blatz, Danielle purchased a box of chocolates for Emma as a thank you for the night before.

"I'm so glad you happened to be with Dominic," Emma told her, the words accompanied with respectful appreciation. Danielle wondered if she was drawn to Dominic because of her emotional state, or was it more physical, the desire to be with someone who was a protector by training and build?

She checked on Monroe one last time before turning off the lights. Monroe had one hand up by her ear, her nose almost touching her little fingers. A beautiful angel, so innocent and pure. Closing the door, she contrasted the emotional connection between her daughter and Dominic.

No, my attraction to Dominic isn't one or the other, mental or physical. It was a combination of his touch and his body, his perspective and wisdom, his experiences unique in her limited scope of men. It was thrillingly different, but she embraced it fully and completely, wanting more.

Heat had started within her chest, and it was still present when Dominic called. He asked her what time she'd like him to arrive, and she answered with the same brevity.

"Now."

As she got ready, Danielle thought about how she was behaving differently with him. Had he been a new acquaintance, she never would have seen him the second night in a row. With Andre, it had been two weeks after their first date and night of intimacy, and for Lars, a lot longer. But time and norms of waiting didn't apply with Dominic. They were comfortable with their attraction and desire, neither pretending a waiting period was required to see each other again.

It's not only desire, she thought. It was probably going to be time management, specifically due to Dominic's schedule. Given his terms of employment, his time off was at Lars' discretion or when Lars was out of town. Dominic had told Danielle that he'd looked forward to the trips she'd taken to Zermatt with Lars because he'd get the entire day off while they were out sightseeing.

For now, that schedule was perfect, but for long term...Danielle put that phrase out of her mind. She was doing what her therapist had recommended, which was to become involved with a new man, and it had occurred entirely by chance.

In the last twenty-four hours, she'd wondered about the circumstances, which had opened the door for her needing comfort, or decompression, as Dominic had called it. That left her vulnerable, needing and wanting a protector, but as Dr. Blatz had said, it wasn't contrived.

"Nor was it forced. You had a platonic acquaintance relationship with Dominic for two years prior to this time," Dr. Blatz had pointed out. "He was safe emotionally, because he'd witnessed your relationship with Lars evolve and end, and had your back, literally, with the situation with Andre in the parking lot. You can hardly be blamed for being attracted to a man who had proven his value. Accept it for what it is."

I can do that.

When the knock came, Danielle straightened the front of her brushed cotton pajama top, checking her hair in the entryway mirror.

Dominic entered when she stepped back, looking her up and down. "That's a sexy outfit." His expression was unmistakable, the desire in his eyes matching her own. She slid her hands around his neck, lightly rubbing his scalp, wanting him so badly she ached. He lifted her legs up and around his waist, pushing her into the wall.

"Down the hall, to the right," she mumbled, barely getting the words out between kisses. Unlike the previous night, where the intimacy had begun slowly, like pouring the foundation of a home, tonight was about adding the designer finishes. Danielle was fascinated with Dominic's body and completely unable to control herself when he touched her. More than once, she had to clamp her mouth shut for fear of waking Monroe.

At midnight, Dominic's kisses turned soft, moving his lips across hers. "I love the way you smell," he murmured, "and move." She hummed a response. "How long can I stay? I want you to get enough rest."

At this, she opened her eyes, just a crack, a playful smile curling her lips. "You think I'll want you in the middle of the night?"

He rubbed his nose against her cheek. "I know you will, because I'll want that too."

Danielle moved her fingers up his thigh, up to his back where her hand stayed. "How could I not? This is incredible."

"Thank you. Now close your eyes and let me caress you to sleep."

As if that's going to happen.

CHAPTER 29

Friday, Danielle was mentally groggy, her performance sub-par. Her mind had already slipped out of the environment, ready for new challenges. Her lethargy was also physical; two nights of unbelievable intimacy with a new man showed she was out of practice staying up late and enjoying herself. Five more months, give or take, she thought time and again.

At the end of the day, Margaret stopped by her office.

"You've done a great job with Jacob," Margaret said from the doorway. Danielle looked up, her face expressionless. She knew why the woman was in front of her, and it wasn't to give compliments.

"I'm sure his new accounts are pleased," Danielle remarked, turning back to her screen. She had no reason to be cordial to the woman. At last, Margaret spoke.

"He posted the top numbers for the day. A first for him and the new team."

Danielle didn't bother to look at the woman, her typing continuing. "Then you're right. I was a good teacher and he a good student." Long after Margaret had left, Danielle's jaw remained tight. Eventually, her chest stopped banging against her inner cavity walls, easing as her anger subsided. Never in all her career had she worked for a company where a person in management had tried to sabotage her performance.

Danielle's pulse had finally calmed when the two-tap came. She was startled, the rate of her heart going right back up again. "I thought you were out of town," she said, her voice as black as her look.

Lars hesitated, absorbing her comment and tone. "Business wrapped up early. Do I need to turn back around?" He had spoken with a bit of levity, but that changed when she curled both lips under, a preventative measure against spewing out the venom she felt towards Margaret in front of him. "I'll take that as a yes."

Danielle's mouth pressed tighter. Now she had another grievance; she wasn't going to be able to see Dominic after work as planned, his duties as driver and bodyguard required.

"You can talk to me," Lars said. Although she didn't want to say a word, fearing Margaret might walk by as she spoke, her words came out in a cold rush of fury.

"Changes occurred in your absence Lars, which could only have been done with your approval, and done so in a very public way, which was unnecessary and unprofessional, neither words I have associated with you or MRD in the past. If you want more details, talk with your co-manager. But just so we're clear, you're on my hit-list right along with her, and that, Mr. Egle, is probably all I'm allowed to say on the matter. Now if you want to fire me, so be it. If not, would you please leave? I've already had one unfortunate visit by Margaret today and don't need another." When she was done, she didn't give him the courtesy of waiting for a response. She looked back to her screen, the dismissal cause enough for termination.

What a horrible, awful way to end the week. *And just when I thought myself bullet proof from circumstances beyond my control.*

"I'll get back to you on this," Lars told her, then left. As quickly as possible, Danielle put on her outerwear and left the building. She saw Lars' BMW limo but Dominic wasn't standing outside, waiting for Lars. *I'd like a serious hug.* Even that was now denied her. Previously, seeing Dominic in public and sharing a congenial hug or kiss would have been perfectly acceptable, now it would be awkward. She'd never been particularly good at hiding her feelings and couldn't risk her deeper passions for Dominic wouldn't be obvious to the world, and their mutual boss, in particular.

Danielle walked by Lars' car on her way to the metro. Having the same boss was ironic, that was for sure. Instead of being blissfully unaware of Lars' comings and goings, she was now going to be acutely informed, because her own personal life depended on it.

A buzz in her pocket alerted her to a text. Dominic was unsure of his schedule for the evening. No surprise. She then received another text. This one from Stephen.

Looking forward to seeing you at the shower tonight.

Caught up in her own life, she'd completely forgotten the baby shower was this evening. Looking out the window from the metro, she called Layda and explained her predicament.

Layda laughed easily. "I'm going to make it really easy for you." She had already purchased an item for Stephen and Eva. "Trust me, it's valuable enough for both of us. You can get a little something later if you want, but this can be a family gift."

At home, Danielle accepted Emma's offer to give Monroe dinner while she showered and changed, wondering if she'd see Dominic later this evening. It wasn't until after she had placed Monroe in the car did she check her text and at once, had the schedule of both men.

"Unreal," she muttered. Lars would be at the baby shower, because Dominic would be driving him and waiting.

So close and so far, she thought miserably. But then again, she should probably thank her lucky self that Dominic was in her life at this moment in time. The aggravating fact that she'd show up at all these social events and see Lars was somewhat softened by the possibility of seeing Dominic too.

"Thank you for coming," Eva said, lightly kissing her cheeks.

"You look beautiful," Danielle complimented, genuinely happy for the woman. "In my next life, I'd like to come back to a gallery that's named after me."

Eva smiled gracefully, leaning in to Danielle's ear. "It was the curse of my grandfather having a girl as his first grandchild, not a boy."

The Galerie Eva Presenhuber was minimalist, concrete floors with a narrow strip of taupe and charcoal, the colors muted enough not to detract from the modern displays.

"Where would you like this?" Danielle asked her, hoping to set down the large gift she held.

Eva pointed to the room where the shower was being held.

Danielle made her way through the gallery, recalling what Layda and Georgy had told her about the gallery. Eva's parents were benefactors to the local hospitals in the area, the gifts in the form of art for the walls plus a new wing for the oncology department at the University Hospital Zurich. Eva's grandfather owned art galleries in both Geneva and Bern, and much of the modern art that Andre had adorned on the walls of his home had been purchased through Eva.

Danielle accepted a piece of prosciutto wrapped cheese from a plate, looking for a familiar face when she saw Stephen.

"Hey, dad-to-be."

He kissed her, thanking her for coming. "Eva is an extraordinarily gorgeous woman, pregnant or not," Danielle gushed. "Is that the pregnancy glow or something more?"

Stephen lowered his voice. "I did encourage her to scale back her time at the gallery and focus on preparing for the baby," he said. "And she took my advice on giving up drinking and forgoing the random cigarette."

She touched his arm, sensing there was more. "And?" she encouraged.

"She also encouraged me to get to know her family, so I've now become the adopted Uncle…" Stephen didn't give her the big reveal she was expecting, but listening to Stephen's recounting of the last few months, Danielle thought how much of a partnership he had with Eva on every level. *The difference between being in love and being friends with a goal, she mused.* And that goal being the comfort and care of a new child being brought into this world.

Stephen left to join Eva, leaving Danielle with her second appetizer when she saw Lars. He was speaking with Johanne, their demeanor relaxed. They must be sticking to the Swiss policy of no work outside the office.

She turned away with the objective of finding a drink to wash down her discomfort. She soon found it and was mid-swallow when a man spoke to her left.

"Everyone around me is spawning like salmon in the fall." Danielle laughed, glad she didn't have more than ice in her mouth.

"Giles, you are so crazy." He put an arm around her and placed a kiss on her cheek. "Are you looking for your mate so you won't be caught upstream without something to fertilize?"

"No way," he muttered. "The worst mistake is to bring a girl to a baby shower. Everything shouts commitment and pregnancy."

Danielle casually glanced around. "There's one woman who is attractive and nice at my office, but she's not here," Danielle said, thinking of

Georgiana. "Maybe some afternoon I'll bring her by the shop so you can meet her."

"I didn't know you had any girlfriends left."

Danielle nudged him with her shoulder.

"Well, good luck to you," she said as he tipped his glass to her. Giles left her to join Lucas and Christian, who were standing with a group of guys near the couch. As Danielle watched, a conversation started between the girls and hovering men, proving that any occasion was enough to start up the fires of romance.

"Hello, Danielle."

Lars had come up behind her. She barely met his eyes before looking away. "Hi, Lars."

"Have you been to this gallery before?"

Danielle gave him a brief smile. She held her glass, unsure where to walk or what to do. He was still waiting for her answer, and she finally gave it. "No, but the art is very nice," she said.

"Danielle, I have two things to say. First, that night with Margaret—"

"Lars," she interrupted, "we are beyond the point of having to explain ourselves to one another."

"Explaining is different than having a desire for understanding."

"That's splitting hairs," she murmured, "and I have no desire to understand what your hand on her neck and lips on her cheek meant." She was about to walk away when she recalled he'd chastised her for lacking respect in the past. Purposefully, she looked directly into his eyes.

"You are staring through my eyes, not into them."

She tipped her head with acknowledgment. Of course, he'd notice the difference.

"The second thing is that I spoke with Margaret and how she handled the changes in accounts. That part wasn't discussed, but her goal was efficiency and transparency. Everyone should know what's going on in the office, thereby saving time."

"It's your office. Change it as you will."

"It's also my life, Danielle. And I would like to change something." He set down his drink and pulled out a blue, velvet satchel. "You can guess what's in this packet, but perhaps not why I want to return it to you."

She made no move to take it from him. "No, I actually can't think of one reason why you would want me to have something of yours. We've both moved on."

"I still have a bedroom full of furniture for a little girl in my home. Does that sound as though I've moved on?"

"Which you may fill with another child from another relationship. Look," she said, not wanting the conversation to turn ugly. "You chose a very public place to make your affections for someone else known, which is perfectly reasonable. So be grateful I'm at peace and working on my own issues, but it's unrealistic for you to think I'm going to ever wear something from a man who isn't in my life romantically any longer."

He moved his hands closer, the pouch still extended. "I'm asking that you honor the past, not predict the future. There's a difference, don't you think?"

"Yes, I *did*," she said, unable to keep the emotion out of her voice. "But it seems you and Margaret are working me out of a job—"

"And I told you my philosophy on bringing her in as a manager."

Danielle nodded impatiently. "Yes, that you are doing what you said: you are giving Margaret room to make decisions, to succeed or hang herself. You are asking me to separate your personal life with her from the business, and then," she emphasized, "you are asking I give you the benefit of the doubt? As though all of this is for my good?"

"Yes, that's correct."

Danielle was stunned. "Okay. Let me repeat this one more time, so I'm totally clear. You aren't trying to get me out of MRD, *but are* expecting me to be okay with you sleeping with other women, while at the same time, wanting to renew or maintaining a *something* with me by giving me back the ring and watch?"

"Almost. While I'm not expecting you to be *okay* with the other women, I do want you to keep what I gave you, and try to remember what it represents. Maintain certainly. Renew, the jury is out on that one."

Growth. Maturity. Danielle took a deep breath. She reminded herself that a short month ago, she'd promised him with all her heart and mind that she would work on both of those things. That she would respect him and show him how much she loved him.

Lars had been watching her.

Danielle held out her hand, palm up. "I don't promise to wear these items."

"No, but you will have them if the remembrance gives you something of value."

Like a pawn shop, she thought sarcastically, instantly regretting her cynicism. Georgy had mentioned Lars could be forcing himself to see other women as a means to disconnect from her. It was plausible. "Danielle," called Stephen, motioning her over. Danielle excused herself from Lars and joined her friend. Slipping the satchel in her purse she comforted herself with that theory.

If it wasn't real then, maybe it's not real now. Not that it matters. She'd moved on, just like she was supposed to.

CHAPTER 30

As Danielle carried on conversations with other guests, Lars was always in her peripheral vision. Lucas and Christian were without dates, and she pointed out two possibilities for both.

"What happened to Max tonight?" she inquired. "Working?"

"Maybe," said Lucas. Danielle looked between the two of them.

"We don't see him at all," Christian elaborated.

It was possible they were aware of the situation at the restaurant, but Danielle wasn't going to go there. Not my problem, she told herself, changing the subject to plans for summer vacations.

The hostess stood, introducing herself as a friend of Eva's, requesting guests find a place to sit so the shower could begin. Danielle was relieved to find that in this culture, a shower was more about sharing snippets of the bride-to-be's favorite things and listening to tributes from her close family and friends than playing games. A major gift from Eva's parents was announced; a babymoon trip for Eva and Stephen to the Mediterranean. Danielle glanced at Stephen, watching for an expression of worry or surprise but he simply put his arm around Eva, and gave her a lovely, genuine kiss. They had naturally evolved from long-time friends, involved with, or married to other people, to hooking up in a time of need. She watched the genuine love on Eva's face, wondering at what point their emotions had clicked over. To the external world, they seemed a typical couple having a baby.

Stephen's arm squeezed tight around Eva's shoulder; protective and caring for the mother of his child and now life partner.

The woman sitting beside Danielle responded to a call and stood, leaving the seat vacant. It was quickly filled.

"They seem to be doing well." Danielle didn't change her focus from the happy couple, responding to Lars without turning her head.

"They have a really good partnership. It started out unconventionally but look at it now."

"Being partners isn't so bad." Danielle thought on that one. She'd rather be alone than be with a man if it was truly just about partnering, where no passion existed. What was the point?

"Lars," she began, turning to face him. "Are you happy being partners with Margaret, in the professional sense of the word? I'm genuinely curious."

He took a sip of his drink, his eyes turning from her back to the couple in front of him. "Happy is the wrong emotion to describe the situation. Being happy and being a partner in the business world for me, is an oxymoron. I much prefer being the managing director."

"Which is emotionless. Or should be." She thought as much. "Why would you go messing up such a good thing?" she pressed. "Did you know what you were getting in to when you constructed this merger?"

A grimace formed on the corner of his lip. "I was and am a pragmatist by nature. Our world is changing, Danielle. The days of the stand-alone investment and wealth management entities are evolving. If I didn't address it proactively, we were going to become obsolete. Not in the next year, but sooner than we'd like."

"Granted, I don't know as much as you do, but I think you're wrong. The largest and wealthiest clients have the means to bring it all in house, but the majority will never have the desire or capacity to go it alone. They'll always need help." She looked at him carefully. "But that's not compelling to you, I see."

He made eye contact. "I like a challenge, you know that."

"The irony is you have created our own challenge by *merging* with Margaret," she said, thinking how strange it was that she was now giving her former love and boss grief about his personal and management situation. They truly had come full circle, so she might as well continue. "Clearly, there is more going on in that brain of yours than you are willing to share. You're sure you know what you're doing?" she asked.

"I think I do."

She shrugged, turning back to the couple. "Well, then let's hope you're right, otherwise a whole lot of people are going to be out of work and coming after you with pitchforks."

Lars chuckled, and they said no more while a few gifts from out of town guests were opened. Their goodbyes at the end of the night were cordial; kisses to the cheeks and a light touch on the lower back by Lars. Feeling the brief warmth of his fingers, it was with a bit of surprise and unexpected anger that she experienced the familiar surge of desire.

Walking in to the cold night, she saw the lights of Lars' car. Dominic emerged from the vehicle, already making his way to the passenger side for Lars.

"Hi, Dominic," she said casually, the emotions from Lars' touch now merging into the excitement she experienced at seeing Dominic, like two lanes on a freeway.

"Danielle," he said, his deep voice low and formal.

"Busy night tonight?"

"Heading up to Zermatt for the weekend."

"Be safe." He told her to do the same.

Amazing. They were both going to be the mountain town tomorrow. Assuming Lars was staying for the weekend, Dominic would be there too.

In fact, they were likely in the very same village.

Danielle sent Dominic a text without receiving an answer before she turned out the lights. They must be driving through the mountains. She was almost asleep when her phone beeped. Turning over, she saw it was a text from Lani, asking about the baby shower. Danielle looked up at the dark ceiling. They hadn't had a meaningful conversation since the blow-out and now Lani was asking about a subject guaranteed to inflict emotional pain. She typed back. *Pleasant*

A minute after pushing send, she got a call.

"So, tell me all about it," Lani asked, sounded tired, irritable and genuinely curious.

Thanks for saying I missed you, sorry I haven't called. Pure Lani.

"You really want to hear this?" Danielle asked.

"Sure. My life is a misery of my own making, so I might as well get it all out there."

"Okay, just don't shoot the messenger." Danielle described the gallery, the décor, food and guests.

"What about the trip to the Mediterranean?" Lani asked with an edge to her voice.

"Yep, that was in there."

"You weren't going to tell me?"

"Believe it or not, I do have my own issues that I'm dealing with, and things that you might care about aren't necessarily what's on my mind."

"Oh, fair enough. What's going on with you?"

"Well, other than Lars dumping me, as you predicted, and then him dating the managing partner from Velocity, the firm that we merged with, nothing much."

"You are kidding me?"

"I can't make up something that bad, Lani. It was made worse because it played out in full display as I was at dinner with Johanne and Dario." Danielle pulled up the comforter. She knew Lani was going to ask for details and she determined it was time to tell her everything. Lani had been her friend since college. Despite how financially irresponsible she had been, and emotionally immature in her own relationship, Danielle had always appreciated her friend's sometimes hard-to-hear but sound feedback.

When Danielle finished catching her up, Lani asked, "So, what now? Do you stay at the office and continue on as before?"

"No change in status. I need a job that pays the bills." Danielle wasn't going to reveal her plan for the future. Lani would find out the same time as everyone else.

"Don't we all?" Lani asked with resignation. "And what about dating other people? Are you giving that a shot?"

"Dating, as in looking for a real relationship, one that involves love and emotions? Not now." To Danielle's relief, Lani elected not to pursue the subject. Danielle had never been a good liar, and Lani would probably call her out.

The call ended on neutral territory. The topics of the men in Lani's life and the financial status of her restaurant were untouched, like the hidden mine that was known about, but avoided.

The next morning, Danielle checked her texts before she got out of bed. Dominic told her Lars owned an apartment in the village of Zermatt, which is where he stayed.

But he could come to me.

She invited Dominic to stay the night, or a few hours, whatever his schedule could accommodate. Happiness returned when she read his response.

The moment I'm free

Her spirits sufficiently uplifted, Danielle imagined Dominic's arms around her. He represented safety, comfort and a magnificent thrill, that latter feeling increasing because being with him was now the forbidden fruit. She ignored the sliver of worry that whispered this scenario couldn't go on indefinitely.

CHAPTER 31

"I'm glad you're staying the night," said Layda as she took Monroe who had stretched her arms out for her grandmother. "We are going to the zoo tomorrow morning because the earliest chicks are now being born."

"That's wonderful!" Danielle exclaimed. "What time are you going? I could come back first thing if you can wait."

"Danielle," Layda began, her voice firm. "We are going to be up and out early, the first ones in line when the zoo opens at eight. Georgy wants to beat the rush, and you know Monroe, she's up at seven at the latest. This way she can be down for her nap when you return."

There was no way around the schedule. Danielle expressed her profound gratitude to Layda, who said it was all part of the job of a grandma. "We are overjoyed to have the opportunity, Danielle. Your free time is not going to last forever, so enjoy it while you can."

As Danielle drove up the pass, she focused on Layda and her comments. Danielle's schedule would surely change with her new work environment; Monroe would start pre-school once she was potty-trained and diaper free, first going one or two days a week, then more. Playdates and school plays would become the norm for Danielle. How did one ever manage children and working without the guilt, let alone creating and maintaining a relationship with a man?

She certainly couldn't consult with Lani. That woman walked out on a dozen years of marriage and left her dream of having a baby with Stephen when the restaurant became successful. Now she was right back to where she was before, working full time, except without a man and zero life balance.

Don't think, just enjoy. Learn and evolve.

Danielle pulled into the parking lot in Tasch and was off the train and into the ice climbing station ten minutes later. It was the third Saturday, and they were going to be heading up the intermediate ice climbs. Not much higher than the beginners, her instructor said, but technically more difficult.

"And it is getting warmer, and even a degree or two matters."

The instructor continued explaining the day's climb. "To this point, you have been climbing alpine ice, which is usually found in the mountain environment. In this scenario, it's trickier, because the frozen water comes over a cliff or is from an outcropping. That means you can't go straight up."

"It's more technical because the flow underneath is somewhat moving?" Danielle surmised, to which the instructor nodded.

"Correct. The alpine ice is rock solid. The water-ice can be soft, hard, brittle or tough," she explained. "And when you have mixed climbing, the ascent is both rock and ice, which is what you will be doing today."

Danielle felt a wave of uncertainty flow through her and harden, just like the ice they were going to be climbing. Was that what Lars had climbed when it broke off? When they were fitted up, the group moved outdoors, taking snowmobiles to an outcropping of water which was a part of a glacier flow. She looked up at the wall, and felt a bigger tug of fear than previous climbs. As if sensing her nerves, the instructor pulled on her chest strap.

"We all go through the fear stage," she said confidently. "You can do this, and we'll be here to help."

Two hours and one slip later, Danielle was mentally fine but her left wrist was bruised. She'd made one of the most basics mistakes, kicking too hard in the same place, weakening the ice she needed to stand on. It cracked, she slipped, and made a second mistake. She instinctively tried to break her fall with the other wrist, twisting it before the safety rope stopped her with a jerk. As she'd hung in place, the instructor calmly coached her to reset her footing, but when Danielle tried to grip the rope, she grimaced. Seeing the reaction, the instructor lowered Danielle down and examined her hand.

"A sprain, and you need ice or it's going to swell badly." She was done for the day, choosing to take an aspirin and ice pack, watching with the team for the final two hours. She learned as much from observing the mistakes of others as she did by listening to the instructors debate the French versus German techniques of placing feet. As she took it in, Danielle experienced similar heart-stopping moments watching others slip on the ice, then the relief that came from the climber regrouping. Pragmatism and reality changed her outlook further: nothing was without risk, not crossing a street and getting hit by a driver who didn't stop to turn, or on the ice. Mistakes in judgement are made, accidents happen and sometimes random acts of nature occur.

Back at Layda's home, she continued icing her wrist.

Danielle knew she was taking a gamble that she'd even be able to see Dominic, but assumed his night would begin when Lars' ended. Ten or eleven probably if Lars was out, but much earlier if he was entertaining at home. *Like he'd preferred to do with me.*

She periodically received texts from Dominic about a tentative time of arrival. One hour went by in the tub reading and soaking the sore parts of her body. The next hour passed and she started getting hungry, deciding to order in because her hand was throbbing. By nine, she had finished and noticed her wrist was starting to purple. She texted Robin that he'd need to get a substitute player for Sunday evening.

Ten thirty came with another text from Dominic, who now couldn't commit at all. She didn't want to know if Lars was out on the town, so she didn't ask for details. At 11, her disappointment was compounded by the guilt she felt for not going home and being with Monroe. She turned on some music, and when a text came through shortly after midnight, she didn't bother check it. The desire to see Dominic had gone, replaced with annoyance that her life was dependent on his schedule.

CHAPTER 32

"Any meetings this morning?" Danielle asked Glenda the moment she arrived at the office on Monday.

"No, but what happened to your hand?" Glenda asked her, eyeing the soft, black brace. "Are you going to be able to type with that?"

"We'll soon find out." When Danielle had returned from Zermatt, Layda insisted on taking her to the urgent care, where the x-rays confirmed a bad sprain and slight tearing of the muscle, but no fracture or bone break. Seeing Glenda's worry, Danielle said, "It hurts which is one reason I was asking about the meeting schedule. It helps to keep it elevated. I think I can hit the important keys, but my ring and pinky fingers are worthless."

"I have aspirin if you need them." Danielle thanked her, sitting down before she saw anyone. She had her hand on the desk when she realized the fault in her plan. The desk was structured so that her right hand was the one hidden from view, and her left was in plain sight. There was going to be no avoiding comments if anyone stopped by.

Danielle's hand lasted until the regular trader meeting at ten a.m. She arrived early, keeping her hands under the conference room table throughout, remaining silent as Margaret informed the group that another staff member would be hired within the week, with shared responsibilities for precious metals and commodities.

"She'll be working under Jacob," Margaret added, giving Jacob a smile. *One more nail in the coffin.* It didn't bother Danielle as much as her wrist. It was starting to pulse from the inside. At least during trading, it had been above her waist, on the keyboard. With every passing minute, the ache grew, making it harder for her to remain still and focused.

Danielle looked across at Johanne, hoping to get his attention, but his eyes were glued on Margaret. So were the other traders. Only Lars was intermittently checking his cell phone, looking up at Margaret when he felt the need to reinforce a point she was saying or answer a question specifically directed at him.

He is almost as checked out as I am, she thought with mild humor. Thinking of him distracted her from the throbs, so she allowed her mind to contemplate his apparent detachment from the firm he'd built. Perhaps he had reached a level of success at MRD that had bred boredom, and he was easing out of the firm in such a way as to not offend Noel. But where would he go? Bigger firms existed, but as she always said, MRD kicked everyone in returns. Retirement? She didn't see him sitting at home and he'd already traveled to most of the places he wanted to see.

Danielle ran out of theories just when she felt a spike of pain in her hand. Why Margaret had chosen this day to have an extended meeting was anyone's guess. The pulsing pain increased, and she wasn't sure how much longer she could sit in the meeting. But getting up and leaving might come across as catty, a way of visually disrespecting the new boss.

Another ten minutes went by and she was desperate. She swiveled her chair to the left, out of sight from Lars, Johanne and Margaret. She casually crossed her right leg over left, the black of her pants and top matching the wrist brace she wore. Gradually, Danielle raised her left wrist above her elbow. There she left it.

Johanne didn't notice, nor Margaret. It was Lars who raised his eyes from his cell phone, his head still down. It was a quick glance that zoned straight in on her wrist. He looked back down, where his eyes remained until the meeting wrapped up.

Back in her office, Danielle had just sat down when the two-tap came.

"You hurt yourself?" Lars asked.

"Carpel tunnel," she answered, dropping her wrist into her lap. It was a mistake. She couldn't affix her earphone without two hands. She had no choice but to keep her eyes up, expectant, hoping he'd leave before she had to do real work. "Can I help you with something?"

"Usually it's the right hand for right handed people or even both hands," he noted. "And the fingers aren't so puffy."

Danielle cursed his observant ways. She had no choice but to lift up her wrist. "Yeah, I over did it," she explained.

"The piano made your fingers swollen and blue?"

"Yeah," she said, blotting out the pain shooting through her eyes as she eased her hand down on to her lap. In two strides, Lars was in front of her.

"Let me see that."

"I don't think you need to use the managing director tone of voice," she said quietly.

"Sometimes it's the only one you listen to," he said, his voice equally low. "Let me see." Danielle kept her hands in place.

He held his hand out and she just stared at it, then him. "Why aren't you letting me see it?" Danielle looked up into his dark brown eyes. Slowly, she lifted her wrist from under the desk. Her fingers were swollen like sausages. "You saw a doctor?"

She nodded. "It's just a sprain, really. Not unlike what you had and will probably heal faster."

"You don't know that," he disputed, touching her fingers gently. "Does this hurt?" he asked, gradually moving the ends of her fingers this way and that, stopping when she grimaced. "That proves it's not broken, but confirms you need to go easy."

"Thanks doctor," she said sarcastically. "The next time I won't bother with the hospital and x-rays, I'll just come to you. Can I have my hand back now?" He let go of her, but stood in place. Danielle gave a little smile. "It's nothing, Lars. Seriously. It was fine all morning, and wouldn't have gotten swollen except that the meeting was eternal and my wrist was on my lap. I can still trade, if that's what you're afraid of."

Lars sat down. "You can barely move your fingers."

"My trading has been, and will be fine," she said slowly.

"Danielle, tell me what happened, and I don't care if we are in the office. I'm a concerned friend. Not your boss or former anything. A *friend*."

Danielle grumped. "If you must know, I was ice climbing, third session. I had been kicking my toe too much, and weakened the ice. I slipped and tried to break my fall with my left hand. Rookie mistake."

She watched his eyes, taking gratification in seeing what she thought was shock or stunned admiration, a bit of fear and ultimately…respect.

"Where?"

"Zermatt. Where you climb, I think, except I'm at the beginner area."

"Did you know I also instruct there?"

She cocked her head. "Since when?"

"About a month ago. On the indoor course, weekends."

"I didn't know," she acknowledged. He'd started teaching before she'd begun her lessons.

"It's been a different experience for me, helping new students like yourself," Lars answered, his eyes conveying more emotion than his voice was letting on. "Why?" he asked quietly. With that one word, Danielle felt emotion rushing up the back of her neck. "You can't answer?" he prompted. She shook her head. "That's a good thing, Danielle."

No, it's not, she wanted to shout. I'm still in love with you, but I'm trying to go forward with someone else, facing my fears, and yet I can't get rid of what I'm feeling for you.

Lars gave her a look that she'd not seen in months, the soft, penetrating gaze that affirmed he knew how she felt.

"Thank you," he said without elaboration.

"I said I'd try."

"Try less hard," he said humorlessly. "None of this will be worth it otherwise."

CHAPTER 33

Two aspirins dulled the pain in Danielle's hand, but she was sure the ache just transferred to her head, because she felt mentally fatigued, the recurring visual of Lars' eyes coming back time and again. With him on her mind, her trades were off, and she was constantly distracted by the people walking past her office, wondering if it were going to be Jacob, Margaret or Johanne. Her phone rang and she saw the caller.

Only in my odd state would I think a call from Lani was a positive distraction.

It was 2:40, with only fifty minutes of trading left, but the ability to make a material difference in her numbers was low. Danielle picked up.

"Hey Lani, how are you?"

"Could be better. Do you have something you want to tell me?"

"Oh, Lani. The last time we went through this it was about Stephen and Eva. I have no idea what you're looking for. Just tell me."

"If you are lying to me, it's the end of our relationship."

Danielle leaned back in her chair, holding her left wrist up. "How can I acknowledge or deny whatever it is you are talking about. You want to tell me now or save this for later?"

"Now. The lawsuit. Max and I are getting sued for fraud by Dario and Johanne."

Danielle sat forward, accidentally hitting her left arm against her desk and gasped. "What?" Danielle asked, trying hard not to hyperventilate from pain. "And no, I didn't know about a lawsuit." It was partially the truth; being told what Max and Johanne *might* do was different from having confirmation prior to the actual filing.

Lani quickly told her the details. She was served paperwork at the restaurant with her assistant chef looking on. Max was tracked down at the gym, getting his papers when he was on his way out the door. "We are essentially being accused of stealing money from everyone."

"What do you think?"

"I think Johanne and Dario want their half a million back and instead of asking for it, decided to be complete and total jerks and make a scene in front of the world."

"Lani," Danielle began, her voice calm. "To what end? Why would they be forced to take this route? Did you ask Max?"

"He said the same thing; he thinks they just got cold feet, and because the paperwork has a three year return on investment clause, the only way they could get their money back was to file a lawsuit."

"Can you go into mediation so it doesn't cost you thousands?"

"Max said no, that would mean we are agreeing with what they are accusing us of."

Danielle feared no matter how she responded, Lani wasn't going to take it well. Offering to help was the best road to opening Pandora's box and a world of destruction.

She chose the safe route. "What now?"

"You call Dario and Johanne and tell them to retract the lawsuit, that's what."

So much for the safe route. "I'll talk with them, but my guess is they are unlikely to listen to me. I think the bar is pretty steep to getting a lawsuit filed, so they must be convinced of something illegal happening. Lani, do you…I don't want to put this in a bad way, but do you think Max is being upfront with you?"

"He's shown me the books and I trust him."

"Lani," she said as gently as she could. "You thought you could trust him before."

"Right, but that was with my body. I'm far more particular about finances."

Danielle sure hoped so. "I'll talk to Johanne after we get off the phone."

"Great," Lani said, relief thick in her tone. "One more thing, and please don't say no until you hear it. Can you lend me some money for legal expenses?"

"That should come out of the business account, not a personal loan," Danielle replied, grimacing at her tone.

"We need it for the business, Danielle. We are barely making it. Some days the cash flow is positive, others in the deep red. We are trying to ensure we have cash, for ninety days."

"Lani, you said ninety days a month ago when I told you no the last time."

Danielle waited for Lani to break the silence. "Max was right," Lani said. "You aren't going to help."

"Lani, I just said I would talk to Johanne. That's what you asked. How could that be misconstrued as not helping? But beyond that, Max is worth a lot of money, I know, because I ran his account before Margaret closed it down. Why isn't he using his funds to defend himself, and now you, by association? Have you asked him those things?"

"I've brought it up," she admitted, "but he insists personal and business funds are separate."

"Bull crap. I put up my own money and so did Andre. As well as Johanne and Dario. How can it be okay for everyone else to take risk but not him? How can *you* be okay with that? And how do you expect me to be okay with that?"

"I don't know," Lani said, sounding deflated. "He's so convincing when I speak with him."

"Sure, and that's what's made him so good at what he does, but Lani, aren't you at least wondering how all these people can be so wrong? Has Max been genuine and transparent with you during this partnership you've had?"

"Yes, he has," she answered, her voice lacking conviction.

"Then you have nothing to worry about, at least legally. Financially, I'd go back to him and hold his feet to the fire about paying for the lawsuit. It's the cost of doing business."

"And I will tell him you are a no."

Danielle sighed. "Lani, as the follow-up to our last conversation, Margaret is in the process of pushing me out of a job. My guess is by the end of the summer I'll either be fired or life will be so miserable I'll quit."

"You are going to be jobless?"

"Maybe," she hedged. "I've got Monroe and her grandparents to think about, and I'll include them in any decisions I make. What about you?"

"I'm going to keep cooking, because for now, that's all I can do. I could stand to use a few more customers, like my friends."

Unsubtle as always. "I'll see what I can do. Good luck with Max."

"Thanks. Bye."

An abrupt ending, but it could have been a lot worse.

Shortly thereafter, Danielle accidentally hit her left wrist again, this time on the armoire that held her winter shoes and jacket. "Dangit," she hissed under her breath.

"Was that an American swear, because if it was, I don't think it counted."

She poked her head around the door, keeping her left hand inside. "Hey Johanne. Guess who I just got a call from? Your favorite lawsuit victim."

"Lani called?" he asked, incredulous.

"Indeed. *Super fun*. I had to promise that I'd talk to you about dropping the lawsuit." She paused, asking him to help her with her coat. Her left arm was stiff and straight, as she directed him to lift up the jacket. "So consider my promise fulfilled. I asked you."

He nodded, lifting up the arm so she could insert her wrist.

She couldn't manage the buttons and he took sympathy on her.

"You're helpless," he said, starting to fasten each one.

"That's what Lars said."

"You're speaking to him?"

"Yes, when it comes to my inability to trade due to my fingers hurting, conversation with the ex-love is fair game."

"There," he said, finishing the last button. "I was rather hoping you'd tell me you hooked him with your left."

"Wishful thinking. I slipped on the ice," she said, which wasn't a fabrication at all. Too bad she hadn't been quick enough to give that line to Lars.

"Clumsy American," he grumbled, walking beside her until they reached his office. "You didn't tell me anything else about Lani. Want to dish?"

Danielle shook her head. "The dish is empty. Oh, wait. I forgot one important item. She wanted money to pay for legal fees." Johanne's eyes popped. "I suggested Max reach into his deep pockets and pay for the legal costs himself, because that's what business owners do. After that, I offered that it might be plausible that not all of us are wrong about Max. She refuted that, wholeheartedly."

"She's going to go down with the ship, then."

"Appears so. See you tomorrow."

"Right. My advice is to put pillows on your left-hand side so you don't roll over onto it."

It was a good idea. When Emma saw her wrist, she wouldn't leave until Monroe was fed, changed, and put in her pajamas, also mandating Danielle change in case she needed help—which she did. Buttoning her top was essentially impossible.

Once Monroe was asleep, she took two prescription pain pills given to her at the hospital and was out thirty minutes later.

CHAPTER 34

Danielle had done as Johanne suggested, propping up her hand on a pillow. It was awkward, but she'd been able to sleep. The next morning she called Robin with the bad news. No playing this week either. She then called the instruction office at Zermatt, asking if she could still attend the last session, just to watch.

"We are likely to cancel this weekend because we are expecting white-out conditions," Danielle was told. The last training and competition would be delayed a week.

Danielle closed her eyes, visualizing Lars again. He'd been so concerned. What had he said? Try less hard, because otherwise it won't be worth it otherwise?

What did that mean? she pondered. *Walking our own path for a while, seeing how we do without one another, while seeing other people?* Dominic. He'd not texted or called, and she hadn't missed the absence. How long had it been since she saw him, four days? Strange, he was all consuming, like taking a hit of helium from a balloon but when it was gone, that was it. The temptation wasn't there anymore.

As much as she wanted to feel the passion for him, it was hard work. When to see him, when she couldn't, not being able to hug him in public, all mental stress that had started to irritate her after only a week!

Georgy's words float up and around her consciousness. Marriage is hard enough, but if it's too much work, it's not meant to be. Maybe Dominic wasn't her forever-guy, but he could be hers for a little while longer.

Tuesday was sheer pain and misery, her trading hitting an all-time low, the combination of the pain killers she was forced to take and being slow fingered. Not since she was hired had her returns gone so far in the red. Wednesday wasn't much better. It would take a few massively wonderful hits Thursday and Friday to make any kind of positive impact.

Research and after hours trading was what she needed to do, but as she told Dr. Blatz on Thursday, it wasn't going to happen.

"And I can't blame my subconscious, because I'm doing this very consciously."

"I'm not sure it would help your resume to be let go," he observed. "Is it your intent to make Lars look bad?"

Danielle had to think about that. "Perhaps," she said sheepishly. "Which is really wrong of me, because all things considered, he's been really great through everything."

"On to the next inevitability. How will you handle Lars learning about Dominic?"

Danielle was caught off-guard. "I never expected him to know about Dominic." When he stared at her, she felt compelled to speak. "I thought Swiss men were all about discretion, and the culture of fooling around on the side was accepted."

After a moment, Dr. Blatz spoke. "You are not in public with Dominic, which means it's in hiding. It's on the side as far as Layda and Georgy are concerned, because you've not told them. Put it all together, that means something else."

Danielle carefully considered her next words. "It means I'm not serious with him."

"How do you feel about that?"

She scrunched her nose in discomfort. "Guilty. He's amazing in bed, but also incredibly well-rounded. I feel so safe and protected, without a stitch of judgement..." she trailed off, suddenly realizing she sounded defensive.

"May I make an observation?" She nodded. "As you pointed out, he's not called or texted. You and he happened to share an experience following a trigger event, but your connection isn't defining your life or his."

Danielle blinked. "I was convenient?" she asked, incredulous.

"And you are single, vulnerable, and beautiful... the 'ands' go on for quite some time. As he said, to know you is to love you, but we both know you will not let that happen, right?" She bit her lip, shaking her head. "Because you both know at some level, conscious or not, that you two are filling the void in one another's life."

Danielle lightly ran her forefinger over the stitching of her wrist brace. "We both live pretty weird, antisocial lives, between our work and personal habits," she said somberly. "Are you suggesting that I not pursue Dominic further?"

"That isn't for me to decide. You know where it will eventually lead. The question is for you to determine if your heart can handle the strain of the journey."

Danielle looked out the window, seeing the clear, blue sky darkening. It was almost the middle of March, the sun melting more snow with each passing day. Another week and the snow would be totally replaced with the first green grass shoots and the cherry trees lining the path along the waterfront would start to bloom.

"How much sooner before you can climb again?" he asked, changing the subject.

"I'm not sure. I hope a week and a half will be enough time to heal."

"Do I detect excitement in your voice?"

An upward curl formed on one side of her mouth. "I've actually missed it."

"You sound surprised."

She tilted her head. "I guess I am. It's kind of addictive, just like Lars said."

"You are combining your physical acumen with mental skills. For someone of your precise, aggressive nature, it makes sense."

Danielle was struck by his words. "Yeah. I guess it does."

Throughout dinner, bath and stories with Monroe, his words were in the back of her mind. All that Lars had told her about ice climbing, she was now experiencing first hand.

"You fear that which you don't understand." She wasn't sure where the quote came from, but now, when she needed it, there it was. Probably Dad, or David, two reservoirs of knowledge and wisdom she'd relied upon so heavily.

I wonder what David would think of my situation? Her former boss, mentor and quasi-surrogate father would probably say she was a trader, a person who placed bets for a living and had a multi-year track record of winning. She knew which bet she should place, and if she wasn't doing it, then she was making the purposeful decision to be a loser.

Danielle then wondered about the one subject she thought Dr. Blatz would bring up for sure: Danielle substituting Dominic for Lars.

Substituting was the wrong word, she decided after considerable thought. A wonderful, lovely, kind, and interested distraction.

She thought back to the question she'd asked Dominic in her half-inebriated, desire-driven state: could he love her. His response was "to know you better would be to fall in love."

Did either of them really want that?

CHAPTER 35

"How's the hand?" Glenda asked as Danielle walked by her desk.

"A lot better. Still sore but I don't need the pain pills. Glenda," she said, glancing down the hallway before she spoke, "I just want to apologize for not getting the returns you've been used to seeing."

"You don't need to apologize to me for hurting your hand."

Danielle glanced left this time, towards the offices of senior management. "It's not all about my hand."

Glenda's eyes squinted, sympathy mixed with real anger. "We all know why, and none of us are happy."

"By none of us, you mean…?"

"The entire support staff has been scaled back on the bonuses we are receiving, so your fall in numbers barely impacts what was already lowered."

Danielle was stunned. She'd never heard of such a thing. "Lars must know," she said quietly, to which Glenda shrugged her shoulders.

"It was like this before Lars' joined the firm, and then he made terrific changes to raise us up. Now it's back to where it was before, so morale is low." Danielle didn't know how to respond, but had the inclination to communicate this to Johanne, maybe even Lars directly. The last thing traders needed were to have their support staff leaving.

"You know what I think?" Glenda asked conspiratorially. Danielle stepped into the cubicle, keeping an eye out for others coming in to the office. "The reason Lars did the merger is because Velocity was failing, and he got a really good price, so he struck before the doors of Velocity shut completely."

Danielle smirked. "I hope he got a *really* good price, like free."

During lunch, Danielle stopped by Johanne's office, scooting the chair close.

"It's Friday," she began briskly. "My numbers are in the tank this week thanks to my medication and the overall state of affairs, so I'm taking a break." Johanne blinked in a one-eye first, then the other type of way, making her giggle. "I have a conspiracy theory for you." She related Glenda's hypothesis, waiting as Johanne's eyes moved beyond her to the hallway before he responded.

"The entire support staff got a slash at the same time the smaller accounts were closed," he said.

"That's a real employee booster," Danielle quipped. "I actually think Glenda might be right about getting the merger for a song, but Lars had no real knowledge of the why behind it."

"It's clear now," Johanne began. "Look at their corporate work. You can get away without having a personality in that environment, but not here. High net worth is all about hand-holding, suave deference and high numbers."

"All the things Lars delivered," she added, thinking of his finesse with others while maintaining his own stature. "Well, now we have an idea of the why, but it doesn't change anything."

"No," Johanne agreed. "We get to wait it out."

"For what?"

"The place to implode."

She titled her head inquisitively. "Are you going to enjoy this?"

"Yes, right up to the time it does."

"Then you must still be getting overrides on Jacob and the new team."

He winked. "You bet your profits I am."

She stood, suddenly hungry. "I'm glad someone is continuing to make money around here."

Back at her office, she took a moment to appreciate the lake view. Now that her time to enjoy the scenery was limited, she regretted taking it for granted.

And lunch. She'd gone to lunch less than a handful of times as well, and she was in the prime location to do so. On a whim, she went directly to her wardrobe, pulled out her coat and handbag.

"Leaving us already?"

Danielle peeked around the wood. She struggled with her coat until Lars helped with her left sleeve. "Thanks. But yes, I am leaving you," she said, her voice flat and look serious until she saw his dismay. "For *lunch*."

"Are you eating alone?"

Danielle looped her purse over her shoulder. "As always."

"Good. Then may I join you?"

She looked at him. "Where? To lunch?"

Lars' lips thinned with a pressed smile. "That would be the idea."

"Can I go to lunch with the boss?"

"Yes," he answered. "It's also allowed between two friends."

"I'm going to Stars & Stripes, and you may be sick of it."

"Not likely. Hold on a moment, if you would, while I get my coat."

Without waiting for her response, Lars left. Lunch, with the managing director, former lover, now friend?

They walked down the hallway, and to her right, in her peripheral vision, she caught Johanne look up, his mouth opening. She didn't wink at him, but wanted to, just to keep him guessing. Today was another episode in the soap opera.

Her thoughts were prophetic when Lars directed her to his car. Dominic was already outside, waiting by the back door.

"We can walk," she offered.

"The clock is ticking. Driving will save ten minutes on either side."

Danielle made eye contact with Dominic as they approached. "Hello, Dominic."

"Ms. Grant." He'd used the same words and inflection he had for two years. The wave of discomfort she felt was fierce as she entered the car. Lars followed behind her.

"It looked like you and Johanne were having an intense conversation just now," Lars started as Dominic pulled into the street.

Danielle smirked, still looking out the other direction. "You don't have anything better to do than stand in the hallway and watch your people?"

"You're injured and your numbers are down. Johanne is in the middle of a lawsuit and the staff is unhappy. So, the answer is yes, I've literally got nothing better to do than stand and observe."

This got her to turn to toward him. "Did he tell you that himself?"

"It's a small community. Word of a high-profile action like that gets around quite quickly, especially when the recipients of the legal paperwork are served in very public places."

Danielle shook her head. "Yeah, can you believe it? Lani told me she was served the papers in the middle of the restaurant."

"Which was proceeded by the processor tracking her down, which necessitated the hotel management…"

"They all know?" she gasped in horror. Lars nodded. "That is so awful." Danielle took in his expression with a sweeping gaze, confirming her suspicions. "You have a right to be smugly satisfied with your predictions. They have come to fruition."

"Not all of them."

She inhaled deeply, turning again to the lake. "Are you going to do anything about the support staff?" she asked him. In the past, she never would have been so forthright in asking a question regarding business management; ever sensitive to crossing the professional boundary lines. Now, if he didn't want to answer, let him make the decision.

"It will be managed."

"Nicely vague," she responded, looking forward. She steeled her focus through the front windshield, feeling Lars watch her profile.

The car slowed and Danielle waited until Dominic opened the door. She looked up at his eyes, but they weren't on her face. His attention was on her hand, which she extended. He gently pulled her up, and held on to it a moment longer than necessary once she was beside him. It was symbolic, their tenuous connection made, acknowledged then broken as he went around to open the door for Lars.

Ironic they were only now going out to lunch, and at a place with so many memories of their life together.

We are still in each other's lives. Would there be a time when they weren't?

CHAPTER 36

"Greetings," Stephen said pleasantly, giving her kisses and Lars a handshake. "A special occasion?" he asked.

"Yes," Danielle replied, before Lars could. "Lunch at my favorite place." She forestalled any further questions by gesturing to the table reserved for the founders of the establishment.

"Of course," Stephen said, leading the way. Danielle took the far side, her view to the sidewalk clear. Dominic was nowhere in sight; probably already back in the car, ever-ready to protect his boss. She looked down at the menu, wondering if Renaldo had changed it recently.

"I like this new you," Lars began, glancing down at the menu.

"Just call me Danielle, Version two-dot-o," she said, closing the menu. "But then again, not all upgrades are improvements. Sometimes they actually screw up things that weren't broken."

"True enough. Speaking of broken, how's your wrist coming along?"

"It's still a little sore, and I'll miss out on the session tomorrow but I am going to go anyway, just to learn what I can."

"The forecast is looking bad," he said, pulling up the weather application on his phone. "I suspect the only climbing that will happen is indoors."

"How do you like teaching? Is it fun or boring to watch others climb while you hold the rope?"

Lars smiled. "The experience of instructing is very different than the act, but in some ways more rewarding. Seeing the changes in a student and their confidence level shoot through the roof is a high."

Danielle nodded, knowing exactly what he meant. "Completely the same thing with sailboarding. I'd never taught before coming here, and it hadn't ever occurred to me until the opportunity presented itself."

They paused when the waiter came to take their order.

Once he was gone, they picked up their discussion about teaching and their experiences with frightened students.

"You would not believe how many of my students are afraid they are going to get hit by the sail, knocked off the board and drown," she said.

"At least the landing is soft in your world."

"Not really," she countered. "When you are zipping across the water at 30 mph and land on the water, it might as well be pavement. But I suppose that's better than the hard ground of ice climbing."

"An unfair comparison," he corrected, "because in climbing, ice or rock, one is tethered by a rope that's nailed into the rock, catching you when you fall."

They went back and forth, comparing and contrasting the environments, concluding each one could be deadly and dangerous.

"I bet you more people are injured in your sport than mine," he challenged.

"Look it up," she retorted, accepting the plate of food from the server. "I already know that the number of people dying while climbing is fractional compared to motorcycle deaths."

As she ate, Lars typed on his phone. "Here it is," he began. "According to the British Journal of Sports Medicine, most windsurfing, or sailboarding injuries as you call it, occur within the first two years of the sport." He read in silence, then summarized. "From a poll of 109 national and international competitors at the elite level... 1.5 injuries per year... ...while the Germans had 1.92 injuries per year. Crazy Germans," he added. Danielle had no idea of the statistics of her sport, but wasn't going to admit it that yet.

"Now this is interesting. The most common injuries are lacerations, jellyfish stings, abrasions and strains, at 29%, 26%, 23% and 19%."

Danielle started laughing. "Jellyfish aren't found in fresh water."

"And contusions occur 16% of the time, which means that of those who are injured per year, you are two times as likely to have an actual head injury." He paused to pick up his fork, taking a bite. "Aerial maneuvers, the kind you like to do, and jumping, result in 22% of the lower back injuries, and 34% of those are recurring. The rest, just about 60%, hit the soft tissue of the lower body, in the knee or lower leg. And here's the biggy: windsurfers have 250% more upper body injuries than race boarding. What's that?" he stopped abruptly.

"Give me that," she asked. She scanned the report, and sure enough, her sport was fraught with injuries, some of which she'd suffered. "Race boarding was allowed in the Olympics in 1996. Seriously? Even I wouldn't do it." She handed the phone back, thoughtful.

"So, what's your conclusion?" he asked her.

"From what Dr. Blatz told me about ice and rock climbing, people rarely get injured, but tend to die if they fall, which happened fourteen times in twenty years, but that's just in Canada. Extrapolate to the places where one can climb, and perhaps—maybe—a hundred a year."

"And in your sport," Lars said, "a person will live, but end up walking around with a cane because of lower back problems and that's in addition having a knee or ankle replaced along the way, unless they have slight amnesia from the head bumps."

Danielle stopped eating. It took her a few moments to digest the implications, but when they did, she'd lost her appetite. "I think I need to choose another sport."

"No," he disagreed, putting his phone away. "You keep doing what you're doing. Obviously, you're so proficient you don't have to worry about injuries." Seeing her shake her head, Lars asked, "You disagree?"

"Lars, I'm not kidding around. I mean, injuries happen all the time, but I just figured it's a way of life, part of the sport."

"You can't possibly hear this information and stop your sporting activity immediately."

She nodded, feeling severe. "I'm all about percentages Lars, as you know. But that's a really high rate of injury and problems. I have one daughter, and God willing, might have another child someday. How many people do you know who have pain issues they have to deal with continuously, and it ruins their entire life?" She went silent.

"Are you thinking of your father?" Lars asked, with gentleness.

Danielle nodded. "The last thing I want is to have joint pains or any type of chronic pain or use a cane on the way to the bathroom."

"Age may bring that on anyway."

"True, but sailboarding is aggressive, lots of banging and whipping. My legs and knees hurt, my thighs and shoulders. Don't get me wrong, I love it but I am sore afterwards. When you climb, all you get is a sunburn when you don't put on protection."

"Danielle, I think you're taking this a little too far."

"Am I really?" she wondered. "Up at the mountain, I've seen men and women in their seventies scaling the rocks. Sailboarding continues *maybe* until your fifties, if you're lucky. And those guys are beat up."

Lars took a drink. "Do they just retire the board?"

"Most go into boating, where they tend to drink a lot." She looked at her watch. "We better go."

Lars insisted on paying until Stephen came over and said it was on the house. "Your baby shower gift will cover you for the next year." On the way to the car, Lars asked what she'd gotten Eva and Stephen.

"It was purchased by Layda, and it was exquisite. A hand embroidered christening outfit and milestone gifts for every three months until one year old, which were sterling silver utensils, plates and a few Swiss-type things that I can't name."

"Sounds like Layda."

Danielle thanked Dominic as he held the door, his look the exact same as always; his professionalism never wavering. In the car, she felt for the seat heater. By the time the car was moving, it had already started to warm up.

"Danielle, look at me. I didn't bring up the statistics to cause you to make any changes. Far from it. I was actually doing it more for the competitive factor."

She made eye contact. "I know."

"Then you should treat it in the vein of the discussion. Statistics, that's it."

Danielle felt as strong as stone as she held his gaze. "Are you kidding? Our life is one big number, comprised of a million little numbers. Once I have the numbers, it's my responsibility to act on them, not sit and become one of them. All those numbers you read about my sport, the injuries, knowing that it means debilitation later on."

She stopped abruptly, looking straight ahead. Dominic's eyes were watching her, his glance between her and the road.

"You won't be a statistic, Danielle."

"Really?" She turned back to him. "Andre was never going to be the statistic either."

"I didn't mean—"

"No, you didn't, but I did. Unlike you, Lars, I am not going to play the odds with my life, or my body. Yes, I can continue sailboarding, but all it takes is that one time and I'm done. Out on the water, face down in the middle of the lake. Who will be there to turn me over? You? No, because you never wanted to learn. I have no one else. And who will be there for Monroe?" Emotion had been swelling in her chest and throat as she'd spoken, but it was like the lava under a volcano, coming up from the groundswell underneath.

"I'm very sorry, Danielle. I promised I never would have even gone there but we were having a discussion—"

"Yes, we were," she broke in. "And you shouldn't apologize. I'm not mad at you. I'm furious at myself." She fought the tears. "I've been such a hypocrite. Expecting you, and Andre before you, to set aside sports I deemed unsafe, and all the while, not looking in my own backyard." She covered her mouth with her fingers, pushing the wet from her eyes. Not only did one man have to see her cry, but two. What a mess she was in, and the entire time, thinking herself so wise. So in control of her life, doing the smart thing, always. What a fool she'd been.

"You know," she said quietly, still looking out at the city streets. "I started ice climbing to get out of my own way, to face the fear of what you were doing. It was for me. Not for you. And look," she continued, turning to him. "My therapist was right. I have changed." Lars' dark eyes held hers. She felt his empathy and sensed his guilt. "Interesting isn't it?" she asked, her voice breaking. "I'll be the one giving up my beloved sport and you just stay the same. Well," she gulped, "that's not true. You have started teaching, which implies you are trying to be safer. Am I right?"

"I never intended this."

A crooked smile lifted her lips and she broke eye contact.

"Sir, do you want me to continue around the corner?" Dominic asked.

"Yes, please."

"No," Danielle contradicted. "I'm not going back to the office. I want to go home."

"Sir, you have an appointment," reminded Dominic.

"Lars, it's fine," she said, wiping away the last of her tears. "Dominic can drop you off then take me home. Is that alright?"

"Of course. I'll let Johanne know you aren't feeling well." Lars rested his hand on hers, squeezing. "Don't be so hard on yourself."

She felt like crying all over again. "How can you say that?"

"I never wanted you to feel like a hypocrite, see you hate yourself and cry because of it. And I certainly never, ever expected you to make a rash decision to stop sailboarding."

"Is it rash?" Danielle questioned. "It's reasonable, something I haven't always been. Well guess what? I'm going to change that, too."

The car stopped in front of MRD. "Sir?" prompted Dominic. Lars leaned over and kissed her cheek, then got out of the car. When the car pulled away, Danielle reached in her purse, putting a thin layer of ointment on her dry lips. When she looked up, Dominic's eyes were on hers.

"Your home?"

Danielle thought of Emma, who would be there with Monroe. "No. Yours."

CHAPTER 37

Danielle wasn't sure if Dominic would say no, and had he done so, it would have been okay. She felt strung out, the Ferris-wheel of emotions coming full circle, from awareness to shock, anger and self-hate, the ride beginning for a second and then a third time.

"Lars was right about the statistics," Dominic told her. She looked up at him. "It doesn't mean you have to like it."

"Dominic, just out of curiosity, are you still involved with dangerous things, like jumping out of planes?"

His eyes crinkled in humor. "You mean in addition to carrying a gun, and serving as someone else's full time protector?"

She let out a laugh. "Yeah. Taking a bullet for someone would qualify as a dangerous thing. Compared to that, I guess parachuting from five thousand feet is sort of inconsequential."

"Danielle, you are an assertive, type-A personality. You demand a lot of yourself and are drawn to others with the same characteristics. Are you truly surprised that your sport of choice is equally, or more dangerous, than the very men you are with, parachuting included? By the way, there are zero injuries in my sport because when something goes wrong, we just die."

"Kind of like ice climbing." He nodded. "Was that meant to be comforting?" she asked with brittle humor.

He stayed serious. "I think the truth is very comforting. You know where you stand and can make the right decisions from there."

The rest of the ride was in silence. Dominic parked in the underground garage, next to his own vehicle. "Please wait," he requested, coming to her door, opening it. He put out his arm, and she curled her hand under his. In a single turn, Dominic's other arm was around her shoulders, careful of her injured hand, and he held her tight.

"I've never seen you sad before," he murmured. "Happy and aroused, yes, which I like a much better." She shut her eyes and nodded. "Let's go in. We don't have much time."

An hour later, Danielle was still in Dominic's bed, the thick, down comforter warm where they'd been wrapped in each other's arms. Dominic was buttoning his shirt, moving the collar just so to get it properly aligned, standing in front of a long mirror on his closet door. Danielle moved her arm under her head. She wanted to make a quip about being a satisfied woman, but it wasn't entirely true. *I am hard to satisfy*, she realized, the harsh reality no less obvious than Dominic's sculpted body.

"I'll take the metro home," she offered. He looked at her in the mirror, nodding. Dominic slid on his coat, the material molding over his shoulders and gave a final tug of his jacket then reached for his cell phone, putting it in his pocket. "And thank you."

He sat on the edge of the bed. "What for, specifically?"

She looked at his lips and eyes, choosing to run her fingers along his leg. "All of it."

Dominic ran his fingers through her hair, pushing it behind her ear. "We are filling a place in each other's lives, which is unbelievably rewarding, from my perspective." She smiled. "But we are temporary fixtures that won't become permanent." Her smile faded. "It doesn't mean I am suggesting we stop. I'm just speaking the truth, so we don't try to pretend this will grow into something that won't ever be. The last thing I want is to cause you more hurt, because that's not what you want or deserve. Do you understand what I'm saying?"

Danielle nodded, having gone a little cold with his words. "You don't want to get involved to any depth because it's not meant to be."

"Not with our lifestyles or schedules. You don't think I haven't considered every possible way to be with you?" His comment lifted her spirits a little. "But I'm a pragmatist, and there's a reason I'm single and will remain so for a long time."

She traced the top of his hand with her finger. "You won't even allow yourself to go there?"

"I know how brutally unfair it is to fall in love, knowing the end will come, and two hearts will be broken. Is the temporary, emotional high worth the following pain?" The question was left hanging. Dominic leaned down, caressing her forehead and cheek with his lips. "You are divine." He brushed her lips, pressing lightly at first, then harder as she responded. "Stay as long as you want."

Danielle waited until he left to get out of bed. When she got dressed, it was as though she were attending a wake. Another man, another relationship done, this one, before it had even started.

At home, Danielle explained away her early arrival as a migraine. Emma promptly called Layda, asking if she could come get Monroe. The guilt compounded her lie and actually did create a headache. Danielle played with Monroe until Layda arrived.

"I promise I'll be over early tomorrow," Danielle told Layda, who looked her over with the eyes of a falcon.

"No, you will come over when you feel well enough." Layda was holding Monroe on one hip, bouncing her gently. "Georgy and I will be infinitely relieved when you are able to change environments. I don't know if you can see what we do, but your work life is manifesting itself in a physical change in you."

"I'm losing more weight?" she joked.

"No. You are aging, Danielle, before our very eyes. Maybe playing piano wasn't the right thing to encourage."

Danielle shook her head no. The truth was far more complex than playing at a jazz club. "No," she sighed. "This has to do with our favorite family subject."

"Men?" offered Layda with a scowl. "Not now. Tomorrow, if you are up to it. We can have a mom-to-daughter talk."

"I'd really like that."

Danielle puttered around the house, suddenly making a bee-line for her cell phone. Johanne answered on the first ring.

"Are you sure it was a headache, or did you get together and then break up with Lars during lunch?" Danielle started to laugh and ended up crying.

"Dear Lord girl, I'm here for you."

"I'm glad, because I'm not here for anyone, including myself."

"True that."

His ghetto slang was so completely non-Swiss, it stopped her tears and got her thinking straight again. "Look, I'm literally home in bed, a complete and utter emotional wreck."

"Then stay there. You can't come out dancing with a wrist brace, because it's hard to find Velcro matching that exact hue, so stay in and ferment like aged grapes. When you come back to work on Monday, that will have turned into fine wine, ready to be poured."

Danielle was struck speechless for a moment. "Did you just liken me to moldy alcohol?"

"Yes, I did. Now go and start your fermenting process. With any luck, you'll be the champagne vintage and not the crappy Pinot. God forbid, you'd be a red. That's so whiny."

Danielle was still laughing to herself when he said goodbye, wishing she could bottle his humor and drink it in sips.

Probably because she wasn't expecting to hear or see Dominic all weekend, she was emotionless when she received a text.

Zermatt all weekend. Text me if you come

Danielle checked the weather. That won't be happening. A weather advisory had been issued for the following day and could come in as early as tonight.

Bad weather. Unlikely, she texted back. *Be safe*

She put the phone on do not disturb because she needed a good night's sleep.

Dominic was unique; filled with understanding, caring, concern and empathy; but he'd told her it was going to start and end with only being physical. Had she been emotionally connected to him, her feelings would have been hurt to a far greater degree but a couple of nights does not a loving relationship make. Interestingly, she was no longer bothered by not seeing him. It was as though the unquenchable desire she'd had for him in the beginning was now like having a cup of Mexican coffee when the mood was right and the perfect ingredients were available. It was divine when she had it, but the rest of the time, it was completely unnecessary.

And it was clear that Dominic felt the exact same way.

CHAPTER 38

The edge of the storm buffering the Alps hovered over the city, turning Lake Zurich a glacier black. Danielle wore her heavy down jacket and wool hat, shivering as she walked to the back door of Layda's home.

At least my hand is no longer sore, just stiff.

She called out a greeting from the back room, hanging her coat in the back-entry closet. The kitchen was oddly quiet, but in a state of half-use; half-eaten food and plates on the counter tops. *Very unlike Layda.*

Danielle went first to Georgy's study on the main floor, finding it dark and empty. She then went upstairs, calling out again, though it was clear no one was home. Monroe's room was made up, as was Layda's. She went back downstairs, thinking it odd they'd have gone out and not told her…

My phone. She'd not taken it off Do Not Disturb. She saw a dozen missed calls from Layda, then Emma and finally, Lars. She was about to listen to the voice messages when she opened the texts.

She grabbed her coat and purse, nearly ripping open the door, running, slipping and sliding to her car. At the same moment, Lars drove up, gesturing her to get in.

"No time. You can't drive. Come with me. Hurry." Danielle was already breaking into sobs and gasping for air as he guided her to the car.

"Breath Danielle. You can't faint now. Down you go. Legs in." Once he'd pulled out of the drive, he spoke.

"I've spent the last thirty minutes tracking you down," he said. "What happened?"

"I hadn't checked my phone," she burst out, "and it was on Do Not Disturb—"

"Georgy's alive," Lars broke in, "barely. He collapsed once, commanding Layda to get the neighbor who's a retired surgeon. He revived him, but Georgy had another heart attack in the ambulance. I'm not going to lie, it's touch and go. Danielle, look at me. I'm ordering you, breath through it. You can do this. You can!"

He gripped her leg, pressing strong enough into her thighs to break the dizzying fog.

"I can't do this," she cried out. "I can't. Not anymore."

"It's not about you," Lars said harshly, shocking her from self-pity. "Its Layda and Monroe, both need you there for them. I do too, Danielle," he said. "Focus. I am here for you, okay? I won't leave your side."

She muffled choking cries, nodding. He drove to the emergency entrance, telling the valet the keys were in the car, rushing her through the entrance and to the waiting area. Layda stood beside with Emma, who held Monroe. The little girl was fine until she saw Danielle teary eyed, then she herself became upset. It was the antidote Danielle required to pull it together. She could lose it in private, but she had to be there for her daughter, just as Lars had advised.

That man. He'd been there for her when her father had died, and he was here now.

Lars briefly left her to speak with a hospital staff member, then ushered herself and Emma to a private room, as Layda insisted on staying in the main waiting area.

"I'm okay," Danielle told him, forcing the panic out of her voice. "Shhh," she said to Monroe. "It's okay, mommy's here." The little girl was whimpering, her mood still being affected by Danielle's tone.

"Sit," Lars ordered. "Take care of that little girl. That's your only job now. She can sense your moods. Find it within yourself to take your love and give it to her, *now*. I'll be back."

Lars kissed her cheek, leaving directly to Layda. The woman broke into tears and he put his arm around her. Danielle felt for Monroe's hand, lifting her fingers up then down. Thankfully, Emma was there.

"I didn't know," Danielle said quietly.

"And it wouldn't have mattered," Emma told her. "It happened so quickly. Had it not been for Layda and the paramedics, Georgy would already be gone."

Lars caught Emma's attention, gesturing her to join him. The woman left, spent a few minutes with him, and returned to Danielle.

"Georgy's still in surgery. Triple heart bypass. The doctors give him fifty percent, but Lars says eighty."

It brought a little lift to her heart. Georgy was a bull, but Lars wouldn't give her false hope either.

Danielle could not, *would not* think about an alternative future without Georgy, who had been such a part of her life for two years. She closed her eyes, saying a silent, fervent prayer for him and for the surgeons who were working to save his life.

Danielle turned Monroe towards her, the little girl gripping her fingers to stand.

"Want down?" Danielle asked her. Soon Monroe had pulled herself up and was holding on to the coffee table, teetering around, bravely moving between the chairs, periodically falling down.

Lars came into the room, holding three cups. "Coffee and tea," he said. Danielle gratefully accepted the tea, the three of them sitting in momentary silence, watching Monroe. "I was waiting for Layda to join us, but perhaps she wants a few moments to compose herself." Monroe turned around, her small hands on Danielle's knees looking up, then moved her hands on the next knee over, which was Lars. One hand extended to the other, her tiny fingers spread on his pants before she looked up, seeming to notice the man attached to the legs.

"What do you know about the surgery?" Danielle asked Lars.

"A triple bypass takes three to four hours."

"What about mortality rates?" He told her it depended on other factors; smoking, drinking, diabetes. "You're saying if he lost weight and cut back on the cigars it would help?"

Monroe was still hovering near Lars' legs, turning to the table then back again. "She must prefer your brushed cotton to wool pants," said Danielle.

"That's what I like to hear," he said, squeezing her hand.

"Come here," Danielle said, attempting to scoop up her daughter. Monroe resisted, her refusal immediately changing to a push. Danielle let her go, unhappy when Monroe moved to Emma, who picked her up, sitting her on her lap.

Another punch to my bruised heart. Her own daughter didn't want to be with her, and it hurt.

"She still loves you," Lars said under his breath, holding her hand tighter still. As if sensing her feelings, Lars moved his arm around her shoulders.

"Thanks," she murmured. Time had passed, but his caring had remained.

"I told you, I'm here for you."

Danielle woke up, her head on Lars' shoulder. Monroe had fallen asleep on Emma's lap, wrapped in the blanket provided by the hospital staff. "What's happened?" she asked quietly.

"Georgy made it. He's out of surgery. Layda is in the room next door with him, where I suspect she'll be for the next four days until he's released."

"Is that all?"

"It may take a year for all the discomfort to pass, and not much heavy lifting, but it being Georgy, I would expect him to be back to normal in a week."

Danielle felt herself sink against Lars, realizing his hand was intertwined with hers. "Thank you again."

"Thank the weather for being so bad last night that we turned around and came back. Otherwise, we all would have missed this entire event, which could have turned out very differently."

She agreed, then reluctantly lifted her head. "I should probably get Monroe home now. Emma?" They agreed she'd stay with the still-sleeping Monroe as Lars and Danielle went to say goodbye to Layda.

They stood together, looking at Georgy, who was sleeping. Layda was by his side, one hand on his leg, the other his shoulder, resting herself. Danielle went in and gave her a kiss, murmuring she'd be back the following day. Lars came to her side, giving Layda a hug and kiss.

"Let me know what I can do for you," he said.

Layda was fierce in her look. "Take care of my family."

"I'll do that," Lars promised.

CHAPTER 39

Lars dropped Emma off first, which set Monroe whimpering. Outside the car, Danielle gave Emma a bear hug of appreciation.

"See you Monday," said Emma, "unless you want me to come over so you can see Georgy. Drop her off here if it's more convenient."

"We'll see how she behaves."

Once in the car, Monroe's unhappiness turned to full-blown wailing. "Sorry," Danielle said to Lars.

He shrugged, seemingly unperturbed. "Part of the journey, right? Happiness and sadness. Tears and laughter. Equal and opposites."

Danielle relaxed her head against the headrest and turned to him. "I didn't realize how much of your perspective I'd been missing."

"I do recall there was a time you never believed you'd conceive or carry a child. Every day is a gift."

"I'll remember that," she said, raising her voice as her little girl wailed louder. Danielle turned to the backseat, digging in the overnight bag Emma had assembled, finding a toy. The little girl's wailing was momentarily abated as her focus became the object.

"That's a little better," she breathed with relief, turning back into her seat. "Are you missing out on any other events at Zermatt, beyond the teaching?"

"A few," he answered. "I have been staying on the weekends to have social dinners with out of town clients who have homes in the area. I do recall telling you I don't go out just to be busy and that hasn't really changed, your recent observations at the restaurant notwithstanding."

"Oh, Lars," she groaned. "Not this again. I told you we were beyond that."

"And you are right. I am beyond that. Ergo, I'm not dating anyone."

"Which you have no obligation to tell me, either."

"You were the one who asked me if I was missing anything," he teased, "but perhaps I should be asking you the same question." For a moment, she said nothing. Could Lars have learned about her discussions with Georgy? No. Dominic? He'd never say a word. "The piano playing? The Jazz club?"

Her relief was infinite. "Did Ulrich snitch on me?"

"I did hear about a five-thousand-dollar song."

"Wait, what? How did you hear about that?"

A pause preceded his comment. "I have stopped by once or twice."

Could he have paid for it? "And you didn't say hello?"

"I didn't want to disturb you. Now can you tell me about Layda and Georgy and your new involvement with them?" Danielle glossed over the details, touching on the family transition aspect.

"In monarchies, it's called generational inheritance. In the real world, it's the transfer of power."

She laughed. "I'd hardly call it that. There is something far more important though…" Lars saw her expression and was expectant. "I call Layda mom now, and she calls me her daughter. Georgy's been my second dad for a while now." She had the satisfaction of seeing his head turning very slowly to her as he slowed for a red light.

"All is moving forward," he said, more to himself than her.

She assumed he was referring to their lives. *Yes, we are on our separate paths.*

"Have you and the others figured out what's going to happen with the support staff?"

Lars' mouth turned down, but his scowl carried a humored look. "It's after hours, I'm not your direct manager and this crosses the lines of professional boundaries, don't you agree?"

Danielle let out a whiff of air. "You think I care about that any longer, given our history together and when death is around the corner? Let me ask you this, then," she continued. "If we were married, you came home from the office, and I could tell something was up and you weren't yourself, would you talk to me?"

"Regardless of our relationship state, if you worked in any capacity that wasn't my peer, I couldn't speak about work."

"I'm so glad we are getting this out of the way after the fact," she said as her home came into view. "What were we even thinking, Lars? If we'd remained together, I'd have to leave the firm or you'd go elsewhere, all so we could have meaningful conversations at home. Ridiculous."

Her monologue elicited a chuckle. "Yes, there would have been some natural consequences associated with the romantic relationship, but don't you think we would have sorted it out prior?"

"Sorted," she drawled.

She was still smiling to herself as Lars turned down her lane, the lake view inspiring even in its darkened state. All is moving forward, just as Lars had said.

"Lars, thanks. I don't think I could have driven to the hospital."

"I *know* you couldn't have."

"There is one thing," she started. "I saw the car seat for Monroe. Have you...has it been in the car this entire time or did you put it in this morning, when everything happened, just to be ready in case we needed rides?" She glanced over her shoulder, seeing Monroe had fallen asleep, her head against the cushion, the toy in her chubby fingers.

Lars turned into her driveway, parking the car. He pressed a button on his side of the door, and Danielle felt heat under her moving up her legs and lower back. "It never left." With two fingers, Lars gently turned over her left hand, opening the fingers. "Any pain?"

"Not, it's just stiff."

"And emotionally?" She didn't know if he was referring to the events of the day, or her overall emotional state.

"Fragile is a word that sums it all up." He moved his fingers from along her skin to the soft brace, crossing the webbing then up the length of the next finger. Her finger twitched out of time with her heart, one erratic, the other calmly pulsing.

"A near death experience will do that to a person." He continued following the outline of her fingers, stopping where the skin met the material. "Do you know what Layda told me?"

"No," she answered quietly, wanting him to keep caressing her skin.

"Layda and Georgy have made you the sole beneficiary of their entire estate. She was telling me about it because their attorneys had filed it all last week. With you on the paperwork, it needed to be recorded and validated for the investment side."

The information stunned her. "How could she even be thinking of money when Georgy was going under surgery?"

Lars slid his palm under hand, cupping it, threading his fingers through hers. "She was so worried that she herself might have a heart attack from grief, she wanted someone to know their wishes beyond the attorneys."

Danielle knew that who Layda conveyed the information to was just as important as the information itself.

Lars curled his fingers inward, leaning towards her. Their foreheads met, the light touch insignificant to the connection they still had. "They love you almost as much as they do me," she said quietly.

He pulled back just enough to meet her gaze. "No, they respect me, that's different from loving me."

"Well, I respect you, which is very different from loving you, so I have to agree with them."

His lips, wide and sensual, closed and broadened with her comment. "Sassy, irreverent, American. Always making jokes when I'm trying to be serious." The back of his fingertips grazed her chin, caressing her jawline.

"Look where it's gotten me," she murmured.

Lars leaned forward. "Do you want me to kiss you or not?" It took only a lift of her face to brush her nose against his. "That's a yes," he said, his lips touching hers through the words, the sensation tickling her.

Danielle put her hand to his chest, feeling his heartbeat through the sweater. She groaned with pleasure, a vibration of pleasure moving through her, the anticipation of what was to come causing a dizzying effect.

"Don't tease me," she begged, gripping his chest harder. He delayed her satisfaction by gliding his tongue along her lips.

"You want to rush this?" he murmured.

"No," she answered, "and yes." She didn't want him to stop period, fast or slow, but was uncomfortable taking him inside her home. It would be too much. *For now.*

Danielle began stroking his neck, drawing back as she found his chin with her thumb. She tugged gently, covering his lips with hers, fully and completely, pressing against him hard before gradually pulling back.

"Now you are stopping?" he complained.

She smiled, lovingly brushing her nose against his. "You have made it clear I can't have any expectations. I'll be honest, Lars. I love you still, and am just at the point of functioning in a world knowing I must see you, can't have you, and not walk around like a wounded dove in spite of it all."

He bent to nuzzle her neck and she kindly, but firmly, lifted him back up. "Please," he murmured.

"You know I'm right." He tried once more for her skin, and when she stopped him. He sighed deeply.

"But I want you. I've missed your lips, your smell…"

"Good," she answered, "but you were the one to tell me that time is a good thing, to help us understand if we can, or should be together. Lars," she said, drawing back a little further, her hand dropping to his fingers in her lap. "I hate to use your words against you, but only time will prove if we are compatible in the long run."

"But I know you want me."

She smirked. "All you have to do is look at my eyes, proving you aren't blind. But if part of my growth is to be the strong one, I will be." To show she was serious, she extended her fingers, unthreading his in the process. "I'll get Monroe."

Lars was by her side, insisting he hold the baby carrier with the still-sleeping Monroe inside, as she handled the overnight bag. Danielle didn't bother removing her, but set her just inside her bedroom, closing the door halfway. Lars was waiting in the hallway.

"Why didn't you take out the car seat?"

He extended his hand to her. She allowed herself to be drawn towards him, the hug becoming a full embrace. "Kissing you wasn't enough of an answer?" She hummed a negative and he caressed her neck with his lips. "Just because I said I can't make a promise didn't mean I gave up hope."

CHAPTER 40

"He said that?" repeated Stephen. It was Sunday morning, before the opening of Stars & Stripes. Monroe was with Emma, allowing Danielle to make a quick stop to see Stephen, share the details of Lars and the situation with Georgy before heading to the hospital. "*And* you resisted him? My dear Danielle. You have most definitely grown."

"You approve then? I did the right thing?"

He nodded. "By playing hard to get? Absolutely."

"No!" she said emphatically. "I wasn't playing. I'm serious about not starting *something* with Lars as I am about eliminating sailboarding."

"Both could be temporary, you know."

Danielle eyed him carefully. "What's up? This isn't the normal Stephen, who in a very stately, and purposeful manner tells me like it is. This is almost sassy. Almost, American."

He smiled mischievously and excused himself. "Stay here." When he returned, he held a cream-colored bag in his hand. "I'd like your opinion on something. Look." He pushed it across the table.

"This can't be what I think it is." He said nothing, his lopsided smile doing the talking for him. With growing excitement, she separated the gold rope, removing the ivory-box. Very slowly, she opened it, the big reveal causing her to gasp and grin. "Stephen…" His lips were pressed, lips wide, grin full. "It's beyond stunning." Danielle held it up to the light, before he shushed her back down. "Sorry!" she whispered, turning her back to the door. She turned it this way and that, leaving the ring in the box. "Rose gold?" she asked, and he nodded. "Has she seen it? Does she know?"

"No to both. I like surprises. Unlike my experience with Lani, who picked the ring, demanded the size, color and type, I got to do it all. Of course, I wasn't a complete idiot," he said, causing her to giggle. He'd never used that word in the time she'd known him. "I did my Sherlock Holmes first, spoke with her parents, got her dad's and mother's and grandfather's permission."

Danielle smiled and shook her head. "Can you tell me how you went from friends who hooked up, to good friends having a baby, all the while still being in love with Lani, to now this?"

"Respect, honesty, and shared values are the underpinnings of good friendships, agree? We had a strong physical attraction, but were emotionally intertwined and hung up on what were ultimately dysfunctional relationships. We couldn't actually appreciate, or fall in love with, one another until we…detached, I guess, from toxic relationships. It was a different path for both of us, and didn't happen at the same time, but when it did, we just kind of sat there, and said: you were here the entire time."

"What a blessing to go through that together." She took one last look at the ring before handing it back. "The square cut is very elegant and timeless."

"The center stone was a gift from her grandfather, an heirloom piece he purchased from some estate. The two, triangular trillion diamonds were given by her parents." Her mouth dropped. "But so you don't think I'm a complete dud, I purchased the wedding band, which she is more likely to wear around the house."

Danielle was glad to hear it. "I was about to think you'd mortgaged your life away!" She asked about the wedding band, expressing enthusiasm for the diamond eternity band. "Classic and timeless."

"You might appreciate that I got the idea from the one Lars gave you, although this is a smaller version. Speaking of which, are you going to start wearing it again?" She hadn't given the ring a second thought in weeks. "As I recall, you took it off in retribution for him seeing Margaret, not because you ever stopped loving him, which last night proves."

"Ahh, dear Stephen. I'm not going to rush into, or back to, anything right now, so let's go back to you. Do you have any ideas on when a wedding would be?" He told her Eva had expressed a preference for short engagements.

"Just enough time to get the venue, flowers and other things before the baby arrives. Why? You think a double wedding might be in the works?"

"Stephen!" she said, then lowered her voice, and her mood. "Why are you so chipper about Lars, when before you were all about my taking my own path for a while."

He put the box back into the bag, setting it on the table. "Because in the last year, I've learned a few things. True love doesn't fade, it can go dormant for a while, like Lars once told you, but it's still there. You needed to, and perhaps still need to, grow and mature in order to handle the ups and downs of a relationship. God knows that I was with Lani for a dozen years, but it might as well been three months for all we grew. I was in a perpetual swamp of stagnation, I just didn't know it. In the three or more months, and really, the last thirty days, you've grown more than you did in the entire two years prior."

"That's pretty harsh, Stephen," she said.

"Do you disagree?"

"Enough," she laughed. "Don't get me all down for my personal and emotional limitations. I'm still coming out of my fragile stage, which, in all seriousness, is still there, especially with Georgy. Can't you give me a little credit for not jumping right back with Lars when that's going on?"

"Danielle," he said, glancing at the door, where a line outside was starting to form. "Position it however you want, but you and I both know you and Lars are in it for the long haul, whatever that means. These things you are going through and working out could just as easily be done within the bounds of marriage. If you choose to use Georgy's health or you working at MRD as a delay tactic, then go right ahead, but don't think you're fooling anyone, not me, Layda and Georgy and especially not Lars. And with that, your brotherly lecture of the day is finished."

She threw her arms around him. "I hope Eva loves you half as much as I love you. Good luck tonight," she told him, giving him a final kiss before leaving.

The happiness she felt for Stephen's newfound situation carried over to her optimism for Georgy's full recovery. She arrived at the hospital anticipating Layda would still be there, and although guessed that she was not likely to eat, brought her a carry-out from Stars & Stripes.

Layda came out of the room and they hugged each other without a word, Danielle assessing her up and down, as if to divine Georgy's state by Layda's appearance.

"I'm okay, just fine," Layda told her.

"Let's sit down for a second," she recommended, but Layda shook her head.

"I've done enough sitting. I need to get home and take a shower." Sure enough, her coat was already on and her purse was around her shoulder.

"I'll drive you," Danielle offered, already turning to walk, but Layda held her firm.

"No, you came to sit with Georgy, not take care of a perfectly able-bodied woman, which I am. Danielle, he needs you more than me. I've already called a car and will come back later this evening. I'll be damned if the last person my husband sees is a nurse beside his bed and not me."

Danielle's throat caught air. "He's that bad?"

Layda scowled. "No, but it makes the point."

"Don't do that to me!" she cried, glad to see Layda still had her spitfire sense of self. "Here. Since you are bound and determined to go home alone, take this. It's soup and some real food. Promise to eat?" For a second, Layda's strong exterior bent, and she nodded, looking spent. "I'll be here until Emma needs to go."

"You take care of that little girl, not me or Georgy, Danielle. We've had our life. We want you to be able to live yours."

The words were so familiar to what her own father had once told her. It must be a parent thing, earning the wisdom to pass on to the next generation, deprioritizing themselves in the process.

"I do have one apology to make," Layda said, her face downturned. "Monroe's birthday. It was to be this week." Danielle's blank stare confirmed it wasn't even in her consciousness and said so.

"I always thought a blowout party for a one year old was too much," Danielle confided, sensitive to Layda's feelings, but was positive on one thing. "Georgy first, you second and Monroe next year, when she's two. Sound good?" Layda nodded, relieved. "I'll work with Emma on letting those you invited know." Danielle got the list from Layda, which was long. She placed a call to Emma, who insisted on talking to everyone, freeing Danielle to see Georgy without being in a rush.

Danielle went to the washroom, soaping her hands before visiting Georgy. He was sleeping, the tubes and wires attached indicating a strong, even pulse. It was some time before a nurse came in, willingly answering her questions about his state. Danielle held his hand. The year before, when her own father died, he was across the shores, with Sheila beside him when his kidneys finally gave out, along with the rest of his body. In some ways, being here with Georgy was the comforting experience she never had, although the nurse gave Georgy a high chance of living a fully productive and healthy life.

"With the proper life choices," the nurse had said.

These men and their food. At least this time around, with Georgy, she had reinforcements like Layda to help motivate him in the proper direction. Actually, she corrected herself, the biggest motivation was likely to be Monroe; the visual of watching her graduate a goal he could work towards.

When Layda returned at six, Danielle left, making it home in time to eat with Monroe and go for a short walk around the block. During the day, rain had poured down, washing down rivers of water from the streets down into the lake. It looks flooded, Danielle thought, seeing the watermark. She'd wait until she saw Giles again to tell him she could be a part-time instructor, as she was the year prior since that wasn't dangerous.

Maybe she wouldn't teach at all, or only once or twice a month. She didn't know. Without a spouse, partner or whatever, the guilt cycle was ready and waiting for her to get on and ride anytime she wanted to engage in a discretionary activity that wasn't work. Piano playing didn't induce self-loathing because Monroe was asleep; she didn't know any better.

Those darn day activities….although the ice climbing center in Zermatt had day care for the kids who didn't ski, and they seemed to have a great time. Monroe might really enjoy that, getting her fill of other kids, an activity Emma and Layda advocated, while allowing Danielle to fulfill her own passions.

Bathing and reading Monroe to sleep kept Danielle suitably occupied, preventing her from thinking about the one man in the center of her emotional life. She elected not to take a bath, because relaxing in hot water was sensual, or could become so if she didn't have discipline to keep Lars out of her thoughts. But that was only a delay tactic, as Stephen would have said. The moment she lay down, he appeared in her mind's eye, she felt his touch on her fingers, and his lips on her neck. It only took the thought of him biting the fine muscles on her neck to start feelings of arousal within her, sensations she didn't want to encourage.

Why was it thoughts of Dominic didn't do the same thing? The answer was obvious; he was a physical stimulant, a wise, patient and interesting man, but dazzling only in person. Lars was stimulating in thought, she didn't need him to be by her side to become excited.

It took an hour of struggling with her wants and desires before she faded with fatigue. She wanted Lars badly, but for the second instance in her time here in Zurich, she was invoking Swiss-style patience with her romantic life. Her future with Lars might be obvious to Stephen, but it had to be the future *she* wanted, one that would be best for Monroe, not just her. One afternoon, reconnecting after a traumatic event, wasn't necessarily the best gauge of future compatibility.

CHAPTER 41

"So you did it," Johanne stated from the doorway. It was 5:50 a.m., standard arrival time for Danielle, but early for her manager and dancing partner.

"What did I do now?"

"You are the beneficiary for the entire Mettleren Holdings. Even Margaret was left without words. Well, that's because the green bile of jealousy was threatening to spew forth from her mouth, but happily enough, she was able to choke it back down long enough for the partners to discuss what to do."

Danielle gestured him in and to shut the door. "How and when did this get around? It just happened last week!"

"Actually, it happened on Wednesday, but the partners were only informed because the attorneys are having serious issues with your employment now."

Danielle was dumbfounded. "How could they possibly have an issue with that?"

"One word," he said flatly. "Conflict. It reminds me of another word. Andre." It only took a second for Danielle to get his meaning.

"I can't believe we are going through this all over again! I will trade more for them because of my vested interest, not less."

"Danielle," he said, lowering his head, his eyes peering over his spectacles. "It's seven billion dollars' worth of vested interest in their direct funds, thirteen billion extended in the network as we already discussed. Since you are now the sole beneficiary behind Layda, why would you even bother to trade for anyone else?"

She was offended at his comment. "I've never treated that family with preference and you know it."

He bounced his foot. "Everyone knows that, even counsel, but rules are rules. You can only guess what the witch wants you to do?"

Danielle's head bobbled in disbelief. "She really thinks I'm going to give up the account, as I did with Andre?"

"You either give them up or she takes them away," he said with a shrug. "And she already has some idea of who it's going to go to."

"Jacob."

"Of course," Johanne retorted. "But actually, she believes you are going to stay, because where else are you going to go?"

"Exactly," she responded. "Now, if you'll excuse me, I'd like to start trading, although I believe I'm going to take lunch today, and for that matter, every day from this point forward. The snow is officially gone and the sun is here to stay, don't you think?"

Johanne's foot stopped bouncing and she could practically hear the wheels of thought turning. "Are you going to do something wicked?" he asked mischievously.

"Will you hate me if I do?"

"Lord no. I told you I get an override on the others, and Max has already come to the table with an offer to settle."

"What??" Johanne explained that over the weekend, Max had offered to transfer the titles of several apartments into an escrow account as collateral. "If we don't get our money back, then we will sell the properties."

Danielle waited for the other shoe to drop. "But if the restaurant is still bleeding money, it's guaranteed you'll have to do that. Why wait?"

"Dario thinks Max wants to save face. He'd rather convert the restaurant over to the hotel like he should have done, giving us money behind the scenes than simply close it down." Danielle wondered what that meant for the employees. "Termination. Oh, I don't mean to be totally rude and callous," he said, the sarcasm thick. "How is Georgy? We were only told he's stable."

"That's what he is, stable. He's a fighter, and the surgeons said the bypass went as well as possible. He has a lot to live for, and his diet and life patterns will be a reflection of just how much he wants to watch his granddaughter grow up. Yes?"

"Well…" he drawled, his foot starting to bounce again. "Anything else you'd like to share? You left with Lars and never came back. He said you were sick…"

Danielle scoffed and put on her headset. "Go away and let me work, you gossip monger. I have to concentrate."

"Yes!" he half-shouted, clapping his hands once and lifting both in the air.

"What—?"

"Don't say it," he interrupted, standing while still facing her. "I know your returns are going to shoot back up again, because there is nothing better than you avoiding a question." He pointed a finger at her. "If you are going to go out, go out big, girl."

When the door opened and he walked out, Danielle clamped her lips together, unable to suppress the smile from forming. Maybe he was right. If she was going to go out, she might as well be at the top.

Danielle didn't notice the passage of time, her zeal for the numbers giving her a thrill she'd not experienced since before Andre's death. It wasn't for the commission checks to Glenda, or stabbing Margaret in the eye, it was for herself. Words of wisdom from her old boss and mentor David came back to her. Friends are fleeting but respect is eternal. Well, she wanted Lars to be her friend, and to have his respect, even if it were for only a short period of time before she was truly ejected from the company or forced to make the choice to leave.

And I'm going to make sure that every last one of them knows the very best thing they had walked right out the front door.

At three, the two-tap came. "Did you have monitors installed over the weekend, because I just shut down."

"And hello to you," he said. Danielle hadn't tried to conceal or suppress her delight at seeing him. "Good trading day."

"Excellent day," she corrected, her smile turning smug. "A renewed motivation."

"Johanne said he spoke to you about discussions regarding the Mettleren family."

Danielle switched off her computer, affirming that indeed he did. "Is there something I can do for you or were you stopping by to thank me for my excellent work? Oh, wait. I think you just did that in your understated way." He laughed, his expression bemused. "Gotta run, so you need to speak fast." He didn't, and Danielle stopped in front of him. Just being near him now was a tease, for her, and she thought—or hoped—for him as well. "Okay then. See you tomorrow."

Danielle said goodbye to Glenda, passing Margaret on the way out. "Good night, Margaret."

Only after she'd passed her did Margaret say, "Danielle."

That evening was the best she'd had in several months, and it only occurred to her over dinner that she'd not seen Dominic outside the office. Or rather, maybe he was there, but she' been so focused on getting home that looking for him hadn't been top of mind.

Another positive step forward. Once Monroe was in bed, Danielle opened her laptop again and researched the latest market trends. By eleven, she had enough information to trade the rest of the week.

Tuesday was a repeat of the day before, with Lars stopping by again as she shut down.

"Is this becoming a pattern?" she questioned.

"A managing director has an obligation to ensure all his traders are happy, which I can see you are, much to the bemusement of the senior staff."

This time, Danielle held the door of the wardrobe open, peering around just enough for him to see her, but no one else. "I'm making sure that all of you will miss me extraordinarily when I'm gone. You, most of all." She shut the door, giving him a sly look. "It's too bad it took me this long to figure out it's rather fun leaving you at a loss for words."

On the way home, she sent Robin a text. Her hand was good enough to play, if they wanted her. She received a text back almost instantaneously.

Yes, please! Was Robin's text.

Danielle hugged and kissed her daughter with delight, ignoring her squirms. Her daughter was just going to have to get used to her love and attention. Danielle knew she was at fault for her daughter's attachment to Emma, but while she was working, she required a caretaker, and to have one at home was far better than leaving Monroe at a center.

"We are going to see Grandpa," she said out loud for her daughter's benefit, first in English, then Swiss-German. At the hospital, she held Monroe's little hand and waved at Georgy through the window. When

Layda came out, Danielle asked if Georgy was well enough to handle her little ball of energy.

"If it kills him, he'll die happy."

"Layda!"

"It was his words verbatim, not me this time. Come on in."

"Hey, Dad," Danielle greeted, giving him an awkward hug and kiss to the forehead. Monroe stretched her arms out to Georgy, and when denied, started to fuss.

"Here, you have to make do with me," Layda said, taking Monroe in her arms, then walking her to the window, pointing outside.

"You look pretty good but how are you really feeling? Are you in any pain?" Danielle asked him.

"My dear, I'm glad to be here. My biggest regret is all the pain and fear I've put Layda and yourself through. I'm so sorry." Danielle touched his arm gently. "And I'm sorry for always having seconds or thirds of your pies."

She squeezed. "I won't take it personally if you only take a single helping...after six months." His promise to eat better and start exercising was witnessed by Layda.

"Georgy, I heard you made some rather large changes in the Mettleren paperwork."

"We love you so much, Danielle," he said.

"Did you know that your love is going to cost me my job?" Georgy's thick eyebrows bunched together in the frown. "This doesn't warrant you having another heart attack, so I won't continue if I see that pulse monitor rise one bit. Promise?" He nodded, though his eyes were still dark. "According to council, we are running into the exact same issue that we had with Andre; familial connection and potential conflicts."

"What are they proposing?"

"Well, they are still working on a proposal, but Johanne gave me the heads up that if I elect to stay, all your money, and the family money goes elsewhere, leaving me with a lot fewer accounts. Alternatively, I leave the firm and my clients follow of their own accord."

Georgy grumbled at the first part of her comment but smiled with the second.

"I know," she whispered. "I'm going to be unemployed pretty soon, and I couldn't be happier."

"Truly?"

She nodded. "I see no reason to push it, because I'm now a trading goddess, sorry to be so arrogant about it. I'll take care of Monroe, you and Layda, and keep to my routine until the rest of our world is sorted out."

"Which means I need to get my butt out of here."

"Which means," she said, squeezing his hand, "you need to do as the doctor orders and get better. Money can be made anytime, but family is not replaceable. Agreed?"

"Yes, ma'am. But that doesn't mean I can't make a few phone calls and keep the ball rolling in the right direction."

"Correction," interjected Layda from the window. "I will be placing those calls, not you."

Before Danielle could add to that, the supervising physician asked the group to leave so Georgy could get his rest.

"Only a few more days," said the doctor.

On her way home, she called Lars with the update, knowing he'd appreciate it.

"It sounds like he's making an excellent recovery."

"Yes, he looked very well. I'm sorry, Lars. I didn't even ask if I was disturbing you. You sound busy."

"I'm still at the office, yes."

"Everything okay? Scratch that. Never mind. I'm not supposed to ask. Just wanted you to know how Georgy was doing."

He thanked her again, ending the call. She had a moment of second guessing herself, and Lars. Was he with Margaret, even though he said they weren't together, and he wasn't dating? Danielle shook her head. She was either going to make the decision to believe him or not.

Yes, she was going to believe he was honest with her.

With that decided, he could be late at the office because of her or other matters involving normal business operations.

But oh, wouldn't it be fun if they were having to stay late talking about her. And what, exactly, were they going to do with the Mettleren accounts? She suspected Johanne was right; Margaret was going to give the ultimatum. Danielle only hoped the timing would work out such that she'd walk out the door the same time as Georgy's money, hitting the firm nicely between the eyes.

CHAPTER 42

Danielle visited Georgy every night after work with Monroe, encouraged by his recovery. His vitals were strong, his mind functioning as it should and with Layda's help, he had developed the transition plan for the new offices of the family management team.

"We are going to build a new wing off an existing building," Layda said, adding they were also buying the adjacent building, in case of expansion. "We'll connect the two structures with a concrete and steel walkway; the permitting taking far less time than the construction itself." Danielle thought it perfect. "I'm glad you agree because the architect will submit the plans tomorrow. With good luck, the permits will be complete by the end of this month and construction will only take four or five weeks."

Friday, Danielle received a text from Dominic, informing her he'd be at Zermatt that weekend. So would she. Her hand was well enough to climb, the weather was cooperating, and the last instruction of the series would wrap up. Georgy, when learning she was going to skip climbing to visit him, insisted she go.

"You do that, or we will have words, my girl." Danielle could only acquiesce, his tone and manner reminding Danielle of her own father. Danielle held off replying to Dominic. In the days following their last hook-up, she acknowledged she wasn't one of those women who could have a casually intimate relationship, at least not for an extended period of time. An end-point had to be on the horizon. That much she'd learned from Andre; falling in love in spite of her goal to have it remain only physical. She no longer believed she could have one without the other, the union of mind, heart and body intertwined was what she wanted.

Too bad I can't just have great sex and call it a day. For that, one couldn't get any better than Dominic, and yet…the singular act of Lars kissing her face and neck was so much more arousing than Dominic had ever been. And unlike her time with Lars, she'd never experienced bright lights during her passionate kissing with Dominic or felt dizzy with his touch. Ultimately, Danielle decided not to respond to Dominic. She was unsure of what to say, *thanks, but no thanks?* She was far more interested in what his employer was doing on Saturday night and where he'd be spending his time.

Sticking to her plan, just as Georgy had insisted, Danielle dropped Monroe off with Layda on Saturday, who said she and Monroe would pay a last visit to Georgy Sunday and ride home with him.

"That seems awfully fast for him to be released," worried Danielle.

"Six days is the norm for a bypass," Layda said, unconcerned. "He is committed to being around for all of us, not just this little bundle of energy." Assured Layda was comfortable with having Monroe for the homecoming, Danielle offered to bring over lunch on her way back from Zermatt.

"Honestly, Danielle, I think Georgy is going to come home and immediately go to bed. And if he feels up to it, I'm going to talk with him about what changes we need to make for our upcoming social calendar. I don't want him overdoing it." Danielle fervently agreed.

"What can we do?"

Layda smiled. "It's not *we*, my dear. It's what *you* are going to do. I thought we had a few months, but it's going to start immediately, as in, the weekend after your birthday."

Danielle took a gulp of reality and swallowed her pride. "I'll trust you on that one. But…" she hesitated, "I'm really going to need your help on one thing; shopping for appropriate clothes. I don't know what your events entail, what I should wear or anything."

Layda's momentary look of concern was replaced with sheer confidence. "Emma can watch Monroe and we can take care of that. How about this…" she began.

"A shopping date with my mom," Danielle said out loud during her drive up to Zermatt, the wonder and excitement of it all causing her to grip the steering wheel a little tighter. "Of course, I'm getting fired, or losing all of my accounts, at the same time," she said. "And Lani is no longer my best friend, which is weird," she said, a little bit of longing in her voice, "leaving me with no best friend, which is doubly weird."

What about Lars? whispered a quiet voice. *He's been there, acting like her best friend through it all.*

"In fact," she said aloud, "he's up at Zermatt this very moment, teaching." If she had time after her own session was complete, she'd walk over and watch him in action.

Danielle arrived early, learning the final day of instruction was on waterfall ice. "Leading and following in multi-pitch settings," explained the instructor. Danielle rotated her left wrist, feeling a few aches but nothing that playing the piano for two hours didn't produce. As the group put on their gear, the instructor came to her side.

"Feeling any nerves since the slip?"

"No, not at all," Danielle answered.

"That's good," she exclaimed. "Beginners either get right back on the ice or they never show up again." Danielle wondered if the woman had taken odds on her, but didn't ask. Giving her a pat on her back, the instructor left and soon they were walking as a group to a nearby frozen waterfall.

The instructor's offhand remark was gratifying to Danielle. After the initial chest-in-her-throat moment, and then the pain of the wrist, it hadn't occurred to her not to go back up the ice. Her mistakes were just that, mistakes, created by her own miscalculations. While on the ground watching the class continue, she'd seen another climber fall due to a broken piece of ice, but he'd been caught by the safety rope. Nearly one-hundred percent of accidents in ice climbing were preventable, she determined, echoing the literature she'd read, random acts of nature notwithstanding. So, if a person watched the weather report and didn't take unnecessary risks, it was a safe, practical sport that kept the legs and upper body in amazing shape. Just look at Lars.

Well, I haven't actually seen Lars' naked body lately, she thought to herself as she waited at the bottom for her turn. Today, she was in the middle of the climb, her attention on climber above and below her as she searched for the right foothold. She knew what loose ice resembled, as well as firm ice by the colorations, pleased that she could discern between the two even with intermittent cloud cover.

At the top, the teenager took a picture of all of them before descending, Danielle again placed in the middle. Near the bottom, she heard a crunch and a yell from the bottom, but seeing nothing, looked up, watching as the oldest man of the group came falling towards her. She didn't have time to move out of the way, and felt his hip crash into her shoulder before his rope caught, stopped him abruptly. He hung just below her, eyes wide open and mouth hanging.

"You're okay," she said, finding her voice. "The rope got you." He gulped and looked down. "Accidents happen. I know this."

When he could talk, the man apologized profusely speaking so quickly in Swiss-German she could barely keep up.

"No, I'm not injured, I'm fine," she assured him, imminently grateful it wasn't his two-inch spikes that had hit her shoulder. The instructor called up to him to continue down, and after a few deep breaths, he started again. When Danielle arrived at the bottom, the instructor was at her side.

"What did you do wrong?" she asked without sympathy.

"I didn't adjust my position to either side."

She nodded, approvingly. "One foot either way would have prevented that, and honestly the incident could have been a lot worse." Danielle thought back to the crampons again. *Yes, much worse.*

The afternoon ended with the group deciding to have drinks together at the outdoor café, enjoying the light and warmth of the heat lamps as the sun had already set behind the mountains. She stayed for thirty minutes then excused herself, heading towards the indoor ice climbing wall. Inside, she wandered around, looking for a board posting the instructors and times, finally seeing Lars' name was on the roster for that morning, before her class had even started.

Oh well, she thought, disappointed. It would have been nice to watch him. She walked from the indoor area to the open rotunda connecting the outdoor activities, stopping for a horse drawn carriage, the only form of transportation allowed in the cute village. She walked by the luxury watch shops of Hublot and Bucherer, thinking of the timepiece Lars had given her, which was still sitting in her drawer at home. At what point was she going to put it back on? Stephen had raised a good point regarding the ring; she still loved Lars, regardless of her temporary anger at him over Margaret, and that was a symbol of all they'd had.

On a whim, she went into the next jewelry shop on a mission. When asked if she required assistance, she told the cashmere-clad man exactly what she was looking for. He found her a very similar ring, and then she asked how much.

"Do you take returns?" she asked, inwardly smiling at his look of disdain.

"We exchange, Madam." Danielle handed him back the ring, thanking him for his time. Now she knew approximately how much Lars had spent on the two items in her drawer at home. Together, they were worth more than her home.

Her next destination was a chocolate stop. She passed the Lindt store in favor of a much smaller boutique, selecting an assortment of truffles, falling for a Matterhorn-shaped milk chocolate, complete with white chocolate dripping from the top.

It was halfway in her mouth when she stopped, seeing Lars in front of her. Her half-smile remained as he came towards her.

"I understand you were looking for me," he said.

"For a minute. I'm over it now," she quipped, eating the remaining half of her treat.

He eyed it, then her. "Is that like a hot, New York second, scalding but fleeting?"

"You wish. More like dry ice on a person's arse up here. Come on, walk with me. It's too cold to stand still."

"I'd love to."

CHAPTER 43

Danielle offered him a bite of chocolate, which he declined, so she nibbled, carrying the bag in the other hand as they strolled. At first, the conversation centered on her reasons for wanting to see him at the ice climbing arena.

"I was interested in seeing how you teach others," Danielle told him. "I've never seen you in that environment and I was curious."

"We had the same inclination then." She glanced at him, perplexed. "I wanted to see how your ice climbing was coming along, arriving just in time to see you get knocked down by the climber above you."

Danielle grimaced. "It hurt a bit more than I let on."

"I imagine. Watching it happen was one of those fast-frame photos where I wanted to shout a warning, but it occurred too fast and probably would have scared you more than anything. Are you sore?"

"Thankfully, no. Don't tell me sailboarding is harder on the joints!" She had said it in a teasing manner, relating what her instructor had told her. "Both times, it was completely my fault. Can't blame the rock for cracking when I pounded it with my toe nor failing to get out of the way from the guy above me."

"True enough," he said, which deserved a nudge from her elbow. She loved the chance to touch him, even it was short and the point of contact wasn't skin to skin.

"Do you give personal instruction?" Danielle asked him, getting the visual of something more intimate out of her mind.

"No, no time or interest. Why?"

Danielle wrapped up the small bag of chocolate, making room in her coat pocket, wishing she'd brought her gloves. "Well," she said, rubbing her hands, "I'm not in the market, but I was guessing that's why you were still in the area."

"I had a client meeting and decided to stick around." He noticed Danielle shivering again. "Weather gear for ice climbing in the sun isn't the fur that's best for the dark. Here. Give me a hand."

Danielle willingly complied, grateful for his warmth. *Skin against skin.* "I've never been in downtown Zermatt at night. It really is like all those pictures on Instagram."

"Better in person, I think." Lars asked about Georgy, laughing at Danielle's recounting of his feigned resistance to changing his bad habits. "He'll do what's required."

"Of course, he will. It's just so funny to hear the old man grumble. Reminds me of my dad."

Lars drew her closer, putting her hand in his pocket with his own. "Better?" She nodded. "Do you miss him?"

"When I think of him, and that happens pretty frequently. Most of the time it's because Layda or Georgy will say something very similar to what my dad used to say. It makes me believe the wisdom of parents is quite consistent; a few of the words change here and there, but the essence is still the same."

They stepped off the sidewalk, and Lars put pressure on her fingers as they waited for a carriage, then crossed the road. The small movement pushed beads of heat up her arm, straight to her chest. It was the little things, the touch or pull that wove the fabric of a relationship, she thought, not just all deep conversations or hot sex.

"When was the last time you saw your parents?" she asked Lars. It was a subject they'd rarely discussed, even when they dated. His father's stroke and Lars' own change in career as a result, were both somewhat tender subjects.

"About a month ago. They asked about you."

She looked at him, trying to read his expression. "How do they even know about me?"

"I'd asked you to come pay a visit before our last issue, if you recall. It was only courteous to tell them what to expect."

Danielle didn't know what to say. "So much for your discretion."

"Your favorite word," he teased back.

"Whatever! It was you who introduced that concept to me in the first place."

"Very true, and I thought I was being wise, however I got it completely wrong. But in my defense, when someone thinks they're going to get married, it's good form to tell the parents, don't you agree?"

That's what they had talked about, then.

"I do. But what's worse is your luck with rings." Lars' head cocked back as he laughed.

"I seem to have very bad luck on that front. She gave hers back and you don't wear yours. Next time I'll just invest the money in hard metals."

Danielle simultaneously nudged him and squeezed his fingers. "Gold and currency, baby. That's where it's all at."

Lars continued to humor her with self-deprecating comments and she enjoyed teasing him. Danielle shivered again, and he switched sides, taking her right hand into his left pocket.

"No ring on this finger either," he observed.

"Did you know that because I'm right handed, it doesn't fit very well over my finger? That's definitely not a one-size fits all ring."

"Convenient," he said, a tone of neutrality.

That was an awfully loaded word. "And too bad," she said, purposefully implying she might have worn it if it had. "But I will tell you, I just happened to pop into one of these jewelry stores and was rather appalled to learn how much that ring you purchased for me might have cost."

"Value is in the eye of the beholder." His comment was backed up with a brush of his fingers against hers.

"I do value you, Lars. A lot. And the ring. I mean, we're here, holding hands and walking like a normal couple, all the while knowing we aren't a couple. It's confusing…I'm confused…" she faltered. They reached a breezeway between two buildings and Lars' hand drew her to a stop.

"I'm only confused as to why I let you keep chocolate on your face this whole time."

"What?!" She exclaimed, trying to remove her right hand from his pocket to wipe it off. He gripped her tight, keeping it in place.

"Here, you'll never find it. Let me." She was unprepared for his lips to find the corner of her mouth instead of his finger, inhaling when he lingered, his tongue touching her lips. When he stopped the sensual caress, Danielle's hand was beneath the collar of his jacket, holding him tight.

"Do I have any more?" she murmured.

"Yes, but it's too cold for me to get your entire face wet." She giggled as he put his arm around her shoulders, turning her towards the train station. Her hand had naturally gone around his waist, and now dropped to the back pocket of his pants, under his jacket.

"As much as I could walk up and down for another hour, exploring dark alleys in this lovely town, you need to get inside."

They walked a block in silence, nearing the train station. "Um, did that count as two people who like kissing each other or are we more?"

He stopped, embracing her. "Let's just say we are like two climbers who were on the same sheet of ice, became separated by a big waterfall and then rappelled over a crevice or two. We slipped but, thanks to our relationship crampons, were saved, and now are on the ground together. Not a tragic fall in sight."

She waited just a moment to speak. "You could have just said yes, we are a couple."

Lars let out a loud burst of laughter. "There you go again…" He kissed the top of her head, the act so quick and natural, she wondered if it had even happened. *The after effects are telling me it was real.*

Danielle waited until they were near the edge of a building, pulled him to a stop and held his arms with both hands. "What is going on?" she asked, her half-smile quizzical. "I like this, but..." She searched his eyes, seeking help when his thumb stroked her cheek, causing her to shiver.

"The incident with Georgy affected me in the same way as you learning about the risks of sailboarding; it was a life-altering event, Danielle. I came to the conclusion we don't have time to waste, not anymore. My father had a stroke and that changed the course of our lives forever. You have no idea how much time I've thought about all the things we could have done but never did. Andre's death changed all of our lives, in yet another direction. Now Georgy. When do we stop pretending we always have tomorrow, when maybe we don't?"

Danielle had been looking deeply into his eyes, feeling his passion and experiencing the depth of his words.

"Now?" she suggested on a whisper.

He nodded. "Yes, now, if you are ready. I know I once said I can't make any more promises, and you asked me for a lifetime of tomorrows;

but that time is now. That means no more waiting for you or you me. All that's happened in the last three months is evidence that we are meant to be with one another Danielle, and we both know it." Before she could respond, he cupped her cheeks in her hands, the force of his conviction coming through his lips, reinforcing all he'd said. She was barely able to grip his jacket through the passion-driven kiss. When he finished, his eyes scanned her for a reaction.

"Am I right?"

Danielle put her hand to his cheek and nodded. The love she'd pushed down, set aside, denied and finally accepted was here again in her life, and it wasn't going away. "Yes, Lars. You've been right all along."

CHAPTER 44

Their kiss was broken by her trembling from the cold. Lars took her hand, walking briskly back to the train, holding tight. Lars looked positively smug on the way to the parking lot. Dominic would be by Lars' car, waiting. She certainly didn't want Dominic driving Lars to Layda's home, waiting outside, knowing or guessing what was going on inside. Even though her time with him had been limited to several encounters, it was disconcerting.

"Since you have a client dinner, why don't I come to your place?" she suggested, hoping Dominic would be back at his apartment by then.

"I'm not sure how long it will last, and you might already be in bed."

"So you would drive yourself?" she offered. Lars cocked his head slightly, as though it were an odd question, and it was. She spoke quickly. "If your dinner runs after ten, then don't worry. Georgy is being transferred home tomorrow and I want to be there to help."

They walked to her car, Lars bending to kiss her once she was inside, shutting the door behind her. She never saw Dominic, her nervous energy dissipating as she drove home. She called Layda, asking about Georgy and if the plans were still on to bring him home tomorrow.

"I'm sure they want him gone as much as he wants to leave."

"How about we shoot for noon for him to arrive at home? That way, I'm there to help and you and I can talk after we get him settled." Danielle would tell Layda in person that the strategy with Lars had worked, contributing to their renewed situation. That was a terrible phrase, but she didn't have a better description for their relationship.

Danielle was relaxing by the fire, a cup of hot chocolate at her lips when her cell phone rang. She glanced at the caller ID. It was never good news if Lani was calling on a Saturday night during prime dining.

Danielle dithered until the very last ring then answered.

"Hey, Danielle. Are you home?" she asked, skipping the greeting in her rush.

"No, I'm out of town. What's up?"

"I need a place to stay. Max evicted me." Danielle held the cup steady, on the edge of her lips.

"I can't believe it."

"Believe it," she said in a rush. "Worse, he's given me twenty-four hours, told me that the place is being sold by the new owners—"

"Wait, back-up. Slow down and walk me through each part." Lani exhaled, took a breath, forcing an even pace to her speech which periodically ramped back up into a near unintelligible garble. At the end, Danielle put down her cup, hearing the doorbell. She walked to the door and gestured Lars inside.

Putting the phone behind her back, she whispered, "You're early!" and kissed his cheek. "It's Lani in crisis."

He shook his head as Danielle sat back down on the couch.

"Lani, I'm not personally involved, okay, so you can't get mad if some of this information is wrong or out of date. Once again, don't shoot the messenger, okay?" Lani swore on her life, but told her to get on with it.

"The titles of several units were to be transferred into escrow, to be held by the investors, namely, Johanne and Dario. The agreement was to keep those in escrow for ninety-days, during which Max was to come up with some sort of plan to keep the restaurant afloat, and/or pay them back."

"Then why would Johanne and Dario kick me out?"

"I'm not sure they would, or are," replied Danielle. "And I can't even confirm that yours is one of the units in escrow."

Lani swore, a half-sob in her throat. "Do you think Max is lying about this as well?"

"Lani, I haven't spoken with Max in weeks. Don't you have any recourse for eviction? And what's going on with the restaurant?"

Lani broke into a full-fledged sob. "He fired me, Danielle. I don't have a job in my own restaurant."

"What?" she gasped, staring up at Lars, who stood above her, drink in hand. He sat down beside her, lifting one of her feet off the ground, removing the slipper.

"Today, after the last group of diners were served dinner. And Danielle," she choked, "he did it in front of the entire staff. I *started* that restaurant. The whole thing!"

At this, Danielle at least felt relief. She spoke calmly, hoping her tone would carry through to Lani. "That's not possible with the structure we had in place. The chef, you, could never be forced out. The only way to get out was to purchase your share, that way you were covered no matter way." The pause was awful. "Lani," she said in horror, "you didn't let him change the contract, did you?"

She sobbed again. "He said it was minor and that he was majority investor, paying for the paperwork…"

"And you didn't have an attorney read it?"

"Obviously not!" Lani exploded. Lars' eyes raised, hearing her explosion. Slowly, he moved the glass under his chin, the sign to cut it off.

Danielle didn't know if he meant the call, or the relationship with Lani in its entirety.

Probably both. A toxic personality literally permeates everything in its sphere.

"It sounds like you need a lawyer now, a really good one," said Danielle. She had no other words of advice to offer, and all those she'd given in the past had been ignored.

"Danielle, have you even heard anything I've said? If I had the money to do that, I would, so clearly I don't have money for an attorney."

"I thought you'd have money set aside for a rainy day. To answer your question, I'm not home and can't let you in, but it's irrelevant. My home is only two bedrooms, and I actually only have one bed."

"I'm okay with sharing, Danielle. Or I can sleep on the couch."

"Lani, my life is not conducive to that right now. Georgy gets home from the hospital tomorrow after a triple by-pass and I have Emma helping out with Monroe while I'm out. I'm really sorry," she said, feeling all the sweetness of a once cherished relationship gone sour.

Lani half-choked a response. "Me, too. But I can call Stephen. He lent me some money last month to cover the rent. Maybe I can crash on his couch."

"Lani...I—that's great he gave you money but isn't that a bit insensitive to his situation?"

"What? He's going to be a dad, not get married. It's not like he even really cares for Eva other than her being the mother of his child."

"Lani, what happens if things have changed with him and Eva?"

"Like what? He still loves me, Danielle. That will never change." Her words were nearly an echo of Lars', who had long maintained Lani's belief Stephen would never stop loving her.

There was nothing Danielle could say that wouldn't get her in trouble. "Good luck to you then."

"That's what Max predicted you would say. You know Danielle," continued Lani, "some people experience death and come out of it the better, but you have become more selfish."

"Was it selfish for me to give you the quarter million to start your business? Or are you suggesting that because you took your inflated ego, walked out on your marriage and the restaurant, leaving us all high and dry, I was selfish by not giving you yet more money? That's not selfish, that's intelligent."

"You bi—"

"Stop," Danielle interrupted. "You have the audacity to think Max was right about me, the same man who literally screwed you physically, then financially, the person who fired you and is now kicking you to the curb? Actually, the person who had it nailed was Lars, predicting you were going to lose it all a year ago. Congratulations, you met his expectations."

The line went dead, the adrenaline racing through Danielle's system still coursing as she put the phone down. Lars watched her, saying nothing.

"Actually..." she said to herself, picking the phone back up. She accessed the contacts and placed Lani on the Block setting.

Lars sipped his drink. "Have I ever been blocked?" She shifted to face him.

"Never."

"Not even during the worst of times?"

Danielle sunk back into the couch, the adrenaline now starting to ebb, the toxic after effects of the call dissipating. "Can I speak honestly?" she asked.

Lars smirked. "When have you not?"

"I don't think we ever had 'worst-of-times,' in the classical sense of the word. The worst was seeing you kiss another woman, but it wasn't like she was giving you a lap dance." Lars choked and she laughed before continuing. "Can we really look back at everything we experienced and say it wasn't worth it? Or that there were any 'worst times' per se?"

Lars put down his glass, slipping his shoes off at the same time.

"The worst part for me was you being with Dominic, and not being able to do or say anything about it. At least with Margaret, you saw all that there was." Danielle's face and gut froze. She felt the sickening tingling of heat in her face, moving down her chest as he stared at her, his eyes going tender, betraying all he knew. "Not that I blame you, given the circumstances. You have every right to be with anyone you wanted, my driver and bodyguard included."

Still dumbfounded, she embraced honesty, the trait she'd just espoused. "Yes, I did."

"What I want to know is why you stopped, so abruptly?"

She had no choice but to answer his question in a way that told him the background. "One night I left work and he politely offered to take me home. On the way, a car almost hit us. I lost it, literally. It was a trigger like the kind where I saw my life flash before my eyes." His eyebrows deepened in concern. "We were unhurt, but I was hysterical and couldn't go home. The only place was his house."

"Logical."

Danielle nodded. "He was very professional, talking me through PTSD and the come down phases. I then learned about his background and honestly, it helped. But Lars, I have to be clear on one thing. It was me who instigated things, not him." She exhaled, continuing. "It wasn't until the third time we were together that he started a very business-like conversation." Danielle stopped, chuckling. "You would have been proud of him. The net was there was no future for us, though he was okay to continue if I wanted to when convenient, but…" she shrugged.

"It's not you," he concluded.

Danielle clasped her hands on her lap. "The therapist wanted me to go out, be vulnerable, experience men and potential heartbreak. All of it. I got three out of the four on the list done. Adding the last was overkill."

Lars' jaw clenched, his chin down, the manner strikingly masculine. "I didn't mean to invade your privacy," he said, sounding apologetic. "It was a bi-product of Dominic and me having a phone application that allows us to track the other person, standard operating procedure for client and bodyguard." She thought through the events. That meant when they dropped Lars off, he would have seen she didn't go directly home, but to Dominic's.

It doesn't matter now, she told herself. The man in front of her is what's important.

"Why aren't you more upset?" she asked Lars, a tad unsettled that if he truly cared for her, his emotions would have risen up, just as hers had when seeing him with Margaret.

"I took consolation in the fact that your numbers remained down when you saw him, but after we spent time together, they shot right up." She thought through the sequence of events. He was absolutely right. "Combine that with knowing the Mettleren account is going to be taken out from under you, and yet your trading continued to be superior…that made more of a statement than any words you could have said."

Danielle drew her legs to her chest, hugging them tight, feeling a prickle of hope spreading like a vine into her extremities. "Anything else?" she asked.

"No more now." He dropped his legs to the floor, sliding one arm under her knees and the other around her back. In a single motion he picked her up, and held her against his chest. "It's my turn."

Lars had never spoken with such authority to her, the directness the equivalent to a shot of steroids. He entered her bedroom not bothering to turn on the lights. In the torrent of passion that followed, Danielle's cries of pleasure matched the longing she'd felt for him, all that had never gone away, now increasing with each movement as she allowed them to flow freely.

In the breathless aftermath, Danielle traced her fingers down the middle of Lars' back, the lean, connective muscles rippling to his shoulders. His body was so different from Dominic, and she reflected on her one-time opinion of Dominic; that he'd been her most gratifying intimate experience.

I was completely wrong. Muscles and strength didn't compare to respect and friendship. And no amount of temporarily comforting warm skin left the heat within her of deep, soul-touching love.

CHAPTER 45

"Do you still love me?" Lars asked quietly, the warmth of his breath moving through her hair. She caressed his arm, his body parallel hers as they lay on their sides.

"I thought my display of passion would have answered that," she answered. With a laugh she rolled over, pressing her skin against his, talking into his neck, kissing between words. "I know, always trying to be serious and I ruin the moment." She stopped talking, holding him as though he were her lifeline. "But Lars," she continued, the depth of her emotion making her subdued. "Nothing I felt for you ever went away. Stephen knew that, so did Layda and Georgy. I'm not very good at hiding my feelings."

"No, you aren't."

She kissed his chest. "Did you mind?"

"Anger is usually a sign of caring. You were pretty angry at the office."

"That was mostly at Margaret," she clarified. "But yes, you were an indirect recipient. P.S. I'm still upset about the sailboarding-ice climbing statistics, but I have fallen in love with the sport."

Lars moved the hair away from her forehead with his lips. "Do you realize we now have that in common? You love it, on your own, without my influence."

"Yeah," she said quietly. "You know what I realized about my beloved sport? It was and is exclusively singular. It fit my lifestyle and personality for that period of my life." She, traced his jawline with her fingers. "My life at that time, with my mom dying and then taking care of my dad full-time was so mentally exhausting, it was my only release. Now…here…I like being with people. I don't have the same stresses but I also have more outlets. Playing piano in a jazz club wasn't something I'd ever have contemplated before, and it's really been fun and invigorating." Lars fingertips moved down her skin, cresting over her hips, down to her thighs and back up. "So many changes, and soon we will have yet another."

His fingers. "Why do you say that?"

"Because I will be leaving MRD."

"You don't have to leave because we are dating. You know the rules."

She silently laughed. "How could I ever forget? Lars, Margaret's actions are wrong on multiple levels. With her scorched Earth policy, the only aspect within my control at the office is what I do, or do not do. It has to do with pride and my sense of self-respect."

He draped her leg across his thigh, holding her tight. "And rightly justified."

"You're not going to ask where I'm going after MRD?"

"No. I don't want to know when or where."

"So you can look Margaret and Noel in the eye." He hummed an affirmation. "The thing I'm not looking forward to is that she's going to respond in some public fashion, maximizing the chance to humiliate the single, American woman." Then another notion occurred to her. "Do you have some special timing in mind for my departure?"

"Hmmm. Let me just say there are optimal and sub-optimal times to leave the firm."

"Are you going to tell Noel about us again, or keep it quiet?"

"This time around, I was going to skip right over Noel and go public, unless you are opposed to the idea."

"Whew," she exhaled. "That's commitment." He hummed, his lips forming a smile against her skin. "Are you going to suffer any adverse consequences of that?"

"Danielle, did you ever wonder why Margaret is giving all the accounts to Jacob, not Georgiana?"

"Because his returns are higher."

"Actually, Georgiana is only about seven points behind him, hardly enough to warrant the amount Margaret has gifted him."

"Are you suggesting they are sleeping together?"

Lars chuckled at her shock. "My kiss to her cheek was apparently nothing to Jacob's ability in bed."

Two things occurred at once, both revealing. "Are you telling me you never slept with her, and that she, sort-of, dumped you for Jacob?"

Lars pulled her on top of him, holding her hair back from her face, his thumbs near her lips, the grip hard. "Yes, and sort of. The fact is that the gravity of what I was starting to engage in hit me in the face when I saw you, and your look of…disappointment. Danielle, it was probably the single worst look I've ever received. And such sadness. No matter how we ended, I never meant to inflict that kind of pain on you." He stopped, kissing her tenderly. "So, that was it for me. She definitely expected more, but the end was immediate, and abrupt. She wasn't very happy with me then, and of course, seeing you there, she connected the dots."

"Hurt pride creates a vengeful person."

"Indeed. But taking the big picture view, if the worst thing to happen is Margaret beds half the firm, let her. My bigger concern is how you are treated, actually."

"Me?" she questioned. "I'll be fine. What else can she do? Nothing. Going back to the timing thing, I've always thought natural transition times are before or after our break in August."

"I agree," he responded in his managing director voice. "But you never know what's going to occur between now and then. Best to be prepared for all possibilities."

Danielle lowered down to his face, teasing Lars with kisses short and sensual, playful and passionate.

"I love you, Lars. All of me." Her kisses turned deeper and longer, the grip on her hips slowing, deepening, causing her breath to turn shallow. She arched, gripping and releasing more of herself to him, and when he thrust up intensely, she cried out. Their physical selves were all that was their relationship had been, the ups and downs, hurts and struggles. Now, they were feeling the elation of celebrating overcoming all the obstacles they'd faced; and they were doing it together.

The following morning, she rose early, making Lars a simple breakfast of oatmeal, sausage and fried eggs. He came into the kitchen with a towel wrapped around him, which she wanted to immediately remove, and apologized for not doing so. She held the frying pan with her left hand, the spatula in the right.

"Trust me, I would stay in the bedroom with you all day, but I need to leave in an hour. We are transferring Georgy from the hospital, and I need to be available to help Layda and watch Monroe."

"Why don't I come help? Another set of hands can only benefit the process."

MEANT TO BE

"You don't have to do that."

"What would you say if I start to act like your....dare I say it...*boyfriend* while out in public? Do *boyfriend* type of things?"

Danielle laughed at his teasing, falling deeper into her ocean of love. "What do boyfriends do?"

He moved next to her and cupped her face in his hands. "I get to help my future father-in-law with coming home." Danielle's heart paused. "It's time, don't you think?"

Danielle's head was nodding before she said the words. "I do."

His dark, chestnut eyes were full of adoration as he brushed his nose against hers, drawing her in with as much intoxicating strength as he'd had when they first met.

"You gave me the answer before I asked, but I should make it formal. Danielle, will you marry me?"

Lars, in his towel, bare chested, his wet hair a sexy mop, standing in the kitchen. It was the most unorthodox setting for a proposal she could have dreamed, and the most romantic imaginable.

Her cheeks lifted high with an uncontainable smile. She nodded first, and as her mouth opened on the word yes, Lars' covered her lips, inhaling all the love she had, making it a part of him.

No. He's had a part of me with him since the very beginning. Now, it was time for the rest of the world to know.

CHAPTER 46

Over breakfast, Lars told Danielle he'd like to speak with Georgy and Layda. "Why the look?"

"It's part skepticism, disbelief and elation, because that's what I'm feeling."

"Breath in," he said, happy and proud. "In the meantime, I was and am serious about helping tomorrow. For the present, it will be done under the guise of being a good family friend."

"I'd suggest you ask Layda. And assuming she says yes, are you going to start driving yourself, or will this torture Dominic to drive you and know what's going on between us?"

Lars lifted a glass of orange juice, looking at her over the rim. "I don't want to completely hurt your feelings, Danielle, but while you are beautiful and intelligent, you are not much more than a blip on Dominic's life. He won't be with me much longer."

Danielle scoured his face. "You're firing him?"

"Not at all. He's leaving at the end of April of his own accord." When Danielle started to apologize for causing a rift between them, he stopped her. "It has nothing to do with you. He's always wanted to open his own training, self-defense and wellness studio, a sort of all-in-one tailored to his unique skill sets. I knew about this four months ago, and have been on the search for a replacement ever since. His parents live in Bern, which is where he'll relocate." Danielle was dumbfounded, and relieved. "It's not that easy finding a man who can protect you, but won't be attracted to your wife at the same time."

She savored the word, but not the implication. "Do you think I would ever step out on you?"

"It's not you I'm worried about. It's the other person being trustworthy. I've not always had that benefit, if you recall." She did, knowing that not all chauffeurs kept their client's private life private.

Danielle dipped her head shyly. "I really liked how you said that, *your wife*." Lars gave her a lottery-winning smile.

"You already do mom really well."

Danielle's swollen heart felt pressed against her ribs.

With the worry of Dominic no longer on her mind, she greeted him without issue when he arrived with Lars.

"More man-power if we need to move beds around," Dominic told her when he emerged from the car in jeans and a turtleneck. He gave her a wink and smile, but it wasn't leering or disrespectful. In fact, it struck her as the opposite, as though he appreciated her ability to accept and appreciate what they'd shared and move on with her life.

Danielle was glad both men were present, because Layda wanted the heavy furniture in the master bedroom rearranged. For the ease of Georgy's work, they relocated a cabinet, desk and chair from the study downstairs to the sitting area beside the bed.

It took less than an hour for the furniture to be moved and arranged to Layda's liking.

"Can we feed you for your services?" asked Layda, including Dominic in her offer.

"Thank you, ma'am, but no," said Dominic. "I'll wait in the car."

Danielle helped Layda pull out the fresh fruits and vegetables from the fridge, noting that the meats were going to be for the other men, not her husband. "Spinach and beans for you," she lovingly told Georgy. As they prepared the food, she periodically heard Lars or Georgy. The words were muffled, but Georgy's booming laughed vibrated the walls.

"They've always gotten along so well," Layda said, tossing the salad.

"How long have they known each other? Five, ten years?"

"Longer," she answered. "Since before Lars left for New York. He was a trader and initially met Georgy at a financial conference in Geneva. They hit it off, and at the end of two days, half the Mettleren clan had met Lars, not that he got the business right away. He had to earn that, and earn it he did."

Danielle could envision a younger, aggressive Lars, lean and elegant in his suits, smoothly introducing himself, maneuvering around a room, meeting the movers and shakers.

"Have the years changed him?" she wondered.

"Now he's a bit more patient, or perhaps relaxed, but I think that's what a certain amount of success does to men. They don't have the chip on their shoulder of constantly having to prove themselves to others."

That, and him being ten years older, was probably why Lars was so even-keeled about Andre, and why, even with Dominic, Lars accepted that she'd been intimate with another man. He was able to completely separate the emotional and physical interactions.

"He was such a strength to me the morning of Georgy's attack. I just…" Layda stopped talking, breathing evenly until she regained her composure. "So firm and stable, all that I wasn't. Then he found you and took care of us all." It was good to be with a respected man. "Did you invite him here today?"

"He offered, then insisted, once he learned what I was doing."

"Ever the gentleman."

When the plates were on the table, Danielle went into the living room, seeing Lars on the couch holding Monroe.

"Where did she come from?" Danielle asked, perplexed.

Lars held the little girl who yawned. "She was squawking upstairs so I went to get her."

Danielle took Georgy's arm, ignoring his grumbling when Lars walked on the other side, Monroe holding him tightly, her little arms around his neck.

"Easy and paced, Georgy," Danielle counseled. "If you don't listen, I have my enforcer here."

Georgy grumbled a retort that made Lars laugh, but she didn't know the translation for what he'd said. At the table, Lars murmured he'd tell her later.

In the small nook off the kitchen, Georgy sat at one end and Layda across from him. Lars sat to her left, with Monroe between them at the corner in the highchair. Georgy began by raising his water in a toast to Lars. Lars modestly accepted the comment, turning the subject towards the rehabilitation regime prescribed by the physician. The three adults laughed at Georgy's gripes about going to the center, which turned to elation when Lars suggested converting one of the spare bedrooms upstairs to a gym.

"You aren't lacking in rooms in this house. Why not?"

Georgy stared at Lars for a moment, pointing his fork. "I'll do that."

"Oh, Georgy," cried Layda, laughing. "Next you'll be putting a lap pool in the backyard."

Georgy looked at her, then Lars. "Is that possible?" Before Lars answered, Layda slapped his arm with her napkin.

"I take it back, Lars," started Layda, her mock scolding tone obvious. "I'm not happy you're here at all. Look what you've started!"

Lars' full bellied laughter affected Monroe as well as herself. The little girl's eyes were fixed on the man to her left as she ate, her fascination with him keeping her attention. Danielle wondered if Monroe remembered Lars from previous interactions. She must, Danielle determined. Monroe hadn't shied away from him, behavior she'd previously exhibited.

Little by little, thought Danielle.

The hour-long meal ended with a desert of sorbet instead of one of Danielle's homemade pies that Layda kept in the fridge at all times.

"It will be my reward instead of my right," declared Georgy.

"I'll keep you to that," threatened Layda, giving him a kiss on the cheek. Lars announced it was time for him to get going, thanking Layda for the food and wishing Georgy fast healing.

"We'll see you next weekend, then?" Georgy asked Lars.

"We were going to have a dinner after my ice climbing competition," explained Danielle, "but with Georgy I'm probably not even going to go. Family here is more important."

"You will too, go," growled Georgy, speaking over Layda, who insisted she not change her schedule. Danielle looked between the two as Lars folded his arms.

"It appears you will be rock climbing," concluded Lars.

"Are you all serious?" Danielle questioned. The three nodded their heads, giving her a taste of they'd been putting Georgy through.

Lars turned from her. "Layda, what were you planning?"

"We were going to get bundled up, including Monroe and head to Zermatt, watch her compete then spend the night at our home," Layda explained. "Danielle, are you sure you won't be nervous with us all there?"

Danielle decided to tease Lars, just a little. "I do recall Lars saying ice climbing is an individual sport, and that one gets nervous with observers. Should I be worried?"

He caught the reference immediately. "Yes, but that was for people who weren't wanted in the first place. That said, let's not make a big deal at your home. The last thing you need is a lot of work. Since I'm literally right down the road from you, I'll have it catered and manage the cleanup. My only request is Danielle play a song or two on piano. Deal?"

It was her turn to grin.

Danielle looked at Layda and Georgy for confirmation, then back to Lars.

"Deal."

CHAPTER 47

Danielle walked Lars to the front door after the meal finished.

"Do you think they are getting the hint?"

Lars smiled. "A man doesn't come over to help move furniture without a motivation."

"What about just being a nice guy?"

Lars brushed her face with his lips. "A nice guy can write a check to cover a mover. A man in love shows up and lifts the furniture. See you tonight."

"I'm playing," she reminded him.

"I know. That's where I'll be able to see you."

Georgy was sipping a chamomile tea when she returned to the kitchen. "This tastes terrible," he pronounced, lifting the cup.

"Then add a bit of sugar, like a good dad should do." Danielle kissed his head, wrapping both arms around him, unexpectedly tearing up. "I love you so much. Don't you ever, *ever* do that again, okay?" Georgy nodded in reply.

"Now," she said, releasing him and sitting down. "Are we really all going up to Zermatt next weekend?"

"I'm serious about seeing you, yes," said Georgy. Layda nodded, placing her hand on his forearm. "Are you trying to get out of this so Lars won't come?"

"No, that's not it at all. That was an inside joke. When he was engaged, he called me for advice—I know. It shocked me too," she laughed, seeing their faces. "He asked me how to disinvite his friend, who I later learned was his fiancé. I asked if her presence made him uncomfortable, and he'd replied it was a focused, dedicated sport requiring concentration."

"Danielle, I think Lars is very much where he was in January, when you refused to see him." Layda was contemplative, worry and compassion making her voice gentle.

"Yes..." she said, unsure how, or if to proceed. "Layda, I believe this proves you were spot on, about me getting out there, living life for the past three months. Oh!" she stopped abruptly. "You. Are. Never. Going to believe what has happened," she said, pronouncing her words precisely. Layda and Georgy shared a concerned look.

"No," she rushed to allay their fears. "It doesn't have to do with Lars, but Lani." When she finished telling the saga, she shook her head. "Thinking about next weekend made me jump to my birthday, and I thought you might be tempted to ask Lani to come up for dinner."

"No chance of that, is there?"

Danielle's burst of laughter set Georgy chuckling as well. "Do you think I did the right thing?"

"You did the only thing," Georgy answered firmly. "Lars was right then and it proved out."

Layda shook her head, her lips pressed firmly together in disappointment. "To think Lani would bring up Max, after all he's done to her, and is still doing. But I am sorry you have lost your only girlfriend. That's a shame."

"My life is pretty full at the moment, and women take a lot of energy."

"Now men, on the other hand, take quite a bit less." Georgy waited until Layda and Danielle were staring at him. "Now, my dear, back to Lars. Update us please on the situation at work. I want to know what else I've missed."

"In the two days since I learned your accounts will be taken away, not much, other than Lars telling me Margaret is sleeping with Jacob, and that probably answers why he has, and will be receiving, all your accounts."

"Indeed," was all Georgy said. Layda changed the topic to Georgy's health, suggesting a nap. Danielle agreed, and left shortly afterward.

She went home, changed and arrived at the jazz club a quarter before six. Seeing Benny at the bar was a wonderful surprise. "Special occasion?" she asked Benny after kisses had been exchanged.

"Just observing," he drawled, lifting a snifter, directing it to her, "along with the rest of the men in this crowd."

She squeezed him with delight. "I'm so glad you're here."

Once she'd placed her things in Robin's office, she glanced around the bar. No sign of Lars. Well, perhaps something came up, or he'd arrive later. It was a mostly full house, three tables in the back still open, but the bar was full and the line at the door forming.

"Welcome this Sunday night," she began, seeing the bowl on the piano already had a few requests. She paused to look through the song titles and denominations, holding up the winning request.

"I'm going to announce this now," her tone threatening. "I'm only going to be playing *Crazy* once this evening, and it's now. So I hope the requester enjoys it, and for the rest of you, don't request it again or it will in fact, drive the audience over the edge."

Danielle sang and the heat rose as the club filled to capacity. The usual favorites were requested, the amounts varied and in between requests, Danielle played Gershwin and Goloka, past and present, mixing it up.

At the break, she saw Lars standing at the end of the bar beside Benny who sat at the counter. She joined them, sliding her hand around Lars' waist, kissing him a welcome.

"I guess that says it all," quipped Benny.

She and Lars laughed, his hand dropping an inch from her waist. It was dark and they were at the corner, but it wouldn't have mattered to her if they were standing in the middle of the room. She agreed with Benny-*finally*.

"When did you get there?" she asked Lars.

"I've been here the entire time," he replied. "Keeping quiet allowed me to see the reactions of the crowd, which was nearly as enjoyable as watching you."

"Cheers to that," added Benny, winking at them both.

Once Leon passed her a club soda, she drank as Lars and Benny discussed the upcoming events for MRD, the annual August event at St. Moritz being one.

"What are you doing next Saturday night?" Lars asked Benny. Danielle pinched his waist, guessing his intent.

"Working."

Lars leaned to her ear, the breath tickling her skin. "That does it. You're playing at your own party."

The break over, Danielle resumed playing, the hour sped by as Lars decided to request his favorites about every other song, bidding up the price. Six songs in, she asked Benny to join her. He promptly nudged her off the bench.

"For y'alls benefit, she slipped ice climbing two weeks ago, and missed playing as she nursed her wrist back to condition. Should you even be playing now?" he asked, cocking his head. "You sing. I'll play."

Danielle gamely agreed, taking the mic with her left hand around her lower back, raising her middle finger. Benny chuckled wickedly, as did a few of the patrons in the front row who observed her gesture.

On cue, Danielle sang, feeling the soul of Etta James. Her love life had come full circle, again, and it felt right.

After the show ended, Danielle gave Benny a hug, who said he was going to remain on stage for another half an hour.

"Great," she said with a kiss. When she saw Robin, she told him to give all the money to Benny for that night. "He gave me half a night off, he deserves it."

Danielle had her coat and purse on when she looped her arm through Lars, thrilled to finally feel like a couple in the traditional sense of the word. She nodded to Leon with a big smile, and he gave the man-version of approval.

"I've been thinking about Layda and Georgy," she began when they were on the street. "I hypothesize that decorum in your social circles means it would look bad to announce an engagement for a while. Is that true?"

"Unfortunately, yes. It's not been a year, and it would come across as very insensitive to the family, which we don't want."

Danielle drew him close. "Then we can be super discrete and keep it to ourselves as well as Layda and Georgy. That way, if Layda wants to plan, she feels like she has adequate time." She was already giddy at the thought of wearing the ring on the appropriate finger. "Just get ready for my numbers to go through the roof."

CHAPTER 48

Monday morning, Danielle arrived at the office with an air of suppressed excitement, her left hand a little heavier than it had been the day before. Both ring and watch were prominently on display, her three-quarter sleeved St. John knit showing off the pieces. She couldn't wait to sit in front of Johanne, and see how long it would take for him to notice, give a jubilant shriek of happiness at the forthcoming numbers sure to exceed her previous record.

Johanne's office was dark and empty as she passed, delaying her moment. With a zeal created from pure excitement, she traded for three hours, utilizing the research from the evening before. After Lars left, she'd worked until midnight, unable to sleep. How could she? Her future now included him, her daughter, and her family of Georgy and Layda.

It was exhilarating.

Ten minutes before the Monday team meeting, Danielle shut off her system and paid a visit to Johanne, shutting the door behind her. He was distracted, briefly glancing up until she sat down.

"Ready for the meeting?" Danielle asked.

"No, actually I'm behind on some paperwork for my boss." He reached over, grabbing paper from the printer, obviously expecting her to leave. "Yes?"

"Have you checked my numbers for today?"

"Danielle, I'm sorry, but of all the times to be coy, which I usually appreciate, this is not helpful. Margaret is going to be sharing yet more news today, and even I'm not sure of all that's coming down the pipe. What's up?"

"This." Danielle raised her left hand up, palm facing her. His focus went from her eyes to her hand, then he caught the wiggle of her fourth finger. "Normally you're so quick to catch these things," she teased. "That's why I wanted you to check the numbers."

Johanne glanced at the clock above her head, then turned to his computer, pulled up the trading screen and cursed. He shook his head, half-grimace, half-smile. "And you couldn't have done this before, when we really needed your numbers to be up?"

She shrugged. "Can't rush these things."

"Well, since I've seen that ring before, I'll assume you're not engaged but back on. I'll expect your numbers to be a lot higher when that happens." Danielle held herself very still, eyes boring in to his. Johanne leaned forward, mouth dropping open. "Is that…?"

She nodded, lips wide with a smile. "It's a lovely placeholder until I get the real thing, given by the same man who asked me to marry him, and I said yes. The short story is that he never went there with Margaret, and all that we have gone through has brought us to the place we were before—and beyond."

She was surprised by Johanne's sober expression. "This is going to be great for numbers, but…it's not going to help."

"Johanne, if you are worried about Margaret, don't be. I've moved so far beyond her and this place it's not even funny."

He frowned. "It's not that. It's a whole lot of things that are going down the drain, and your bright spot is the bubble floating up from the mess in the sink." His horrible analogy made her laugh.

"Speaking of stinking utensils in the sink, I learned this weekend one reason I was required to train Jacob, and why he's gotten my accounts. She slept with Jacob when she couldn't have Lars." Johanne's face when black. "True story."

"No wonder…" he muttered, pulling his lips under his teeth. A rap at the door was followed by Glenda poking her head in, reminding them of the time. Danielle stood, touching Johanne's arm when he came around the desk.

"Look at it this way. Everything is temporary. What else can she do?"

He gave her a look of naivete. "You have no idea."

They entered the conference room together, he taking the far side on the corner, nearest the door, and she across from him, her back to the lake. Georgiana greeted her, and Danielle pulled out a chair for her. As Margaret was late, the group made small talk. Danielle leaned closer to Georgiana. "Have you started seeing anyone since we spoke about meeting people?" Georgiana's shook her head no. "Good. I have a wonderful friend who I think you'd like."

"Really?"

Danielle nodded. "I'll tell you about him later." They swapped cell phone numbers just as Margaret entered, subduing the mood. As Margaret spoke, Danielle glanced around the table, making eye contact with Jacob, then noticed Ulrich to his right. Lars wasn't present; perhaps that was why Ulrich was attending, the presiding representative from the group of partners.

Someone to keep Margaret in line, if that was even possible.

"We are continuing with the evolution of the firm," Margaret started. "Both the corporate and individual trading will be affected, as well as commodities." A look to Johanne confirmed he knew what was going to be said, but unlike Ulrich's detached expression, Johanne's jaw was tight and eyes overly focused behind his glasses.

"Firstly, all the gold held by Johanne will move to Jacob. Georgiana will trade currency under Johanne. Also, all the Mettleren accounts will also be transferred from Danielle, split between Jacob and to a lesser degree, Georgiana."

Margaret gave no time for questions or comments. In a single decision, Margaret had taken away billions of dollars from Danielle and Johanne's management and eliminated hundreds of thousands of dollars in overrides for himself and staff.

She was nearly back where she started, two years prior.

Danielle didn't express any emotion whatsoever. She was going to excel until the day she walked out the door.

As Margaret continued to drone on, Danielle was daydreaming about wedding dresses, honeymoon venues and Monroe wearing a beautiful, miniature white replica when she felt her cell phone buzzing. It buzzed again, stopped, then buzzed again. As subtly as she could, she pulled it out, under the table, looking down.

Danielle collected her things and stood, looking at Johanne, who was still her manager. "Gotta go," she said, under her breath. He raised his eyebrows, but nodded.

"Excuse me, Danielle. You're leaving?"

"Yes, Margaret. A personal matter to take care of. Johanne can brief me on anything else I miss."

Margaret leaned forward. "This is a mandatory meeting, required by all traders."

"Understood. But I have a personal matter that is urgent and must be attended to. I hope you'll understand."

Danielle paused long enough for Margaret to answer her, and when she didn't, Danielle nodded to Ulrich, who inclined his head.

"Ulrich, I believe our employment contracts stipulate traders are required to attend all mandatory meetings," Margaret said.

"Correct, although exceptions have always been made for personal matters."

"Where life and death are hanging in the balance," Margaret said, sounding awfully like the paperwork. "Danielle, is this a matter of life and death?"

"Unclear at this moment. It's very significant however."

"Danielle, during your tenure here, your life has been riddled with personal matters that have caused great disruption to the clients and the firm. The management has been overly lenient with you, in my opinion, but you will not find me so. If you cannot provide a reason for leaving us during this important discussion, then you might find yourself out of a job upon your return."

Danielle held her eye, not bothering to look at Ulrich or Johanne. This was all about her and Margaret.

"You do what you have to do," Danielle said evenly. She walked out, told Glenda she had a personal matter and left, the hallways of the office quiet as the large, glass front doors opened and shut behind her.

Ten minutes later, she was at Stars & Stripes. "She still here?" Danielle asked Stephen. "How bad?"

"Drunk is drunk," he replied gravely.

Danielle looked around the dining area. The first lunch patrons were already seated, the bar counter half-full. "I'm sorry you have to be the one to do this Stephen, but you have to call the police. She doesn't listen to anyone when she's been drinking and might just lose it when she sees me."

He nodded once, turning his back to the floor as he placed the phone call. Danielle's pulse quickened with each step towards the kitchen. The servers emerging from the kitchen with plates looked worried, but nodded with relief as she passed by.

"Ivan," Danielle called, seeing him by the drink counter. "What's going on?"

"She's raving, Bella. Saying it's her kitchen, Renaldo has no right to be there, it's hers and she wants it back." Danielle glanced over his shoulder. She recognized Lani's voice, but couldn't understand her words. "Keep doing what you're doing. I'll handle this."

When Danielle entered the kitchen, Lani's back was towards her. Her right hand was in the air, gesturing as she told Renaldo what he was doing wrong. The hollandaise on the eggs benedict had too much lemon and not enough cayenne pepper. "You need to butter the muffins, not leave them plain…"

Renaldo nodded his head as he continued to work and quietly direct the chefs around him to prepare the dishes. Renaldo placed a grilled cauliflower on a plate, handing it to an assistant when Lani intercepted it.

"No—no!" Lani interrupted, "you need to do it thissss way."

Danielle walked over, put her hand on Lani's forearm and held it firmly. "You will proceed as Renaldo directed," Danielle told the server. "Lani, stop."

Lani seemed stunned, her eyes glassy, taking a moment to digest that she was being told what to do.

"This is my kitchen and you have nooothing to do with it," she said loudly. Danielle gripped her arm harder.

"He has customers to feed, and you started the restaurant to feed customers, right?"

"Don't you *dare* talk to me that wayyy," she hissed. Danielle maneuvered herself between the chef and Lani. She moved closer to Lani, requiring her to back up. "Are you pushing me?" Lani demanded. "I'll sue you for threatening me and, and… intimidation," she finally got out.

Danielle nodded, knowing her words were going to be useless, but said them anyway.

"Lani, you are not an owner of this company, and you are trespassing on private premises. Further, you are in violation of health and safety rules, which could result in a large fine."

"Good!" she yelled. "You deserve it, kicking me out of my own kitchen."

"Which you left voluntarily," Danielle reminded her, taking another step forward, her intent to guide Lani to the back-entry door.

"I started thissss," she yelled, her voice echoing down the hall. "What are you going to do?" Lani demanded. "You can't throw me out of here…"

Danielle nodded her head, continuing to force her through the kitchen. She glanced over Lani's head to a server who came near. "Have Stephen bring them to the back door," Danielle murmured. "Lani, you had a good run here. Your time was special, and yes, you helped us create a wonderful restaurant," she went on, hoping flattery would calm her down, each time taking a step forward. "But it's over for you now. Renaldo is the chef, and he needs to make food for the diners, don't you agree?"

"They are my diners!" she insisted, pounding her chest. "My work area! I helped design it!"

"Yes, you did," Danielle affirmed. "We all helped out, and you did a fantastic job."

"And Ivan," she pointed when he came in the kitchen. "Me! I'm the one that interviewed him. He wouldn't even be here if it weren't for me." Ivan picked up a plate, and left, firing Lani up more. "And he won't even talk to me. This is mine, Danielle! Mine!"

They were two steps from the door when it opened. Two police officers appeared, Stephen beside them. "Not any more, Lani," Danielle said quietly. Lani looked around her as the officers took either arm. She looked up at Stephen, betrayal and confusion in her eyes. "You're trespassing," Stephen said to her in English. He wasn't unkind; he was civil, which was far more than Lani was being. The next words were in German; Danielle could understand them, Lani could not.

"She'll be held at the station where we'll file a report," said one officer. "If you want to press charges, an owner needs to come down. Otherwise, she'll be held overnight for drunk and disorderly conduct and not released until she pays the fine associated with the charge."

"What'd they say?" slurred Lani. Stephen didn't respond. Lani craned over her shoulder, looking at Danielle, imploring her to answer.

"You're being arrested, Lani." Danielle's friend started sobbing, no longer resisting the officers who escorted her out of the kitchen.

Stephen told the waitstaff and kitchen workers he appreciated their poise and grace under the circumstances, and asked they keep it a private matter. "Lani will be mortified when she sobers up, and this will only add to her pain. I'd ask us all to remember her contributions with pride, because she helped lay the foundation for what we have." Those assembled nodded in agreement. Stephen looked to her. "Do you have anything to add?"

"Only my statement of gratitude for all you have done. Let's keep making this restaurant awesome."

"Yeah! Bella," cheered Ivan, who started clapping. The others joined in, and Stephen raised his hand.

"I do have one final thing," Stephen added. "I was going to wait until this weekend, when the announcements goes out, but I want you all to know I'm getting married and you all are invited to the wedding."

The clapping turned to spontaneous cheers, Danielle giving Stephen a massive hug. As the others took turns congratulating him, she said goodbye, telling him they'd catch up later.

"I'll still probably give her some money to get her back on her feet," murmured Stephen.

"Only if you clear it with Eva, promise?"

"Yes, sister of mine."

Danielle kissed him on the cheek and took a cab back to the office. An unreal day, and it wasn't even noon. When she arrived at the front doors, she paused, feeling a hunger pang. She took a right and walked a block to a noodle shop. She stood at the bar eating, thinking about Lani. Stephen giving her money was downright saintly, but that had to stop. He had bigger priorities, like supporting a wife and family. Lani was completely employable, and with her reputation she could find a job anywhere. In fact, Max firing her was probably a blessing, because it might insulate her from lawsuits down the road. Regarding Margaret, Danielle felt bad for Johanne, who'd probably taken the brunt of Danielle's walk out, but Margaret couldn't hurt him more than she already had. Although Ulrich was in the room, and he was a pillar in that organization, he too might step in if Margaret got crazy.

She already has. If that had occurred in the states, a mutiny would already have occurred in the ranks, but here, people were so downright polite, they'd probably just stage a sit-in at their desks, boycotting the coffee.

Danielle finished her meal, taking her time on the way back. Work was going to be there for her whether or not it was a positive environment. She only had another few months, and after what she'd endured so far, she could handle that.

CHAPTER 49

Danielle walked through the glass double doors and was stopped by security.

"I'm sorry Ms. Grant, you must wait here. Hold please," he requested, putting out his hand. Danielle glanced at the receptionist, who called for Jacqueline Layder, the head of human resources. In the minute it took her to arrive, Danielle had already processed what had occurred. Margaret had called her bluff, letting her go.

Jacqueline arrived with Ulrich by her side.

"Will you please join us in the front conference room?" Ulrich requested. Danielle nodded, following them in, watching with a bit of humor as the security guard stood outside. For a moment, she visualized herself running down the hall, willy-nilly, like the raving lunatic Lani had been the hour before. Danielle subtly removed her cellphone from her purse, holding it in her hand. As they sat opposite her, she folded her hands on her lap, under the table, turning on the voice recorder.

"We are regretfully taking this action at Margaret's request," Ulrich began. "Lars was just informed, as was Noel. I'd like to reiterate that this was, and is, exclusively Margaret's decision, as she oversees human resources, which includes the hiring and firing of individuals." He then gave her his profuse thanks for all she'd done for the firm.

Danielle nodded, analyzing the man. He used words judiciously and for a purpose. To reinforce this was all Margaret's doing meant he and Jacqueline were following instructions, pure and simple.

Ulrich turned to Jacqueline, who went over the policy regarding infractions and insubordination. Danielle could tell that Jacqueline, who Danielle respected and liked, was sure MRD's position was bullet-proof, because Margaret was working within the letter of the law.

"Non, life-threatening reasons for leaving the firm, are, unfortunately, not covered," Jacqueline said to her. "And therefore, your leaving during a meeting where your superior requested you stay is insubordination, and therefore, grounds for firing."

"What does life-threatening mean, exactly?" Danielle asked. Jacqueline and Ulrich looked at one another, as if she were asking an obtuse question. "Does this include threats upon the safety of employees, friends and partners?" Jacqueline considered the categories and nodded. That wasn't good enough. Danielle needed her to be recorded. "I'm sorry, I'd like you to be clear. Could you tell me if it matters that friends, employees or partners of an MRD employee were in physical danger, then it would count as life threatening?"

"Well, yes of course," Jacqueline said, as though she were slightly offended friends, relatives or employees wouldn't count.

That was all she needed to hear. Danielle placed the phone on the table, the equivalent to holding out a gun, barrel forward.

"You have just admitted firing me for reasons unjustified and are therefore in breach of employment law as written by MRD. I left to protect the innocent lives of friends and my business partner by a drunken, hostile woman who had entered my restaurant and was threatening violence. For evidence of this, you may look up the police report that I, as the co-owner of the establishment, had to give. The person is now being held at the police station." Danielle appreciated the look of horror on Jacqueline's face, and disgust and regret on Ulrich's. She knew it wasn't towards her, but at Margaret, who had put them at risk; it had been her judgement call, and now they were going to be sued. "Had Margaret stopped to ask the question, we wouldn't be having this conversation, but that was not the course of action she chose." Danielle paused.

"I'm going to make this easy for all of us. MRD can offer me a settlement wherein I am not compelled to take you to court for breach of contract, discrimination, unlawful firing and an abusive and biased work environment. I have evidence showing all four occurred. As a culture that values privacy and discretion, I'd hate to think what would happen to all the clients who realized their accounts were being transferred from the number one gold trader in the industry to another young man, who received them solely on the basis of sleeping with the operating director. That would be Margaret." They'd been played, and now got the privilege of cleaning up the mess. "You have until Friday to return with an offer, or you will be hearing from my attorney."

"Now, on a personal note," Danielle continued, her voice less severe, "I'd like you both to know I respect and admire you, tremendously. I've enjoyed working with you and being here, until the Velocity-MRD merger. I personally wish the two of you nothing but the best and hope that when the occasion arises, we will continue to have a congenial relationship. You may courier my personal items to my home at your convenience, but no later than ten tomorrow morning."

Danielle rose, and Ulrich stood when she did, his hand out. "We'll be in touch," he said somberly. Jacqueline was right beside him, also ready to shake her hand. "Thank you," she said, her eyes conveying more words that she was at liberty to verbalize. If there was a universal karma train, perhaps she'd helped them in some small way deal with the demon that was Margaret.

Danielle walked out the door, took the elevator down and saw Dominic standing by the car. "Dominic!" she said, as gayly as she'd ever been. "Give me a hug." He opened his arms, squeezing her so tight she huffed.

"Did you hear I just got fired?"

"That did crackle through the airwaves." He glanced above her head. "I think I see a nuclear cloud above the offices, but that could be black rain."

She laughed heartily. "And do I hear correctly? You are going to Bern to open your own shop?" He affirmed the truth, and that he'd been working towards it for quite some time. "I'm glad for you, really," she said, squeezing a thick bicep. "This bodyguard stuff is only a small part of what you are capable of."

"I know, but I did it and do it very well."

"That you do, Dominic. Thanks," she said, turning sincere. "And I mean that. Thank you so *much*. You were there when I needed you, and that was a critical moment for me. I do think we are all where are meant to be at the right place and time. So, from the bottom of my heart, I want you to know that you're awesome." A slow, appreciative smile curled his lips. For a man who genuinely wanted to protect and help people, that comment probably eclipsed any romantic moment they'd shared. "Give me another hug."

"Good luck Danielle," he said in her ear. "And much happiness from here on out. You deserve it."

Dominic's words were wings on her butterfly, making her walk back to Stars & Stripes akin to bouncing along the pavement. The sun was out, glistening across the lake, the sporadic clouds creating metallic spots that dissipated into blue. Perhaps in the summer she'd add rock climbing to her activities as the ice melted. It was something she, Lars and Monroe could do as a family, especially if they were with Georgy and Layda up in the mountains.

A family. Her head was ringing with the phrase which sounded like golden symbols.

At the restaurant, it was too busy to have a long conversation with Stephen, but they covered the essentials. She was now unemployed, but informally engaged to the man of her dreams. Danielle grinned, displaying her ring finger for evidence. "What about you? I never got the details on the proposal."

"It was simple yet romantic. The way both of us tend to be. The formal invitation should arrive this weekend, so a heads up. The date is for August, which is what the ladies need to adequately plan the wedding."

Danielle thought about the timing. "When is the baby due?"

"September-ish. I know. Eva's going to be as big as a house."

"Doesn't matter," Danielle dismissed. "She's just going to be more beautiful than she is now."

"Yep. More to love." She squealed, giving him a kiss and a hug.

On the way home, Danielle stopped by the flower mart, wondering what was going down at the office. Johanne and Georgiana….Ulrich and Jacqueline…Lars and Noel. She was almost as excited about the tsunami taking place there as she was to tell Emma she could have the rest of the afternoon off.

Danielle told Emma she'd had to take care of an emergency today and ended up getting fired over it. Emma's eyes grew dark and angry. "Suffice it to say that once the right people were in possession of the facts, they realized it was unlawful, and are now in a sticky situation of having to cover themselves."

Emma's eyes brightened back up at this. "Good for you, bad for them."

"My thoughts exactly."

Danielle changed her clothes, Monroe watching her from the floor where she toddled around. "I think it's time for a walk, little one." Ten minutes later, Danielle was pushing Monroe in her stroller along the pavement, enjoying the spring heat on her back, wondering just how long it would be until she heard from Lars.

CHAPTER 50

Danielle called Layda and Georgy later that evening, revealing she'd been fired. Very methodically, she described the circumstances and the final meeting with Ulrich and Jacqueline.

"I like how you handled this," complimented Layda. "Detached and yet you softened it with the personal touch at the end."

"Beyond liking the two of them as people," Danielle emphasized, "I'm going to see Ulrich at the Opera for years to come."

Georgy grunted, acknowledging the truth. "But you've not heard from Lars?"

"No. I suspect he may still be dealing with the fall out. In the States, this type of sudden turnover is rare and usually causes issues with clients who have millions sitting with a single trader."

The conversation transitioned to the buildout of the new offices and what to do with the Mettleren family and business accounts prior to that time.

"I'll demand they remain under Johanne, or I will pull every last dime," stated Georgy without hesitation. "I'm going to call Noel once we hang up. If he's unavailable, I'll go down the line to Lars and Ulrich."

"No Margaret?" Danielle asked sweetly.

"That woman does not exist for me." Georgy excused himself from the conversation as she and Layda continued.

"Now," said Layda briskly, all business yet parental. "Since you are now suddenly free, I say we enjoy some female time."

Danielle could only smile at her change of manner and the delight she felt through the phone. "I'm not even sure what it means!"

"I'll show you."

Before heading out, Danielle sent off two texts, one to Johanne the other to Lars, inquiring if all was well. Johanne responded immediately, Lars not at all.

Maybe I'm not supposed to be in contact with former employees, she thought. She looked at the time and called David on his cell phone.

"To what do I owe the pleasure?"

"Oh, you know," she started, teasing. "The usual. I'm calling about men and my employment status." Her former boss and manager chuckled, telling her he was ready to hear about the latest challenge in her life. His good humor ended with her words, his questions precise, his judgement measured.

"You have them in a sling for the firing," he concluded.

"Do you think there's more to this story that I'm missing?" she asked.

"Absolutely. Margaret was clearly waiting for a chance to fire you. With a firing, word gets around and you have a harder time finding a job where the clients will follow you. What'd you do to get on her bad side, other than being beautiful, American and having dated the boss?"

It was essentially what Stephen had said. "I believe she wants me to leave Zurich all together."

"After you telling me she was hitting on Lars and is bedding Jacob, that would be the betting man's gamble."

"Hey!" Danielle said, abruptly. "Why can't they just go to you? The accounts she's removed from me or taken from Johanne."

"You mean transfer them to Russelz? No reason."

Danielle loved the idea. In the tight-knit world of high net-worth people, they all knew who managed each other's money; the greed factor causing many to jump ship to get to the best trader. Georgy would talk, giving his recommendation for Russelz. At least some of the clients who were annoyed with MRD would find a new home for money management with David's firm.

"I do have one word of caution for you," inserted David. "You initially called me about Lars and what to do about contacting him. If my guess is right, what he's going through is not pleasant. Plus, until you review the documentation they will want you to sign, best stay on the right side of protocol. Keep it cool and wait until he contacts you."

"There is one extenuating circumstance David..." she started, rolling the ring on her finger. "Lars asked me to marry him. I'm wearing the ring he gave me last year, and he's going speak with Georgy and Layda before it's official."

He uttered a congratulations, then went right back to business. "But you've not told anyone, it's not public?"

"No. That may not happen for a while."

"That's good. You may not be speaking with Lars for some number of months, because it will, or could, be seen as a conflict. You simply don't want to have to deal with those types of issues."

"But David," she said, exasperated. "The firing and management changes preceding it were done under Margaret. How could that ever be misconstrued?"

"Because you *were* fired, and you reaching out to a director of the firm for any reason is against protocol, black and white. If you want that settlement, which you very much deserve, put your hormones and heart on hold until this is out in the open."

Danielle felt like the flat side of a plank had hit her chest, crushing her. He was absolutely correct and she knew it. To leave millions on the table, rightfully earned, was financial irresponsibility. David advised her to work through Georgy if Lars were to be contacted because theirs was a legitimate client-broker relationship.

Danielle's next call was from an officer at the police station, asking her to come down and complete the paperwork regarding Lani's arrest. It needed to be filled out the same day or the charges would be dismissed.

This is the right thing to do, I'm sure. Still, she called Stephen. He'd received the same call from the station.

"I've spoken with Eva," Stephen informed her. "Eva is sympathetic towards Lani, as is her family, especially her grandfather. They believe her chances of being employed elsewhere are low if she has this on her record."

"Is that true?"

"Yes," he answered somberly. "The Swiss do not look upon a police record with a forgiving eye."

Danielle understood, but was certain the best course forward was to let Lani deal with the consequences of her actions. "Lani is so bull-headed, I don't believe she's going to learn or change if she gets a simple slap on the wrist, do you?"

"I'm less worried about that than her always coming back to me or you for more money, which she is guaranteed to do if she doesn't have a job."

"No, there has to be a better solution, especially with your altered world. A new wife and baby are more than enough for a lot of people. Adding an unstable, potentially unemployed and vindictive ex-wife is not on anyone's bucket list."

"Danielle, it's still Lani."

She sighed audibly. "And that's the problem. Lani hasn't changed but you and I have! I get it, Stephen. But for once, I'm going to look out for you and do what needs to be done."

"What is that?"

"I'm going to sign the papers at the station. If I've learned one thing from my time here in Switzerland it's that the immediate pain can be worth the promise of a good future."

"I can see your point. Every time you endured tremendous suffering, the end result was always better."

"Not just me Stephen, you as well. You lost a wife, who you thought was your best friend. But life is so much more than that, which you realized. It was a blessing Lani left, because you have what you always and truly did want: a family. Plus, you have the restaurant to boot."

"I should thank you," Stephen concluded.

She laughed. "Yes! Now let me get going. I can tell you don't want to go on record against her, so I will do it for both of us."

Stephen gave his support. "You are right on this one Danielle. Thanks for being the brave one."

Brave or stupid.

Danielle wished she could call Lars and get his advice but made the safe choice and called Georgy back, relating David's advice about not calling him, then her decision about Lani.

Georgy promised to speak with Lars and get back to her.

Danielle bundled Monroe up and drove to Layda's. "Georgy's still on the phone with Lars," Layda informed her in an undertone.

Danielle told Layda she only had an hour to visit the station, and really had wanted Lar's opinion on what do with Lani. Layda nodded, leaving the room, returning moments after.

"Lars agrees it's the only way Lani will learn. Also, Georgy said you can't contact Lars."

"Layda, it could be months before I can talk to Lars again." Layda sat in front of her, asking for more information. "David is sure my paperwork includes an industry standard clause, which means we can't communicate unless we have some kind of formal relationship."

Layda crossed her legs, leaning forward on her elbows. "For how long?"

"I'd have to check the paperwork. David thinks a year."

"Well, I'd be surprised if it will be that long," predicted Layda, her voice and eyes mischievous. "The way Lars looked at you while carrying heavy furniture up two flights of stairs was enough to show me all a mom needs to feel confident he'll soon be proposing."

"Layda," Danielle whispered. "Lars asked me to marry him yesterday, before any of this occurred. We weren't going to do or say a thing until he had a chance to talk with you and Georgy and get your permission, which he insisted was an absolute must, and I agree. Please don't say a word until Lars can speak with him. More than anything, we are sensitive to your feelings and how things might look in this town." Seeing that Layda's surprise was equal amounts happiness, Danielle extended her left hand. "You recognize this. A temporary place holder until it's official."

She stopped talking when Georgy returned.

"That was interesting to say the least," he boomed.

"Anything you can reveal?" Danielle asked pleasantly, watching Layda's face in her peripheral vision.

"Yes," he said firmly. "If they thought it was bad before, it's a going to be a brown snowstorm now."

"Why don't you just say a crudstorm?" asked Layda tritely.

"Don't you dare use that kind of language!" Danielle howled. "That's my territory as the uncouth American." When the laughter subsided, Danielle became somber. "Is it going to be okay?"

"We will be fine. They are clear Johanne gets all our accounts or my money is pulled tomorrow."

"If you don't already have a place in mind, would you consider Russelz, my former employer? They are one of the top firms in the States."

"Good plan," rumbled Georgy. "I now need to excuse myself and make a call to the contractor. He indicated the timeframe for the family offices could be cut in half with the right people and the right amount of money, and I have plenty of that."

"Georgy, wait for a second," Layda requested, her eyes on Danielle, her expression thoughtful. "I'm thinking that we don't really have to rush, do we? Danielle could take a vacation, which is what most people do when they transition from one position to another. Don't you think that would be possible?"

Georgy paused for a moment and chuckled. "It's our money. We can do with it what we want. If Margaret digs in her heels, we park the funds with Russelz and wait for Danielle to be on board. In fact, if you want more time, I can get in a consultant to start the paperwork required for structuring, which means attorneys, accountants and the like."

A spring breeze flowed into Danielle's soul. "You mean for the first time in two years, I can actually take a vacation when I want?"

Layda reached up and clasp Georgy's hand, nodding with satisfaction. "It's settled then," Layda announced. "Go finish your business downtown and then come back for a nice dinner. It's time to relax, and tomorrow you can sleep in."

Danielle prepared to head out, dropping by Georgy's study, where he already held his phone in hand.

"I really can't talk with Lars at all, can I?" she asked, already knowing the answer.

"Unfortunately, no, until the paperwork is done and the term limit satisfied." Her heart sunk a bit, but didn't entirely hit the floor. It was only a matter of time.

This time, I'll wait for him, because we are worth it.

CHAPTER 51

Danielle thought the four-story, grey and taupe building used for the Zurich Polizie resembled a classic bank more than a municipal building.

That's what happens when the majority of crimes are probably white collar, not violent offenses. Danielle wondered which category Lani would be placed in, but soon learned it didn't matter. Trespassing and making physical threats were serious offenses in the country of Switzerland, and Lani faced a fine of five thousand francs.

It took roughly thirty minutes for Danielle to provide her sworn statement, sign her signature, and consign her friend to stay in the basement holding area until the fine was paid. No exceptions. No bail. On her way out, she texted Stephen, imploring him not to pay the fine. Lani must sober up and recognize that she was in jail, and it was of her own doing.

Danielle's next thoughts were of Johanne. She'd checked her texts every few minutes, hoping to hear back from him. With her being fired, his accounts being taken, then Georgy demanding he retain full control of the Mettleren accounts, he had to be sitting in the hot seat. But Johanne should be able to respond, since he wouldn't be bound by the same no-contact laws as Lars.

Finally, Johanne responded.

Meltdown

Danielle put her phone away, gazing out the train window.

What in the world had Lars been thinking when he created the merger? Job preservation is what he'd said, but in a rare moment of massive miscalculation, he'd not considered the people aspect, only the financial picture.

It's not always about the numbers. That was the line he'd used with her when she was focused on making money to the exclusion of all else. Now it was his turn to learn that in spades.

After she returned to Georgy's home, she and Layda spoke about the schedule for the next few weeks. The first item was Danielle's birthday party. Layda's enthusiasm overshadowed any lingering worry she had. It was time to let her issues go and embrace the life she had. Her time here had taught her few things were permanent, and she should enjoy every second.

A half-hour later, Danielle was making a cup of tea and laughing with Layda about the resale value of wetsuits when Georgy entered.

"Good news," he remarked. "We will have a fully functioning business office ready for art and furniture in three weeks and will sit idle until you are ready. Regarding the family office consultant, I have arranged an introduction this weekend to see if you two get along. I also gave him a heads up that even when you do start, your hours may be cut back a little. I'd like my granddaughter to see more of her mother, not less with this new role."

It didn't take much convincing for Danielle to agree to reduce her workday by ninety minutes. It would get her out of the office at 2, allowing her to participate in the afternoon music playgroups, art classes and all the activities young children required.

"Now," continued Georgy, "you may be unsurprised to know that not only did Margaret ignore my request, she also removed my extended relatives and their accounts from under Johanne. She will now suffer the financial consequences of her decision." Danielle started to ask a question, but he raised his hand. "No. You are no longer working. Let me handle this."

He was so adamant that Danielle agreed. The mental freedom allowed Danielle to enjoy her evening and she gave Emma the next day off. Layda joined her and Monroe for breakfast, then together they visited the zoo. By the monkey exhibit, Monroe was getting restless, fussing through the lion exhibit. By the time they reached the indoor penguin sanctuary, she was asleep. Layda and Danielle ate soup and pastries at the indoor cafeteria, the freshly made buffalo mozzarella caprese delicious.

"Have you heard anything from Lani?" Layda asked Danielle. She hadn't, and was encouraged by Layda to reach out to Stephen.

Stephen answered. "Yes, she called me first thing. She'd sobered up, apologized profusely and asked me to pay the fine."

"And?" Danielle prompted.

"Eva's grandfather learned of the situation and called her last night. He proposed an idea which I'm sharing with you." Danielle stared into the distance as she listened to Stephen's words. "What do you think of that?" he finished.

"I think Eva's parents really, *really* love you."

"No, they love Eva, and to her grandfather's point, getting Lani out of town is just the ticket for us to have a new life together."

Eva's grandfather offered to pay off the fine, and in return, Lani would accept a job at one of his restaurant's in Geneva as a secondary line chef.

Quite a comedown from her work in Zurich, but it was employment. He'd also made it clear to Lani that Eva was engaged to Stephen, and Lani was not to contact them any longer. If Lani could agree to that, she'd get out of jail, have a job, and receive a gift of the first and last month's rent paid for at an apartment owned by the family. "Are you okay with all of this?" Stephen asked.

"Yes," she answered. "It will give Eva relief, allay any guilt you might have and remove her from our line of sight."

"Good. You are only required to do one thing. Drop the charges, or it will be on her paperwork."

Danielle looked at the time. "I won't make it today, but tomorrow afternoon I can do it. I make no apologies. She's made our life misery, Stephen. Another twenty-fours might solidify the gravity of her mistakes."

"You know, Layda," Danielle began when she was off the phone. "I just realized I'm mad at Lani, as in, really furious. All that she did, dropping out on us, hurting Stephen, not being there for me, all of it."

"And now you have lost a friend."

Danielle nodded. "For good."

"Let me ask you this," Layda started, her voice more compassionate than normal. "Even if this hadn't happened, do you believe you were really a good fit for each other now, given your life choices and style?"

Layda raised an interesting question. "No. We don't have a lot in common."

"It's best not to force some things, don't you think?"

Danielle thought once again about Georgy's words. If you have to work too hard, it's just not meant to be; just like her relationship with Lani.

CHAPTER 52

Wednesday, Danielle attended a musical playdate with her daughter, her first ever.

The experience was all that Danielle could have imagined, but never before enjoyed. When she went home, she laid down for a nap, the luxury of a mid-day break wonderfully new. Working already seemed like another world. The role of being a mother, with no obligations to dress up, go in to the office, rush home to turn around and leave again, was all consuming. That notion was reinforced when Danielle dropped Monroe at Layda's prior to going to the club. Monroe fussed and was clingy with Danielle.

"This is different," Danielle observed, trying to gently disconnect Monroe's little fingers from her blouse.

"But not uncommon," Layda said. "Until now, she hasn't been used to spending time with you during the day. Two days in a row is enough to disrupt her schedule, but also let her know how much fun it is being with her momma."

"I'm making it harder on myself, aren't I?"

"It's very difficult to manage both motherhood and working because children like routine, particularly when they are young." Layda brought over the scooter, but Monroe turned her head over Danielle's shoulder. Finally, they lured Monroe out of Danielle's arms by moving into the playroom,

Danielle spent a few minutes on the floor, engaging her daughter with a miniature horse. She quietly exited the room as Layda kept Monroe occupied, and made her way past Georgy's office.

"Hey!" Danielle scolded in an undertone. "Aren't you supposed to be upstairs sleeping?"

"I needed a file and you caught me."

"What's new?" she asked.

"Johanne has now tendered his resignation, as did Georgiana and Ulrich. As of tomorrow, all our accounts go to Russelz."

"All?" Danielle asked in a wickedly-happy whisper.

"All thirteen billion."

"Whew," exhaled Danielle. "How is Noel handling things?"

"No idea. We haven't been talking. It's all been through Lars."

"Okay," she held up her hand. "Say no more."

"One last item. You are scheduled to meet with the consultant on Saturday, after the competition but before our family get-together. It will be short, I promise."

Danielle left early in order to stop by the police station before she headed to the club. Although Eva's grandfather had paid the fine the day prior, Lani was still locked up until Danielle signed off. What she didn't anticipate was the speed at which the officers would release Lani. Danielle heard her name called and stood frozen as her former friend walked towards her.

Lani was disheveled, pale and looked to be on the verge of breaking down. The officer removed her cuffs and Lani made straight for Danielle. Wanting to step back, she told herself that law enforcement were all around, and Lani would at least be smart enough not to attack her there.

Danielle's dread turned to shock when Lani put her arms around Danielle and sobbed. "I'm so sorry," she cried, her voice muffled in

Danielle's shoulder. The anger Danielle had towards her friend melted away with Lani's words, a mixture of acknowledging her faults, and her idiocy for drinking and demanding the restaurant be returned, for trusting Max, and her shame at calling Stephen, having no idea he was engaged to Eva.

"I've been such a stupid fool," she sobbed. "I'm so sorry, and now I'm being forced to leave—well, no, I take that back, I'm being given another chance by Eva's family and..." her words were lost to Danielle then as Lani sobbed harder. Danielle led her to a corner of the room, holding her and listening. It was all she could do.

When her tears finally dried, Danielle asked her if she had money to get home. "I have no home, remember?" Lani said, not bitterly, just factually.

"Hold on." Danielle called Georgy, who promised to follow through on her request and get back to her. He did so within minutes, and Danielle relayed the details. "Johanne said he'll meet you at the apartment in thirty minutes," she told Lani. "He and Dario will let you in. Johanne said you can stay only as long as it takes Eva's grandfather to move you out. Is that acceptable?" She nodded, more tears sliding down her cheeks. Danielle texted Georgy the confirmation, and then took out a twenty franc. "Here. This will get you home."

Lani stared down at the bill, rubbing the paper with her thumbs. Looking up, she was broken.

"I can't believe it's come to this, Danielle. Do you think Johanne can forgive me for all the money that's disappeared?"

"You didn't know Max was spending it, Lani. It wasn't all your fault."

"But I didn't listen. Not to you, or anyone. Can you—will you ever forgive me for how I've been? Will we still be friends?"

Danielle embraced the honesty she wanted from those in her life. "I hope so Lani." As if knowing it was all Danielle could give, Lani silently shook her head, more tears falling. "Come on. I'll walk out with you."

Curbside, Danielle hailed a cab. She gave Lani one last hug "Take care."

"You, too."

Watching the cab move down the street, Danielle thought *that's how a decades-long friendship ends.* A series of bad decisions, hurts which were like bruises, being hit over and over until the skin breaks and blood is spilled.

Danielle walked to the metro for the short ride to the club. For the first time, she didn't feel like playing in front of a room of strangers. She wanted to be with her man and daughter, at home by the fire, as a family.

Not yet, but soon.

CHAPTER 53

Danielle arrived at the club early enough to sit at the bar and have a drink before going on stage.

"You want something in your next drink to cheer you up?" Leon had noticed her glum mood.

"It's been a particularly rough week," Danielle told him, "and no number of Mexican coffees are going to change that reality."

"Tell me what constitutes a bad week for a person like you. This, I have to hear."

Leon placed both palms on the counter, inspecting her, skeptical.

"Getting fired," she answered, ticking off the items with her fingers. "Your best friend being put in jail for threatening others. Going to the prison to press charges. Not being able to talk with your boyfriend due to employment contracts. Would you like me to continue?"

Leon shook his head, making a drink. "This one's on me. It's a double." He passed her a tall glass of sparkling water and they both laughed.

Danielle still had ten more minutes until her set when two figures entered to her right. "Is this becoming your full-time job?" Johanne cracked, his face straight. Dario came around to her other side, giving her a side hug before Johanne wrapped both arms around her. Danielle scanned Johanne, worried. "Are you okay? I heard you quit."

"He's perfectly fine," interjected Dario, "and I'm beyond thrilled."

Johanne sat beside her. "Yes, to both. It was a blowout of insane proportions, which I will happily relate over a good drink." She glanced at the time, telling him he could give the reader's digest version now or wait for the break in forty-five.

"Speed talk," encouraged Dario, ordering drinks for both of them. "Go."

"Word got around you were fired under false pretenses. Ulrich threatened resignation and Margaret called his bluff. He walked out the door that afternoon."

"I didn't hear that part at all," Danielle whispered, still in shock.

"It's being kept quiet, as more clients might defect, but it will happen anyway, once people start talking. When I saw that even a partner wasn't immune, I was concerned but was still going to stay, right until I learned Georgy demanded I keep all the Mettleren accounts, and without consulting me, Margaret gave them all to Jacob. Glenda told me what had transpired. What was I supposed to earn money on, air? Now the entire upper management is in question."

"Where was Lars during all this?"

"Absent from my line of sight," Johanne replied, shrugging. Dario chuckled, raising his drink to Robin who walked by.

"Five minutes," he said to Danielle.

"The firm couldn't possibly fold, could it?"

Johanne took a sip of his drink. "It would be perfectly fine if they'd fire Margaret, but for whatever reason, that's not happening, or hasn't yet. Glenda is my only source of information, so we'll have to wait until tomorrow for the latest. But I don't really care now do I?" Johanne said with a lilt in his voice. "Because I received the most amazing, out-of-the-blue call from Georgy about a job offer." He scowled at her. "You dirty-dog. You wanted me to leave all the time, didn't you?"

Danielle gave a coy smile. "You have been the best to me, Johanne. Do you think we could stand to work in a no-pressure office together?"

"Yeah, and I'll even let you be my boss if you want."

"Ha. No way. I like you taking all the meetings."

The lights turned down and Danielle gave them both kisses. "You can tell me what's up with Lani later."

"Nothing is up," Dario told her. "We are letting her spend one last night, since the movers come tomorrow. Pretty good of us, huh?"

Danielle was proud of them and said so. They could have made it a whole lot worse for Lani.

She started her set giving a shout out to her friends sitting at the bar. The evening was slow, with few requests being made and the room half-full. She assigned it to the weather, the warmer, sunnier evening more conducive to walking along the lake than staying inside a darkened room. No wonder Robin moved the venue outdoors with the change from winter to spring.

During the break, the three discussed the latest with Max.

"Here's what I think happened," Dario began, tapping his fingers one by one on the counter. "Andre passes away, Max is lost. He had already been eyeing the sex appeal of Stars & Stripes and wanted it for himself. He sleeps with Lani, breaking up her relationship with Stephen which was already on the rocks. Then, when he realizes that the new restaurant Lani chose was terrible, he faces facts that you were the brains behind the last venture. He gets mad, but instead of talking with Lani to change the menu or reinvest more money into the décor, he gets people like us to invest more money, but it's hemorrhaging. The leg needs to be cut-off, not given a tourniquet."

"But Dario," she exclaimed, "where did all the money go?"

"Believe it or not, a fair amount was spent on the overhead associated with that place. They were paying thirty grand a month in rent."

Her mouth dropped. "But that's more in line with a high-end retail shop, not a restaurant."

"And that's what you get for having an owner who has no idea about the business. The remaining money was being spent on his lifestyle, which could best be described as wine, women and song."

Danielle was flabbergasted. "But why in the world would someone with his net worth use other people's money when he had his own?"

Johanne wagged his finger. "You just said it. Other people's money. OPM. I did some digging on the account he had with us. He made a good living, but his money with us was his trust fund. It must be invested and only ten percent spent in any given year."

"No," she whispered.

"Yes," confirmed Johanne, nodding his head. "In the last six months, he started spiraling. He fell into the trap of so many start-up CEOs, seeing how easy it was to get money from the investors and betting on future revenue to pay back the debt. It supported his lifestyle but was unsustainable. The oldest scam in the book."

Danielle shook her head, recalling the first time she met Max, who was dining with a group of friends and Andre. It was Andre who paid, and Stephen had said he always did.

"Max was basically a siphon," she concluded.

"A charming, handsome siphon," corrected Dario.

Dario explained how they could get their money back by selling the two apartments, but they were considering keeping one to rent out. "Unless Max can get his family to repay us in the sub-ninety days he has left."

She left to finish out her set, the evening ending quietly. She'd half expected and hoped Lars would show up, sit at the bar, subtly sipping his drink and they'd chat, but no. It was still silent, and rightfully so. She maintained the long view, that her settlement and their relationship was worth the silence.

Thursday, she and Monroe took a long morning walk, stopping at the deli for cheese and bread. Danielle slept when Monroe took her nap, and after Emma came over at two, Danielle visited her therapist. It took the first half of the session to catch him up on recent events, and the second half was spent working through her lingering emotions about Lani, and how Danielle would keep her sanity until she and Lars could be together.

"You are making it sound like it will be months until you see him," Dr. Blatz observed. "All that's waiting is the settlement offer, which will be proposed tomorrow. Once done, there are no barriers between you and Lars."

"It depends on his contract."

Dr. Blatz nodded, watching her curiously. "Danielle, you told me that when it comes to Lars, you have underestimated his love for you, and the lengths to which he would go to be with you, correct? After all you've been through, do you really think now will be the time he will break his pattern?"

She hesitated, scared that what she so desperately wanted was going to disappear, and told him so.

"It's the penultimate test for you," he affirmed. "The big question is just how much you are willing to put on the line for this man?"

She didn't hesitate. "All of it. No question."

"Then that's how you proceed. Take that conviction and be unbending. Your future self will thank you."

CHAPTER 54

Friday morning Danielle and Monroe attended a music play group then it was naptime. She did laundry, cleaned the dishes and the house, then realized she had nothing for dinner. With each hour that had passed, Danielle had a renewed respect for Emma and the stamina it took keeping up with an active child. More than once, she thought working was far easier to manage than her young daughter. When Monroe woke grumpy, Danielle called Emma, relating it was her third straight day.

"Is she sick, or am I doing something wrong?" The older woman laughed, saying the trick was getting her down at the same time, and waking her up from her afternoon nap at precisely ninety-minutes.

"Regulating the sleep patterns is the most important aspect of managing your child." In the craziness that occurred after Andre and then working, she'd stopped reading the books on kids and childhood development. Now she was playing catch up. Danielle's frustration continued when the next night, she was half-way out of the city and realized she'd forgotten the portable crib. She returned, retrieved the crib, arriving at the Village feeling like a complete failure as a mother. Andre had been only half-right when he said that millions of kids had two working parents and turned out just fine; that part might be true. What he hadn't predicted was the part about parental guilt and challenges when circumstances changed.

At Georgy's home, he read the instructions as she assembled. "I think we'll be buying one of these," he called to Layda. "Sorry," he mumbled, not realizing Layda was on the phone. She walked out of hearing distance. "Art and furniture for the new space, I believe."

"Things she can more than handle, and I'm so glad of it," remarked Danielle. When she finished, Danielle plopped beside Georgy, defeated.

"I forgot the blankets."

"That, my dear, we can solve."

As Georgy searched for linens, they talked of Johanne and Dario's kindness to Lani, and her imminent move out of town. "I have one question," Danielle began, watching him closely. "Did you have anything to do with Eva's grandfather deciding to help Lani? You two have been friends for years."

Georgy turned, holding sheets and a blanket. "Do fathers have to share secrets?"

"The same ones who pretend to have discretion? Unreal," she muttered to herself.

"Are you saying you are unhappy with the outcome?"

"No, and that's the problem. I'm thrilled, for both Stephen and Eva, and also for me. It's a great relief, and I'm feeling bad I don't feel bad." Hearing her words, Lars came to mind. He'd pointed out her use of the word bad was overdone.

Georgy grunted. "You don't think Lars knows? My dear, he was the one who suggested it, not me. I was just the conveyer of the message."

"I love that man," she said automatically, thinking nothing of the tongue in cheek phrase.

"I know Danielle," he said, seriously. "So do we."

Their moment of bonding was broken by Monroe starting to cry. "She's hungry and I'm starved," Danielle said, standing up. Georgy suggested Chinese takeout.

Danielle took Monroe downstairs, placing her on the floor and she immediately crawled into the living room. It was of similar size to Lars' home in the village, but the layout was slightly different. While both living rooms faced the Matterhorn, in this home, the open concept dining room was glass enclosed. Because she'd never spent much time downstairs during her overnight stays, she hadn't fully appreciated the room until Layda turned on the lights.

"Wow," Danielle exclaimed. "That is so beautiful." The chandelier gave the room the illusion of being one with nature, hanging over the rock ledge below.

When the food arrived, Danielle pointed out the oversized table made their small dining group look even smaller. It was a table for twenty, the plush, woven back chairs as ornately elegant as Layda's other furniture. A different style from Lars', but she liked both equally well, even if Lars' home had a special meaning.

"Layda, do you mind if I go in a couple of hours early before the competition? I'd like to watch the other climbers before it's my turn."

"Go," she encouraged. "We'll come up around 11:30. Is that a good time or will it distract you?"

Danielle smiled. "I think I'm good with distractions." If she had time, she'd make her way over to the indoor climbing area. She'd checked the boards and learned Lars was instructing that morning. It had been five days since she'd seen him. The next morning, she rose early, ate and played with Monroe until Layda came downstairs. With a kiss, she left, eager to get to the mountain.

It was a windy day, the gusts pushing her forward during the walk from the parking lot to the train. It was worse on the mountain, though the east side of the rock where they climbed was mostly shielded. She checked in at the reception center, confirmed their start time and went to the indoor training facility. Climbers were already scaling the hundred foot sheet of ice.

She heard Lars calmly calling out instructions, and it took her a few minutes to find him. He was guiding another student who held the bole rope, while a second instructor stood by as a back-up. Danielle made her way to his left, watching his profile.

"Slowly now," Lars cautioned a climber who was searching for a foothold. "Take your time," he continued. She could have watched him longer, but doing so would have increased the ache she felt. As subtly as possible, she removed her phone and took a picture of him, then zoomed in, lifting her phone higher to get a good shot. She was snapping it as he turned and looked, a candid smile lifting his cheeks, barely long enough for her to catch it on film. She smiled and he turned back to the ice, the interaction only a second or two.

He must have sensed someone watching. Or, she thought happily, the magnetic attraction pulled them together no matter where they were or what they were doing.

Maybe he will come and watch, and that would make me nervous, but also happy.

Her group was assembling in the gear up area, the mood jovial and fun. It was a competition of their own skills against the clock, but given the conversation, everyone expected the young woman in her teens to be first, the older man to be last and Danielle and the two others somewhere in the middle. She was harnessed when Georgy and Layda arrived with Monroe all bundled up.

"And where did she get this outfit?" Danielle asked pretending to scowl at Layda.

"It wasn't me, this time," she grinned back. "You can blame her grandfather."

Danielle felt the soft, sheepskin fur, admiring how it cocooned Monroe like a seamless blanket. All that was exposed was her little face, squished and happy to be in the arms of her papa.

"If it gets too cold, go back inside," Danielle counseled. "This isn't the climbing Olympics."

"No, but it's your birthday," Georgy said. "Happy birthday Danielle."

"Yes, happy birthday," said Layda, kissing her cheek. "Do well."

CHAPTER 55

The competition was less stressful and a lot more fun than Danielle expected. It consisted of three climbs, two on parts of a frozen waterfall and then a straight up climb of ice over rock; each scored on time and technique. As Danielle prepared for her first climb, Georgy and Layda stood with Monroe behind a low fence. In her peripheral vision, she saw Lars approach, spiking her nerves. As a consequence, she rushed, slipped once on the way up and again on the way down, finishing second to last in time. On the second ascent she'd completely forgotten her spectators, totally focused on the waterfall outcroppings, carefully and precisely kicking once to establish a foothold, her confidence increasing on the descent. She'd climbed up the rankings to third, feeling that she might even come within a minute or two of the young woman who seemed to scurry up the ice like a monkey with cleats. When her instructor gave the word for the final climb, Danielle clamped with her feet, pushed with her thigh, scoping her pick placement in coordination with her ascent.

In that moment, it occurred to her why the competitions were valuable: with a time constraint, it was a vertical game of chess, figuring out the moves fifty feet in advance. It was mentally consuming, ending with her body stimulated and exhausted, but her mind cleansed.

The descent was her fastest and cleanest yet. When she placed both feet on the ground, her time was called and she heard a woop from Georgy. Looking up, she saw the final climber descending, the young woman. Danielle watched her foot slip, the force of the drop causing her to lose her grip. She hung, suspended for a few moments until the swinging ceased. When she finished, her time was a full thirty seconds over Danielle's. Danielle ended in second place overall, behind the young woman, immensely pleased. She'd accomplished what she hadn't believed possible.

The group of five congratulated one another on completion, and Danielle hugged her instructor. She then looked for Lars, catching his eye. He was so proud, those dark orbs holding hers, conveying his love with restraint. He kissed Layda's cheek and shook Georgy's hand before leaving.

On the short train ride to the lot, Danielle sat by Georgy, leaning close. "Lars looked awfully happy," Danielle said.

He eyed her, knowing full-well what she was asking. "He and Noel came to an agreement last night regarding all things MRD, and that's all I can say on the matter."

"Georgy!" she exclaimed in hushed tones. "Are you kidding me? Noel's entire company is imploding and that's all I get?"

Georgy shrugged. "Sorry." She hmphed, still in shock that the information she wanted the most was being denied. "On another note, the consultant will be coming by around five-thirty."

Long enough to take a quick soak in the hot tub, which is what she did. She walked in with her towel around her, heading for the shower.

"Happy early birthday!" Layda announced from the hallway. Beside her was the same masseuse Danielle had previously used. "You get to enjoy an hour of well-deserved pampering."

Danielle was thrilled but reminded Layda of the man coming over. "I delayed him a bit." Delighted, Danielle disrobed in the massage room and tried to relax.

It was hard. Her thoughts were on Lars, the glow of pride and their still-private relationship. Eventually, she felt her mind exiting the fast lane of the interstate, the masseuse releasing her muscles, getting her to downshift, take the offramp, and pull over.

It was then she fell asleep. Though short, it did wonders for her. Danielle chose a dark red for her lips, combing her hair straight. She'd parted it on the side, the lift of her long bangs giving a single flip, elegant but not overly done, like her black slacks and short heels, perfect with her cashmere top. The outfit was somewhat professional for the discussion with the consultant, yet comfortable for dinner.

"That's lovely," complimented Layda, standing at the bottom of the stairs.

"I know it's a bit underdressed for dinner," Danielle confided. "But I didn't want to overdo it for the meeting."

Danielle finished her make-up and went downstairs.

"Danielle, Georgy would like to see you in his study before the consultant arrives. Oh, and I forgot to tell you I asked Emma and her husband to come up for the party. I hope you don't mind. They are downstairs as well."

"That's great!" Danielle said, thrilled. Emma had been such an important part of her life since Andre died, Danielle was happy she could be part of this special day.

Georgy was sitting in his chair waiting, and Danielle took the seat closest to the fireplace, on the plush couch.

"Now, I thought it wise to have a pre-conversation first, because we have never talked details about what you require in terms of an employment contract or even salary."

"What? You missed the negotiation where you give me the chalet in St. Moritz, my own private plane and an apartment in Geneva when I need to meet with the other members of the extended family? Seriously, Georgy. You know what I was earning before…"

"And we talked of you earning more here."

"Right," she grinned, crossing her legs. "So, what's there to discuss?"

"*Much*," he answered, emphasizing the word. "First, you won't have a private plane yourself, as you'll use mine, but honestly, the train is far faster, because of the scarcity of air strips in this great mountain country. Second, you won't be needing a chalet in St. Moritz, as you already have this one."

"Two down," she quipped. "What's left?"

"A home in Geneva, because all our family sans us, reside there. On this one, I have to say it will be chosen with the input of your new partner."

"Partner?" she asked, her mouth going dry.

Georgy nodded somberly. "I'm sorry to drop the news on you like this so suddenly."

"But…" she stammered, "the entire point of working with you was based upon the understanding I'd be leading the family trust and trading group. Yes, I need someone with the proper credentials, and I always thought I'd at least have a hand in choosing that person."

He lifted his hands palms up. "Well, Layda and I have done some observing over the last week and spoken with other family members. We realized that it may be unrealistic to expect you to want to stay in a full-time position until Monroe goes to pre-school, which is two years. We also learned from the consultant that managing a family office at thirteen billion requires a broader skillset than what you presently have, and frankly what you will ever have. That's far beyond a person who is simply credentialled."

Danielle's shock had completely taken away her ability to respond. What in the world was she going to now: quit her role at the family office before she ever began and start working for a total stranger? At least when she'd jumped to MRD, she'd been able to speak with Ulrich and Lars on a conference call.

Georgy caught her attention. "I did, however, want to make sure I was going down the right road and called David. He concurred that our plan of action was wise."

Danielle tried to regain her composure, restating the obvious. "You discussed this with him?"

"In detail."

"Okay," she hedged, assembling her thoughts. Georgy was, after all, the grandfather of her daughter and her default dad. He loved her and wouldn't do anything that would purposefully hurt her. Besides, if David was on board, then it couldn't be entirely to her detriment.

"You have done this for my benefit, and that of the family," she began, forcing a calm she didn't feel. "And you and Layda believe that I will not only accept this arrangement, but be able to work with the individual you are bringing on to be my partner, without my input or involvement."

"I do."

"Well, then I will support your decision because honestly, I trust you."

He sat forward, beaming. "I'm so glad. Because the consultant I've been using is the one I'd like to be your partner."

"Now?" she asked. "He must have impressed you quite a bit."

"You have no idea." He raised his voice and said, "You can come in now."

The door swung open and Danielle's mouth dropped.

"Hello, Danielle," Lars greeted her calmly. She leaned back into her chair, in total disbelief.

Lars and Georgy shook hands, the older man clasping the younger one's shoulder. "I'll let you two work out the details."

Once the door shut, Lars sat beside her on the couch.

"Are you my new partner or my boss?" she asked in exasperation.

One side of Lars' lips lifted slightly. "Technically, I'm the managing director, but you can choose whatever title you believe would best fit your role, so we can be peers and talk at home without reservation."

Danielle's eyes were fixed. "And the place in Geneva. Georgy said I'd need input from my new partner…" Danielle's voice trailed off as he took her hand.

"I spoke with Georgy over a week ago and asked him a single question, one that would throw my position with MRD in jeopardy." He closed his eyes when his lips touched her palm, opening them with a soft, proud smile. "I asked him for permission to marry you."

"I didn't know!" she exclaimed in a whisper.

"I previously said I'd leave my world to be in yours," Lars said intently. "And that's what it came down to."

"But…how could this all happen and it be okay?" she asked, overjoyed, thrilled, and worried at the same time. Lars brought her fingers to his lips, caressing them gently.

"It had to play out in a certain way, Danielle. All of it."

"Can you please tell me what happened?" she repeated, the explosion of her emotions making it difficult to concentrate.

Lars nodded. "Leaving my world for yours had to be done in such a way that all the people I wanted to come along with me did so on their own accord, without my influence. And it was vital that Noel would want to get rid of me, or at least be pleased I had left."

Danielle blinked, his face coming into focus as she drew back.

"Are you telling me that you orchestrated this…from the beginning?" she questioned in wonder.

Lars smiled. "Do you recall when I started the discussions with Velocity?" It took her a moment.

"It was right after Andre's death," she answered in disbelief. "You knew then…"

"I suspected, and hoped, we would be together some day, yes." The magnitude of his plan nearly overwhelmed her. As if sensing she needed time to absorb his words, Lars traced the top of her hand. "As you were coming to grips with being alone, I was planning our future, one that required a way out of the business for me such that wouldn't hurt my relationship with Noel, or my reputation in the industry."

She looked deeply into his eyes. "But Lars, your reputation is hurt now. People leaving…the Mettleren account…" she trailed off.

Lars' fingers continued to caress her as he spoke. "On the contrary. To the world, the merger made, and still makes, complete sense. Family offices are sprouting up. MRD needed to extend and broaden its base. At the same time, I knew—or rather, made an informed guess—at some point you'd leave to manage the Mettleren accounts. Georgy has been after you nearly since day one. It was one reason I was so adamant, and unhappy, about you dating Andre. I didn't want them poaching you."

"Selfish," she interjected.

"Yes, but for an entirely different reason. At the time, I didn't know, or love you in the slightest. I was competitive and protective. Then as we evolved into something more, so did my thinking." He turned her palm over, tracing her life lines.

"What about the bad decisions Margaret was making?"

"Ironically, her territorial and greedy nature accelerated us being together."

"And with Margaret firing me, and Johanne and Ulrich resigning, you are blameless."

Lars lifting her palm up to his lips, then cheek, cupping her hand against his skin, a vulnerable gesture for a man so in control of his surroundings. "This is where I want you, Danielle. Next to me, always. Day and night, weekdays and weekends."

"You put me through hell," Danielle told him, feeling nothing but love for the man she held in her palms.

"And you did the same to me. Now you know why I was so distraught when you rejected me in January. I'd literally spent four months planning our entire world, preparing to move mine around, having you move in with me…"

"And I destroyed it because I was afraid."

Lars lowered her hand, clasping it between his palms. "At that point, I had to let fate take its course. You had to go through your own stages of growth, without my intervention."

Danielle leaned into him, needing to be held. Learning that he'd structured his entire life and career around their being together, and she had nearly destroyed it, distressed her anew. "I'm sorry," she whispered.

"Don't be," he said, stroking her hair. "On your own, you saw a therapist and experienced ice climbing. We proved our relationship was real; we could and did coexist, laugh and talk no matter what state we were in, even when we weren't intimate or even physical with each other. You can't make that up, Danielle. It either is, or isn't."

Danielle walked her fingers up his chest. "Georgy told me if it was meant to be with you, it would just work out. It might not be easy, but it would come together."

"And it did. Noel accepted my resignation, appreciating that I took full responsibility for the situation at MRD. He knew, as did I, that clients wanted and demanded a change of management at the top, which they got. Of course," he continued with a bit of levity, "he doesn't blame me, or you, for the loss of the Mettleren accounts. He'd expected that since you became engaged to Andre."

Danielle slid her hands around Lars' neck, lifting her face at the same time, breathing in his skin.

"All those things you said," she murmured. "You said to try less hard, when it came to ice climbing, or none of this will be worth it. All the time, you were giving me little hints." Lars kissed her forehead, nodding. She nuzzled against him. "My brilliant, handsome, incredible man who I love so much." Her words caught on her emotions. "Was it you who paid for me to sing Crazy?"

"Of course," he murmured. "It was a bit obvious, but I had to see you sing. That was the closest I could get to you with all that had been going on."

Danielle kissed his skin, her tears made up of sorrow and regret she hadn't had more faith in him, but also of joy that their journey had finally brought them to this point.

"Now, Layda and Georgy did have one condition of me marrying you," Lars explained. "I was taken aback, shocked but incredibly grateful. Would you like to know what it is?"

Danielle leaned back, trying to stem the tears from falling. "Do I have a choice?"

"Of course. They did say it was dependent on you also agreeing." Lars stood, walking to Georgy's desk, opening the top drawer. "He told me I'd find it here," he said under his breath. "Ah, there it is." Danielle could barely breathe as he walked to her. He bent down on one knee, holding out a small box.

"This was…" he stopped, his own eyes filling with emotion. "This was originally given to you by a man who loved you with all his heart. The one who gave you that beautiful little girl, who I will have the pleasure of raising with you." Danielle blinked back tears as he spoke. "This will keep the memory of Andre alive in our lives, because without him, we wouldn't be here, right now, as a family."

One tear made its way down Danielle's face, where it stopped on her lip. "With this ring, will you be my wife?"

"Forever," Danielle answered. Her hand stopped trembling as he slipped the ring on her finger, as if it too, knew where the ring belonged.

"We were meant to be, Danielle. Always."

CHAPTER 56

Lars and Danielle walked out of the study and down the hallway.

"I'm not sure I am going to be hungry after that emotional life changing event," she said honestly.

"Well, you're going to have to work up the appetite, because I don't think your guests are going to want to eat alone."

"Emma and her husband---" Danielle started, her words cut off in shock.

"Surprise!!"

The living room was filled with her friends who stood under canopies of streamers and balloons that floated up from vases full of flowers. Johanne and Dario, wearing expressions of undiluted delight, Stephen, his arm around Eva's shoulders, her hands on her growing belly, Glenda and her husband, along with a grinning Ulrich and his wife. Georgiana stood beside Giles, who gave Danielle a mischievous wink, and there was Benny, who pointed to a portable digital piano. That dog; he'd said he was playing Saturday night, just not where!

"David?" Danielle squeaked, suddenly seeing him and his wife, who had been hiding behind a column. "I can't believe this!" She then noticed Noel, who raised a glass to her. Georgy held Monroe, Layda's arm linked under his, beaming with happiness.

Lars raised his free hand, still holding on to Danielle as the cheering, laughing group settled down.

"Thank you all for helping us pull off what may go down as being the best surprise birthday party ever, because it was, in fact, a surprise."

"Cheers!" called Johanne.

"And what would a surprise party be without one more announcement," Lars asked, gesturing to Georgy, who took over.

"On this, Danielle's thirtieth birthday, I'm pleased and proud to announce that my daughter…" Georgy stopped, clearing his throat, "is engaged to Lars, a man I've known and now love as a son. Join me in saying congratulations!"

The yells of congratulations and well wishes were now exuberant, growing louder when Lars lifted Danielle's hand up in the air, turning her fingers so the group could witness the truth. She was laughing and crying, the hugs she received from her dear friends heartfelt, and no less earnest than the ones given Lars. She'd never seen him stand so tall or smile as wide as he did now.

"Fin-a-ally," said Johanne, kissing and hugging her. "After what you two have been through, I need a drink for all of us."

"Dario," Danielle said as Johanne joked with Lars. "Aren't you feeling downright satisfied?"

"That I told you he wasn't serious with Margaret?" he asked in an undertone. "Yes, because I saw how he acted afterward, and it was pure regret."

Stephen approached next, joking about a double wedding. "See? I was right after all," he said, while Danielle kissed Eva.

Ulrich beamed, still shaking his head. "I think I was about the only person who didn't know what was going on, so congratulations on that alone," he complimented Danielle. "If you can keep working with Lars and date him at the same time, you're the one who should run the firm."

Lars gave Ulrich a pleased, proud smile. "Be careful. She might be doing so one day."

Giles and Georgiana hung back, coming up individually, Georgiana thanking her for giving her number to Giles, who kissed her and mumbled, "Smart, fun and yet not so brilliant I can't handle her." Danielle hugged him, happy and in agreement with his assessment.

David came up with his wife Jolene.

"Congratulations," they said with enthusiasm. While still shy, Jolene's demeanor was much improved from the last time they'd met. For many of those assembled, their last gathering with Danielle had been at Andre's funeral luncheon. They had an uncommon bond of love and suffering; the bond of life.

Noel came at the end, when the others had gone to the buffet line for the food.

"I'm so happy for you, Danielle," said Noel, kissing her cheek.

She thanked him, then couldn't help herself. "And you're okay with Margaret, truly?"

The older man nodded, his salt and pepper brows furrowed. "She is focused and dispassionate, two traits that have proven highly effective in this business. Unfortunately, you never saw the good she was doing for the company in other areas, which were significant. That said," he turned slightly, leaning in, "I'm unhappy about the way you were treated, which was horrendous and uncalled for. The settlement can't undo her actions, but hopefully is large enough to ensure you are satisfied."

Danielle felt confident she would be. "And how long do you think it will be until Margaret gets swept off her feet like all the other gorgeous, intelligent people I've met during my two years in this wonderful country?" Danielle teased.

Noel raised an eyebrow, watching Giles and Georgiana. "Longer than you, and perhaps even longer than Lars. As we've seen, the woman will put her work above everything, her personal life included. Granted, the changes have been hard, but the firm needs someone who has the commitment for the next five years, maybe longer if we're lucky."

"All it takes is one," she quipped, which got a laugh from the man.

He clasped Danielle's hand warmly. "I'm going to miss you Danielle. Good luck with Georgy, and a long life with Lars." Danielle slipped her palm from within his grasp and put both arms around him.

"Noel, I'm officially making you my honorary Uncle, which means I get to hug you at every event from this time forward instead of shaking your hand." She kissed his cheeks and he did the same.

When Danielle moved into the living room, Georgy approached, a slight smile on his face.

"You just expanded our family, I hear."

She grinned. "Noel isn't going anywhere so I just made it formal."

"Wise move." They stood, side by side, watching everyone mingle. They represented all those she'd loved during her time here, and David and his wife were all of her past life that she was carrying in to the future.

"We are a family, Georgy, as you always said." She looked up at him, full of affection and pride. "I love you so much. Thanks Dad."

They observed Lars holding Monroe, the little girl gripping his collar like a rider does the reins on a horse. "He's an incredible man, Danielle. You are going to be very happy."

Danielle smiled. "I already am." She kissed him again and walked towards Lars and her daughter. Their journey wasn't ending with the wedding. Marriage was only a milestone. Their journey would last a lifetime.

ABOUT THE AUTHOR

Before she began writing novels, Sarah Gerdes established herself as an internationally recognized expert in the areas of business management and consulting. Her two dozen books are published in over 100 countries and translated into three languages.

BOOKS IN PRINT

Sarah Gerdes

Suspense/Thriller

Above Ground
Global Deadline
Incarnation Trilogy
- Incarnation (book 1)
- Incarnation: The Cube Master (book 2)
- Incarnation: Immunity (book 3)

Romantic Suspense

In a Moment
Danielle Grant Trilogy
- Made for Me (book 1)
- Destined for You (book 2)
- Meant to Be (book 2)

A Convenient Date

Non-Fiction

Chambers (5 book series)
- Chambers (book 1)
- Chambers: *The Spirit Warrior* (book 2)

Non-Fiction

The Overlooked Expert: 10th Anniversary Edition
Author Straight Talk
Sue Kim: The Authorized biography
Navigating the Partnership Maze: Creating Alliances that Work

Resources

Instagram: sarahgerdes_author
www.sarahgerdes.com